KEN W. SMITH

Shot at Redemption

A Jay Mendes Thriller

First edition

ISBN: 978-1-7372317-0-7

This book was professionally typeset on Reedsy.
Find out more at reedsy.com

This book is dedicated to our everyday heroes.
Our military, homeland security, first responders, and private citizens
who risk their own lives for the public good.
Also, in memory of Westwood friends:
USMC Lance Corporal Michael J. Devlin, 1962-1983. Killed in action, Beirut, Lebanon
Cadet Julia Babineau, 1960-1981, US Coast Guard Academy

"True redemption is seized when you accept the future consequences for your past mistakes."

— EDWARDO MACEDO

Contents

III   Part Three

Preface

It was a beautiful, sunny day in the peaceful Italian village. The view of the blue-green water of Lake Albano was eye-candy for all who visited. But Ivan focused on one site—the third-floor balcony of Castel Gandolfo—summer home to the Pope. He focused the scope of his powerful sniper rifle on the balcony window—nothing in sight. There was a slight breeze, and he adjusted his rifle to compensate. If successful, this shot would bring home the biggest paycheck of his career.

The third floor of the apartment building on the Corso Della Republico housed several units. Ivan lived in a two-bedroom suite with one bedroom serving as a small command center. The second bedroom housed computer workstations and sophisticated electronics for eavesdropping. Ivan made sure no message entered or left the small village without his knowledge.

To maintain his cover, Ivan worked as the cafe's general manager on the first floor. It opened at five in the afternoon and closed at two in the morning. The schedule suited him well, allowing him to get to know his neighbors while gathering intelligence about the local political scene.

* * *

The tall, dark-haired woman was considered one of the most beautiful people in the world. People magazine proclaimed that fact at least three times. As a child actress raised in Hollywood, Angelica Bonham won several acting awards before launching her solo music career at the age of fifteen. With a light and distinctive voice, her pop album sold millions of records. She went on to star in situation comedies on the Disney Channel. Then, at eighteen, she had an affair with a movie executive twice her age. While the scandal ended his career, Angelica rode the wave of tabloid news to fame. As an adult, she starred in several action blockbusters, becoming one of Hollywood's most sought-after and highest-paid actresses. Once again, Angelica gained notoriety for a steamy relationship with one of the hottest leading men until a nasty drug problem derailed her career and forced her to escape to private life. Now she had a new mentor. One that had no cares about fame and wealth, only retribution.

In the street below Ivan's apartment, Angelica browsed the designer storefronts wearing a large sun hat and dark Gucci sunglasses. She kept her face hidden as she listened in on a conversation at a local cafe. Her targets were two uniformed police officers and a plainclothes detective.

The detective spoke first, "I heard the Holy See would be making a series of clandestine visits to our village. He is working with senior officials on a more liberal direction for the church. However, the Vatican wants to maintain secrecy until the final draft is complete. Therefore, we will need all uniformed officers to be extra-vigilant to secure his safety. Do you understand?"

"Yes," one of the officers replied. "How will we know he is coming?"

"The local pastor, Father Cavatelli, will let us know. He is in communication with the Swiss Guard and the Vatican travel office."

"Very good. We will do everything we can to keep our Holy Father safe."

Angelica smiled and walked away.

* * *

Ivan observed movement behind the balcony window. This could be the chance he had been waiting for. Ivan opened the window enough to allow the barrel of the rifle to protrude between the wood shutters. He picked this location because it was one story higher than the adjacent building. His spot offered a clear view of the balcony without being exposed to security personnel in the piazza below. Ivan lay prone on top of his wooden dining table, released the trigger, and chambered the round.

The window began to open. Ivan took a deep breath and blew it out through his nose. The doors pulled open a bit further. Ivan closed his left eye to help him see better through the scope. A person wearing black opened the window. It could be one of the guards or servants since the target would never open the door himself. Ivan turned on his laser designator, and a small red dot appeared on the person's forehead. He pressed his finger against the trigger. The guard stepped onto the balcony and waved at a few tourists. He scanned the cafes, shops, and buildings along the perimeter of the piazza. Ivan knew to stay still and patient. The guard was not his target. But if the guard spotted him, he would fire to prevent himself from being discovered and invoke his escape plan. The man continued scanning and waving, but luckily, he never looked directly at Ivan. He turned and stepped inside, leaving the doors open.

Ivan waited. Would his target step out on the balcony? He often traveled to Gandolfo at night to spend a private weekend away from the Vatican. His public holiday would not happen for several months in July. But this Pope liked visiting Gandolfo, unlike his predecessor, who preferred staying in Rome. Ivan watched as another person stepped onto the balcony. This one wore a white robe, a white skull cap, and a large gold chain and cross. Ivan's red dot fit cleanly behind his target's eyes. He blew out his breath and began to apply pressure to the trigger. The young priest, a local pastor, waved his hands to the audience below. Ivan relaxed and lifted his finger off the trigger. Ivan was shocked to see the priest, Father Cavatelli, look at him and smile, then stepped back off the patio. Ivan smiled, too. The priest provided intelligence for an extra weekly offering and received a donation to an offshore bank account. Ivan pulled the rifle out of the window and closed the shutters.

There was a knock at the door. Ivan stowed the rifle and mattress in a closet. He moved the table back to the middle of the dining room and returned the chairs to their proper place. The knock repeated.

"One moment, please," he said in Italian. "I am coming."

He opened the door to see Angelica's radiant smile. He embraced her as they kissed. The scent of her perfume and the touch of her lips sent a wave of pleasure through his body.

"I'm glad I can get your attention, Ivan," Angelica whispered into his ear. "I have some good news. Do you still have time for a little afternoon pleasure before the cafe opens?"

"Always, my dear," Ivan replied as he pulled her inside and closed the door.

I

Part One

Chapter 1

Jay woke up in an empty bedroom. He didn't know where he was or how he got there. Without warning, the door to the bedroom opened, and a tall slim man with graying temples walked in.

"Where are we?" Jay said.

"In Kuwait," the man replied. "I can't say anything else."

"What the hell happened last night? I must have passed out from drinking."

"I can't tell you for your own good. Some friends helped us out of a hairy situation, and now you have a plane to catch. I'm giving you a ticket, a new passport, cash, and a cell phone.

"Where's my stuff?"

"When you are on the plane, you'll receive a phone call that will answer your questions."

"Why am I here? The last thing I remember, I was awaiting my trial verdict. Did I get off?"

"Yes, but you're wanted for questioning by a bunch of people, including the Iranians, who placed a bounty on your head. Follow my instructions, keep your head low, and this whole episode will blow over."

"I'm a SEAL. I don't run from fights."

"This is different. Trust me. Follow my instructions, and

when you return home, this situation will be gone."

"How will I contact you?"

"You won't. I'll find you when you complete the job."

Jay was shocked and confused, "What about my friends? My girlfriend, Natalie? I need to call them."

"I'll reach out to them and let them know you're safe."

"Why are you doing this to me?" Jay said. "What did I do wrong?"

"You didn't do anything wrong. They want you to stay alive. It's better that you don't know."

The man walked out.

Jay wondered, *who are they?*

* * *

Forty hours later, Jay strained to see the shoreline of the distant archipelago from the window. The pilot said they were on the final approach—their destination, the Mount Pleasant RAF base on East Falkland Island.

The self-governed British territory was best known for raising sheep and breeding penguins. That was until 1982 when Argentina tried to reclaim the island from the Brits. A short but bloody war followed, taking over 800 lives. The history books called it the Falklands War.

The plane crossed over the cluster of tiny islands on its final descent into the RAF airbase.

It had been a long trip. Jay flew commercial from Kuwait to Amsterdam. From Amsterdam, he traveled straight to Buenos Aires. Then after a twelve-hour layover, he flew the final leg to Mount Pleasant.

The jetliner stopped near the terminal. The flight attendant, doubling as the baggage handler, handed Jay his two duffle bags. One filled with clothes and the other with dive gear. Jay departed the plane, stretched his legs, and breathed in the Falklands' cool, dry summer air.

A rusty, blue Land Rover pulled up next to the plane. An overweight, dark-haired woman stepped out. She wore a ratty navy pea coat, a black knit cap, and ragged blue jeans. In her hand was a small cardboard sign with *Mendes* scribbled in red crayon. Jay walked over. He could smell the alcohol on her breath from ten feet away.

"Jay Mendes?" the woman said with a scowl. "I'm Dora Williams. I'm the ship's executive officer."

"You're Williams?" Jay said. "Show me some ID."

She towered over Jay's five-foot-six-inch frame. It looked like she outweighed him by at least one hundred and fifty pounds. She grabbed Jay by the collar of his green polo shirt and shoved a knife against Jay's sternum. "This is my ID. Get in the car, or I'll gut you like a fucking sea lion. Understand?"

Jay looked up into her eyes. He was too exhausted to play this game. Plus, her lousy breath was making him nauseous. Jay dropped his duffle bags. He wrapped his right hand over her wrist and squeezed. Her scowl evaporated as pain shot through her arm. Dora's eyes opened wide, and her face turned red. Sweat poured down her forehead as she struggled to hold the knife. Jay wouldn't let go. He squeezed harder, twisting her hand until the knife dropped to the ground.

"How's that for ID?" Jay said.

He pulled her wrist down towards the ground until she dropped to her knees. He looked her straight in the face and said, "Don't ever pull a weapon on somebody if you don't intend to use it. Do you understand?"

The woman nodded, and Jay let her hand go.

"You're the right guy," Williams said. "My boss told me you don't take shit from anyone. Follow me."

Jay got in the back seat of the car. They exited the Mount Pleasant airbase and turned left onto Darwin Road. The name made sense since it was miraculous any life survived on this barren island. There were no natural trees, only lakes and rock outcroppings. Thick peat-moss-like growth covered the rolling landscape. Jay saw a few brick houses with thatched roofs surrounded by grazing sheep.

"So, Mendes," Williams asked. "How did you become qualified for underwater inspections?"

"I was a diver in the Navy," Jay said.

"The agency said you were more than just a diver. You had combat experience."

"I did a tour in Yemen. Things got a bit hairy from time to time."

"I didn't believe your record. That's why I did it."

"Did what?"

"Pull the knife on you. I wanted to make sure you didn't make that shit up."

"Well, was I lying?

"No, I believe you now."

Williams turned around without saying another word.

* * *

Jay thought about the last year as he stared out the window.

They pulled his unit out of action after Kathleen Amejian filed her complaint against him and his team. He sucked up his pride through the secret military tribunal and held his temper as the bitch lied about him. Kathleen told the military panel he killed her husband in cold blood. The claim was bullshit. Jay knew it was a lie because he never pulled the trigger of his gun. Someone else shot first. He still had fragments of the bullet in his neck and shoulder to prove it. But Kathleen's power and influence scared the Navy brass. So, they caved and charged him with war crimes. The second charge, dereliction of duty, was for not following the rules of engagement. That is, for not identifying himself as an enemy combatant. Pretty hard to do when the enemy shoots first.

Pete, his JAG, wouldn't let him take the stand and tell his own story. Too dangerous, he said. So he sat and listened to her lie. Kathleen was so convincing. An international war correspondent married to one of the richest men in the world. Why would she lie? She was a grieving widow. Her husband's brain splattered across the cave floor in front of her. She cried and went on about loving him and how Jay ruined her life, how he stole her dignity and her future. She should have won an Oscar for her performance.

Then his Infinity Squad teammates testified. Gunny Mack told the jury how Jay saved his life in Fallujah. McCoy described how Jay pulled hostages off a burning container ship. Gia testified how she went undercover to rescue Goddard and Amejian, and she almost fell to her death and described how Jay saved her and Antonio on the container ship. Then she told them how the anti-tank rocket blew apart the Land Rover with General Andrews inside. With tears in her eyes, she described how Jay carried Michael Goddard to the helicopter under fire and how Michael died in her arms. There wasn't a dry eye in the house—twelve senior officers dabbing their eyes with tissues.

Gia testified how she found the murdered pilots in the plane wreckage in Pakistan. Her testimony was riveting. Finally, she described the rescue operation and how Jay asked her to identify the hostages. *Gia explained how the cave was so pitch black she couldn't see the shooter. But once the gun fired, Gia saw blood running down Jay's arm. She said he did everything possible to keep the hostages alive.*

Jay was hopeful. Gia's testimony was so believable. That was until Kathleen's slick London lawyer destroyed her on the stand. He questioned her testimony and claimed she was too emotional because of her loss. For some reason, Jay's memory after that point was blank. He assumed he was found not guilty since he wasn't in the brig. But he couldn't recall the verdict or anything else. He didn't even know why Steve Bonner was with him in Kuwait. Jay remembered Steve as a Marine instructor at sniper school, but that was it. Did he help Jay escape from the brig? Was Jay in witness protection? He wanted to know the answers.

* * *

The Land Rover drove into the town of Port Stanley. Home to 2,300 residents, ninety percent of the island's population. Most of the inhabitants descended from the original English settlers who arrived in 1832. Today, the Falkland Islands maintain the charm of a British colony.

They pulled up in front of a small white building with a brown, thatch roof. A blue wood-cut sign hung above the door. Gold lettering read *The Crown*.

"I'm hungry," Williams said. "We can grab a bite to eat and a drink before we go out to the ship. No alcohol allowed on board."

"Sounds good," Jay said. "How long has the ship been in the Falklands?"

"A few days. I'll explain everything once we place our

order."

Jay thought he walked into a London pub. Dark paneling covered the walls. Union Jacks and Falkland Island flags flew from the ceiling. A picture of Queen Elizabeth adorned the wall behind the bar. Another photo showed Prince Charles visiting wounded British soldiers during the Falklands War.

Williams pulled up a stool at the bar. A few local fishermen dressed in plaid wool shirts and filthy coveralls sat at the other end. Two older women sat at a table in the back corner next to a red-felt pool table.

"Try the bangers and mash," Williams said. "It will fill you up. What do you want to drink?"

"I'll have a black and tan," Jay said.

"Make that two," Williams said to the bartender.

"Did Bonner tell you why he sent you down here?" Williams said.

"No. If he did, I can't remember."

"You're assigned to the R/V Nereus II. It's a U.S. research vessel owned by the Navy but operated by the New England Marine Institute. It's in the Falklands on a research expedition. Our security officer had a heart attack last week. We flew him to Buenos Aires for medical care. We've been waiting for you to arrive to finish our voyage.

"How long will the ship be here in the Falklands?"

"Another week, then we sail back to Falmouth."

"Falmouth, England?"

"No, Falmouth Massachusetts. On Cape Cod. You've heard of it?"

"Hell yeah. It's my hometown. I have relatives there."

"No shit. It's a small world."

"Where are you from?" Jay asked.

9

"Here and there. I was a Navy brat. Grew up on bases around the world. The last port of call was Newport, so I went to Mass. Maritime and traveled the world on rusty freighters. I landed the job in Woods Hole a few years ago. It's been the best gig I've had. They treat you well, and the pay is the best in the business."

"Why do you need a security guard?"

"Pirates. They're taking everybody hostage. They don't care who you are or what country you call home. As long as they can extort a few million from the ship's owners, they're happy."

"I thought they ended the pirate operations off Somalia."

"Yea, they did. I'm talking about South American pirates. They're coming out of Brazil, Venezuela, and Colombia. A lot of them work for drug cartels."

"You look pretty dangerous," Jay said with a smile. "And you handle that knife pretty well. Why aren't you in charge of security?"

"To be honest, it's all an act. I haven't fired a rifle or handgun since the academy."

Jay ate his food and drained the beer in a manner of minutes. The English sausages were bland for his taste since he grew up on the spicy Linguica and Chorizo common to Portuguese cooking.

Williams drove down the street and parked the car in a small parking lot next to a fishing pier. Jay and Williams boarded an ancient Boston Whaler.

"Welcome aboard," said the captain of the boat, an overweight man with a thick white beard. "My name is Charles Moody. I'm a direct descendant of the first Colonial Governor. I'll be taking you out to your ship."

"Nice to meet you, Captain Moody," Jay said as he tossed his gear onboard. He thought the man reminded him of Jolly Ol' Saint Nick.

As they pulled away from the dock, Jay noticed the wreck of a sailing ship sitting in a shallow harbor.

"Captain Moody, what's the history behind that ship-wreck?" Jay asked.

"What, that old hulk in Whalebone Cove?" Moody said. "That's the Lady Liz. She's an iron barque. It was damaged sailing around Cape Horn back in seventy-nine—1879, that is. The ship sat in our harbor until 1936. Then a storm ripped her from her mooring, and she beached."

"Why is she still there?"

"Some locals say it's a memorial to the power of the sea. It reminds us not to get too cocky and respect the force of nature."

"What do you say?"

"The island governor is too cheap to pay for the salvage fees. Either way, It's part of the island's lore."

Captain Moody piloted the boat south along the eastern coast of the island. Then he headed west. A small island lay ahead with flocks of birds flying over a large beach.

"You might want to grab that pair of binoculars on the console," Moody said. "We're approaching Sea Lion Island."

Jay picked up the binoculars and trained them on the beach. To his amazement, he spotted three large sea lions lying in a cluster. Their large, blubbery bodies meshed together like a giant Jello pie. Sea Lion pups flopped along the beach while doting mothers kept a close eye on them. Thousands of penguins scurried around. At the edge of the beach, individual penguins sat tall on grassy nests scattered across the sand. Other penguins waddled through the sand with fish in their mouths.

"This is amazing," Jay said. "Can you go onto the island?

"Of course," Moody said. "You can even stay overnight at Sea Lion Lodge. The island is a nature reserve. In fact, one of the research teams from your ship is studying the sea lions right now."

Jay took out his iPhone to take pictures of the giant sea lions basking on the beach.

"Look to your port side. There's your ship. She's a beauty."

Moody turned away from the beach and headed towards their destination. The *R/V Nereus II* sat anchored in the calm waters of Falkland Sound with its white superstructure rising high above its dark blue hull. The square fan deck rode low over the water with a large gray gantry standing high above the deck. Jay saw people milling about. A few people started waving.

"There's your greeting committee," Moody said. "Hang on, and I'll take you in."

The Captain maneuvered the small boat towards the large ship. One of the crewmen lowered an aluminum platform off the fan deck.

"Mendes, throw that mate the bowline," Williams said.

Jay followed her order and threw the nylon line to the crew member. A few minutes later, Jay followed Williams onto the ship.

After many introductions, Williams led Jay below deck to the crew quarters. He entered the stateroom with two bunks, a small desk, and a closet. Luxurious compared to the cramped crew quarters on warships.

"You'll have the cabin to yourself since you're the only

security guard. I'll give you a tour of the ship later. Take an hour to get settled and catch a nap. The evening meal is at 17:00."

Jay dropped his duffle bags onto the floor, stripped down to his briefs, and lay down on the top bunk. Not so bad, he thought. He could get used to this duty. A second later, Jay was sound asleep.

Chapter 2

A loud banging on his door woke him up.

"Mr. Mendes?" a young female voice said. "The Captain needs to see you on the bridge."

"Okay," Jay said as he shook the cobwebs out of his head. He jumped off the bunk and opened the door. An attractive African American crew member named Perry stood outside his door. Her eyes opened wide when she saw Jay's chiseled muscles and scars.

Jay sensed something was wrong.

"Sorry about that," he said as he grabbed a t-shirt from his duffle bag.

"Please, don't apologize. I haven't seen a body that sweet for months. But we must hurry."

Jay got dressed then followed her through the winding corridors to the ship's bridge. The Captain stood looking out the window. A tall, gray-haired man, he wore a white dress shirt and dark blue slacks. He stood looking out the window with a pair of binoculars. Without turning, he said, "Welcome aboard, Mendes. I understand you have diving experience?"

"Yes, sir," Jay replied. "Fourteen years as a Navy diver."

"You brought your scuba gear?"

"Yes, sir. Everything except the tanks."

"We have tanks. Perry will show you where they are. Get suited up. We have a situation. Two of our scientists are on a rigid hull inflatable on the sound. They've been tracking a pod of Sei whales. The propeller of their boat got tangled in a fishing net, and they're stranded. I need you to cut the net free."

"Sounds pretty straightforward," Jay said. "I'll get my gear." He turned to move towards the door.

"I hope you brought a dry suit," the Captain said. "The water temperature is forty-three degrees this time of year."

Back in his cabin, Jay searched through his duffle bag. The last time he went scuba diving, he was in the Persian Gulf. The water temperature was seventy-five degrees. But Jay brought several suits with him.

Thirty minutes later, Jay sat on the sidewall of the inflatable fifty yards away from the disabled boat. Jay could see the brown fishing net floating in the water.

Jay dropped off the side of the boat. The shock of the cold water took his breath away. He sank until his feet hit the rocky bottom. The water was sparkling clear, and he could see where the net tangled on a pile of rocks.

Movement off to his right caught him by surprise. A quick flash. Then nothing. Jay swam toward the net as fast as he could, his powerful strokes working his muscles to fight off the cold. He saw another flash. He turned to see a sleek, gray shape fly by him.

Jay focused on the net, using his knife to slice through the hemp until it floated free. Task one accomplished.

As he swam to the surface, he saw the flash again. This time he saw a sleek body and powerful flippers. It swam closer. Jay thought it might be a shark, so he prepared to defend himself. Then he got a closer look. His guest was a dolphin. It stared at him with curious eyes as he swam by. It seemed smart enough to stay away.

Jay continued to cut a path through the net. All around him, fish swam free. As he worked his way towards the boat, he noticed movement near the water's surface. The shape was gray, but not a fish. What if it was a shark? Jay held the knife in front of him, ready to strike if the beast struck out. Then the head turned. Two round black eyes stared back at him. Then he heard a soft whine like a sheep.

It was a baby seal. Too small to be a sea lion pup, it was five feet long and had fuzzy gray fur. Jay swam closer to see one of its flippers caught in the net. The seal looked like it was injured. "Mendes, are you alright?" Perry said in his earpiece. "What's going on?"

"The net's free from the bottom. I'm working my way toward the boat's propeller, but I have a situation."

"What situation?"

"I found a baby seal. It's entangled in the net."

"Well, cut it loose and let it swim away. You're running out of time."

"I can't. It's stuck in the net. If I leave it here, it'll die."

"Mendes, you'll freeze to death if you don't get out of the water in five minutes."

"I'm cutting him free. Radio to the crew on the boat and tell them I'm bringing a passenger on board."

"But Mendes...," Perry said, but Jay didn't listen. He focused on the seal's flipper.

The seal watched his every move. Then it stopped moving. As if it knew Jay was there to help it. He spotted the seal's rear fin caught in the net twisted at a strange angle. Likely broken, Jay cut the net away from the fin, careful not to cut the seal's skin. Then he reached out and held the fin steady with his left hand while he cut the net away with his right. The seal didn't move.

When he finished, the seal splashed around and grunted. Jay swore he saw the seal smile at him as they floated to the surface together.

"Over here!" a voice shouted. "Bring the seal to the boat, and we'll lift it in."

Jay turned to see two researchers waving towards him from the edge of the inflatable. He pushed the baby seal towards them. The poor little guy didn't have the energy to resist.

The two researchers extended their hands down, and Mendes pushed the seal into their arms. They pulled him onboard.

"Great job Mendes," Perry said in his earpiece. "Now cut the net away from the boat's propeller and get back here."

Jay followed orders by cutting the net, then swam back to his rigid hull. Perry reached down and pulled him out of the water. He peeled his suit off and wrapped himself in thermal blankets. When he was ready, Perry gunned the engine, and they headed back to the ship.

The researcher's boat followed close behind, pulling up to the aluminum dock at the same time. Jay jumped off his inflatable and went to help with the seal.

One of the researchers, a young dark-haired woman, waved to Jay.

"Hey, thanks for saving this little guy. Can you help us carry him off the boat?"

"Sure," Jay said. "I'm glad to help. Is he going to be okay?"

"His body temperature is very low," she said. "We need to warm him up in the medical ward. We weren't planning on having any sea mammal guests on this trip, but we brought a few tubs in case of an emergency."

"What are tubs?" Jay said. "You mean bathtubs?"

"Yes, designed for injured marine mammals. They have to stay in the water to survive."

Jay helped the woman carry the seal to the medical ward. There a medic and a nurse examined the seal. The medic pulled a portable x-ray unit over and snapped an image of the seal's rear fin. The doctor reviewed the image on the machine's LED screen.

"Sorry, it's broken," the doctor said. "It won't be able to return to the ocean. I'll have to euthanize it."

"No," Jay said. "You can't kill him. Can't you do something?"

"I'm sorry," the doctor said as he walked over to a medicine cart and removed a hypodermic needle. He filled the syringe with a clear fluid.

Jay stepped between the doctor and the seal. "You're going to have to kill me before you kill that baby."

"Mendes," Williams said, standing in the doorway. "Stand down. That's an order."

But Jay didn't budge. He stared the doctor in the eyes.

"Mendes, I said stand down."

"No, it's okay," the dark-haired woman said. "I'll take care of him. If he recovers, I'll take him back to the aquarium in Woods Hole."

Jay looked at the woman. She was going to save and care for the baby seal. The woman stepped over to Jay and placed her hand on his arm. Jay relaxed. The doctor turned and put the needle down.

"Mendes, I'm putting you on report," Williams said as she turned and stormed out of the medical ward.

"Let me complete my examination," the doctor said. "Then we can discuss what to do with him."

The woman took Jay's hand and led him out of the ward. They went out a door onto the outside deck. The woman wrapped her arms around Jay's shoulder in a warm embrace.

"This is nice," Jay said. "But I don't even know you."

"Jay, you don't recognize me?"

"How do you know my name? We weren't even introduced?"

"I'm Olivia. Olivia Cataldo."

Jay searched his memory. *He grew up in Maravista. A village in Falmouth, Massachusetts, on Cape Cod. His next-door neighbors were Walter and Maria Cataldo. Olivia was their daughter. She was fourteen when he joined the Navy. His brother Joseph's age. Then the memories flooded back to that horrible morning.*

The ship's PA system blurted, "Mendes. Report to the bridge. Immediately!"

Jay held Olivia's hand for a moment longer. Then she pushed him away and said, "You don't want to make Williams angry. We can talk later. How about after supper?"

Jay laughed, "Sounds great. It will be fun to catch up."

"Good luck," Olivia said with a smile.

Chapter 3

The view of Falkland Sound was breathtaking. A mile away, the water erupted in foam. A large dark form broke through the surface, and a fountain blew into the air. Behind the whale, he saw Olivia taking pictures while Stephanie, another researcher, piloted the inflatable. She was trying to get closer to the elusive Sei whale.

Jay watched the action from his boatswain's chair high above the ship's deck. He was painting as punishment for insubordination. Jay didn't mind, though. He enjoyed the fresh air and scenery, a stark contrast to the last four days spent traveling.

Jay saw crew members and researchers on the fan deck building an enclosure and pool for the seal. Olivia told him the research team named the seal Jojo in memory of his younger brother.

After finishing his duties, Jay grabbed a quick sandwich in the galley and went out onto the fan deck. He heard a sharp screeching sound. It sounded a bit like a sheep. As he approached Jojo's pool, he saw movement. Then a dark gray head popped out of the water, and Jojo bleated Baaaaa again. Jojo dove back under the surface and spun around in circles.

Olivia walked up and hugged Jay. "What's he doing?" Jay

asked.

"He's cleaning himself. Fur seals spin around in the water to remove sand and other debris from their fur."

"It looks like fun," Jay said. "Do you know how old Jojo is?"

"We think he's six months old. He's eating fish, which means he's weaned off his mother's milk."

"Does he live here in the Falklands?"

"Yes, there's a small colony at Dolphin Point on Sea Lion Island. The majority of the Antarctic fur seals live on South Georgia Island."

"Are they endangered?" Jay asked as the little seal attempted to growl at Jay. It came out sounding more like a purring cat.

"Not anymore," Olivia said. "They were almost killed off for their fur in the early nineteen hundreds. But when they banned whaling activities, the seals rebounded. There are now over one and a half million Antarctic fur seals."

"That's incredible," Jay said. "He is cute. How's his flipper?"

"Not good," Olivia said. "He can swim alright, but he's not able to walk on the beach. The doctor also thinks he injured one of his eyes. We won't be able to tell until a specialist examines him."

"What does he eat?" Jay asked.

"Krill. The microscopic fish that whales eat. They also eat small fish, like sardines. Do you want to feed him?"

"Sure. Tell me what to do."

Olivia picked up a metal pail and handed Jay a small fish. It was slippery and fell on the deck. Olivia laughed as she picked it up and gave it back. Jay threw the fish into the pool, then watched Jojo swim over and suck the fish into his mouth.

"So, what are you going to do with Jojo?"

"Falklands Conservation permitted us to bring him back to the Institute for rehab. They don't believe he'll survive in the wild."

"That's great. When do we head back?"

"Soon. We're finishing our research in the Falklands. Our last stop is South Georgia Island to weigh the seals and count the penguins. Then we head north."

* * *

The research ship pulled anchor the next morning and headed out into the open ocean. The seas were rough, and Jay almost fell on the rocking deck. At lunch, he noticed many of the researchers leaning over the railing. Since few people were eating, Jay piled his tray with sandwiches and fruit. He grabbed a chair in front of the television to watch the Global News Network (GNN).

"Hey, sailor," he heard from a familiar voice behind him. He turned to see Perry taking the stool next to him. "How can you eat out here on the open ocean?"

"I'm lucky," Jay said. "I've never suffered from seasickness."

"Why's that?" Perry said with a scowl. "I spent the day in my cabin puking my brains out."

"I'm not sure. I grew up on my father's fishing boat. The ocean off the New England coast is as rough as the South Atlantic. We survived some nasty gales."

"What kind of fish did you catch?"

"Whatever we could find," Jay said between bites. "At first, it was cod and haddock. Then those fisheries dwindled, so we turned to sea scallops."

"Is your father still fishing?"

"No, he passed away three years ago."

"That must have been a difficult funeral. I lost my dad when I was ten years old."

"How?"

"He died in prison."

Jay almost choked on the apple he was chewing on. "What happened?"

"He was busted for selling drugs. I was a baby, and my family didn't have any money. My dad tried smuggling cocaine into the country from Columbia but got caught by the Border Patrol. Somebody shanked him in jail trying to steal his shoes."

"I never went to my dad's funeral," Jay said. "I wanted to, but I was on a ship in the Persian Gulf and couldn't leave my unit."

"Were you a SEAL?"

"No, I was a Navy diver. I also worked as an MP."

"So that's why Jojo loves you," Olivia said from behind Jay. "He can sense your love of the ocean."

"Were you eavesdropping?" Jay said, turning to Olivia, who was holding a cup of tea in her hand.

"Hey, I gotta get going," Perry said. "I'll leave you two lovebirds alone."

"Lovebirds?" Jay and Olivia said in unison. "We just met," Jay said.

"That's not what I heard," Perry said. "We saw you two on the deck last night huggin' and kissing."

"We were just hugging," Olivia said, turning a bright shade of red as she sat down.

"I guess it was a reunion of sorts," Jay said. "We're

childhood friends."

"Sure. Whatever you say." Perry stood up and picked up her tray. "I'll let you have some private time."

"Sorry about that," Jay said. "I hope she didn't embarrass you too much."

"No, I don't mind," Olivia said. "I have a question, though. Why didn't you come home?"

"Like I told Perry. I was in the Persian Gulf."

"No. I mean, why didn't you ever come home? You were in the service for years, and you never once came home on leave. Why?"

Jay looked down at the table. "Come on, let's take a walk."

Olivia finished her tea, and they went outside onto the deck. The wind howled as the ship plowed through ten-foot-high swells. Jay pulled the hood of his sweater up over his head.

Jay and Olivia held on tightly as they walked to the bow of the ship. They found shelter behind a drum winch and sat down on the deck. Jay noticed Olivia shivering, so he wrapped his arm around her and pulled her close.

"Losing Jojo was the toughest thing I ever went through," Jay said. "I blamed myself for the accident."

"Why Jay?" You didn't do anything wrong."

"I told him it was okay to go out with his friends that night. Mom and Dad were in Boston. I was the oldest son and was in charge."

"Jay, what happened? The reports in the newspaper didn't make a lot of sense."

"Jojo went out with two of his buddies. His friend Anthony was showing off in his father's car. They drove out to Provincetown. It was well after midnight before they left, and they knew they were in trouble. His friend was trying to get them home."

"But they were in their own neighborhood. How did they get in an accident?"

"The fog was thick, and the visibility was down to zero. Anthony was on Maravista Ave. It was straight, and there were no cars on the road. He gunned it, and…."

Jay stopped. It had been years since he thought about that horrific night—the call from the police and then going to the scene of the accident.

"He never stopped and drove straight across Menauhant Road and into the ocean. The crazy thing is, Jojo had his seatbelt on. He couldn't release it and drowned in five feet of water."

Olivia didn't say a word. She cried. Deep, heavy sobs. Jay held her closer.

"I never told anyone this," Olivia said after a few minutes. "Jojo and I were dating. He thought my father would object, so we kept our relationship a secret. He was going to take me to our homecoming dance."

"I didn't know, Olivia. I'm so sorry."

"Jojo looked up to you. You were his hero. He went to every one of your football games. He talked for hours about the fishing trips."

"He was a great kid," Jay said. "He loved to sing. Jojo was the life of the party. It wasn't fair he had to die at such a young age. Why did I get to live?"

Olivia stared at Jay. Then she held his head in both of her hands. "Jay, you listen to me," she said. "You are in this world for a reason. You're special. We can't bring Jojo back. But you can make a difference for him. Make him proud of you.

He's watching from heaven."

"I lost so many close friends on the battlefield. I've had to kill others. Life seems so meaningless when you're in a firefight. You do everything you can to stay alive and keep your buddies alive. You don't forget. I know the name of everyone I served with. I know how they died and where they died. I relive those moments in my sleep every night."

"Jay, you've also saved lives. You protected us here at home. Not many people would make the sacrifices you've made for your country."

"Mendes, where are you?" William's voice barked over his radio speaker. "We need you on the bridge."

"I'm sorry, I need to go," Jay said. "Olivia, thank you. You're the only person I've ever been able to talk to about my brother."Olivia leaned close to Jay and kissed him on the lips catching Jay by surprise. Jay kissed her back.

"Mendes, where are you!"

Jay pulled back from Olivia. "I've got to go, or Williams is gonna make me walk the plank."

* * *

Williams met Jay on the bridge. He could tell by the scowl on her face that she was not pleased.

"Captain Michaels wants to see us in his office," Williams said as soon as she saw Jay. "Now!"

Jay followed Williams into the Captain's office. A simple metal desk held a laptop and two computer monitors mounted on a swivel arm.

"I received a warning message from the US Navy," the Captain said without looking up. "There are several reports of pirate activity along the coast of South America. We're advised to stay out at sea and avoid the ports. Unfortunately, we need to make a refueling stop in Salvador de Bahia, Brazil, and a stop to restock our food supplies in Georgetown, Guyana."

"What type of activity?" Williams said.

"Attacks by small boats. Several kidnapping attempts. In one case, pirates kidnapped a couple on vacation in Trinidad."

"Any signs of the couple?" Jay said.

"They found the husband's body on a beach in Playa de Las Salinas, Venezuela. No sign of the wife. Venezuelan authorities are not cooperating with the FBI investigators."

"What do you need me to do, sir?"

"First, I need you to inventory the ship's weapons and assess our defense readiness. Only officers or security personnel can carry sidearms. You can find our long gun weapons store on the bridge. Make sure our weapons are clean and working. You can shoot off the deck of the ship when the researchers are on South Georgia island. As long as you don't shoot any seals and penguins, you'll be okay."

"Yes, sir," Jay said and turned to leave the office. "What about the researchers' sir?"

"Don't shoot them either, Mendes," Williams said.

Jay smiled and said, "I mean, shouldn't they be aware of the threat? Do the crew members receive any protection when we go into the ports?"

"This is on a need-to-know basis right now, Mendes," the Captain said. "The researchers don't need to know anything. Is that clear?"

"Yes, Sir."

"You're dismissed, Mendes," Captain Michaels said.

"Williams will show you the weapons store."

* * *

The profile of South Georgia Island rose from the sea like a shadowy ghost ship. One hundred miles long, the island featured towering, snow-capped mountains. Human habitation was sparse. There was one small town dating back to the heights of the whaling industry. Now there were less than one hundred residents. Two species dominated the islands, penguins and fur seals.

Jay peered through his binoculars as the ship approached their anchor point. Hundreds of thousands of penguins blanketed the beach. Large birds called Petrels tended their young on the grassy hills above. Mixed in with the penguins were hundreds of fur seals. Some were sunning themselves on the rocks, while others tended to the adorable babies. Young seals performed their barrel rolls in the cold ocean waters.

Icy glaciers flowed down on both sides of the beach, creating a natural photo opportunity. Jay snapped images with his cell phone from the ship's deck. He watched an Albatross disappear into the calm waters of the bay. It emerged seconds later with a silver-colored fish in its beak.

"I can't believe how many penguins there are," Jay said to Olivia, who was also taking photos. "I thought they were an endangered species."

"Not down here. There are millions here on South Georgia Island."

"What kind of penguins are they?"

"There are eight types," she said. "Macaroni, King, Gentoo,

and Chinstrap are the most popular. The Macaroni penguins are the most abundant in the world. Over nine million breeding pairs worldwide. Three million on this island."

"That's amazing. What are those gigantic seals hanging on the rocks?"

"Those are elephant seals," Olivia said. "They can weigh over 3,000 pounds."

"Those guys are hideous," Jay said. "They look like they have short trunks."

"Are you going to come with us to the island? All the researchers are going."

"No. I have an assignment from the Captain and the best time for me to do it is when you guys are on the island."

"Oh," Olivia said. "Anything to be concerned about?"

"No, routine maintenance stuff. Have fun. I'll look after Jojo while you're gone."

"Keep an eye on him. He likes to get into mischief."

* * *

Jay waited for Olivia and the other researchers to board the rigid hull boats and head to the beach. Then he went to the bridge and entered the weapons store. Jay was disappointed. He expected to find a wall rack with wire doors and a dozen or so weapons. Instead, he found a rusty, steel storage cabinet with a pair of hinged doors. Jay tried the handle, and the doors opened. Oh crap, he thought, someone left the cabinets unlocked. Inside there were two disassembled AR-15 rifles and an ancient shotgun. There were three cardboard ammunition boxes on the bottom shelf of the cabinet. Inside, a handgun box was open, with the weapon missing.

29

Jay dug through the cabinet and found a partial bottle of cleaning oil and one dirty rag. This was a disaster.

Next to the cabinet was an old wooden desk filled with trash. Jay swept the garbage onto the floor. He opened the top door of the desk and found the handgun, a standard-issue Beretta M9. He pulled out one of the AR-15s and stripped it down. He then cleaned and oiled the handgun. He found the ammunition box was less than half full with enough cartridges to fill two thirty-round magazines. Jay loaded the AR-15s, cleaned the shotgun, then searched the cabinet again. He found a second ammo box with a dozen shotgun shells.

Jay turned on his radio and called Williams. "Could you come to the weapon store?" he said.

"I'll be right there," she responded.

Williams stared at the four weapons on the desk. "That's it?" she said. "You have to be kidding?"

"No, ma'am," Jay said. "Unless there are guns in other parts of the ship, this is the extent of our weapons cache."

"Do they work?" Williams asked.

"Can I test them?"

"Yes, go to the fan deck. Make sure you shoot away from the island."

Jay picked up the weapons and left.

Once on the fan deck, Jay found an old life ring and tossed it overboard. As he waited for it to float away from the ship, he heard a high-pitched noise. Jay turned to see Jojo standing at the door to the enclosure. His big black eyes were staring at him. The baby seal bleated away like a sheep. Jay tried to shoo him back into the pool, but Jojo didn't budge.

The life ring was floating farther away, so Jay had no choice but to fire the weapon. He picked up the first AR-15, aimed, and fired. The water splashed four feet away from the ring. He tried again. This time the bullet missed by over a foot.

Jojo screamed from the loud noise and backed away from Jay.

Not wanting to waste ammo, Jay picked up the second rifle. This time both bullets struck the life ring. Next, he shot the handgun without any problems. Jay loaded a shell into the shotgun. He placed the gun against his shoulder and fired.

Jay screamed as a searing pain ripped down his spine to the sole of his right foot. The pain was so intense, Jay dropped the shotgun and fell to his knees. The pain wouldn't stop. He placed his head in his hands and tried to will the pain away, but nothing worked. A loud ringing filled his head. Jay looked around for help, but Williams was gone. He stayed still for several minutes. They seemed like hours.

Finally, the pain in his head and leg subsided as strength returned to his arm. He gathered his wits and stood up. Jay looked around again to make sure nobody was watching. The coast was clear, so he grabbed the weapons and headed back to the bridge. Before leaving the fan deck, Jay visited Jojo in the pool. But when he looked around, the enclosure door was open, and he couldn't find Jojo anywhere. Jay called Williams on the radio.

"What do you mean you lost the seal!" Williams screamed into the radio. "How do you lose a seal, Mendes?

Jay didn't answer. He put the radio back in its holster. "Jojo, where are you?" he said, searching the fan deck.

After searching the ship for ten minutes, Jay found Jojo rummaging through the galley kitchen. His nose was in the refrigerator, and he was demolishing a leftover tuna casserole. Jay picked up the fifty-pound youngster with his left arm and pulled him out. Jojo licked Jay's cheek, leaving behind remnants of tuna and egg noodles. Jay smiled to himself and returned the seal to his pool. Then he made sure he closed and locked the makeshift wire enclosure. The young seal scampered up the ramp to the pool and dove into the water.

Jay wiped his face with his sleeve. Then he called Williams to file his report.

Chapter 4

Ten days later - Off the coast of Salvador de Bahia, Brazil

J ay knocked on the door of Olivia's stateroom. He double-checked to make sure his suit coat was wrinkle-free and that every strand of his thick, dark hair was in place. Olivia opened the door, and Jay's jaw dropped open. Her tight-fitting black party dress accentuated every curve in the best possible way. She ironed her curly hair flat, and her make-up accentuated her dark eyes. Four-inch heels completed the package.

"What do you think, Mendes?" Olivia said as Jay stood in the door. "Are you ready to hit the town?"

"You look amazing," Jay said. "What did you do with little Olivia?"

She slapped his arm. "Cut it out, Jay. You look like you've never seen a lady before."

"Not one this beautiful. Now, are you ready to enjoy the nightlife? They say Salvador is the best party town in Brazil. You deserve a break."

"I can't wait to see if you still know how to dance," Olivia said. "You were pretty good at your senior homecoming dance in high school."

"I don't remember going to a dance with you."

"You didn't know I was there. Jojo and I snuck in a back door."

* * *

The ten days of open sea sailing had taken a toll on crew and scientists alike. Despite the pirate warnings, Captain Michaels stopped in Salvador de Bahia to refuel. He agreed to let the researchers go into port. Not because the city had the lowest crime rate of any of the ports in Brazil, but because Jay was providing security.

Jay agreed to chaperone the six female researchers. He knew they wanted to have a good time, and he would make sure they stayed safe. Williams joined him as a chaperone. Perry piloted the small boat.

The short ride to the downtown marina was uneventful, and the girls located the Zen, a wild dance club.

The club was loud and crowded. But the drinks were cheap, and the patrons were friendly. Jay's Portuguese was rusty, but he remembered enough to have a few brief conversations. The researchers danced together in a group and managed to fend off the local males. As the night went on, a few girls staggered off with guys. Williams followed close behind.

Jay kept his distance from Olivia and her friends. His job was their safety, and he couldn't let himself get distracted. He'd have plenty of time to nurture his romance with Olivia when they returned to Cape Cod.

He took a sip from his glass of Coca-Cola when he heard a familiar voice, "Hey Mendes, what brings you to this dive?"

An overweight, dark-haired man stood next to him. He wore a nondescript blue polo shirt and khaki slacks. He looked familiar, but Jay couldn't place the face.

"Do I know you?" Jay said.

"It has been a few years, but yes, we met on a mission in northern Brazil. You were working with the U.S. DEA to hunt down a notorious drug lord."

"Right, Ernesto. Ernesto Cabral," Jay said. "Now I remember. You're with the Federal Police. You coordinated the search through the Amazon basin. I'll never forget the monster mosquitoes in that area."

"There you go, my friend. What brings you to Salvador? I notice you're not in uniform anymore."

"You're observant. I left the Navy a few weeks ago. I'm now working with a maritime security company aboard a research vessel. We stopped in port for supplies, and some of our researchers wanted to let their hair down for the evening."

"You're babysitting rich college kids."

"Bingo. You were always observant. Why are you here? I thought you worked out of headquarters in Rio?"

"I'm investigating a rash of drug-related deaths in northern Brazil. Very sad because most of the victims are young adults between the ages of 18 and 25."

"That's awful. What kind of drugs?" Jay said.

"We call the shit Jungle Fury because some of the ingredients grow in jungle plants. Plus, a Brazilian drug cartel is doing most of the production. On the streets, it's simply Fury.

"How are the people dying?"

"It seems to be causing instant strokes in some people.

Others are dropping dead. There isn't even a cure or antidote. Our government is funding research to try to find a way to treat strokes. It's awful."

"Are they smuggling it out of Brazil yet?"

"We think so, but we're not sure. It's one of the reasons I'm here at the port. Since it's a liquid, the cartel can't transport it by commercial airlines. The smugglers are using container ships. You don't need a lot of liquid to make a lot of money. They're using two-liter Coke bottles."

Jay's phone buzzed in his pocket. He saw the call was from Williams. "Jay, we have a situation. I'm outside the ladies' room."

"Hey, Ernesto, I gotta go. Let's stay in touch."

Ernesto handed Jay a business card then said," My pleasure. It was great seeing you, Jay."

* * *

Jay reached inside his jacket to check his gun, then pushed his way through the crowd.

Several drunk young men surrounded the researchers. One girl, a tall blonde named Stephanie, was screaming at one of the local guys. Jay could tell she was drunk, and the young man was trying to calm her down. He pushed his way through the crowd and stood between Stephanie and the man.

"That basshtard felt me up," Stephanie said in a drunken slur. "We were making out, and he, you know…" she held her hands up and cupped her fingers.

There was no way Jay would referee this argument, so he looked at Stephanie and said, "Williams, time to go."

Williams grabbed Stephanie's arm and escorted her out of the club. Olivia and the rest of the researchers followed behind.

When they were outside, Jay turned to see if they were being followed. The coast was clear, so they headed back to the launch.

Someone grabbed Jay's arm, and he turned, reaching for his gun inside his jacket. He relaxed when he realized Olivia had clamped onto him.

"I'm freezing," she said. Jay wrapped his arm around her.

Once on the small boat, the crew members counted their researchers. Satisfied everyone was present, they left the dock.

Jay kept an eye out for anybody following them. Williams watched the bow.

Olivia curled up next to Jay and fell asleep with her head on his shoulder. It was one o'clock in the morning.

Jay's phone buzzed. He saw Captain Michael's name on the screen.

"Mendes, our radar is showing two small boats approaching your launch. One from the port side and the other from starboard. They're moving fast. Assume they are not friendly."

"Aye aye, sir," Jay said and hung up. He pulled his gun from his holster. Perry noticed the look on his face and sped up.

Jay heard the small outboard motors before he saw them. They were half a mile from the ship—plenty of time for mayhem.

"Olivia, wake up," Jay said. When her eyes opened, he yelled, "Everyone down on the deck. Don't look up!"

A moment later, bullets whizzed inches over Jay's head

from the starboard side. The sound of the automatic fire followed a split second later.

"Hit the gas," Jay said to Perry. We need to get back to our ship!"

Gunfire erupted from the port side boat. Jay and the researchers were being attacked from two sides. Jay held his fire. He only had a single ammo clip, and the boats were too far away to do any damage.

The boat on the starboard side was fast and closed in on the inflatable. Jay saw a driver and at least two passengers. Each was armed with AK-47s. Jay crawled to the center console of the boat. He opened a side panel and pulled out the two AR-15s, tossing one to Williams. He grabbed the shotgun and gave it to Perry.

"Nobody boards this boat!" Jay said. "That's an order!"

Jay scrambled back to the starboard side. The outboard was only one hundred yards out, shooting without any effect.

He aimed at the pilot of the boat, released the safety, and squeezed the trigger twice. The driver's head disappeared from view and veered off to the right.

Jay adjusted his aim on the second gunman and squeezed the trigger twice again. The man fell back into the water. Two more shots and the third gunman was down. Six shots. Three kills from a moving boat. Jay hadn't lost his shooting skills.

"Did you hit anybody?" Olivia said from down on the deck.

"No," Jay said, lying. "I scared them away."

Jay looked towards the ship. Only three hundred yards to go.

A metallic clang caught his attention. A grappling hook pulled tight on the aft of their boat, which lurched to a stop.

Jay flew forward, missing the corner of the center console by inches. He reached down to stop his fall, dropping his rifle in the process. He landed on top of Stephanie, who didn't say a word.

"Are you alright?" Jay said. "I hope I didn't hurt you."

Stephanie shivered in fear, "I'm scared I'm going to die. Please stop them."

Several of the other girls screamed. A dark-skinned man with an AK-47 stood at the bow of the outboard.

"Perry," Jay yelled. "Shoot him!"

She pointed the shotgun at the man but didn't pull the trigger. She froze. Jay stared at her, but there was nothing he could do. He couldn't risk wrestling the gun away from her.

The man pointed his rifle at Perry.

Olivia sprang up from the deck of the boat. She yanked the shotgun from Perry's hand, racked the barrel, then pulled the trigger. The blast echoed across the water.

The bright muzzle flash blinded Jay. When his vision returned, he saw the attacker was gone.

"Jay, watch out!" Olivia yelled. He looked up to see a giant hand grab him by the collar and pull him out of the boat. He punched the man in the face with his right hand, then wrapped his left arm around the man's neck and pulled down. They both fell into the water.

The attacker grabbed Jay around the neck as they sunk into the dark, murky water. Jay punched him in the head. The man punched back. Jay hit him again and again, but the man's grip didn't loosen.

Jay struggled to hold his breath, knowing that he would drown if he gave into the natural reflex to breathe.

As an underwater diver, he trained to deal with stressful

situations. He learned how to fight underwater and survive. Jay knew his attacker didn't have the same training.

Jay reached down into his right pant leg and pulled out his desert dagger. He punched the razor-sharp point into the back of the man's neck and twisted. Jay pulled the knife out and then slammed it into the center of the man's chest, slicing through the heart. The man's body went limp, and Jay pushed him away.

With several powerful kicks, Jay was back on the surface. Looking behind him, he saw the pirate's small boat was empty. He cut the rope to the grappling hook, then replaced the knife in its holster. Jay swam back to the inflatable.

"Olivia, use the shotgun to punch a few holes in the boat's hull," Jay said as he crawled back onto the boat.

She obeyed his orders and placed several shots under the waterline until the boat sank.

Williams and Perry helped him aboard. Jay collapsed on the deck, relieved to be alive. Olivia dropped the shotgun and scrambled over.

"Oh my God, Jay," she said. "Are you alright? I can't believe you saved our lives."

"It's the other way around," Jay said with a big smile. "How did you learn to shoot like that?"

"Jojo and your Dad taught me how to skeet shoot when we were kids."

Chapter 5

The Nereus II sailed into Martha's Vineyard Sound early on a Sunday morning. The March air was crisp but not cold. Seagulls swarmed over the ship's fan deck, looking for scraps of fish, but Jojo wasn't giving up a single bite. Now seven months old, the fur seal pup weighed close to one hundred pounds. He splashed in his pool, scaring away the pesky gulls.

Olivia and the other researchers scrambled around, securing the last of their gear. The fan deck was full of equipment harvested on the return journey.

Jay viewed the Falmouth shoreline for the first time in fourteen years. It felt good to be home. He wondered how his family would react to seeing him.

"Hey, Mendes," Williams said. "Don't you have anything better to do?"

Jay ignored her, which he knew irritated her more than coming up with a sassy answer. She grunted and returned to her navigation screen.

As the ship approached the Woods Hole dock, Jay picked up his duffle bags.

"Remember, you have ten days' leave," Captain Michaels said. "I don't want to see you back a second sooner. You deserve a break. You did a great job, Mendes. Especially what you did in Brazil, I can't thank you enough."

"Thanks, Captain," Jay said. "I was doing my job."

Jay scrambled down the ladder to the fan deck. The boisterous fur seal swam over to him. Jay reached into a metal pail and held up a fish. Jojo grabbed it out of his hand and splashed back into the pool, forcing Jay to jump out of the splash zone.

"You have to work on your footwork," Olivia said from behind as she wrapped her arms around his waist. Jay turned to hug her back but stopped himself short. Mud covered Olivia from head to toe, her dark-blue coveralls soaked in seawater.

"Wow do you look sexy," Jay said. "Thanks for sharing."

She laughed. "Welcome to the fashionable world of marine biology."

"What are you doing now?"

"I'm going home to sleep," Olivia said. "Three hours of sleep in four days isn't hacking it. But I'll stay awake long enough for my father's party. He's throwing it for us at the Portuguese Veterans Club. He's inviting a bunch of old friends to celebrate our return."

"That's great," Jay said. "I didn't know your father liked me."

"He loves you, silly. You saved my life."

"Well, I'll have to let him know he's wrong. It's the other way around."

* * *

That night was a blur. Jay saw so many friends and neighbors he couldn't keep their names straight. He gorged himself on stuffed quahogs, lobster, and clam chowder, drinking enough beer to last a lifetime. Olivia and Jay dnced late into the night then went back to her apartment.

The next morning, the couple sat on her porch looking out over the small Wood's Hole inner harbor. Jay drank a strong cup of Colombian coffee and enjoyed a thick slice of Portuguese bread. Olivia cuddled next to him wearing an oversized Red Sox t-shirt. She kept staring at him with a sparkle in her eyes.

"Did you have fun last night?" Jay said with a sly grin on his face.

"You know I did. But I didn't get any sleep."

"Can't you sleep in today?"

"Not quite. I have a ton of work to catch up on."

"I hope you can save a little time for me. I only have ten days before the next trip."

"What were you thinking of doing?" Olivia said.

Jay glanced towards the bedroom. He stood up and held out his hands to Olivia, who accepted them. Jay pulled her to her feet and gave her a long, passionate kiss. She moaned and melted into his arms.

"Not sleeping," Jay said as he picked Olivia up and carried her into the bedroom.

* * *

The next ten months flew by for Jay. The ship's calendar was full, and the maintenance schedule was demanding. When he was home, he spent all of his time at Olivia's apartment.

Most of the research trips were short, from a week to ten

days. On the last trip, the Captain called Jay into his office. He managed to stay clear of Williams and stay out of trouble, so he wasn't sure why the Captain summoned him.

"Mendes, you have a visitor," Captain Michaels said as he stood up from his desk. "I'll leave you two alone for a few minutes.

Jay turned to see Steve Bonner walk into the office. "Hey, Mendes. Great to see you."

Jay stared at Bonner, "I have a few questions for you."

"I'm sure you do."

Chapter 6

T he Bonner Maritime Security Agency shared a small office with a construction company. The agency hired former special operators for security jobs on commercial ships. Steve Bonner, the owner, was a former Marine. He had a good reputation because he paid well and only placed his employees on American vessels. He had a dozen openings on container ships and tankers based in Bahrain and the UAE. Most assignments lasted for twelve months. They paid well and the considerable profits wer tax-free. Best of all, he had no problem filling assignments.

New job requests came in through his website. Today he received a strange request. A U.S. marine research vessel needed a security agent with diving experience. They needed someone fast and offered him twice his standard rate if he sourced a candidate within twenty-four hours. That meant he had to find a Navy SEAL. He made a few calls but came up empty. He would have to go out and do some active recruiting. He knew exactly the place to go.

* * *

Jay felt alive for the first time in six months. The bed in the Ramee

International Hotel was soft and covered with fine silk sheets. The feel of Natalie's soft skin was even smoother. She curled up next to him in the king-sized bed. Her head on his shoulder, and her legs wrapped around his torso. She grazed her fingers across his sweaty chest.

"You lost so much weight," she said. "Was it bad in prison?"

"It wasn't a prison. It was a Navy detention center. The inmates were sailors, so they didn't give me a hard time. They looked up to me. But I spent most of my time in my cell."

"Then did they starve you?"

"No, but the food sucked, and I didn't eat a whole lot. I tried to stay fit doing sit-ups and push-ups, but over time, I lost my enthusiasm."

"I missed you a lot," Natalie said as she kissed him on the cheek and ran her hand down his chest and between his legs.

"I can tell. You won't stop."

An hour later, Jay admired Natalie's slim, naked body as she crossed the room towards the shower. His cell phone buzzed, and he looked at the screen. "Pete says he'll meet us at Rocky's at 17:00," Jay said. "That gives us an hour. He booked us on a commercial flight to Norfolk for 06:00 tomorrow morning."

"He's a great guy," Natalie said as she stepped into the shower. "He paid for this room out of his own money."

Jay's phone rang. He answered. "Mendes. What? Are you guys in the bar already? Yes, we'll come down. Order us some food. We're starving."

* * *

The bar at Rocky's Cafe was empty except for two linebacker-sized men sitting at a high-top table. They each coveted a pitcher of

46

beer. *Gunny Mack's half-full pitcher contained a light pilsner while McCoy savored a dark Guinness stout. A third pitcher of Sam Adams sat on the table with two glasses. Baskets of Buffalo wings and french fries filled the middle of the table.*

"Now, this is what I call a healthy meal," Jay said as he entered the bar. He slapped Gunny on the back and sat down. Natalie sat down next to him. Jay poured each of them a beer, and he raised his glass.

"Here's to the best friends a guy could have. I wouldn't be here now if it weren't for your testimonies and support."

"You deserve it, Chief," McCoy said. "You saved our asses so many times on the battlefield. It's the least we could do."

Gunny downed his mug, then asked, "What's next, Jay? Where are you going? Have you thought about it?"

"No. I figured I'd go back to Norfolk with you guys and take some time off to figure things out. You know, do a lot of fishing and scuba diving. Maybe go down to the Bahamas for a few weeks. I may even go back home and spend some time with my family. It's been fourteen years since I left for boot camp."

"How about law enforcement?" Natalie said. "You could get a job with the FBI or Secret Service."

"That's not a bad idea. I haven't thought about my options. I didn't know I was going to beat the charges."

An attractive dark-haired waitress came over to the table. She gave McCoy a friendly smile, who blushed when she placed her hand on his shoulder, "Are you going to order any more food?"

"How about cheeseburgers all around," McCoy said. "And another round of beer. You're welcome to join us."

"Maybe later when my shift is over, sweetie."

The night flew by. Jay and Natalie danced to fast rock and roll songs then clung to each other for the slow romantic songs. The bar filled up with Marines and sailors, and Jay felt he was back in Virginia Beach. Gunny Mack kept the beer flowing, and Jay excused himself to use the men's room. As he waited for his turn, someone tapped him on the shoulder.

Jay turned to see a tall, slim man with gray-speckled hair. The man's face looked familiar, but Jay couldn't place it.

"Are you Jay Mendes?" the man said.

"Yeah, who's asking?" Jay said a bit warily. He wasn't expecting anybody to know him outside of his small circle of friends.

"Steve Bonner. We met at the Marine sniper school about five years ago."

"Bonner. That's right. You were one of the instructors. If I remember, you were a Gunnery Sergeant."

"That's right. Retired now. I wondered if you had a few minutes to talk. After your visit, of course."

"Sure, I'll be right out."

Jay and Bonner stepped out the front door of the bar and onto the sidewalk. The sun was setting. A crowd of men in white robes and women in black burkas huddled across the street. Otherwise, things were quiet.

"Jay, are you still on active duty?"

"No, I got out today. I'm heading back to Norfolk in the morning. Why do you ask?"

"Have you ever thought about staying here in the Middle East? Work as a private contractor."

"No. I haven't been home in a long time and miss the states. Why do you ask?"

"I run a small maritime security agency. I hire ex-SEALS and Marines to work on commercial vessels. They train the crew in self-defense and protect them against pirates."

"Sounds interesting, but I'll pass for now."

"The pay is great, and it's tax-free."

"Thanks anyway. Like I said, I'll pass."

"No problem," Bonner said. "If you know of anybody interested, I'm looking for someone right now." Bonner handed Jay a business card.

Jay took the card and shook his hand. "Thanks for the offer. I'll keep it in mind."

Jay turned to go back into the hotel when he noticed the small group of men and women had grown. Several of the men held signs in Arabic.

"Hey, Bonner, what's going on?"

"Oh, nothing to worry about. It's the nightly demonstration."

"What do you mean?"

"They're Shiite Muslims protesting against the ruling Sunni dictator. They've been doing this for years. They want a change in government and want the Americans out."

"Why are they gathered outside the front gate of the base?"

"They harass the American sailors. Try to provoke a confrontation so they can use it against us. Ignore them, and they won't be a problem."

* * *

Jay looked at Steve and realized his memories were returning. "So why are you here?" Jay asked. "Is there a problem?"

"Your contract is complete. Unfortunately, the Institute isn't offering an extension. Apparently, the ship is hiring a new full-time security officer as well as a diver. They're hiring two people to replace you."

"That's reassuring, but it doesn't help me. What am I going to do for work?"

"You could take another assignment in the Middle East."

"No, thanks, I've had enough overseas deployment. I want to settle down here on the Cape with Olivia."

"I'm sorry, Jay, but all of my contracts are offshore. So, I need to run since I have to grab a MAC flight at Hanscom Airbase later this afternoon."

II

Part Two

Chapter 7

Jay escorted Steve off the ship and said his goodbyes to the Captain and the ship's crew. By the time he disembarked, it was after supper, and Jay was starving. He thought about going straight home, but instead, he walked to his old Jeep Cherokee parked in the employee's parking lot. Jay bought the car from a crewmate for one hundred dollars and a round of beers at the Landfall. He liked the great deal he got. But Olivia thought he was crazy for driving a dark orange car. Jay intended on painting it but never brought it to the body shop. He opened the door, and the smell of mold almost killed him. He threw the bags in and shut the door fast. Walking seemed a healthier idea.

"Phew, can't you clean that junk heap?" he heard a familiar voice say from behind him. He expected to see his little sister Jessie. He imagined her dressed in a cheerleader outfit, waiting to bound into his arms. Instead, he turned to see a tall, slim supermodel. Now twenty-one years old, Jessie Mendes was drop-dead gorgeous. She towered over Jay's five-foot-six-inch frame. Her long, dark hair was pulled back by a jeweled barrette framing her sparkling blue eyes. A perfect set of white teeth smiled back at him. Her thin legs were wrapped in a sleeveless, knee-length dress with four-inch red stiletto pumps completing the package.

"Look at you, Jess!" Jay said as he hugged her. She returned the hug with little kisses on each cheek. "You look amazing! Are you on the air?"

"Not yet. I will be."

"Who's your next victim?" Jay said with a smirk. "I mean subject."

"You."

Jay looked past Jessie to see a cameraman setting up a tripod. The satellite truck with a large six on the side sat in a parking space across the street in front of the NOAA office.

"I don't think you want to interview me. I'm a boring old crewmember."

"Are you kidding? You're my brother and a Navy hero! My friends told me about the party Mr. Cataldo threw for you. I'm sorry I missed it. I was working on a project. I need one more interview to finish it."

"I'm not sure about this. When did you land the new gig?"

"Well, it's not a real job. I mean, I'm still in college. It's for practice. My professor will review it and give me a grade. The cameraman is my classmate, Roger. The station loaned us the van."

"Wow, that's cool. Promise nobody will see this interview? Otherwise, I won't sign a consent form."

"Promise. The farthest it will go is my professor's computer."

"Okay, you have a deal. Ask away."

"We'll do a practice run to test our lighting and camera angles."

Roger fussed with the equipment for a few minutes. He

gave Jessie the thumbs up when he was ready.

A red light went on.

"This is Jessica Mendes from Channel Six News," Jesse said, looking into the camera. "We're here tonight with a new hero. My brother, Jay Mendes. He's a..." Jessie turned to Jay.

"Jay, what's your rank?"

"Cut!" Roger screamed.

Jessie snarled at him. "Roger, you don't have to yell, cut. We're not filming yet. This is only practice."

"Oh, sorry. I like saying it."

"You're not a Hollywood director," Jessie said. "You're a journalism student."

Jay smiled. He loved the banter between his sister and her friend. It reminded him of their childhood when they would fight about everything.

"Okay, Jay," Jessie said. "What's your job and rank?"

"I'm not in the Navy anymore. My rank was Chief Petty Officer. I worked as a security officer on a research ship until a few minutes ago."

"Okay, let me start again. This is Jessica Mendes from Channel Six News. We're here tonight with a new hero, my brother, Jay Mendes. He's a security officer aboard the R/V Nereus II. The ship is a research vessel operated by the New England Marine Institute. Jay, can you tell me about any stories aboard the ship?"

"Sure, Jessie," Jay said with a serious look on his face. "I was escorting a group of researchers visiting Salvador Brazil for a night on the town. On our way back to the ship, pirates attacked our launch. I shot three of them from a moving boat at a distance of two hundred yards in the middle of the night. Then fended off two other pirates attempting to board the boat. I killed one by stabbing him in the neck. One of the researchers killed the other one."

Jessie stared at Jay with her mouth wide open. "Cut," she said. "Is that true?"

"Naw, I'm joking. Thought you would like something exciting for your broadcast."

"Oh my God, Jay. You had me going. What happened?"

"Pirates harassed us, but nobody got killed. That would have caused an international incident."

"Okay, do you mind filming the interview one more time? Then we're done. I'll get a good grade on this one. Do you want to grab a bite? The school gave me some money. We can go to the Landfall."

"Sure, let me call Olivia first," Jay said.

"Olivia, who?"

"Cataldo. You remember our next-door neighbor in Maravista."

"Of course I know, Olivia. She was Jojo's girlfriend. You mean you two are a thing?"

"I guess you could say that."

"How? When? You need to tell me all the sordid details?"

"They won't show up on the evening news, will they?"

"No, Entertainment Tonight."

* * *

Jay called Olivia's phone, but it went straight to voicemail. He wasn't sure if he was annoyed or concerned. He wanted to see her.

They were able to get a table at the Land Ho, a popular seafood restaurant without waiting. It was still the off-season on the Cape. The summer would arrive in two months, bringing swarms of tourists.

Jay ordered a beer for himself and Roger and a glass of Pinot Grigio for Jessie.

Jay raised his glass for a toast. "To Jessie for her first legal drink with her big brother. May, you become a successful and not too snobby television reporter."

Jessie laughed, almost spilling her drink.

Two of Jay's crewmates passed their table on the way to the bar. More crew members streamed in behind him. They were celebrating another safe return—a sailor's tradition dating back hundreds of years.

"Hey, Mendes," Juan Alvarez, a coxswain mate, said as he walked by. "We're telling Olivia you dumped her for a hot chick."

"She's my little sister, Alvarez. Cool your jets."

"Well then, is she single?"

"Not for you. She has higher standards."

Alvarez laughed and pounded Jay on his shoulders. "Hey Mendes, about that night in Brazil. The girls told me you were one mean-ass shot with that AR-15."

Jessie glared at Jay. "You said you were joking!"

"I was," Jay said. "He's talking about shooting on the range. He was part of my security team."

"Yeah, sure, Jay," Jessie said. "I don't believe you. You're probably one of those Navy SEALS but can't tell me, or you'll have to kill me."

It was Jay's turn to choke on his beer.

Time flew by fast as Jay and his sister reminisced about the fun they had growing up. They told stories about taking their Dad's fishing boat for a joyride and getting stuck on a sandbar. They wrapped up the night by walking back to Jay's Jeep.

"Jessie, it was great to spend time with you. Don't be a stranger. I want you guys to meet Olivia."

"Jay, Roger, and I are friends. We aren't dating."

"You could have fooled me," Jay said, elbowing Roger in the arm.

Roger glared back at him. "No, she's right. Jessie has a boyfriend."

Jay turned to her. "You're kidding. You two aren't a thing?"

"No," Jessie said. "I'm dating a guy named Andrew Bessie, the third. He goes to Brown in Providence. I met him through a sorority sister. Andrew works for a newspaper in Providence.

"His father owns it," Roger said.

"Jay, he asked me to marry him when we graduate. We're engaged. You didn't notice?"

Jay looked down as she spread the fingers of her left hand out. A sparkling diamond ring adorned her ring finger.

Jay stared at it. His little sister had grown up.

Then a thought came into his head. "You said his name is Andrew Bessie. That means your married name is going to be Jessie Bessie?"

Jessie stopped and put her hands on her hips. "Stop it, Jay! Don't laugh. Andrew's family is very well regarded in the Rhode Island social circles. They have a ten-room mansion in Newport. His father owns a fifty-foot yacht."

"Jessie Bessie? It's like the movie *The Wedding Singer*. Drew Barrymore's married name was going to be Julia Gulia." Jay couldn't stop laughing. Roger joined him.

"Cut it out, you two!" Jessie said with a pout. "Stop making fun of me."

Jay wiped the tears from his cheeks with this sleeve. "I'm sorry, Sis. I didn't mean to get you upset. I'm sure he's nice, and I'm very happy for you."

He hugged her and kissed her on the cheek. "I'll see you soon. Be careful out there."

Jessie hugged him back and wiped the tears off his face. "I love you too, Jay. You stay safe. Stay away from those pirates."

Chapter 8

J ay drove the quarter-mile to Olivia's apartment in less than a minute. He bounded up the stairs two at a time. The door to her apartment was a bit ajar, but he didn't seem to notice. Jay wanted to scream hello at the top of his lungs. Then he realized it was almost one in the morning. He should wake her gently.

When he was able to push the door open, he knew something was wrong. Jay dropped his duffle bag. The bedroom door was open. He saw sheets and a floral comforter lying in a pile at the foot of the bed.

Was she alone? Was she hurt? Perhaps sick or drunk from a late-night party? Jay stepped into the bedroom doorway and looked in. Olivia was sprawled on her back, naked and sound asleep. A pool of fluid stained the bed sheets between her legs.

There was a noise in the bathroom—a toilet flushing. The bathroom door opened. A tall man with salt and pepper hair stepped out. He was only wearing a pair of underwear. The man was older but in incredible shape: Six-pack abs and no body fat. The muscles in his chest and arms bulged. When he saw Jay, his face turned flush red. He ducked back into the bathroom, slamming the door behind him.

Jay vaulted over the bed, lowered his left shoulder, and plowed through the bathroom door. Splinters flew from the hinges as the door smashed inward. Jay slammed into the sink, bracing himself for a fight—but the bathroom was empty. The window next to the sink was open. He ran over and looked out. The street was quiet. Then he heard a car engine start. He caught a glimpse of a car leaving without its headlights on.

Jay went back into the bedroom and found Olivia still sleeping. He realized he was at a crime scene, and it appeared that the stranger drugged and raped Olivia. Jay stepped out of the bedroom and closed the door. Then he pulled out his phone and dialed nine-one-one.

* * *

Jay spent the rest of the night and the next morning in the ER waiting room. Finally, a nurse emerged from the exam room.

"Are you Mr. Mendes?" the nurse said. "Olivia asked for you to come in."

Jay found Olivia lying in bed. Her face was pale, and her eyes bloodshot.

"Olivia, are you alright?"

She shook her head.

"Tell me what happened."

She looked up at him with tears in her eyes. "I don't know."

"What do you mean? Did that man hurt you?"

She nodded. "The doctor said they found semen…."

"Oh God no," Jay said. "I'm so sorry."

Jay leaned over to hug her, but Olivia shook her head. "I

need some space," she said.

"Do you know the man who attacked you?"

"I don't know. All I know is I went to a dinner at the Institute. I ate and had a glass of champagne. The next thing I know, I'm waking up in the hospital."

"Were you drugged?"

Olivia nodded, "The doctor said they found traces of something called GHB in my urine."

"What does that mean?" Jay said.

"He said GHB is a common date-rape drug. It comes in a clear liquid, and you mix it with a drink."

"Like your champagne?"

"It could be. I don't know."

"Do you remember seeing anybody suspicious at the dinner?"

"No, Jay, I can't remember anything."

* * *

It took the rest of the day for Olivia to shake off the effects of the drug. She was distracted and said she wanted to rest. Jay didn't argue, deciding to visit his mother and wash his laundry.

Jay missed Olivia and wanted to do something to help. He tried calling her, but his calls went to voicemail. He spent his time job hunting and working out.

A week later, she finally responded and told him he could come over.

Jay found Olivia doing work in the kitchen. She gave him a quick kiss but returned to her books. He felt something was wrong but couldn't put his finger on it.

After supper, he asked her to take a ride to one of his favorite spots in Falmouth. They drove north on Route 28A past old houses with gray, weathered shingles and antique shops. He took a left towards West Falmouth harbor and pulled into the parking lot for Chapoquoit Beach. The wind was blowing hard, and the surf was up. Several people in wetsuits were kitesurfing.

The sun dropped toward the horizon. A few wispy clouds turning various shades of pink and orange. People lined up in their cars to watch the nightly ritual.

Jay and Olivia walked through the surf. The fine sand squishing through their toes. Jay stopped to skip some rocks while Olivia gathered seashells. When they reached a granite breakwater, he climbed up, and Olivia followed. They walked out to watch the waves crashing over the piles of granite boulders.

Jay held Olivia's hands and pulled her towards him. "I wanted to say something to you for a long time."

"Wait," Olivia said as she resisted. "I need to be honest with you."

"What do you mean?" Did I do something?"

"No, Jay. That's not it. I won an award for the research report I wrote about our trip to the Falkland Islands. It included a grant to continue my studies for my Ph.D. I received a full scholarship to continue my research."

"That's great news. Did you got your first choice at the Institute?"

"I got my first choice. It's not here."

"Where is it?"

"I'm going to study at the Scripps Institute of Oceanography in San Diego."

"I thought you were getting the job at the Falmouth Aquarium? You were going to care for Jojo?"

"Stephanie got the trainer's job at the aquarium. She's staying at the Institute to work on her degree. There was only one slot available. He's in good hands."

"What will you be doing?"

"Sea mammal research. They have the research ship Sally Ride. We'll be traveling to Alaska to study killer whales and seals."

When do you leave?"

"Tomorrow. I was going to tell you sooner, but you know what happened."

Jay turned his back. He tried to gather his composure.

"Jay, what were you going to tell me?"

Jay put his hand in his right pocket. He fingered the small box with the diamond engagement ring. The one his father gave to his mother over thirty-five years ago. He contemplated popping the question. But he knew that wasn't right. He had to let her go.

"Nothing," Jay said as he turned to look at her. "Olivia, I love you. I'll be here when you return."

Chapter 9

The water was murky and cold as Jay approached the ship. Large strands of kelp floated in sinewy clumps around the motionless propellers. Jay watched for errant dock lines dangling in the water. Left by sloppy deckhands, they could entangle a diver, cutting off his oxygen supply. Barnacles covered the hull of the ship. The tiny, razor-sharp crustaceans could tear through the thin nylon work gloves on Jay's hands. They weren't poisonous, but human blood attracts predators. Recent reports of great white sharks feeding on harbor seals were fresh in Jay's minds. Even though the sightings were off the Outer Cape beaches, nothing stopped them from swimming into Woods Hole Harbor.

As Jay drifted towards the two propeller assemblies, he turned on his headlamp. The bright LED lights blinded him for a brief moment. Jay turned on the mini GoPro camera mounted on his helmet. He dove in close to the rudder, the rectangular blade behind the propellers, then worked his way forward, looking for rust, foreign debris, and broken welds. He recorded his observations as he swam.

When he finished the inspection, Jay swam to a ladder on the side of the dock and climbed up. He removed his headgear, placing it on the pier.

A slim, aging dark-haired man in blue coveralls approached Jay and said, "How does she look, Jay?"

"No signs of damage, Al. No obvious rust or decay, and all weld seams appeared to be intact."

"Jay, are you sure about that?"

His words stunned Jay. Al Flores was a long-time friend and the Chief Maintenance Manager at the Marine Institute. He never questioned Jay's findings before. "What are you saying, Al? You don't trust my inspections?"

"Jay, I like you and trust you. But, the Captain of the ship is questioning the quality of your work. Follow me. I want to show you something."

He peeled off his wetsuit and scuba gear, following Al into a two-story brick building. They entered an office filled with computer equipment and video monitors.

"Take a look at this video. A robotic inspection system called the Trekker recorded these images last week."

Jay watched an image in bright orange, reds, and blues. It showed a jagged orange line running across the bottom of the hull.

"That's an infrared image," Jay said. "It's showing a fissure between the third and fourth bulkheads."

"That's right. It picked up a fissure that you missed."

"But I don't have infrared equipment. I don't remember you asking me to use it before. How can you compare my visual inspection to an infrared inspection?"

"We're not trying to, Jay. The Trekker includes acoustic imaging as standard equipment. It relays real-time video streams while conducting inspections. It also creates a log, so we don't have to enter manual reports."

"What are you saying?"

"You know we're friends, and I've gone to bat for you since you returned from the Navy. I know you're having a tough time with PTSD and all. The cost of the robot system is half of what we pay you."

"I can get infrared gear. I won't charge you extra. You have to…."

Jay couldn't finish his sentence as Al stood up and pulled an envelope out of his desk drawer. "Here's your payment for today's inspection. It's the final one."

A feeling of dread overwhelmed Jay. His throat felt dry, and a pounding feeling gripped his chest. Jay felt his anger rise, and he tried to control it but to no avail.

"Thanks for nothing, Al," Jay said as he grabbed the envelope and stormed out of the office.

Jay picked up his dive gear, then pushed his way through the security gate. A security guard stopped him. "I'm sorry, sir," the young guard said. "I need your security pass."

Jay pulled the pass off his t-shirt, threw it at the guard, and then stormed out to the parking lot. He opened the rear liftgate of the Cherokee, tossed his gear in the back, then slammed the door. He gunned the engine, leaving smoke and rubber behind.

* * *

He couldn't think about the consequences of what happened. Not yet, at least. Jay headed north on Woods Hole Road and turned east on Route 28 through Falmouth Village. He ignored the town square lined with ritzy gift shops and cozy restaurants and continued driving into East Falmouth, winding his way through groves of scraggly pine trees and cranberry bogs. He turned down a pitted, sandy dirt path that ended at a white, single-story building. A few pick-up trucks and broken-down SUVs lined the side of the building. A small sign over the side door read Portuguese Veterans Club.

Before Jay went into the club, he pulled off his wet t-shirt and threw it into the back of the Jeep. He reached into a white duffle bag, pulled out a clean white t-shirt with USN on the front, and pulled it on. Jay pulled his shoulder-length hair back away from his face and put the cap on. He ran his fingers through his beard and rubbed his bloodshot eyes, then stepped out of the Jeep.

Jay entered the private bar in the back of the club. Since Jay's father helped build the club, Jay had lifetime privileges. He knew the bartender and members like they were his own family. After his discharge, it has been a home away from home.

Inside the dim clubroom, a ragged pool table sat ignored in the back corner. A few round tables sat empty. Plain pine paneling adorned the walls with photos of past barbecues and other events. One black and white photo showed a group of men standing in front of the hall. Jay's dad knelt in the front row, holding a hammer across his right knee.

The bar had room for about twenty patrons, but now there were two guys at the bar. Jay slid onto a stool in front of the flat-screen television above the liquor shelves. The Global News Network played on the TV.

"Hey Sal," Jay said to an overweight bartender with a shaved head and three missing teeth. "Give me a double Jack on the rocks."

The bartender grabbed a bottle of Jack Daniels, added a few ice cubes then filled the glass to the top. "Here you go, Jay. Starting a bit early, aren't you? Having a tough day?"

"Yeah, you could say that," Jay said as he took the glass and downed the liquor in one gulp. "Give me another."

Sal obliged, and Jay drank half the glass, put it down, and put his head down on the bar.

"I've known you since you were a kid," Sal said. "I built this club with your old man. Tell me what the hell is going on. I've never seen you down like this."

He looked up at Sal and shrugged. "What the hell. I can't afford a shrink. I lost my job today."

"You didn't fuck up, did you? You never fucked up a job before."

"No, I didn't fuck up. I didn't do it as well as...."

"As what? Another diver?"

"No. I lost my job to a fucking robot. Some mechanical camera found a crack I didn't see. I couldn't see."

"You gotta be shitting me. A lousy robot? What the hell is this world coming to? Here, have another drink on me."

Jay laughed. "Yeah, I need one. Give me...."

The reason Jay stopped mid-sentence was the broadcaster on television. It was Kathleen Amejian, Jay's accuser from Pakistan. She was standing in front of a hospital in Italy.

"Sal, turn the TV up, will you? I want to hear what the bitch has to say."

"Sure, Jay, whatever you want. Why did you call her a bitch? She's one of the world's most famous reporters."

"I've got my reasons. Now turn it up."

Sal grabbed the remote control and turned the volume up.

An aerial view of an ancient hospital appeared on the

screen. A small box with Kathleen Amejian's face appeared in the bottom left corner.

"This is Kathleen Amejian reporting from Castel Gandolfo outside of Rome. Inside sources have informed us that Pope Pius XIII is being treated for a gunshot wound. Details are very sketchy, but sources tell us that a sniper shot the Pope on the Vatican's official vacation residence's balcony. Our calls to the Vatican and the Swiss Guard have gone unanswered. On a side note, local priest Edwardo Cavetelli's body was found floating in Lake Albano three days after being reported missing. According to police, he had a gunshot wound to the side of his head. The coroner reports the cause of death as a suicide, even though police found no weapon. Stay tuned for continuing coverage."

He felt his blood pressure rise as he listened to Kathleen's voice on the television. He then said, "I can't listen to her anymore."

Jay grabbed his glass off the bar and threw it at the television. The glass shattered, spraying ice and shards across the bar. A large crack appeared on the screen. Then the TV went black.

"Ah, Jay, what the hell is the matter with you?" Sal said. "Get the hell out of here. Now!"

"I'm not going anywhere. I need another drink."

"You're done for today, Jay. You need to go before I call the police."

One of the guys sitting at the end of the bar stood up and walked over to Jay. He stood about six foot three and built like a weightlifter. "Come on, Jay," the man said. "Don't cause any trouble."

Jay ignored the man and shouted, "I want another drink,

Sal!"

The big man grabbed Jay by the right shoulder and yanked him around. "Come on. You're outa here!"

Jay screamed as pain surged through his arm. Fueled by anger, frustration, and embarrassment, Jay turned and punched the man in the face. The man's head snapped back, and he dropped to the floor. His buddy, about the same height but with a huge pot belly, jumped out of the way. He then took two quick steps and threw a wild roundhouse punch at Jay's head. Jay ducked out of the way and punched the man in his soft midsection. The fat guy bent over in agony, and Jay laid him out with an uppercut.

Jay looked back at the bar to see Sal on the phone. "I need a police cruiser and ambulance at the Portuguese Veterans Club. I have an out-of-control patron."

"Sal, what are you doing?" Jay said. "You don't need to call an ambulance. These guys aren't hurt."

"It's for you, Jay," Sal said as he smashed the half-empty bottle of Jack Daniels down on Jay's head.

Chapter 10

Brian McCoy sat in his office in the Emergency Command Center. His job at the Department of Homeland Security (DHS) coordinated with other agencies during terrorist attacks or natural disasters. The view of Boston Harbor from his tenth-floor office was spectacular.

McCoy didn't pay any attention to the scenery. When he last saw Jay, they were in a bar in Bahrain the night he disappeared without a trace. The only information he had was from a cryptic phone message on his cell phone. It said Jay was okay, but he had to go away for a while. The voice scrambled, and the caller ID blocked. McCoy tried to trace the source of the call without any luck. He missed his roommate and felt guilty for escaping punishment after the Pakistan debacle. He also knew Natalie, Jay's girlfriend, and Gunny Mack, the two former teammates with Jay that night in Bahrain, also missed him.

The other former Infinity Squad members stayed in touch. CJ and Madman finished their enlistment and returned to New Hampshire. Gia Khalil returned to civilian life and concentrated on raising Rameera, her adopted daughter. At the same time, Michelle Goddard moved from London to

New York to run Goddard Aviation. He tried calling her several times but was turned away by her assistant.

Andrea, his administrative assistant, walked in and handed him a newspaper. "I think I found him. Look at the police report."

"Oh, thank goodness," McCoy said. "I thought you had an obituary. He's not dead."

"No, but he is in trouble."

* * *

Jay awoke to a pounding headache. He could tell he was in the hospital by the familiar beeping from unattended monitors. He tried to sit up but screamed when a surge of pain blasted through his head. The pain wouldn't stop, and Jay put his hands to his head, trying to cope with the intense throbbing. A nurse ran in, hearing his scream. She administered pain medication through the IV drip, and Jay fell back asleep.

When Jay awoke, he saw an enormous figure standing in the doorway to the treatment room. The person blocked the light in the hallway so Jay could only see a silhouette. The person moved closer to Jay until he stopped at his bedside. Jay noticed the person was a large man in a police officer's uniform.

"Jay? Jay Mendes, right?" the police officer said.

Jay nodded.

"Don't you recognize me? I'm Marty. Marty Hernandes. Do you remember now?"

Jay thought to himself, who was Marty Hernandes? The name sounded familiar, but he couldn't place it.

"I think I know you," Jay said. "From when I was a kid?"

73

"Yeah. We were best friends. Your dad worked for my dad in the cranberry bogs when he wasn't fishing. We played football together. I blocked for you when you ran sweeps."

"Yeah, now I remember you. My head is a bit fuzzy. I had a tough day yesterday."

"Well, actually, it was three days ago," Marty said. "You've been in and out of consciousness since we brought you here."

"So why are you dressed in that uniform?" Jay said. "Are you a cop?"

"You might say that. I'm Deputy Chief of the Falmouth Police Department. Jay, I'm here to read you your Miranda rights and inform you of the charges against you."

"Charges? What charges? Marty, what did I do?"

"The Commonwealth of Massachusetts is charging you with two counts of assault and one count of disorderly conduct. You broke Mike Alvarez's cheekbone, and you busted Sal's TV at the PA club. Our fathers built that club with their bare hands. How could you disrespect their memory?"

"Shit, was I that drunk? I usually don't blackout when I drink."

"No, Sal hit you over the head with a bottle of Jack Daniels."

"That explains the glass in my skull. So now what? Am I going to jail?"

"Most normal human beings would go to jail. But Jay, you're not human. You have friends in high places."

"God?"

"No, you idiot, me," said a voice from outside the treatment room.

Jay looked up to see a second man standing at the doorway to his room. This man was as tall as Marty but much slimmer.

He had short, blonde hair cut tight to his head. Unlike Marty, Jay recognized his voice immediately.

"McCoy?" Jay said. "What the hell are you doing here?"

"To do one thing, Mendes. Save your sorry ass."

Chapter 11

J ay needed to know what the verdict was.

"McCoy, what the hell happened in Bahrain? Was I found innocent or guilty?"

Then the flood gates opened. Jay closed his eyes as the memories of his last day in the Navy washed over him.

* * *

Jay paced outside the courtroom at Naval Support Activity (NSA) Bahrain, home to the US Fifth Fleet. The knots in his stomach tightened when his JAG, a military lawyer, Lieutenant Commander Pete Medici, told him the jury was back. Jay straightened his dress uniform and put on his cap.

"Let's do this," Jay said to nobody in particular. The Navy MP led him into the courtroom. He saw his Infinity Squad colleagues sitting in the empty gallery. His girlfriend, Sargeant Natalie Choi, USMC, looked at him and smiled back. He reached out to her as he sat down at the defendant's table. She squeezed his hand back and said, "It will be okay, Jay."

Sitting next to Natalie, Petty Officer Brian McCoy and Gunnery Sergeant John "Gunny Mack," McCauley whispered. McCoy was his roommate. Gunny Mack was the Infinity Squad's operation commander and Jay's good friend.

As he sat, he saw his accuser, Kathleen Amejian, and her high-priced lawyer at the prosecutor's table. They sat next to a female JAG lawyer.

The bailiff, a bulky Navy Master Chief, stood up and said, "All rise."

The JAG judge, Colonel Tyler Matthews, walked in, sat down, and looked inside a plain manila folder. He put the folder down.

He banged his gavel, "Call in the jury."

"All stand," ordered the MP.

A Marine General led the procession of twelve military officers. Nine men and three women from Special Operations commands around the world. They took their seats without looking at Jay. Was that a good sign or a bad one? Jay couldn't figure them out.

"Have you reached a verdict?" the judge asked.

Jay felt his stomach knot tighten and his palms sweat.

"Yes, we have your honor," the Marine general said.

"On the count of war crimes, what do you find?"

Jay flashed back to Dubai and the crash of Matthew Goddard's helicopter. The search for his friends Gia and Antonio, Michael Goddard dying in Gia's arms, and the shootout in the Pakistani Cave. This verdict was the moment Jay's entire career was hanging on. Fourteen years of hard-fought service could go down the drain. But even worse, he was looking at spending the rest of his life in jail or even death row. He hoped his defense would be enough to save his bacon. He was about to find out.

The jury foreman opened a small envelope and read, "Not guilty."

A wave of relief swept through Jay's body. He heard a moan from Natalie and two cheers from McCoy and Gunny Mack. But they weren't done yet.

"On the count of dereliction of duty, what do you find?"

"Not guilty."

Not guilty on both charges. After six months in a military jail, he was a free man.

"Ladies and gentlemen of the jury. Thank you for your service to this court. You are now dismissed. Chief Petty Officer, Mendes, you are also dismissed."

Jay watched the jury leave, shook Pete's hand, and turn to embrace Natalie."

Before he had a chance to leave the defense table, a woman walked into the courtroom, "Chief Petty Officer, Mendes?"

"Yes, that's me."

"Rear Admiral Brown requests your presence and Lieutenant Commander Medici's presence in his office."

The woman turned and left the courtroom.

Jay turned to look at Pete, who shrugged his shoulders, "Pete, do you know what this is about?"

"No. It's a mystery to me."

"Jay, is everything all right?" Natalie said as Jay embraced her outside the courtroom. "What could the Admiral want?"

"I don't know, but it isn't good. Why don't you go back to the barracks, and I'll call you when I'm done."

"No way, I'm waiting for you. No matter what the Admiral tells you, you're a hero in my eyes."

* * *

Jay and Pete entered the Admiral's office, saluted, and stood at attention in front of his desk.

"Gentlemen, at ease. Chief Mendes, congratulations on your acquittal. You have shown courage and honor during your entire

career in the U.S. Navy. However, I have three letters on my desk, and I must make a decision. The first letter is a recommendation for a Navy Cross, the second-highest medal in the U.S. Military. It is to recognize your courage and bravery during the battle of Mosul and your efforts to rescue over thirty Iraqi civilians in a thirty-day period. This award will be presented to you by the Secretary of the Navy upon my approval.

The second letter on my desk is a recommendation from the Medical Evaluation Board. Due to your post-traumatic stress and the shrapnel embedded in your neck, they recommend a medical discharge. You do not have to accept the recommendation, and you can choose to remain in an operational unit. However, if the shrapnel moves, you could be paralyzed or worse. You might endanger your fellow sailors and your own well-being.

The third letter is the one that I do not want to sign. It is a referral to the Navy SEAL review board related to the dereliction of duty charge. If the board finds you disobeyed orders, they can remove your TRIDENT, and you will no longer be able to serve as a Navy SEAL. You will be reassigned to a non-combat unit. Needless to say, I will withdraw the Navy Cross recommendation. Do you have any questions?"

The Admiral's words shook Jay's conscience. He was a proud and honorable sailor and did not want to accept a medical discharge. But if he did retire, he wanted to retire as a SEAL. The thought of facing the review board and losing his TRIDENT was beyond terrifying. The Admiral was right. If he returned to active duty, the shrapnel could kill him and endanger his squadmates.

"Sir, what about the Infinity Squad? Will it continue to operate?"

"No, I am afraid without General Andrew's leadership, the Infinity Squad and other HRTs are being disbanded. If you decide

to finish out your current enlistment, you will return to your operating team."

"Sir, may I have a minute to review my options with Lieutenant Commander Medici?"

"Of course, Mendes. You can use the conference room outside my office. Take your time."

Jay saluted and walked out of the office and into the small conference room. Pete closed the door behind them.

"Pete, what do I do? I don't want to retire. I'm too young. Plus, I love being a SEAL."

"But what about the shrapnel? Didn't you tell me you're having numbness in your arm?"

"Yea, but it might never move. I can deal with the pain and numbness."

"But if it does move, it will paralyze you. Make you a quadriplegic. That's no way to live."

"Being a SEAL is the only job I've ever had. I don't know what else to do. I can't go back to being a fisherman or working in some lame office job."

"Jay, if you stay on active duty, you will have to face the review board. The transcripts of the trial will be enough evidence for them to find you negligent. They don't have to prove anything within a reasonable doubt. If even one board member has something against you, you will lose everything. The Navy could give you a general or even dishonorable discharge. It will ruin the rest of your life."

"Damn, this is not a decision I want to make. But, it seems my only option is to accept the medical discharge. Will I receive benefits?"

"Yes. You will receive a disability payment for the rest of your life plus full VA healthcare and other benefits."

"Okay, let's go see the Admiral."

Jay and Pete returned to the Admiral's office.

"Admiral, I will reluctantly accept the medical discharge, as long as I can retire as a SEAL."

The Admiral signed the Navy Cross recommendation and the medical discharge papers. Then he ripped up the review board recommendation.

"Mendes, It is an honor to tell you how much the United States Navy appreciates your service. You are dismissed."

"Thank you, sir."

* * *

Jay walked down the corridor back towards the courtroom. Shocked and dismayed, he couldn't even think about what life would be like outside the Navy. How was he going to make a living? Would Natalie still want him?

"What do you want to do now?" Pete asked outside the Admiral's office.

"I want to see Natalie, then get wasted," Jay said. "But I don't know where to go. I've been in a jail cell for the past six months."

As Jay returned to the lobby outside the courtroom, Natalie ran up to him and jumped into his arms. He caught her petite body and hugged her close. She kissed him until his lips were sore. He placed her down and said, "Let me thank these guys."

Gunny Mack shook his hand and embraced him. McCoy wrapped his mammoth arm around his shoulder and escorted him out of the building.

As they turned to leave, Pete handed him a small khaki bag and said,

"Here's your duffle bag. You'll have to change into civvies.

That's the rule in Bahrain, no uniforms off base. Why don't we meet at Rocky's Cafe at the Ramee Hotel? It's right across the street from the base, and they have homebrew and the best cheeseburgers this side of Dubai."

"Sounds great," Jay said.

Pete reached into his pocket and handed Jay a rectangular plastic key. "I got you a room. It's the least I could do."

"You did everything. You got me off, Pete. I'll never be able to repay you."

"No, you and your friends got you off. Now have some fun, and I'll meet you at five. I have some retirement paperwork to process."

Jay looked around to get one last look at Kathleen, but she was gone. She put him through hell, but he had won. At least for now. Something told him she wasn't done.

Chapter 12

Twenty-four hours later, Jay walked out of the hospital with part of his head shaved and wrapped in a white bandage. McCoy waited for Jay outside the emergency room entrance in a beat-up black Chevy Suburban. Marty sat in the back seat.

"Where are we going?" Jay asked. Nobody answered. They drove in silence for ten minutes until they reached Woods Hole one block from the ferry. McCoy turned into the parking lot of a three-story Victorian building. A coffee shop occupied the bottom floor. A small sign in front of the parking space read, *Reserved for Maravista Security.*

McCoy opened a plain white door on the side of the building. The stairs led directly up to the second floor. He unlocked the door and walked into an apartment almost void of furniture. A square card table and four chairs sat alone in the middle of the floor. A black handgun sat in the center of the table. Jay noticed a steel circular staircase going to a loft above.

"You're scaring me," Jay said. "What is going on? Is this a safe house?"

"Be quiet and sit down," McCoy said. "You were once the top SEAL in the entire Navy. You never fucked up, and we never lost a single hostage until Pakistan. You didn't kill Matthew Goddard, but you took the fall for us. I've been waiting for a year to thank you."

"But now you're going to kill me?"

"What are you talking about?"

"The gun on the table. The empty apartment. You're going to make it look like I committed suicide."

"Man, Sal hit you too hard," Marty said. "We don't want to kill you. We want to help you. Discuss a business proposal."

Jay looked at Marty and McCoy. Then looked at the gun. It all fell into place.

McCoy sat down and put his hand on Jay's shoulder, "We want to offer you a partnership in our new company, Maravista Security. This apartment will be the headquarters. The loft will be your office. The gun is yours. We're giving you a shot at redemption."

* * *

The fire roared all around him, running up the walls and across the ceiling. The flames danced with a life of their own. Reaching out with tentacles of heat, then retracting back. The smoke poured from the tips of the fire, blurring his vision, creating shadows and images that played with his soul. The heat was overwhelming, even inside the fire suit. The sweat poured down his forehead into his eyes and mouth. The temptation to pull off his face mask and wipe the sweat from his brow was overwhelming. A fatal mistake if he tried.

Jay fought back the fear building in the back of the brain. The little voices were saying, 'This is it. Your times up. You've rescued your last hostage and saved your last life. It's easier to die than to fight back. Give up.' But Jay fought back. He suppressed the voices and anxieties. He thought of the torture he endured during his BUDS training—the drill instructors urging him to give up. Just ring the bell, they said, and ease your pain. You don't have to endure this hell any longer.

Jay trained the hose on the fire in front of him and released the valve. A wall of water attacked the fire. He sprayed a wide, arcing pattern in all directions. The thick black smoke turned to white steam, scalding him alive if he wasn't wearing the fire suit. Then the flames retreated, and the heat diminished. Jay worked his way into the kitchen until he found a pile of rags. He sprayed the pile for over a minute until the kitchen floor filled with water. It kept rising. He tried to escape, but the heavy suit prevented him from swimming. Water seeped into the suit, filling up until it reached his neck, then his chin. It inched up until it poured into his mouth. He screamed for help.

* * *

Jay bolted upright. His screams were echoing off the empty walls. Sweat poured down his forehead, soaking the inflatable mattress he slept on. He looked around to find himself in the living room of the empty apartment.

He crawled to his feet and stared at the Baretta. It was one option. One way to stop the nightmares and cold sweats. A way to stop the pain and embarrassment tormenting him. One squeeze, and it was over. He had pulled triggers thousands of times. No, millions, since BUDS training. Most of the bullets launched into harmless targets. Plywood dummies made to resemble real threats. But many shots found their home into flesh and blood. Extinguishing the lives of men he never knew and hoped he would never meet in the afterworld.

Jay sat down on the folding chair and stared at the gun. Picking it up, he admired the smooth cold steel and workmanship. Jay learned to love and respect firearms. They were a simple tool to complete a task. Guns saved his life and the lives of his buddies countless times. Harmless one moment, deadly another. One simple pull. A few ounces of pressure, and they transformed into an instrument of death. But the gun didn't fire on its own.

Jay released the magazine and let it fall to the table. It was empty. He cocked back the chamber and found it open too. No bullets. No death. Clean and simple.

He stood up from the chair and walked into the tiny bathroom with a simple white sink, toilet, and tiny shower stall without a curtain. Above the sink, he looked into a small, unframed mirror. The sight was horrific. A ragged, tangled beard framed his pale face, and hollow bloodshot eyes stared back at him. Jay stared at the image without recognizing the person. He stood back so he could see the rest of his torso. Once hard as a rock, his stomach was loose and flabby. Scars crisscrossed his chest—reminders of hard-fought battles. His arms were thin, and his muscles soft. How could Marty and Brian think this person could be their business partner?

Jay reached back and pulled the bandage off his head, dropping it on the floor. He looked around the bathroom and found a small closet. Inside was a single towel, a razor blade, and a pair of scissors. He picked up the scissors and began the transformation.

* * *

Thirty minutes later, a new man emerged from the bathroom. With a shaved face and head, he looked like a different person. He found his duffle bag and pulled on his favorite USN t-shirt, a pair of shorts, socks, and running shoes. He pulled a dark-blue USS America cap onto his head to cover his stitches. Then he ran down the stairs and out into the brisk morning air.

Jay took a deep breath. He felt like a new man. He ran down the narrow street towards the Martha's Vineyard ferry terminal, then followed a painted path through the vast parking lot. The Shining Sea Bikeway followed a former rail line. In the eighteen hundreds, it transported tourists from Boston to Cape Cod, weaving through woods for about a mile. Then the trees gave way to the spectacular ocean view of Vineyard Sound.

Jay stopped at the intersection of Surf Drive to catch his breath and take in the view. He remembered coming to the beach when he was a small boy. A hurricane washed away large chunks of the bikeway and street. He remembered seeing the ruins of oceanfront cottages scattered across the rocky shore. One small house even sat on the opposite side of Oyster Pond beached on an ancient stone wall.

The early-morning ocean was as smooth as glass. Jay watched loons gliding a few feet over the water, searching for their morning meal while Osprey chicks called out from nests overlooking the beach.

Jay crawled down the large granite blocks separating the bikeway from the beach. He pulled off his hat and shirt, removed his running shoes. and waded into the clear, cool water. The water stung his wound, but Jay knew the saltwater had healing power. He swam out far enough to clear the breakwater then swam parallel along Shore Drive. Jay swam until he reached the breakwater at the opening of Falmouth Harbor. He touched one of the granite blocks, performed a flip turn, and pushed off back to complete his circuit. He returned to the beach, tired but refreshed.

Jay sat on the beach to dry off. He thought about Olivia and their romance. She was a sweet kid, and he loved her, but she was better off on the west coast. Anyways, Jay needed to get his shit together before he tried another relationship. He lay back in the sand and began to drift off to sleep. Then he heard the sound of screeching tires and a loud metallic bang.

Someone screamed, "Hey, you asshole, watch where you're going!" Jay jumped up and ran towards the bike path to see what was going on.

He saw a slim, red-haired woman lying on the ground next to a crumpled bicycle. An older white-haired woman sat in her gray Mercedes convertible, staring ahead in a state of shock.

Jay ran over to the woman on the ground. She wore a skin-tight yellow spandex biking shirt, black shorts, and bike shoes. Jay saw blood on one of her knees but didn't notice any other injuries.

"Are you alright?" he said. "What happened."

"The bitch didn't stop. There's a crosswalk there for a reason, and the bike path traffic has the right of way."

"Do you want me to call the police?" Jay turned to look back at the lady in the car, but she was gone. "Well, I guess you could report a hit and run."

"What? Did she leave? That's great. Now, what am I going to do."

Jay pulled the bike from between her legs and placed it on the ground next to the bike path. The woman tried to stand but screamed out in pain when she tried to put weight on her leg.

"Do you know what time it is?" she asked.

"No," Jay said. "I don't have a watch."

"Can you reach into the handlebar bag on my bike? My cell phone is there. I'll call my son to pick me up."

"Sure," Jay said as he walked over to her bike and pulled out her phone. "Are you sure you don't want me to call the police and report the accident?"

"No, I'll tell my brother. He's a Falmouth cop."

"I better get back to my run," he said. The woman was on the phone and didn't seem to notice.

"Kyle, it's Mom. I was in a small accident on the bike path. Can you come to pick me up? Yes, you have my okay to drive the car by yourself. You have your license. I'm at the crosswalk on Surf Drive. Okay, don't take long. I have to get to work."

Jay put on his shirt, hat, and running shoes then went back up to the woman. "Are you sure you're okay?" Jay said. "I can stay with you until your ride's here."

"No, I'm fine. Thanks for the help."

Jay ran back to the apartment in Woods Hole, feeling like a new man. He took a quick shower to wash the saltwater off, then he called McCoy and told him he would accept the offer to join Maravista Security.

Chapter 13

Dartmouth, MA - South Coast of Massachusetts

Butterflies whipped knots up in Jay's stomach. Not because he was on his first assignment for Maravista. But because he didn't know if the beat-up Suburban Marty bought had proper armor. That's a detail most security people don't overlook. But Maravista was a start-up, and that meant working with a limited budget.

Marty assured him this former Secret Service vehicle had Class II protection. But if the rattles and noises were any sign, Jay wasn't feeling too confident.

* * *

The Pope's assassination sent the world into a chaotic frenzy. Catholic leaders blamed Muslim terrorists, who in turn blamed Israeli intelligence. Demonstrations broke out around the world, and threats against Catholic leaders increased. The National Security Administration (NSA) reported increased terrorist threats and rumors of mass suicide bombings filled the airwaves.

All of the uncertainty was a boom for the fledgling Maravista Security firm. The Fall River Archdiocese hired Maravista to protect their leader, Bishop Rafael Ramirez.

Jay's job was to drive Bishop Ramirez to a meeting with wealthy donors. Bill Shannon, an off-duty Falmouth police officer, rode next to him. A former Army MP, Bill served in Iraq and Afghanistan. He had a spotless record and was considered a rising star in line to be a detective.

The meeting started at four o'clock, followed by a cocktail reception, then dinner. The Bishop's sister hosted the event. She managed a charitable foundation that supported many non-profits, including Catholic Charities. The annual meeting reviewed the foundation's finances and new grant applications.

The house was a charming five-bedroom summer cottage. A wrap-around porch on the oceanside overlooked Buzzards Bay. In front of the house, a narrow path led two hundred yards downhill. It wound through marshy scrub to a small, sandy beach. Private, but not too secluded, the location seemed secure to Jay.

After dinner, the group moved to the porch. The Bishop's nieces and nephews lit a bonfire on the beach. They invited the guests to join them.

Jay didn't like the venue change, but he trained for any scenario. He stayed close to the Bishop. Shannon patrolled the beach on the opposite side of the bonfire.

While some guests sat in the sand, the Bishop stood talking with his sister.

Jay enjoyed the heat from the fire, but the bright light disrupted his night vision. He found it difficult to see past the flames. He also wasn't happy that the Suburban was parked in the house's driveway, over two hundred yards away.

At nine forty-five, Jay's phone rang. It was Marty.

"Hello," he said.

"How is everything going with the Bishop?"

"Fine so far. No problems."

"How's Bill doing?"

"He's good. He's on the beach near the water. He checks in every five minutes."

"When do you leave?"

"In fifteen minutes."

"Okay. Give me a call after you return the Bishop to the rectory."

"Will do," Jay replied and hung up.

Ten minutes later, the guests began to head back to the house. Jay prepared to escort the Bishop back to the Suburban when he heard what sounded like a faint pop.

He moved closer to the Bishop and pulled out his firearm. He spoke into his radio headset.

"Bill?" Jay said. "Is everything okay?"

No answer.

"Shannon, respond, please." Still no answer.

Then there were screams.

Children ran past him in a full panic. Out of the bonfire, two shadows emerged from the smoke walking toward him. One held a handgun with a silencer. The other an assault rifle. The attackers pointed their weapons at the Bishop.

Jay tackled the Bishop to the ground as a deafening blast of gunfire erupted. Tracers tracked inches over his head.

When the gunfire stopped, Jay jumped up into a crouched position. He turned and pulled the Bishop into the thick scrub brush next to the beach. It wasn't very high but offered some protection. He pointed his gun at the man with the silenced handgun and fired.

Two holes emerged between his eyebrows. Then the man dropped to the ground. The other attacker with the assault rifle stopped to look. Jay took this opportunity to escape. He grabbed the Bishop and flung him over his right shoulder, running up the sandy path as fast as he could. He put the Bishop down in the front yard.

"Sorry about that," Jay said. "Are you all right?"

"Yes, but shouldn't we warn somebody."

"Someone call 911!" Jay said. "There are men with guns."

The people on the porch laughed. Then went back to their conversations.

Jay glanced back to see the man with the assault rifle running up the path. Then saw the man raise his rifle.

"They'll figure it out," Jay said. "Now run to the Suburban!"

Jay ducked down as the bullets ripped into the siding of the house. He fired at the shadow to give the Bishop a head start. The attacker dropped to the ground.

Jay sprinted around to the rear of the house and found the Suburban. Someone had parked their high-end BMW in the driveway blocking him in.

Jay looked inside and saw the Bishop lying on the floor of the back seat. Jay opened the driver's door as he heard another round of gunfire. Sparks flew off the side of the SUV. Jay felt a burning sensation in his left calf. He looked down to see blood on the floor. Before he had a chance to close it, the door jerked open.

A hand reached in and grabbed the front of his shirt. It tried to pull him out of the driver's seat.

Jay pressed the gun against the bicep and pulled the trigger.

93

The man screamed but didn't let go. *Damn, this guy was tough,* Jay thought.

Jay leaned forward and threw all his body weight against the door, knocking the man back. He grabbed the door handle and slammed the door on the man's arm. Jay heard a loud crunch of bones as the attacker screamed in pain. Jay opened the door enough for his arm to fall out, then slammed the door, punched the ignition button, and put the vehicle into drive.

Before he slammed the accelerator to the floor, Jay looked out the window, catching a glimpse of movement. He saw the man lying on the ground, wearing a black ski mask and a tight-fitting black sweatshirt. Then he saw the bulletproof vest. The man peered at Jay with icy gray eyes. It looked like the same man who raped Olivia.

The man pulled the trigger. The roar was deafening. A fusillade of bullets slammed into the Suburban. The windows held. Jay released the brake and slammed his foot on the accelerator.

The large SUV leaped forward, plowing into the front of the BMW. Jay kept his foot on the gas, pushing the car back down the driveway. More bullets slammed into the rear of the Suburban. When he reached the street, Jay hit the brakes. He watched the BMW continue rolling until it slammed into a tree on the far side of the road. Jay spun the wheel to the right and punched the gas.

Jay's leg was in excruciating pain, but he couldn't stop. He needed to put space between him and the attacker.

"Bishop?" Jay said. "Are you alright?"

He didn't answer. Then Jay heard movement.

"Yes, I am alright," the Bishop said. "How are you?"

"I'm okay. Don't worry about me. I need to get you someplace safe."

"I smell blood," the Bishop replied. "You must not lie to me."

"You're right. I can't lie to you. He shot me in the leg. It's a flesh wound."

"We need to take care of your wound. Pull over so I can take a look at it. Then I'll drive. I know these roads well. I grew up in that house."

Jay looked into the rearview mirror to see the Bishop's face full of concern. He looked at the road behind him, but it was dark—no headlights following them. Jay saw a sign for an athletic field on his left. He cut the wheel, squealing the tires as he slid through the turn. He pulled into the dirt parking lot, driving past a youth baseball diamond, then hit the brakes and spun the wheel, completing a perfect one-hundred-eighty-degree turn. The Suburban pointed straight out towards the street. Jay looked back at the Bishop, but the back seat was empty. Then the driver's door opened.

"Let me see your leg," the Bishop said. Jay watched him unbuckle his pants belt.

"Bishop, what are you doing?" Jay said.

"You need a tourniquet to stop the bleeding. I know what I am doing. I was an Army medic in Vietnam before I entered the priesthood."

Jay turned towards the Bishop and stuck his left foot out. The Bishop cinched the belt around his thigh and pulled it tight. The pain was excruciating.

The Bishop knelt to inspect Jay's leg. "The bullet singed the muscle," he said. "There are no holes, but I must stop the bleeding."

"Thank you. We must hurry, though."

"Do you have a first aid kit in the car?"

"Yes, in the back."

The Bishop went to the back of the Suburban and opened the tailgate. A minute later, he returned with the first aid kit. He pulled out a bottle of hydrogen peroxide and poured the liquid on the wound. Jay cringed from the sting of the antiseptic but didn't say a word. The Bishop then placed a thick gauze pad on the wound and wrapped it in a bandage.

"Unfortunately, all the kit has is Advil for the pain. I suggest you take eight of them."

"Sounds good," Jay said. "Now I have to call Marty."

Chapter 14

Three days later, Jay and McCoy stood in line with hundreds of police officers to pay their respects at the local funeral home. Bill Shannon was very popular and well-liked. The police fraternity was here to honor him and support the wife and three young children he left behind.

As they walked in, McCoy whispered to Jay, "Marty said he was a great cop. It's a real shame."

"I should have been on the beach," Jay said. "I didn't have a family."

McCoy put his arm around his friend's shoulder, "You couldn't know Jay."

Jay winced as pain shot down his right arm, but he didn't say a word.

"I need to get back to the office. I'm meeting with some agents from the FBI and Secret Service. I'll be back tomorrow for the funeral. I understand Marty is hosting a mercy meal at the Portuguese Veterans Club. Will you be there?"

"Yes. I have to bring a new television for the bar."

As he walked in, Jay thought about the past funerals he attended. General Andrew's at Arlington National Cemetery. Michael Goddard's in London. *When would it end?*

Inside the funeral home, Jay greeted Bill's wife. Her six-year-old son played a video game while her eight-year-old daughter held her hand tightly. The baby, eight weeks old, was at home with a relative.

Jay knelt next to the open casket. He said a prayer and looked at Bill's pale skin. He could see the stitches covering the bullet hole in his temple. Otherwise, Bill looked normal. Jay vowed to avenge his death.

* * *

The next morning, St. Patrick's church was filled. Jay and Jessie were lucky to find a pew in the last row. Somebody tapped him on the shoulder. Jay turned to see McCoy standing behind him. Next to him were several familiar faces. Ones Jay hadn't seen for over a year. Gia Khalil stood next to McCoy. She placed her hand on Jay's shoulder, then leaned down and kissed him on the cheek. Standing next to Gia were CJ, Madman, and Gunny Mack. Natalie Choi stared ahead without looking at Jay. He could feel her pain and anger without her saying a word. Behind them stood Michelle Goddard.

McCoy brought the entire Infinity Squad to Falmouth.

"Who are those people?" Jessie asked Jay.

"Good friends. No, terrific friends."

After the funeral, Jay drove to the Portuguese Veterans Club. They had tables set up with food and several kegs of beer.

"Jessie, go ahead and get some food," Jay said as he double-parked outside the bar entrance. "I have some business to take care of in the hall."

McCoy joined Jay as he opened the back of the Jeep.

"Thanks for helping out," Jay said. "I can't carry the TV with one good leg."

Without saying a word, McCoy removed the large, flat box and carried it into the bar.

"You are great," Sal said to Jay as they walked through the door. He walked around the bar to help McCoy with the TV. "I heard about what you did to save the Bishop. Too bad about Billy though, he was a great guy."

"Thanks, Sal. Nice work with the bottle of Jack. The doctor removed the stitches yesterday."

"Yeah, well, you didn't leave me a choice. You were out of control."

"I know. And I'm sorry. It was a tough day."

"Hey, don't worry, kid. We all have those days. I nearly burned my house down when I got laid off from the shoe factory in Fall River. My wife wanted to take the kids and go back to the Azores."

"Let me help you put this up," McCoy said.

"Don't worry about it now," Sal said. "I'll get a couple of the guys to help me. Join your family and buddies. No matter what happens, Jay, you're always welcome here."

"Thanks, Sal. You're the best."

Jay went back outside, where he saw Michelle talking on her cell phone. He thought she looked fantastic and couldn't believe she was here with the guys in Falmouth.

"Hey McCoy, I'll catch up with you in a few minutes."

Jay straightened his tie as he waited for her to finish her call. He admired how striking she looked in her black pantsuit. What a difference since the last time he saw her in Pakistan.

"Hey, Michelle," Jay said. "It's nice to see you."

"Jay!" She walked right over to him and hugged him. "I can't believe you're here. We went nuts looking for you."

"What are you talking about?"

"McCoy didn't tell you? Natalie flew back to Norfolk without you. She thought you would come on a later flight, but you never arrived. "Where did you go?"

"It's a long story," Jay said. "I was recruited for a private security job. "What have you been doing?"

"Trying to run Goddard Aviation. But I'm spending more time fighting with Kathleen Amejian."

"Fighting over what?"

"My father's business empire. What else? Kathleen claims she is Matthew's heir apparent and deserves his share of the family business. He made her President of GNN. But she wants everything, including the financial and transportation businesses. And she wants me out as President of Goddard Aviation. I've spent more time in court than flying."

"That's ridiculous. Kathleen can't kick you out, can she?"

"No, but she can make my job bloody difficult. She's threatening to ruin our reputation. Chase away our clients. That woman will do anything for power. She has no shame."

"Michelle, I want to hear more, but I also want to see the rest of the Infinity Squad. Can we get together later?"

"Yes, of course. Why don't you stop by the house I am renting. It is a charming cottage in Falmouth Heights. I'll text you the address. Invite your friends. I'm going there now to get some work done. Running an international business isn't all fun and games. Cheers."

Jay expected her to give him a quick peck on the cheek. But Michelle surprised him when she kissed him on the lips. Then turned and walked towards her limousine.

Michelle intrigued Jay. She was the daughter of Matthew Goddard, once one of the richest men in the world. He raised her with a silver spoon. Unlike many children of upper-class gentry in England, she didn't live on her trust fund. Instead, Michelle joined the Royal Air Force, becoming the first British woman to fly combat missions in Afghanistan.

After she left the military, she worked for her father's transportation business. She built it into the largest private aviation operation in Europe. She bought the best jets and hired quality pilots and crews. She even donated helicopters and planes to volunteer mountain rescue teams.

Jay met Michelle when she flew rescue missions for the Infinity Squad. She was heartbroken when her brother died in Pakistan. The last time Jay saw her was at Michael's funeral.

Jay found Marty behind a folding table handing out sandwiches and plastic cups of beer to the police officers milling about. McCoy was hanging with the rest of the Infinity Squad members. Jay grabbed a sandwich and a bottle of water then approached his friends.

"Where's the beer, Chief?" CJ said.

"It's too early for me. Plus, I'm trying to cut back. Drinking is hazardous to my health. Has anybody seen Natalie?"

"She left right after the funeral," Madman said. "Something about getting back before her next shift."

"Did she say anything? You know, about Bahrain."

"No," CJ said. "It was the first time any of us saw her since the night of the trial. Since you disappeared."

"Damn," Jay said. "I wanted to talk to her. Try to explain and tell her I am sorry."

"Looks a bit late for that now," McCoy said.

* * *

The cottage turned out to be a five-bedroom, three-story mansion in Falmouth Heights. Located on a bluff, it offered breathtaking views of the ocean. Jay remembered riding his bike by the house when he was a kid and fantasizing about what it would be like to live here. Now he knew.

The first floor was open and simple. The best feature being the wraparound porch. Most of the bedrooms were on the second floor, and the third floor consisted of a single master suite.

When Jay arrived, Michelle sat at the kitchen table with several of her staff members. She greeted Jay and asked him and his friends to wait on the porch. There was a cooler with beer and several bags of chips. Michelle knew how to entertain.

Jay didn't mind. It gave him a chance to catch up. He learned Gunny Mack was now with the FBI, and Natalie worked with the Secret Service. CJ and Madman were back home in New Hampshire. Gia left the Jordanian intelligence service and lives with her daughter and brother in Amman. He also learned Antonio taught mountain climbing and snowboarding in Interlaken, Switzerland.

McCoy sat down in a rocking chair next to Jay and cracked open a beer.

"You did good, Chief," McCoy said as he stared out at the ocean. "You saved the Bishop's life. You did your job. You can't blame yourself for Billy's death. It's time to move on."

"How do you move on? He left behind three little kids. Every time I see his wife at the supermarket or in the bank, I'm going to feel responsible for his death."

"Marty and I agreed, we can't use part-time cops. We need to hire professionals like you. We're fighting against an enemy as brutal as the Taliban."

"I swear that guy on the beach was the same guy who raped Olivia. He was tough and in shape. Plus, he knew how to fight. He had to be in Special Ops."

"Security cameras caught Olivia leaving the dinner with a Canadian professor visiting the Institute, but nobody has seen him since the night of the assault. The Bishop's attack is classified as a domestic terrorist event, so the FBI is now involved. We have an all-points bulletin out across New England."

"We have to find this guy before he hurts or kills somebody else," McCoy said.

"I agree," Jay said. "Especially since his target appears to be me. Excuse me, guys, I need a few minutes alone."

Jay strolled across the street and took a rickety wooden staircase down the bluff to the water's edge. A light breeze stirred up small waves that broke gently against the rocky shore. Jay walked along the quiet beach and gazed across the water at Martha's Vineyard. The cool sea air helped him think straight as he pondered his future. Jay felt terrible about Bill's death. He signed up for a part-time job, not a military-style mission. Bill wasn't expecting to be ambushed, and he didn't know anything about his adversaries. Jay should never have put him in such a situation, and he should have learned more about the mission. He needed more intelligence about his customers and their threats. He also required special operators, not part-time cops with minimal combat experience.

He heard footsteps coming down the staircase and saw

McCoy trying to sneak up on him. Some things never changed. Despite his size and new government job, McCoy was still a kid at heart. Jay played along with him and acted surprised.

"Hey Chief, we need to talk about the business. Are you ready to get more involved?"

"I thought I was involved. I completed our first assignment, attended our first funeral, and even destroyed our first vehicle. I'm not sure I'm ready to work as a security guard, never mind run a business."

"You were our team leader on the Infinity Squad. You made life and death decisions every day."

"No, that was General Andrew's job. I followed orders."

"But Jay, you ran the team. You planned the operations and got us out of some hairy situations. I'm talking about hiring a few security team members and training them. Then going out and drumming up some business. Bishop Ramirez wants to know if you'll be his regular bodyguard."

"Let me think about it, okay?" Jay said. "I need to head home. It's been a long day."

"Sure, I understand. But don't wait too long. The phone in the office hasn't stopped ringing. Marty wants you to contact people as soon as possible."

Jay and McCoy returned to the cottage in time to say goodbye to his friends. Michelle waited for him by the front door.

"I thought you left without saying goodbye," Michelle said with a slight frown on her face. "You are welcome to stay or come back later. My staff has gone out, and I was hoping to spend more one-on-one time with you."

Jay should have said yes. He always liked Michelle. And

he never knew what she saw in him. But tonight wasn't the night.

"Thanks, Michelle," Jay said as he hugged her. "I need some quiet time. I have some decisions to make."

"I understand," Michelle said. "I'm going back to New York in the morning. You have my number. I'm always available. You know. To talk."

Jay smiled, "Don't worry. I'll take you up on that invitation sometime in the future. Just not tonight."

As Jay drove back to his mother's home, his phone rang. He peeked at the caller ID and saw Olivia's name. He contemplated whether to answer the phone or not. It had been a month since she went to San Diego, and they spoke only a few times. He didn't answer. He pulled into his mother's driveway and played the voicemail.

Hi, Jay. It's Olivia. How are you? I wanted to run something by you. The Director of the Scripps Institute needs a Director of Security. You could stay with me. I have a beautiful apartment on the ocean in La Jolla. Let me know one way or the other. Jay, I miss you. Call me.

Jay thought for a second. Her offer intrigued him. He loved San Diego, having spent a lot of time there while stationed with Seal Team Six. He returned the call but got her voicemail. He didn't know what to say, so he didn't leave a message.

Chapter 15

Jay didn't sleep that night. He rarely did. The nightmares, while different every night, always ended the same. With him screaming himself awake. He tossed and turned, trying to decide whether to move to San Diego or stay in Falmouth. Then he thought about Michelle. She was amazing but out of his league. Why would she go out with him? Around four-thirty, he fell asleep.

At five, the doorbell rang. Jay stumbled down the stairs and opened the front door. Gia, CJ, and Madman were standing there dressed in tank tops and shorts.

"C'mon, Chief," Gia said. "It's PT time."

"Why are you guys here?"

"We're your new employees," CJ said with a smile. "Let's go."

"But I still have stitches in my leg."

"What's a little pain for the DOAT," Madman said. "Come on. You're getting soft."

"What's the DOAT?"

"Deadliest of All Time," CJ said with a smile.

"All right. You guys are crazy. Give me five minutes to change."

* * *

They ran along the oceanfront through Falmouth Heights past Michelle's rented cottage. Then around the harbor to Surf Drive. They jumped on the Shining Sea recreation path and stopped at a small bridge.

The pain in Jay's leg was excruciating. At first, he could only limp along. His team stayed with him. After a mile or so, the pain subsided to a dull throb, and Jay got into a rhythm.

"Take your shoes and your shirt off, Mendes," Gia said. "We're going for a swim."

The cold saltwater felt great on his leg. It was a lot easier for him to swim.

They swam along the beach until they reached the break-water at Falmouth Harbor. Instead of turning around, Jay scrambled up the slippery granite blocks and plopped down onto his back.

"What's the matter, Mendes?" Madman said. "You're getting soft."

"You guys are gonna work with me?" Jay said. "Are you insane?"

CJ laughed. "You know we'll follow you anywhere in the world. From a cave in Pakistan to the mountain ranges in Afghanistan and even dusty hellholes like Iraq."

"You guys already did that," Jay said. " We're retired now."

"We're not retired," Gia said. "We're in a career transition. And we want to work with you. "We're a team, and you can't break up a great team."

"Think of Bird and McHale," Madman said. "Brady and Gronk. Orr and Esposito." They were all greats. And they worked together."

"Can you think of any analogies that aren't Boston sports stars?" CJ said. "How about Jekyll and Hyde?"

"They were the same man, you idiot," Madman replied.

"Okay, guys," Jay said, laughing. "We were a great hostage rescue team. But I don't know shit about running a business. What if we go bankrupt or, worse, get audited by the IRS?"

"Jay, you hire smart people like lawyers and accountants to deal with the business," Gia said. "Do you think my oil baron uncle in Saudi Arabia knew anything about running an oil field?"

Jay stared at Gia. "Did you say oil baron uncle in Saudi Arabia? I thought you were born in Jordan."

"What, I never told you my story?" Gia said. "I must have at one time."

"No, never," CJ said. "Now spill your beans, Princess."

"Well, my real name was Maher...."

* * *

The ultra-long Mercedes limousine waited outside the Anne Fontaine designer outlet on Rue des Saints-Pères in Paris. Inside, personal shoppers gathered around the two young Saudi princesses in the private fitting room.

"Mother will love that," Sama bin Abouzzi said to her younger sister. "It is so chic."

Thirteen-year-old Maher bin Abouzzi smiled, "It is lovely. The silk is so soft on my skin, and the lines are elegant. How many different colors are there?"

The manager of the upscale boutique answered, "Eight. We can have them sent to your hotel or shipped to Riyadh.

Maher smiled. "Can I keep the outfit I have on? The others you can ship to the palace."

"Of course, your highness."

"I want to go to Gucci, then Ives Saint Lauren," Maher said to her sister. "We only have a few hours left in Paris."

"We must go to Metal Flaque first."

"Why, that is a bridal shop?"

"I know. I wanted to surprise you. I am to be married."

"I am so happy for you, Sama. Who is the lucky man?" Maher said as she hugged her older sister. Just sixteen, the dark-haired beauty looked down at her feet. "I do not know. Father has not told me yet."

"You do not know who your husband will be?"

"No. He is a Prince from the United Arab Emirates, but the Sultan has several sons, and he has not yet finalized his decision."

"Why are you shopping for a bridal gown now?"

"Oh, I have a gown. It will be our mother's. We need to find a dress for you and the bridal party. Will you be my maid of honor?"

"Of course I will!" Maher shrieked too loud. A tall, burly man dressed in a black suit entered the fitting room.

"Is everything okay, Princess, Maher?"

"Yes, I am sorry. I am fine."

Maher and her sister climbed into the backseat of the limo.

"Look, here are pictures of the princes," Sama said as she pulled out her cell phone. Six handsome men dressed in custom suits and Arab headdresses lined up in an official state photo. "There are six that are single. The youngest is seventeen. The oldest, twenty-eight."

"Ooh, I like the one in the middle. He is adorable."

"That is Sinrah. He is twenty-one. He is a student at Cambridge University, and he is studying to be a lawyer."

"Oh, what about the youngest one?"

"He is Rian. He is an Olympic football player."

"He has such a rugged, handsome face."

Sama's phone rang. She answered, "Yes, mother. We are on our way. Did he? Which one? Okay, thank you."

Maher saw her sister's smile disintegrate into a scowl, "What is wrong?"

"My husband will be Sharouk, the eldest son. I will be his fifth wife. I leave for Abu Dhabi in the morning."

"Why are you sad?"

"I have heard on the internet that he is very mean and treats his wives like possessions. One of his wives tried to escape and seek asylum in Canada, but his security team stopped her."

"What happened to her?"

"I do not know. She hasn't been heard from since."

"You can't go. You must tell Mother and our uncle no."

"That is impossible. This is the way. Uncle Farouk will pay a large dowry for the wedding. I will not have a choice."

Maher buried her head in Sama's shoulder and broke down in tears, "But there must be something we can do. I will miss you so much."

But Sama left and was married. Two years passed without a word from her sister. Maher's mother showed her pictures of Sama's two daughters, Nura and Layla. However, the Prince wanted a boy. Sama was declared useless and divorced. She returned to Riyadh, a broken woman. Her children, deemed the Prince's property, were kept in Abu Dhabi.

The morning after her return, Maher found Sama dead in her bedroom. Several bottles of sleeping pills open on the floor next to an empty bottle of scotch.

Maher decided she wasn't going to be some dreadful Prince's

possession.

She convinced her mother to let her play on the Saudi junior girl's soccer team that competed all around the Middle East. Professional bodyguards escorted the team, and several of the King's staff made sure the girls stayed in line. Maher's mother also traveled with the team.

The final soccer game of the season was held in Amman, Jordan. Maher had become friendly with one of the Jordanian team members, a fifteen-year-old girl named Keera Khalil. She took her with her to the ladies' bathroom and led her into a stall.

"What are you doing? I do not like girls," Keera said.

"Do not worry. I want to talk to you, not kiss you. I want to know if you will help me escape from my team. I want to seek asylum."

"Why? Aren't you a Princess?"

"Yes, but my Uncle plans to marry me off within the next month to some brute in Qatar. I cannot go. Please help me."

"What do you want me to do?"

"Help me sneak out with your team. I just need to get away from the bodyguards, and then I will find the Canadian embassy. I have sent asylum requests to all Western governments, and they were the only ones that answered. I just have to get to the front gate, and they will let me in."

"Okay, I will ask my mother to help you."

Maher hugged the girl, who backed off at first, then hugged her back.

"Don't worry, I won't kiss you," Maher said, laughing.

When the girls left the bathroom, Keera took Maher by the hand and led her to her team's table, where her mother was eating dinner.

"Mother, you must help my friend," Keera said. "She is quite ill

and needs to see a doctor."

Keera's mother, Shinabi Khalil, was a civil rights attorney in Amman and understood more of the story. She also knew a lot about how the Saudi royal families treated their teenage girls. She recently represented a Saudi Princess who fled to Dubai, only to be recaptured by her family. The girl locked herself in a hotel room and demanded asylum.

Shinabi looked around the room, then said, "We must go quickly. My car is parked out back."

The two girls followed Shinabi through the kitchen and out the back delivery entrance of the restaurant. But as Shinabi pulled out of the parking lot, Maher heard shouting. She looked back to see a Saudi bodyguard pull out a gun and fire.

The back window shattered, spraying glass throughout the interior of the luxury BMW. Shinabi pressed the gas pedal to the floor and sped away.

"Are you girls alright? Are you hurt?"

"No," Maher answered.

"I'm okay too," said Keera.

"Stay down. The Canadian Embassy is five kilometers away."

The rush hour traffic in the city was heavy, and Shinabi had difficulty weaving in and out of the congested streets. She took a quick left, then a right, sending the girls sprawling onto the floor.

"I'm sorry," Shinabi said. "I will try to be more careful."

Two more gunshots rang out.

Maher peeked out the back window to see a large black Mercedes sedan gaining on them.

"That's okay. Drive as fast as you want!"

After several more quick direction changes, Shinabi was able to get away from the Saudi gunmen. She pulled into a narrow alleyway and stopped the car.

"Maher, is there somebody you want to call? Your mother, perhaps?"

"No. Nobody can know where I am, or they will be in danger. Please take me to the embassy."

"Alright. We will be there in a few minutes."

Shinabi drove up to the large, light-gray embassy building in downtown Amman. A low brick wall topped with barb wire surrounded the modernistic complex. Several uniformed Canadian soldiers manned a gatehouse. But as they approached, a black Mercedes pulled up to the gate. Shinabi stopped half a block away.

"It looks like your Saudi friends beat you here."

"How can that be?" Maher said. "I didn't tell anybody."

"Did you use your cell phone?" Keera said. "Perhaps you can email or text the embassy?"

"I will look. Wait, where is my cell phone? Oh no, I must have left it at the restaurant. That's how they know. They found my phone. I cannot go there. I must find a different option. Perhaps the Americans?"

"You will come home with us," Shinabi said. "I will find a way to help you. Now let's go before they spot us."

* * *

Gia stopped for a moment to gather her thoughts, "Shinabi took me in. I changed my name to Gia, and a few years later, she adopted me. My uncle found out and demanded I be returned, but the King of Jordan intervened on my behalf. I didn't see my mother for many years. Then when I worked with the Jordanian Intelligence Agency, I traveled to Riyadh and met her outside the palace.

"You are a real Princess," CJ said. "That's amazing."

"Now you know why it was so important for me to find and adopt Rameera. She reminded me of myself at thirteen. I would never have earned my freedom if I stayed in Saudi Arabia. I had to take a chance, and it paid off. But I sacrificed a lot and risked the lives of my mother and my adopted family. In the end, it was all worth it. Jay, is it decided? Will we come to work for you?"

"I'm honored to have all three of you on my team. Gia, will you be my head of intelligence?"

"Of course."

"CJ and Madman, you two will run my security operations and help me find new operators."

"Sounds like a plan, Chief," CJ replied.

Madman patted Jay on the shoulder, "I have one question. Where are we going to sleep? It's a long commute from New Hampshire."

"It's even farther from Amman," Gia added.

"Stay at the office in Woods Hole. It will be a little tight, but we'll find a bigger facility. Gia, what are you going to do with Rameera?"

"She will stay in Amman until I get settled, then she will move here. She is very excited to live in America."

"Welcome to Maravista Security," Jay said as he dove off the breakwater into Falmouth Harbor.

Chapter 16

The *Boston Globe* religion writer described it as a modern miracle. Three weeks after the Pope was assassinated in Gandolfo, the Vatican conclave elected a new Pope. The world was shocked. Boston's own Cardinal Sean O'Reilly will be known as Pope John Paul the Third. Today, the first of June, is inauguration day in Rome.

The early morning streets of Fall River were quiet when Father Eugene Berle arrived by taxi. The priest from the St. Bonaventure Parish in New Bedford looked forward to praying with Bishop Ramirez before they rode to Boston. Cardinal Sean O'Reilly's inauguration as Pope was remarkable, and he looked forward to the excitement and fellowship of the celebration.

A priest for over fifty years, Father Berle was well-loved in New Bedford, especially with the Portuguese fishing community. Every year he presided over the Blessing of the Fleet, a three-day festival held every summer.

He was about an hour early and planned to pray the rosary inside the St. Mary of the Assumption Cathedral until the Bishop was ready. As he walked up the stairs to the Cathedral entrance, a blond man in a black trench coat approached him from behind.

"Excuse me, Father, may you have a few minutes?" the man said with a Russian accent.

"Of course, my son. What bothers you?"

"My mother is quite ill, and she would like to receive communion. She is sitting in my car behind the rectory."

"That is quite unorthodox. There is an eight o'clock mass in the Cathedral."

"Please, Father. It will only take a moment."

"Of course."

Father Berle followed the suspicious man around the corner into an alleyway behind the church. A twenty-year-old Continental sat idling with the back door open. As the priest bent down to enter the backseat, the blond-haired man removed a Makarov handgun with a silencer from his coat pocket. He placed the silencer to the back of the priest's head and pulled the trigger. The elderly priest dropped to the ground. The man picked up the Father's body and stripped off his vestment and clothes. He then picked up the naked body and threw it in a dumpster.

Inside the limo, a young man pulled the vestment over his suicide vest and stepped out of the back seat. He checked to make sure his contact lenses and the rest of his disguise were in place. Then he blessed himself and walked up the steps and into the Cathedral.

The gunman watched the suicide bomber go inside, then called his boss, "The goods are delivered. Be ready to go."

* * *

Two hours later, Jay Mendes scanned the parking area around the rectory. He had his new armored Chevy Sub-

116

urban as the lead car and two rented armored Mercedes limousines for the ninety-minute trip to Boston. He drove with Gia in the Suburban while CJ and Madman drove the two limos.

"Any sign of trouble, CJ?" Jay said into his headset radio.

"Negative. All clear from up here," CJ reported as he peered through his sniper scope from the rooftop of a school building across the street.

"Why don't you come down. Gia, who are we waiting for?"

"The Bishop, Father Berle from New Bedford, and Father Pastorini from Westport."

Two minutes later, the door of the rectory opened, and two Priests came out. Jay asked them their names so he could verify his attendance sheet.

"Father Bellevue, from New Bedford," the younger one said.

Jay scanned his security app on his iPhone, "I don't have you on the list."

"Sorry, eh. I ah, am replacing Father Berle. He has a bad headache."

Jay stared at the Priest. Something was off, but he couldn't figure it out,

"Como se escreve seu sobrenome?" Jay asked in Portuguese. The Priest stared at him.

"I mean, how do you spell your last name?"

The priest spelled it out and proceeded to climb in the back of the second limo. Then the Bishop exited the rectory.

"Is everything okay, Jay?"

"Yes, Bishop. We are ready to leave."

* * *

117

The trip to Boston went off without a hitch. When they arrived, Jay learned he was the only security team member allowed in the Cathedral. A burly State Trooper at the entrance told him the Cathedral was over capacity.

"Everyone stay outside with the cars," Jay said. "I'll go in with the Bishop."

Jay looked up in amazement as he noticed the Cathedral of the Holy Cross for the first time. The large stone edifice soared over his head. Constructed in 1866, the Boston Archdiocese mother church stood 120 feet high and seated nearly 2,000 people. Jay led his group through the outer foyer and into the main sanctuary, where colossal marble columns supported ornately carved arches. A large white marble altar ordained the front of the Cathedral in front of majestic stained-glass windows. The early morning sun shone through the windows illuminating the Bible scenes depicted by the multi-colored glass.

Jay passed his gun through the x-ray machine and then stepped through the metal detector. Oddly, there was no sign of any bomb-sniffing dogs who were always present at high-profile public events.

After they passed through security, the Bishop took Jay by the elbow and whispered in his ear. Jay smiled.

"The restrooms are in the basement," Jay said. "Who needs to go?"

"Sister Madonna, Father Bellevue, and me," the Bishop said.

"The stairs are around the corner."

"I know where it is since I have been here many times. Unfortunately, the Sister has a bad hip, so we will need to take the elevator."

"Of course," Jay said.

When they arrived at the lower level, Jay stepped into the men's room and scanned the urinals and stalls. When he came out, he told the Bishop the room was secure.

Sister Madonna finished first and stood next to Jay outside the restrooms and said, "It's quite cold in here. I don't know why they keep the temperature so low.

Jay smiled but didn't respond. The Bishop came out. However, the priest took several additional minutes.

Something about Father Bellevue bothered Jay. He had shifty eyes and seemed to be quite nervous. He had an odd accent for a New Bedford priest, and he didn't speak Portuguese. Most priests in New Bedford spoke the language because of the large immigrant population from Brazil and Portugal. When he exited the restroom, Jay noticed that the priest was sweating profusely and refused to make eye contact.

Jay escorted The Bishop and Father Bellevue to the procession forming in the back of the Cathedral. He planned to sit with the priests and nuns towards the front of the nave. However, before they reached their aisle, a uniformed officer stopped him.

"Sorry, buddy, private security officers are not allowed in the pews. Not enough room. You'll have to stand on the perimeter."

"Sure, no problem," Jay said as he watched the Bishop take his position in the procession. Jay's cell phone buzzed. The caller id showed it was from Marty.

"Mendes here."

"I received a call from Fall River police," Marty said. "They found a naked body in a dumpster near the church. It was an elderly priest named Father Berle. He was from New Bedford. You have an imposter in your group."

Jay thought about his encounter with Father Berle's replacement and his comment about his headache. "He told me his name is Father Bellevue. Likely an alias. How was the Priest killed?"

"Close contact shot to the back of the head. Assassination style."

"I know who it is. Call McCoy. Have him alert the officer in charge of security. Tell them I'm not a bad guy, and we may have a situation in the Cathedral." Jay hung up.

Organ music began playing, and a priest appeared on the altar, "Will everyone, please rise for the opening procession." He raised both hands, and the congregation stood.

* * *

The lead altar server carried an ornate gold-leaf cross and led the procession down the central aisle. It reminded Jay of his youth when he served. He couldn't remember the last time he went to a mass that wasn't a funeral or a wedding.

"Everybody, I need your attention," Jay said on his radio. "Police in Fall River found a dead priest behind the rectory. A close-contact shot to the head killed him. We have an imposter either inside the Cathedral or in the vicinity. A Boston Police tactical team is activated, but I need you to search the area around the Cathedral's perimeter. Look for any accomplices, snipers, or getaway cars. Notify a police officer if you see anything. Do not engage unless it is self-defense. I'll handle things inside the Cathedral. We have to find him."

As Jay watched the procession, he spotted the Bishop and Father Bellevue towards the rear. A strange sweat pattern appeared on the back of Bellevue's vestment.

Jay thought for a moment, where did he see a stain like that before? Then he remembered his second tour in Iraq.

He was accompanying a Marine detachment in Fallujah. They searched house-to-house when he saw a woman wearing a burka walk up to a Marine security team outside a hotel. She had a similar stain on the back of her burka. She offered them bottled water, but the Marines declined. A second later, the IED vest exploded, killing the woman and the soldiers.

Jay pushed his way towards the altar, but a police officer grabbed him on the right shoulder. Wincing in pain, Jay tried to shove him aside, but the officer held on and pulled him down a cross-aisle.

"What's going on?" the officer said. "Why did you shove me? Who are you?"

"I'm a private security agent," Jay said, showing his ID badge. "There's an imposter in the procession. He may be a suicide bomber."

"That's crazy," the officer replied. "Wait a minute. You look familiar. Were you at Bill Shannon's funeral?"

"Yeah," Jay said, fearing the cop's response. "We worked together."

"Oh shit, you're Jay Mendes. Everyone in the precinct is talking about you. They say you're a hero for saving the Bishop. I want to shake your hand. I'm Joe McCarthy from Quincy."

"That's great," Jay said as he pried the officer's hand off his shoulder. "There he is."

The procession was halfway down the aisle. Jay pointed

towards the priest near the back.

"He looks normal to me," McCarthy said.

"Hold on a minute, and I'll show you."

Jay watched the procession pass by. He nudged the cop, "Look how much he's sweating. It's too cold to sweat."

"Aw, come on, your nuts."

"Do I look like I'm nuts? Look at the pattern on his back. I've seen the same pattern in Iraq. He's wearing a suicide vest. The sweat soaking through the robe is outlining the straps and pockets."

McCarthy released his grip on Jay's arm then reached down to draw his firearm.

"No, you'll cause a panic," Jay said. "I'll handle this."

"What unit were you in?"

"Navy. SEAL Teams Three and Six. I did multiple tours."

"I was in the Marines in the second fight for Fallujah. You guys saved our butts there. Go ahead. I'll cover your backside."

The procession climbed the stairs to the altar. The servers split off to the right and left while the Bishops and Priests proceeded to several rows of chairs towards the back. Bishop Ramirez stood in front of a sizable satin-covered chair.

The Bishop said an opening prayer and explained they would watch the inauguration on the TV screens and then celebrate mass.

Jay and McCarthy pushed their way through the police officers lining the perimeter of the church. They worked their way to the front aisle but needed to get to the center to have a clear shot. Unfortunately, the Governor of Massachusetts and the Mayor of Boston stood surrounded by security guards in the front row.

McCarthy pushed his way in front and cleared a path through the dignitaries so Jay could get into position.

The large screen televisions showed an overhead view of St. Peter's Square. The televisions were showing the GNN coverage from Rome, Boston, and New York. In Rome, Joanne Roberts was reporting from a helicopter above the packed plaza. The image zoomed in on the balcony where the new Pope would address the crowd. Jay watched the screen with one eye and kept an eye on his suspect with the other.

"And here he comes," Roberts said. "The doors to the balcony are opening. I can hear the roar from the vast crowd below. Thousands of American Catholics traveled to Rome to participate in this special occasion."

Loud applause rose from the clergy inside the Cathedral.

Jay watched in amazement as the TV screens showed hundreds of thousands of people at the Vatican. The crowd seemed to have a life of its own as people sang and swayed back and forth. Close-up shots showed many were schoolchildren in Rome for the first time. Then the windows on the balcony opened, and the Pope waved to the crowd. The congregation in the Cathedral exploded in applause.

The Pope raised his hands to greet the crowd, who cheered even louder. Then, he raised his hand to his forehead.

The sweaty priest stepped out of the back, carrying a prayer book in both hands. He stepped in front of the Bishop.

The Pope said, "Let us Pray."

Jay watched in horror as the fake priest held a detonation plunger in his hand.

The congregation inside the church didn't notice. Instead, they focused on the television screens.

Jay heard CJ's voice on his earpiece, "Any sign of the bomber?"

"He's on the altar standing in front of the Bishop."

"In the name of the Father," the Pope proclaimed, raising his hand to his forehead.

The bomber turned around to face the congregation and raised his hand with the plunger.

Jay saw a faint green glow through the bomber's vestment.

Jay squatted in the middle of the center aisle. Nobody seemed to notice. He dropped to the floor, pulled out his handgun, assumed a shooting position, and chambered a round. He didn't aim at the Priest's head or chest but instead aimed at the green light.

"And the son." The Pope lowered his hand to his chest.

The sweaty priest pressed the plunger down. The light turned red, activating the bomb.

Jay focused on the red light.

"And the Holy Spirit."

The bomber released his finger, yelling, "Praise the Master!"

Jay fired twice, then awaited the bomb blast that would send him to the afterlife.

Chapter 17

Outside the Cathedral, the sound of explosions rocked the mobile television screens causing dozens of police officers to duck. CJ didn't move. He watched the TVs in horror as five mushroom clouds simultaneously filled Saint Peter's Square.

CJ thought he heard gunshots from Jay's headset right before the explosion, but he wasn't sure, "Jay, are you okay?" But there wasn't an answer.

Then he saw the Cathedral doors fly open. A wave of priests and nuns ran out in a panic. As the first priests made it to the bottom steps, gunshots rang out from a high-rise apartment building behind him. Automatic gunfire rained down on the panicked clergy in a steady stream of death, mowing them down like sitting ducks. Trying to escape from the gunfire, the survivors turned around and ran back into the church, creating more mayhem.

Piled high like driftwood on the beach, the priests lay dead and dying on the front steps of the Cathedral.

CJ turned around to look for the sniper when a bullet hit a Boston Police officer standing two feet away.

CJ knelt behind the driver-side door of the armored limo for cover and yelled, "Sniper!"

That's when the bullets rained down on him. Bullets smashed into the armored exterior, causing sparks to fly. Luckily for CJ, none penetrated the thick steel.

Kneeling behind the door, CJ searched for the shooter. It looked like the gunfire was coming from the roof of the ten-story apartment building behind him.

"Madman, can you see the shooter?"

"Negative."

"Gia?"

"No, I'm pinned down behind the Suburban. I dragged an injured nun next to me to protect her."

"I need to get up higher, but my rifle is in the back of the SUV."

A State Police tactical squad ran past him with assault rifles drawn. A bullet struck the last officer in the chest, who fell to the ground in front of him.

CJ instinctively reached out and pulled the officer to safety. Then, he pulled off their helmet and learned the officer was a woman.

He picked up her assault rifle as she lay on the ground gasping for air. He inspected her Kevlar vest and found the bullet hole. He unstrapped the vest but couldn't see any blood.

"What... are you doing... with my gun?" she said.

"I'm going to shoot the sniper."

"But you're a... civilian."

"I was a sniper in the Army. Rangers. I need to stop him before more people die. Stay here, and you'll be safe."

She smiled. "I made it... to the last week of... Ranger school. Then became an MP."

"Did you know Bill Shannon?"

She closed her eyes and nodded. "He was… in my Reserve unit."

She reached for her utility belt and unsnapped a pocket, "Here, take more ammo."

CJ looked out from behind the door. The sniper pinned down the SWAT team near the entrance of the building. He reached in and grabbed the bullet cartridges and stuffed them into his pants pocket. He took a deep breath and sprinted towards an alley next to the apartment building. He was halfway across the street when the sniper spotted him and turned the gunfire in his direction, but CJ was too fast.

He made it to the alley and searched for a way into the building. He found a fire escape and leaped up to grab the bottom rung but missed. Finally, after three more attempts, he caught it. The ladder slid down far enough for him to climb up. It went all the way to the top floor.

CJ stopped at the top platform covered in sweat. There was no access to the roof. Instead, he found himself outside a penthouse apartment. He scanned the inside to make sure the adjacent room was empty, aimed at the window, and fired. A thin line appeared in the thick glass. He unloaded a full magazine into the window until the crack turned into a spider's web. Then he kicked the web, and the glass fell into the apartment. He slid through the small hole and found himself in a bedroom.

He ran through the upscale apartment and into the hallway. He looked both ways and found the stairwell door. He prayed the alarm to the door was shut off as he slammed it open. To his annoyance, a loud siren blared. He ignored it and ran up the stairs to the roof. He stopped at the exit door, reloaded the rifle, then took a deep breath and pushed the door open a crack.

Anticipating a barrage of gunfire, CJ stayed in place, then opened the door further.

No gunfire. He pushed the door all the way open.

CJ found the sniper's empty lair. Copper shell casings littered the roof, and a foam mattress topper covered the black roofing material. Next to the mattress, a nylon gun bag lay open on the ground. He also found a food wrapper and an empty coffee cup. Finally, he spotted a piece of paper lying next to the bag. It was a picture of Jay Mendes taken this morning from outside the Fall River Cathedral.

* * *

Jay placed his handgun on the floor. Then he felt the cold, steel barrel of a revolver jammed against the back of his head.

"You're under arrest," McCarthy said loudly. Then he bent down and whispered in Jay's ear, "Go along with me. I have to make it look good for my boss."

Officer McCarthy knelt on Jay's back, squeezing the wind out of his lungs. He wrenched Jay's arms behind his back, ready to slap handcuffs on, when Jay said, "Wait, don't move."

"That's my line," McCarthy replied. "You're not supposed to say it to me."

"Why aren't we dead?" Jay asked.

"The bomb didn't explode. Your shots stopped the bomb vest from detonating."

"So that means the bomb is still alive even though the bomber is dead. Why didn't it explode? Let me up."

"I can't do that."

"Let me up, or we're all going to die!"

McCarthy let Jay get up. People were running away in panic all around him, but Jay walked towards the satin-lined chair on the altar. Toppled over backward, the bomber lay with his arms spread out wide—like Jesus hanging from the cross. Underneath him lie Bishop Ramirez. A pool of blood stained the ancient chair. Jay couldn't tell if it belonged to the bomber, the Bishop, or both.

"McCarthy, do you have a knife?"

"Yeah."

"Give it to me. Hurry."

"What are you going to do?"

"Don't ask stupid questions. Just give me the knife."

McCarthy handed Jay the utility knife and stepped back but kept his gun aimed at Jay.

Jay knelt next to the bomber and grabbed the collar of his vestment. He inserted the knife and sliced it down to his waist. Then he slit a horizontal line and peeled back the vestment.

"Oh shit," McCarthy said. "Now, what do we do?"

Jay didn't answer. He stared at the black nylon suicide vest. It held four pouches on the front, each containing a clear plastic bag. Inside each bag was a second smaller pouch with a clear liquid. Inside each pouch was a strand of white material cut into strange shapes like stars, crosses, and spikes. White wires ran down the side of the vest and converged on a small, rectangular circuit board. There were two bullet holes. One in the board's center, embedded in a circular LED light—the second hole, a half-inch higher than the first.

"Where's the bomb squad?"

"I don't know," McCarthy said as he nervously looked around for support.

"Use your radio to find out. But, first, we need to extricate Bishop Ramirez from underneath the bomber."

"How are we going to do that?"

"I don't know. But we have to be very careful, or it's the last thing we'll ever do."

* * *

"Madman, Gia," Jay said into the radio. "Where are you guys?"

"In front of the Cathedral," Gia said. "We're helping the wounded."

"What do you mean, wounded?"

"There was a sniper. Shot dozens of people as they ran out of the Cathedral. CJ went after him."

"CJ, where are you?"

"On the roof of the apartment building across the street. I'm talking with a SWAT commander and answering questions from Boston Police detectives."

"Did you find the sniper?"

"No, he was gone when I got to the roof. But I found something else. I'll tell you later. Where are you?"

"On the altar. We have a situation."

* * *

As he stared at the bomber, Jay prayed to himself. He couldn't remember being so scared in fourteen years of active duty. One tiny mistake, and it was all over. He would rather face a hundred Taliban than a single IED.

Reaching down, Jay placed two fingers against the Bishop's neck. He felt a pulse.

"I'm still alive," the Bishop said, startling Jay. "Just praying to Jesus."

"Are you injured?"

"Yes, one of the bullets you shot is inside me."

"I had to shoot. Father Bellevue was a suicide bomber."

"I'll forgive you since you saved my life."

"It's liquid explosive," McCarthy said from behind Jay. "Probably TATP. It's a homemade liquid popular with terrorist groups. But I don't know what the white pieces are made of."

"Looks like ceramic," a familiar voice said. "It isn't metallic and has a high melting point."

Jay turned to see his old friend Victor Salinas standing behind him dressed in a full bomb suit."

"Salinas, when did you get discharged?"

"About a year ago, the same time you disappeared."

"You two know each other?" McCarthy asked.

"This is Victor Salinas, the best IED tech in the entire Navy. We served together for many years. He saved my ass countless times."

"Well, I hope he saves both our asses one more time."

Jay stood up and faced Salinas, who was about the same height and stature as Jay. They could be twins. His oversized bomb suit said State Police Bomb Squad on the front.

"You need to leave," Salinas said. "Now. Please evacuate outside of the blast zone. This is no place for civilians."

"I'm not going anywhere," Jay said, "I'm responsible for Bishop Ramirez's safety."

"My rescue team is on the way. They will extricate him. For now, I am going to inspect the vest."

"We can't wait. The Bishop will bleed out. McCarthy and

I will help. But, you need to tell us how to handle the dead bomber."

"Okay, let's see. First, we need to hold the bomber up, then slide the Bishop and the chair out from under him. Then we'll need to place the bomber on the floor without jarring the vest. TATP is very unstable."

"Okay, we can do this. But first, one question. Where were you guys before the celebration? I didn't see you when I passed through security."

"There was a flurry of bomb scares right before the start of the inauguration. The Boston squad went to a call in the Back Bay. The FBI went to a call in Worcester at Holy Cross stadium, and my squad went to Alumni Stadium at Boston College."

"Did you find anything?"

"No. All were false alarms."

"Sounds like they were deliberate. Okay, what do you need me to do?"

"You and I are going to hold the bomber while McCarthy pulls the Bishop out. Once the Bishop is out of the Cathedral, I'll remove the vest from the bomber for disposal."

"I'm going to help, too," another familiar voice said from behind him. "We need to preserve the vest as evidence."

"Screw the vest," Jay said. "I want to stay alive."

Jay turned to see Gunny Mack standing behind him dressed in a suit and FBI windbreaker. Mac said, "Let's get to work."

* * *

Jay helped Victor remove his bomb suit. Then they stood on

each side of the bomber and knelt. He reached underneath the bomber until he felt Victor's hands, then intertwined their fingers.

The stench of the corpse was nauseating, but Jay focused his mind elsewhere.

"I'm ready," he said. "Please hurry."

On the count of three, Jay and Victor lifted the bomber while Officer McCarthy and Gunny Mack slid the chair backward. As they pulled, Jay felt the weight of the body increase. Jay held on tight as his right arm throbbed. Pain shot up into his spinal cord as he struggled to adjust his grip. He used his legs to hold most of the weight, but he wasn't going to last long.

As the Bishop inched back, Jay felt a spray of warm liquid come out from the Bishop's abdomen, "Hurry, moving the Bishop is releasing the pressure on his bullet wound. He's bleeding out!"

"C'mon, McCarthy," Gunny said, "we have to move him fast."

They yanked the Bishop out, and the sudden movement caused the bomber's body to drop. Jay panicked. Then he dropped to his knees using every last ounce of strength and stopped the body from hitting the floor with an inch to spare. Jay and Victor lowered the body gently to the floor.

Exhausted, Jay pulled his arms out then rolled over onto his back. Drenched in sweat, he lay still for several minutes, holding his hands on his temple, trying to will the searing pain away, without any luck.

"Are you okay, Chief?" Gunny Mack asked.

"Never better."

"Good, because we have to leave. The rest of the bomb

squad is here."

* * *

McCarthy called his Commander, who agreed to let Gunny Mack take Jay into FBI custody for questioning. Even though it was apparent the shooting was justified, Mack had to follow FBI protocol.

"You can't call me Gunny Mack anymore," he said as they left the Cathedral. "It's special agent McCauley."

"You'll always be Gunny Mack to me," Jay said. "But I'll call you Mack to respect your new job. Is that okay, Special Agent?"

Mack laughed and punched Jay in the right arm. He almost fainted from the pain.

Mack led Jay to an unmarked moving van parked on a side street two blocks from the Cathedral. Mack opened a door on the side of the trailer and walked in. Jay followed.

Inside, dozens of law enforcement officers sat at computer workstations. A large flat-screen television hung from the front of the trailer.

Jay looked at the TV. He cringed at the sight of Kathleen Amejian reporting on GNN but stayed calm.

"I'm reporting live above Saint Patrick's Cathedral in New York City," Amejian reported. "The once majestic Cathedral, now a pile of rubble. According to eyewitness reports, a suicide bomber detonated his bomb on the altar, killing the New York Archdiocese's entire leadership. First responders rushed in to aid the injured and evacuate the Cathedral when a second, more powerful explosion leveled the structure. At this time, we're not sure if it was a second bomb or a gas explosion. The Mayor of New York, Victor DiMarco, said it was the worst attack since nine eleven. Investigators and rescuers are digging through the rubble searching for survivors."

The scene changed to an aerial view of the Cathedral in Boston. The taped footage showed people running out of the Cathedral in a panic, then mowed down by the rooftop sniper.

"In Boston, an anonymous shooter killed a priest in cold blood. Then as the panicked clergy fled the Cathedral, a second unknown sniper fired into the crowd. At this point, the death toll stands at eleven. If not for the brave actions of an armed citizen and the Boston SWAT team, the body count could have been much higher. Instead, it took hours for local police and the FBI to search for the sniper and declare the area safe. The Boston Police have evacuated the entire neighborhood. Now we will go to the Vatican for an update."

The image switched to an aerial view showing an empty St. Peter's square in Rome. A sea of white sheets covered victims from the five explosions. Blue and red flashing lights from emergency vehicles lit up the scene.

"This is Joanne Roberts reporting live from the Vatican. People worldwide are in a state of shock today after an unknown terrorist group launched multiple coordinated suicide attacks, killing at least three hundred worshipers in St. Peter's Square. The attacks occurred at the beginning of the Pope's inauguration. Despite heavy security measures, bombers beat the systems. At this time, we don't know if the Pope is dead or alive."

* * *

Jay and McCoy studied the video image from the bomb squad robot. The body lay where Jay left it, on the wooden floor with hands raised above his head. The detonator is still in the right hand. The bomber had sandy brown hair underneath a dark-haired wig. He had a light complexion, a short, well-trimmed beard, one blue eye, and one brown eye. Not your typical Islamic terrorist.

"Why two different eye colors?"

"Contacts," Mack said. "We found a second brown contact a few feet away."

Jay stared at the two bullet holes in the circuit board. Each hole is a half-inch in diameter. "Victor said he found the first bullet embedded in an LED. The second bullet severed the detonating wires and the PC board, but the fragment was in Bishop Ramirez's abdomen."

"Amazing," Mack said.

"What is?" Jay replied.

"Your shot placement. It was perfect. A fraction of an inch in either direction and the bomb explodes."

"Dumb luck."

"No way, my friend. You're way too modest."

"I'm making an audio log for the evidence file," Salinas said. "I'm going to secure one of the explosive packets from the vest for the lab to analyze. Then I'll take the rest of the packets for detonation and preserve the vest and electronics board. TATP is most stable when kept cold, so I will remove the pouch from the pocket and place it in the disposal box filled with dry ice."

Salinas opened the toolbox and removed a pair of wire

clippers, then continued his narration, "I am going to clip the detonation wires of each pouch."

Jay watched Salinas clip the first wire. "There is something odd about this detonation wire," Jay said. "The conductor is white instead of copper."

"That's a plastic conductor called PEDOT," Salinas said. "It's used in bombs built to pass through an x-ray machine. It's printed onto a substrate using 3D printers. We don't see it used too often by non-government terrorists because it is expensive to produce and difficult to store."

"Are you saying whoever built this bomb is a government agency?"

"Not necessarily. They just have a lot of money. Okay, let's continue. I am now going to cut away the tape from the top of the pouch."

Salinas replaced the clippers and removed a small knife with a sharp, triangular blade. He inserted the blade above a pocket holding the pouch. He pulled the knife along the top edge, being careful not to puncture the plastic.

"Now, I am going to pull the pouch up and out of the pocket."

Salinas tugged on the top of the pouch. It didn't move.

"What's holding the pouch?" Mack asked.

"I found a small piece of clear tape at the bottom of the pocket," Salinas said as he pulled out the knife and sliced the tape. The tip of the blade cut through the bottom of the pouch.

A thick, clear liquid oozed out of the pouch. When it hit the air, it started bubbling.

"Shit," Salinas said. "I punctured the pouch. It's leaking."

Jay braced himself for the explosion.

Several seconds passed, and the bomb didn't explode. Jay held his breath as Salinas inched the pouch out. Once the pouch was clear of the pocket, he placed it in the disposal box. He then proceeded to remove the other three pouches from the front of the vest.

As Jay watched the process on the computer screen, he remembered the white strands inside the pouches.

"Victor," Jay said. "Can you show us a close-up of the pocket?"

Salinas removed the camera from his helmet and held it up close.

Jay studied the clear liquid, "I saw before that there are coils of thin, tightly-wound white material inside the pouch. There are miniature needles, stars, and razor-like blades with a thin white core connecting them. The pieces were very uniform - like a machine produced them. Most IED vests contain nails and ball bearings. Have you ever seen anything like it?"

"No, but I did see the same material in the sample we removed."

Mack stared at the screen next to Jay, "Let's make sure we send samples of the strands to the lab."

Salinas returned to the job of removing the vest. He inspected the printed circuit board with the magnifying glass. Victor also examined the bullet lodged between the board and the vest.

Salinas pulled a plastic connector from the clip holding the circuit assembly and placed it in his vest pocket.

"It appears the only metal components of this bomb vest are in the control board. It looks like the inside of a cell phone with a receiver, battery, and detonation switch. It's my theory that the bomber carried the board inside his cell phone. When he went into the bathroom, he removed the board from the phone. He then snapped it into the clip and attached the wires. That's how this system defeated the metal detector and the x-ray security system."

"That's ingenious," Jay said. "Have you seen that before?"

"Once. I watched a presentation by a technician from a French bomb squad. He saw the same device used in Paris in 2015."

Salinas placed the pouches into the disposal box. Then, he pulled the vest off the bomber and put it in an evidence bag so the crime scene investigators could tag it and record it as evidence.

Jay and Mack accompanied Salinas to the bomb disposal trailer. He placed the pouches inside and closed the door. Moments later, there was a muted bang. Then smoke rose out of the edges of the container. When he opened the trailer, a thick layer of white shrapnel coated the inside of the vessel.

* * *

McCoy drove Jay back to the DHS command center in South Boston. The center was full of agents following up on tips.

McCoy led Jay to a locker room. Jay stripped off his clothes, placing them in an evidence bag. After a hot shower, Jay dressed in a dark blue pair of DHS coveralls and a set of shoe covers. He joined McCoy in the command center conference room.

Jay answered questions from dozens of law enforcement officers. They also questioned him about the attack on the Bishop in Dartmouth. After four hours, The FBI finally declared it a clean shooting and released Jay.

Jay called CJ, "How's the Bishop?"

"He's out of surgery," CJ said. "The doctors said it's touch and go, but they expect him to make it."

Chapter 18

Woods Hole - Two days later

The compact Cape Cod Catholic High School bus turned into the Woods Hole Ferry parking lot. The driver, Mildred McCallister, a plump, middle-aged woman with no sense of humor, opened the door.

"The ferry!" she yelled, but the boy ignored her. Instead, he was engrossed in writing a new algorithm for his after-school hobby.

The driver shook her head. She looked into the large rectangular mirror hanging over her driver seat and spotted Kyle, her suspect, but he didn't lookup. His entire focus was on the screen of his iPad. None of the other students on the bus bothered to look up either. They knew this was Kyle's stop.

"The ferry!" Mildred yelled again, watching to see if Kyle moved. He didn't.

The driver's son, Art, and his best friend Tony sat behind Kyle. Art looked upfront at his mother. She nodded at him. Art reached in front of him and slapped Kyle on the side of the head.

Kyle ignored the slap and kept typing.

"Hey, geek boy," Art said. "Time to get off the bus. Last time for this year."

* * *

Three rows back, Charlotte Cranmore was mad. Mad that Art slapped Kyle, the shy boy who helped her pass her physics final. Annoyed that Art's obnoxious mother encouraged him and angry that the school principal never did anything about it. She thought Kyle was cute. He had great green eyes and wavy red hair. Charlotte never told her friends how she felt because Kyle was the school's leading geek, and she was scared to be bullied by Art, who considered Charlotte his girlfriend. More like a conquest or possession. She despised Art, but he was captain of the football team and known for his quick temper. She finally had enough of watching Kyle get picked on.

Charlotte nudged her friend Carla sitting next to her, playing a game on her cell phone.

Charlotte said in a whisper. "Do you think Art will ever stop slapping Kyle?"

Carla looked up with an annoyed expression on her face. "Art's harmless."

Charlotte took a chance to tell her true feelings, "I think Kyle is kinda cute."

Carla stared at her like she had three heads. "Maybe. Not my type," she said. "You better hope Art doesn't hear you say that."

Carla went back to her app.

"Screw, Art," Charlotte mumbled under her breath as she stood up, grabbed her backpack, and approached Kyle. "Hey, Kyle. Do you want to grab a frozen coffee with me? My dad opened a new store here in Woods Hole."

"I'm not sure. I have to meet my Mom when the ferry arrives."

"C'mon, we'll have some fun together."

"Okay, I guess."

Kyle stowed his iPad and followed Charlotte off the bus. Carla, not wanting to be left out, hurried after the couple.

Mildred stared into the mirror, then yelled at Art, "Hey, stupid. Are you just going to sit there and let that geek steal your girlfriend?"

Art, who was in a state of shock, nodded his head and got up off the bus. His sidekick, Tony, followed close behind.

When Art stopped to get out of the bus, his mother whispered to him, "I wanna hear how you put that kid in his place. Do you understand? I'll park the bus down by the aquarium."

"Yea, Ma."

* * *

Kyle stopped at the dock where the Martha's Vineyard Ferry boarded. A line of cars and SUVs waited for the next ship to arrive.

"What does your Mother do for work?" Charlotte asked Kyle.

"She's an officer on the ferry. She works on the bridge."

"That's cool. Do you like ships?"

"Not really. It's her thing. She went to Canada to get her

degree."

"Why did she go to Canada?" Carla asked. "Mass. Maritime offers degrees in commercial navigation."

"It was a joint program," Kyle replied as he walked without looking at Carla. "The Canada Maritime Institute offered a degree focused on ferries."

Kyle's cell phone buzzed. "It's my cousin, Brendan. He says my Mom's been trying to reach me. Unfortunately, the ferry has mechanical problems and is still at Oak Bluffs. His Dad is going to pick me up at the Coffee Shack."

"It's Cranmore Coffee now," Charlotte said. "My Dad just bought the two local Coffee Shacks in Falmouth."

"That sucks," Carla said. "They're my favorite coffee shops."

"They aren't changing the menu too much, and my dad tries to maintain the charm of the local shops he buys."

Kyle turned to walk up the sidewalk towards the center of Woods Hole, "Well, I guess I have time to kill."

"I'm gonna pass on the coffee," Carla said. "I'll check out the t-shirts in the shop across the street. Leave you two alone."

Charlotte smiled but didn't say anything. Kyle didn't seem to notice.

The small shop had a few wooden booths decorated with nautical gadgets and hand-painted portraits of sea captains. Kyle ordered two frozen coffees with whipped cream, while Charlotte ordered a chai tea. They found a table on the front deck.

"I never had a chance to say thank you," Charlotte said. "You know, for helping me in Boston. You didn't have to stay with me at the hospital. It was kind."

Kyle smiled and thought back to that tragic day in Boston.

* * *

Inauguration Day, Hyannis, Mass.

Singing to a church full of priests was not Kyle McPhee's idea of a fun-filled day. But at least he didn't have to sit in class. Since he almost forgot his choir robe, he was the last one on the bus and had the front seat to himself. He was relieved since the three-hour ride from Cape Cod Catholic High School in Hyannis to Boston would be long enough without sharing the seat with another student, especially if that student was Art McCaskill. Kyle prayed the bulky football player would leave him alone, just once.

The engine of the bus started up. Kyle turned sideways to put his feet up on the seat, plugged in his earbuds, and opened the physics book on his iPad.

The bus started, then abruptly stopped. Kyle rolled forward and stopped himself from falling on the floor by putting his hand against the driver's seat. Then the door opened.

"I'm so sorry," Kyle heard a girl say to the driver.

A tall man with short-cropped hair followed the girl onto the bus and said, "Charlotte, there's room in the front row next to Kyle. Driver, we're all set to go. We have forty-two passengers."

Thank you, Mr. Flores. Is Carla here?"

"Yes, she's in the back."

Charlotte saw her friend waving from the back row. Then she turned to sit down, but Kyle was still sitting sideways.

"Excuse me, Kyle," Charlotte said. "Can I sit down, please?"

Kyle looked up. He thought he had gone to heaven. Charlotte wore a simple white cotton dress. Her cobalt-blue eyes sparkled in the morning sunlight, and she wore her silky blonde hair pulled away from her face exposing her perfect cheekbones and petite nose. Her skin seemed to glow.

"Kyle?" Charlotte said. "Can you let me sit down?"

"Oh yeah, sure," he said. "I'm sorry."

Kyle swiveled forward, squeezing his legs into the narrow space in front of him. He felt a little embarrassed as her leg touched his when she sat down, but she didn't move away. Maybe the trip to Boston wasn't going to be all that bad after all.

"Can you believe our class is singing at the mass to celebrate the Pope's inauguration?" Charlotte said. "This is so exciting."

"Yeah, I guess so."

Are you studying for the Physics final?"

"Yeah."

"Would you mind if we studied together? I'm really having a hard time understanding quantum mechanics."

"Sure," Kyle replied. He pulled off his headphones and held out his iPad so she could see the page he was on. "It's not that hard."

***

Kyle and Charlotte were the first ones off the bus. Kyle's heart sunk when he saw Art and Tony get off and head towards them.

"Hey, Charlotte," Art said. "I didn't see you get on the bus. What were you doing sitting with geek boy?"

Charlotte answered Art while looking at the ground. "It was the only seat left."

"Ain't that sweet," Art said with a sneer. He then grabbed Charlotte by her arm and pulled her a few feet away from Kyle.

"Art, let go of my arm," Charlotte said. "What are you doing?"

"I don't like that kid. He gives me the creeps."

"He's nice to me. He doesn't talk much, but he's not mean like you."

Kyle watched the two talk. He liked Charlotte but didn't understand what she saw in a bully like Art.

Tony, Art's best friend, was still standing next to him, "You

146

know Art and Charlotte are going out, don't you?"

"No," Kyle responded. "I mean, yeah. I guess so. I don't really pay attention to that kind of stuff."

"Art told me to tell you to stay away from her, or else."

Kyle wanted to reply or else what, but instead, he didn't say anything.

Kyle looked up at the large TV screens mounted outside the Cathedral for the public to watch. The mass was reserved for Priests, nuns, and other members of the Archdiocese of Boston.

The Central Catholic liturgical choir joined the other high school and college choirs and filed into the church and up a steep staircase onto the choir balcony at the back of the church. He was separated from Charlotte but found a spot in the front row overlooking the nave below.

Two large LED television screens stood on the far sides of the altar. The monitors showed the huge crowds in Rome swaying back and forth. The large TV screen showed the balcony where the Pope would address his church for the first time. The windows opened, and the Pope waved to the crowd. The congregation in the Cathedral exploded in applause. Kyle took his iPhone out of his pocket to record the mass.

***

Kyle watched in shock as explosions ripped through St. Peter's Square. Smoke and flames obscured the close-up shot of the Pope's balcony, but he was nowhere to be seen. The TV screen switched to aerial images showing mushroom clouds filling the sky.

There were two gunshots inside the Cathedral. Kyle instinctively ducked, but when there wasn't an explosion or return fire, he looked back up and saw a priest lying on his back on top of the Bishop.

There was silence. Then someone screamed, and the shock

turned to pandemonium.

On the choir balcony, there was a mad rush for the stairs. At first, Kyle was satisfied to let everyone else trample each other in an attempt to escape. He sensed the danger was in the panic, not from the shooter or a bomb. Kyle scanned the crowd for people he knew but couldn't find anybody. He caught a glimpse of Charlotte's blonde hair moving towards the staircase. Kyle called out to her, but there was too much noise. He spotted her again at the top of the steep, narrow staircase. Then someone pushed her from behind, and she disappeared down the stairs.

"No!" Kyle screamed out.

The sense of claustrophobia was overwhelming as Kyle was squeezed from all sides. The air was hot. All he could smell was perspiration and smoke from the gunshots. He worked hard to suppress his own fear and deal with his only goal—to find Charlotte.

Finally, Kyle started descending. He scanned the floor below and saw Charlotte curled up in a ball at the bottom of the staircase. People were stepping over her, and some even stepping on her.

"Get out of my way," Kyle screamed to nobody in particular as he pushed people out of his way. "That girl, she's my friend."

"Which one?" a voice said. He was the tall man from the bus: Carla's father, Art Flores.

"Mister Flores, It's Charlotte, the blonde girl on the floor."

"Let's go get her before she's crushed to death."

Al Flores took the lead. He moved people out of the way without making them fall. When he got to the bottom of the stairs, he worked his way to where Charlotte lay on the floor curled up in the fetal position. Blood soaked her face, and she wasn't moving.

"Kyle, I'll block the crowd and make them go around us. You help Charlotte. Move her over to the side chapel out of the flow of

people."

Kyle leaned over, grabbed Charlotte's collar, and pulled her off the floor. He placed her left arm over his shoulder and wrapped his right arm around her waist. Al Flores cleared a path to one of the alcove-like chapels. He placed Charlotte on the floor underneath a statue of Saint Raphel, the patron saint of healing. Charlotte wept and kept her hands wrapped around her torso as if she was holding her insides together.

"Thank you," she said in a faint whisper, "I can't breathe."

Then a trickle of blood appeared at the corner of her lips.

"She has internal bleeding," Al Flores said as he appeared next to Kyle. "Probably broken ribs, too. She needs to go to a hospital."

* * *

Kyle smiled at Charlotte and said, "No problem. I'm glad you were okay. But, unfortunately, a few people died from being trampled."

"Oh, no," Charlotte said. "That's awful. And all of those people shot on the front steps. I was so scared. And you were so brave to carry me out and find me a paramedic. She reached out and touched the back of his hand.

Kyle froze. Then he took a big gulp of his drink.

Charlotte pulled her hand back, "What are you doing this summer?"

"I don't know," Kyle said. "Hanging out, I guess. How about you?"

"I work as a lifeguard at Old Silver Beach."

"That's cool."

"Do you ever go there?"

"Where?

"To the beach."

"No. I burn if I spend too much time in the sun."

Charlotte giggled, "You know there's such a thing as sunscreen."

This time Kyle giggled back, "I know. I don't like hanging out without anything to do. I'm taking a class at the Institute in marine electronics. It's part of a joint program with MIT. I want to go there for college."

"Don't you have to be really smart to go to MIT?" Charlotte asked as she took a sip of tea.

"I guess," Kyle replied. "I never thought about it. The admissions counselor says I have the grades. I hope my Mom can figure out a way to pay the tuition. My Dad used to teach there before…."

"Before what?"

Kyle didn't answer.

"Kyle, what's wrong?"

Kyle slid his chair back away from the table, then pointed over Charlotte's head.

Art and Tony stood behind Charlotte. Art reached down and grabbed Charlotte's chair, and pulled her away from the table. Tony stepped up, grabbed the small, round aluminum table's edge, and flipped it over.

Charlotte screamed, "Let me go!"

Tony grabbed Kyle by the collar and pushed him to the floor.

"C'mon, Charlotte, we're going home."

"What are you doing? You have no right!" Charlotte said as she struggled to get away from the brute.

"I told you to stay away from geek boy. You're my girl."

"I'm not anybody's girl. Now let me go!"

Kyle, who hit his head on the deck, slowly got off the floor. Blood flowed from a gash on his forehead.

"Hey, what did you do to him?" A teenage boy in a Falmouth High School windbreaker said. "And let her go."

"Who the hell are you?" Art said.

"It doesn't matter. Now let her go."

"Make me."

"Okay," Brendan Hernandes, Kyle's cousin, said as he cocked back his right arm and snapped a lightning-fast right jab, smashing Art in the nose.

Tony lunged at Brendan, who stopped him with a sidekick to the solar plexus. Tony grabbed his stomach and doubled over in pain.

"Hey, what's going on here?"

Kyle looked up from the floor to see Brendan's father, Marty, standing at the foot of the stairs. His massive bulk filled the entire deck. A small crowd gathered on the sidewalk.

"This kid beat us up," Art said, holding his nose. "He attacked us for no reason."

"He's lying," Carla said from behind Marty. "I saw the whole thing. Art and Tony started it. They were bullying Kyle. They do it all the time."

"I need statements from all of you kids, including you, Brendan."

"Sure, Dad. No problem."

Marty pulled a handkerchief out of his pocket and handed it to Charlotte. "You have some blood on your face, young lady."

"Thank you, sir."

"What's your name?"

Charlotte looked at Art, who was glaring at her, and said under his breath, "You better not say anything."

Charlotte turned her back on Art and said, "My name is Charlotte Cranmore. I was having a drink with Kyle when Art grabbed me from behind. His friend Tony then turned the table over and pushed Kyle to the ground. Carla is right. They bully him all the time."

Marty took out a small notepad and wrote down the kid's names. "You all know each other?"

"Yes," Charlotte replied. "We go to school together."

"What school? Falmouth High?"

"No, we go to Cape Cod Catholic."

"Pretty unruly behavior for Catholic school kids," Marty said. "I went there. If I even thought of hitting someone, the nuns would make my life miserable."

Marty paused, but Art and Tony just stared at the ground.

"Boys," Marty said. "Do you have anything to say?"

"Sorry," Tony muttered under his breath.

"Well, it's time you all go home. Kyle, you come with Brendan and me."

He turned to look at Art and Tony, "I don't want to see you in Woods Hole ever again. You understand?"

"Yes, sir," Tony replied. Art said nothing.

Kyle stood up. Charlotte went over to him and touched him on the forehead, "You're bleeding. Let me get something from inside the store."

"I'll be okay," Kyle said.

Brendan stood on the sidewalk next to Carla and asked her, "Do you need a ride home?"

"My Dad is going to pick us up," Carla said. "He'll be here in five minutes."

"I can drive you home," Brendan said. "My Jeep is parked around the corner. Is that okay, Dad?"

"Sure, stay away from those two boys. I don't want any more trouble."

Chapter 19

Quissett Harbor, Falmouth

The evening sky was a multi-colored pallet as the sun slipped behind a few wispy clouds. As a boy, Jay watched the setting sun from the bow of his father's fishing boat. He often dreamed of sailing around the world chasing pirates and rescuing maidens. But, instead, he wanted to spend time with a good friend and drink a lot of beer.

Marty's home sat on Quissett Harbor's shore, a quaint body of water near Woods Hole. Tucked behind a thin peninsula known as The Nob, the picturesque harbor was home to a few dozen sailboats owned by the members of a small yacht club. The three-story home featured light-gray weathered cedar shingles and floor-to-ceiling windows. A green manicured lawn sloped to the harbor where two boats bobbed against a wooden dock.

Marty's grandfather built the home in 1899, and he inherited the estate five years ago. Marty converted the carriage house into a garage with an apartment on the second floor.

Jay took a swig of his beer and said. "It's still a shock to me.

I can't believe the Catholic church took such a beating."

"Nobody saw it coming," Marty said. "The world was celebrating the first American Pope. Who could have imagined terrorists would inflict so much destruction considering the level of security."

"Marty, I feel guilty."

"How come?"

"Because I survived. I shouldn't have."

"What are you talking about? You're a hero. There are hundreds of people alive because of your quick reactions and skills. Nobody could have made the shot you made."

"Thanks, but I still feel like I could have done more. How did I miss the imposter? He snuck into the limo right under my nose. Why wasn't I more diligent checking the priest's identities."

"Because you're Catholic, and you trust priests. By the way, have you heard anything about the Pope?"

"I have no idea," Jay said. "Nobody has seen him since the attack."

"Don't you think that's strange?"

"Not really. If the Pope is dead, the Vatican will want a smooth transition. If he's alive, they'll want to keep him safe until they find who's behind the attack."

Jay noticed movement behind him. He turned to see Marty's wife Lindsey putting a pot of water on the gas grill.

"Hey, Marty," Lindsey called out from the house. "Jillian and Kyle are here for dinner. Can you come in to say hi?"

"Sure," Marty said. I'll be right over."

"Oh, hey Jay," Lindsey said. "I didn't see you there. Long time, no see."

"Hi Lindsay," Jay yelled back. "It's nice to see you too."

"Can you stay for dinner? Marty's going to cook up some lobsters, and I'm preparing a good old-fashioned clam boil."

"That sounds great."

"Jillian?" Jay asked Marty. "Your sister?"

"Yeah, her son Kyle was one of the choir singers at the Cathedral. He saved a friend from getting trampled."

"I haven't seen her since we were kids. So what has she been doing?

"She went to a maritime academy in Newfoundland and then worked on the Nova Scotia ferry that runs from Portland, Maine to Yarmouth. After that, she returned home to work for the Steamship Authority. She's now an officer on the Martha's Vineyard ferry out of Woods Hole."

"The last time I saw her, she was in braces. And Kyle's her son? I didn't know she had a kid."

"Yeah, she got pregnant during her first year of college," Marty said. The guy's name was Daniel. A brilliant but weird guy obsessed with drones. He disappeared when Kyle was four. Jillian has been raising him on her own ever since."

"Wow, what a story," Jay said. "What do you mean, Jillian's husband disappeared?"

"Yeah, he vanished into thin air. Daniel took Kyle to the beach one afternoon. When they didn't return on time for dinner, Jillian went searching. She found Kyle playing in the salt marsh by himself. We searched the entire Cape but never found him."

Jay followed Marty into the large, open kitchen lining the back of the main house. A slim, attractive red-haired woman leaned against the kitchen counter. It was the woman from the bike path.

"Jill," Marty said. "This is my business partner, Jay Mendes."

Jay noticed Jillian staring at him. Like she had seen him before but couldn't remember where.

"Hello," Jillian said. "Oh my God, I know you. You stopped to help me."

"Hi, it's nice to see you again," Jay said. "But we knew each other a long time ago."

"We did?"

"I knew you when you were a kid."

"Really? I don't remember you."

"I was one of Marty's friends growing up. I lived in Maravista, but we used to hang out here all the time."

"Oh my God!" Jillian said. "I remember you now. You were a short, skinny kid. You always picked me for your street hockey games. Wow, you've grown up. What have you been doing?"

"Well, I spent a few years in the Navy and now work with Marty in Woods Hole."

"Don't let his modesty fool you, Jill," Marty interrupted. "Jay was a Navy SEAL. One of the deadliest men on earth."

Jay glared at Marty, who shrugged his shoulders. "Jay, you don't have to be shy."

"Well, it sounds intriguing," Jillian said. "You'll have to tell me some war stories later."

Jillian turned to her son on the couch. "Kyle, come over here and be social."

Kyle didn't answer.

"Kyle, please, can you come over?"

Still no answer.

Jillian turned to Jay and Marty.

"Can you excuse me? My son's rude."

Jillian marched to the couch and grabbed the cell phone

from Kyle's hand.

"Mom," Kyle yelled. "I'm in the middle of something."

"Kyle Matthew McPhee, you take a break and say hello. You'll get your phone back when you show some respect."

"Yes, Mom." Kyle walked over to Jay and reluctantly extended his hand.

"Hi, Mr. Mendes. It's a pleasure to meet you."

"Hi Kyle," Jay replied, returning the handshake. "The pleasure is all mine."

Kyle rolled his eyes, turned around, and flopped back down on the couch. Jay saw Jillian's pale, freckled skin turn bright red. "Jay, do you have teenage children?" Jillian asked.

"No, I'm not married."

"Well, you're smart then. You can have mine if you wish."

Lindsey handed Jillian a glass of wine, which Jillian guzzled down in one large gulp.

"Lindsey, that was great. Do you have anything stronger?"

* * *

The hot tub water swirled around Jay's sore muscles as he enjoyed getting reacquainted with Jillian.

Lindsey sat on the opposite side of the hot tub with Marty. She looked at Jillian with a sly smile. She had been trying to matchmake for her sister-in-law since she returned to Falmouth, without any luck—until now. She needed to get Jay more involved in the conversation, "Jill, do you remember the time we snuck into the Woods Hole Aquarium? We wanted to swim with the harbor seal?"

"Oh my God, we were in high school and playing truth or dare."

"That's right, I remember," Marty said. "I asked which of my friends you had a crush on. You took the dare. You never told us who the friend was."

Jillian looked at Jay with a smirk. She was drunk and giggling like a schoolgirl.

"Come on, Jill," Lindsey teased. "Tell us who it was?"

Jillian leaned over, wrapped her arms around Jay, and pulled him towards her. He wasn't expecting her to grab him and slipped off the seat into the swirling water.

When he was underwater, she said a little too loudly, "It was Jay!"

Jay pulled himself out of the water and wiped his face off.

"I heard you," he replied, smiling. "Why didn't I know about that."

"You left us and joined the Navy," Marty said.

"What would you have done if you had known mister sailor boy?" Jillian asked.

"I don't know. Ask you out on a date?"

"Well, it's never too late."

Lindsey elbowed Marty in the side. "Honey, it's time to call it a night."

Marty didn't answer. He looked at Jay. Then he looked at his little sister, making eyes at his friend.

"Marty!" Lindsey said as she stood up.

Marty finally climbed out of the hot tub.

"Have you guys seen Brendan and Kyle?" Lindsey asked.

"No, but we'll take a walk and look for them," Jay said.

* * *

Jay stepped out of the hot tub and grabbed a towel. When

Jillian stood up, she wobbled around and sat back down. Jay lifted Jillian up and held her steady until she regained her balance. She wrapped her arms around Jay's neck, and she held on for a long moment. When Jay was sure she wasn't going to fall, he wrapped a towel around her shoulders.

"Come on, Jillian," Jay said. "Let's take a walk. You could use some fresh air."

They walked down a narrow dirt path towards the water. The trail ended at a small dock where Marty had his two motorboats. One was a twenty-four-foot Boston Whaler Vantage, and the other was a thirty-six-foot Baja cigarette boat. Jay turned right to follow the shoreline along the edge of the small harbor. The large moon lit the sky enough, so they didn't need a flashlight. The dark water shimmered in the moonlight, and the waves rocked the sailboats in the harbor.

"Where are you taking me, sailor boy?" Jillian asked with a slight drunken slur.

"I want to share a favorite spot with you. It's been years since I've been to the Nob."

"Okay, lead the way, but don't let go of my hand. I may fall in the water."

"That's okay. I can save you. I'm a sailor boy, remember."

* * *

Kyle sat with Brendan by the fire pit. He thought his Uncle Marty's new friend was leaving after dinner. But the adults decided to hang out and drink in the hot tub. He wasn't happy.

"What's the matter?" Brendan said. "I thought we were

160

gonna work on the bots tonight."

"My mom took my cell phone away. I was in the middle of a new algorithm."

"Well, relax. Our night is about to get more interesting."

"What do you mean?" Kyle asked.

"Remember those two girls from your school? The cute blonde you helped in Boston. And her friend, the feisty brunette."

"You mean Charlotte and Carla?"

"Yea, those girls. I invited them over."

"Why did you do that?"

"I thought you'd be happy?"

"Why would that make me happy," Kyle said. "Did you forget about this afternoon already? Charlotte's boyfriend, Art? He's a real brute."

"No, he isn't. He didn't even fight back when I punched him in the nose. He's just a typical bully who picks on the weaklings but doesn't have the guts for a real fight. Plus, I got the idea that Charlotte likes you."

"Art will find out and beat me up."

"I thought you told me they broke up?"

"Yeah, but Art doesn't know that."

Brendan's sister Melissa opened the back door from the kitchen. Charlotte and Carla were following her. She pointed at the fire pit, and the girls walked over.

The girls sat down on the opposite side of the fire pit.

Kyle thought Charlotte looked cute. Charlotte gave Kyle a shy wave. She was wearing a pink hoodie sweatshirt and white capri pants. Carla was more rugged-looking with olive skin, dark eyes, and several tattoos on her upper arms. She cut her hair short with a purple tinge in her bangs and wore a black t-shirt and jeans.

Kyle noticed that Carla liked Brendan. He was her type, strong and athletic. Brendan and the girls exchanged some small talk. Kyle wasn't in the mood for talking too much, so he listened in. After about an hour, the girls got up and went to the bathroom.

"Kyle, these girls are nice," Brendan said. "How come you didn't introduce me before?"

"I don't know. They go to school with me, but I don't know them very well."

"Charlotte does seem to like you. How do you know her?"

"She's in my Physics class, and we sing in the choir together."

"What's the deal with Carla?"

"Her Dad was in the Coast Guard. So they moved around a lot. He retired last year and now works at the Marine Institute in Woods Hole. He also owns a mixed martial arts studio in Wareham. Carla teaches there."

"She teaches MMA? Holy shit, that's badass. Does she compete?"

"Yeah, I heard she's ranked in the top five in New England."

"That's cool. When the girls come back, I'll sit with Carla. You sit with Charlotte and talk to her."

"I don't know. She's pretty popular. I don't know what to say to her."

"You'll think of something. Now sit down, here they come."

* * *

"What were you guys talking about when we came in?" Charlotte said.

"Brendan and I are working on my microbots," Kyle replied. "I'm trying to get the night vision feature working. But, first, I need to test it.

"What do you mean by microbots?" Charlotte asked.

"They're cool flying robots. You know, like drones, but better. I build them, and Brendan helps me test them.".

"Cool," Carla said, butting into their conversation. "Can we see how they work?"

"I... I don't know," Kyle stuttered. "They're nothing special. A hobby I've been fooling around with."

"Stop being so modest," Brendan said. "They're really cool. Let's show them how they work. Then, we can go down by the water."

"Yeah, show us," Carla said.

"I'm not sure," Charlotte said. "Where are we going?"

"Don't worry," Brendan said. "It's nothing dangerous. We'll go to the Nob on the other side of the harbor. It will take a few minutes."

Kyle and Brendan came out of the carriage house carrying a black carrying case and an iPad.

"Hey, Kyle," Carla said. "Your Mom and that guy Jay left the hot tub and walked towards the water. She seemed a bit drunk. Shouldn't we make sure she's okay? Who is he anyway?"

"He's a friend of Brendan's Dad. I don't know him."

"What does he do for work?"

"I don't know. I think he's a security guard."

"Like a mall cop?" Charlotte giggled. "Does he drive around on one of those silly Segways?"

"Did you call Jay Mendes a mall cop?" Brendan said. "Are you nuts?"

163

"What? What did I say?"

"Jay Mendes is a hero."

"How do you know that?" Carla asked.

"I overheard my Dad talking to Jay. He was a Navy SEAL. When something went wrong. Someone claimed Jay killed an innocent hostage, and he got drummed out of the SEALs. That's why he came home."

"Who claimed he killed a hostage?" Carla asked.

"My dad said it was Kathleen Amejian, the reporter from GNN," Brendan said.

"Oh my God," Charlotte squealed. "My mother knows her."

"How is that possible?"

"My Mom works for an ad agency. She met Kathleen at a dinner party in London. There's a picture of my mom and Kathleen in her office.

Kyle was half listening and half watching his mother stumbling and hanging all over Jay. *She was so embarrassing. Why was my mother doing this? She's still married. If my dad knew she liked this guy, he'd be mad.*

"I don't like him," Kyle said. "Let's go see where they're going."

"What?" asked Charlotte. "You want to follow them?"

"No, not exactly," Kyle replied with a sly grin.

* * *

Jay led Jillian around the harbor and up a narrow, sandy trail onto the Nob. It was dark in the woods, and the path had exposed tree roots and rocks. He held Jillian close to him so she wouldn't trip. The trail was short, only about half a mile. When they emerged from the canopy, the panoramic view of Buzzards Bay took their breath away.

They walked across the neck of the Nob, a narrow strip of land with water on both sides. At the end of the neck, stone stairs climbed to the top of the rounded headland. A few acres around, the small hill rose fifty feet above the water. Smooth granite blocks lined the waterline to prevent erosion.

At the top, they sat on a granite bench overlooking the ocean. The moonlight glistened off the calm water, and the sound of the gentle waves lapping against the granite was enchanting. A bell on a distant buoy clanged in the breeze.

"It's so beautiful tonight," Jillian whispered. "The view is magnificent."

"It's magical," Jay said as he stared at Jillian. He noticed she was shivering, so Jay slid closer and wrapped his arms around her.

"Do you come here often?" Jillian asked.

"Not since the night of my brother's funeral. I decided to join the Navy that night. Needed to do something different."

"That was so tragic," Jillian said. "I remember going to the candlelight vigil at the beach. I knew Jojo and his girlfriend, Olivia. They were nice."

Jay was surprised to hear Olivia's name. First, he felt a brief pang of guilt. Then he remembered she was in California.

Jillian looked at him and smiled. "Did you hear me say I had a crush on you? You were underwater."

"I wasn't all the way under."

"I still do, you know."

"Do what?"

"Have a crush on you," Jillian said, staring into Jay's eyes. She placed her hand behind Jay's neck, pulling him forward, and pecked him on his lips. Jay kissed her back.

Jillian pulled away and looked at Jay in his eyes. She placed one hand on his cheek.

"That was nice," Jillian said. "It's been a long time since I've kissed a man like that."

"You don't have to stop now," Jay said with a grin.

She leaned to kiss him again, but he held up his hand to stop her.

"What's wrong?"

"I hear something."

"What?"

"A faint buzzing sound."

Jay couldn't find the source of the annoying buzz. But he did see a strange reflection of the moonlight. Jay stood up and stepped towards the sound, then tripped over a granite block. He fell flat onto his stomach. Laughter erupted from a few feet away.

The fall knocked the wind out of Jay's lungs. After a few deep breaths, he gathered his composure, stood up, and sat back down with Jillian.

Jillian recognized the source of the laughter.

"That's my son and his friends," Jillian said.

She was about to yell something, but Jay put his finger to his mouth.

"Shh," he said. "I have an idea. I'll give them a bit of their own medicine. Why don't you walk around to the other side of the hill? Act like you're searching for the noise."

Jillian was still a bit tipsy, but she went along with Jay's plan. While she walked back and forth, Jay crawled to the edge of the hill so nobody would see him.

Jay worked his way down the slick granite blocks and slid into the water. The cold water felt good to him. As a Navy

SEAL, Jay trained to swim and work in the fifty-degree water of coastal Virginia.

Jay swam with his head above the water until he saw the four teens at the base of the headland. The two girls were wearing strange headsets. Kyle had a remote control in his hand, and Brendan was holding an iPad. He crept out of the water and approached the group. He snuck right up behind Brendan. Peering over his shoulder, Jay saw the iPad screen was lit up in the eerie green mode typical of night vision scopes. He watched Jillian stumbling around, looking for the bot.

Jay was so close to Brendan that a few drops of cold saltwater dropped on Brendan's shoulder. Brendan wiped the drops away then turned to see Jay crouching behind him.

Brendan screamed! Then the girls screamed louder.

Jay laughed. He noticed Kyle looking at the iPad and saw Jillian waving at him.

"Gotcha!" she said.

Chapter 20

New York City

S moke seeped from the piles of rubble once known as Saint Patrick's Cathedral. Located in the heart of Manhattan, St. Patrick's twin towers were a reminder of the city's Irish Catholic roots.

From street level, the front of the Cathedral appeared unscathed. The twin spires soared toward the sky. But that's where the beauty ended. The circular stained glass windows ordaining the front facade stood empty and vacant—the mahogany front doors—now piles of charcoal on the blood-stained granite steps.

There was an eerie silence in this busy, bustling part of the city. Barriers closed off the area around the Cathedral, restricting access to Rockefeller Center. The Mayor of New York objected to the closures, but he gave in when reminded of the carnage of the 9/11 attacks.

"Ewww," Jessie said. "What's that smell?"

"Death. Rotting flesh. Bodily fluids," her cameraman and classmate, Roger, replied.

"Do you have to be so morbid?" Jessie said as she held her hand over her nose.

Roger shook his head in amazement, "I have a question. Why are we here?"

"We're investigative journalists. We're here to find a groundbreaking scoop."

"But we're still journalism students. We don't graduate for another month, and we don't work for anybody yet."

"I told you all this on the ride down from Kingston. Weren't you listening to me?"

"Not really. You're always talking. I can't remember everything you say."

"Well, we both better shut up," Jessie said. "Because here comes a cop. I'll sweet talk him, so he lets us in the Cathedral."

"Let us in where?" It's a pile of stone."

"Shut up!"

Jessie primped herself for the police officer. Her tight red dress squeezed her breasts tight, accentuating her cleavage. She smiled to show off her perfect teeth.

"What are you two doing here?" the police officer asked, waving his hands. This is a crime scene. No media allowed."

"But officer, we're investigative reporters. We want to share a tip with you."

Roger looked at Jessie. She ignored him. She was on a roll.

"What tip? Do I look like a tip line? Pick up a phone and drop a dime. Now scram."

"Then can you bring us to the officer in charge? It's a vital tip."

The officer looked annoyed.

"Please, Officer," Jessie said with her little girl pout.

"Listen, missy, what's your name?"

"Jessie. Jessie Mendes."

"What news organization are you with?"

"Channel Six in Providence." She flashed her intern ID then returned it to her pocketbook. He reached his hand out. She placed the ID in his hand. He studied it and gave it back to her.

"Sorry, kid. No students are allowed either. Now take off before I arrest you for lying to a police officer."

Roger grabbed Jessie by the arm. He looked back at her in amazement. "Come on, Jessie, let's go. We'll wait for somebody to come out."

Jessie and Roger peered at the historic Cathedral.

"Roger, let's get some b-roll footage. Then, we can walk around outside the perimeter of the site."

Police cordons blocked one lane of Fifth Avenue to allow traffic to pass. They also blocked off the entrance to East Fiftieth Street.

Jessie observed a row of closed-down storefronts, "Look; the debris shatter the windows at Louis Vuitton. I was gonna get a new bag."

"Too bad," Roger said, shaking his head. "I know that's a top priority for you."

"Look at the piles of debris," Jessie said. "It looks like a mountain of rubble. Let's take a closer look."

"What about the cop?"

"What about him. He said we couldn't go into the Cathedral. We are technically not going in."

Jessie slipped between two of the wooden barriers, and Roger followed. Once past the barricade, they could see right inside the Cathedral.

The main sanctuary was now a pile of stone and plaster.

Only three of the great pillars remained standing—sticking out of the rubble like lone sentries. Crumpled stainless pipes lay underneath piles of roof tiles—the only remnants of the once majestic pipe organ.

Rescuers dressed in white hazmat suits led dogs over the top of the rubble, looking for human remains. Along the street, coroner vans lined up, waiting to remove the bodies.

Jessie stopped Roger and pointed to the top of a pile. Two FBI agents carried a body bag down. One of the officers slipped, and the bag's zipper opened. A headless torso wearing the remains of a nun's habit rolled out. One agent grabbed it, pushed the body back into the bag, and zipped it up.

Jessie stared in shock. The stench of death overwhelmed her, causing her to throw up.

Roger waited while Jessie finished retching. When she stood up, tears were streaming down her cheeks, smudging her thick mascara.

"Are you alright?" Roger said. "We can leave if you want."

Jessie shook her head. "I'll be okay. Did you get that on the camera?"

"Yeah, I got it."

Jessie looked up. A young Hispanic man wearing a white hazmat suit stood in the street in front of her. The man's large dark eyes stared at her—his arms on his hips.

"You know you're not supposed to be here, Jessie."

That was creepy; she thought, "How do you know my name?"

"Your brother, Jay, talked about you all the time."

"How do you know my brother?"

"We worked together," the bomb squad officer said. "My

name is Victor Salinas, and I'm with the Massachusetts State Police Bomb Squad. I served with your brother overseas. One of the agents in Boston tipped me off that you may come here to practice your investigation skills."

"We'll leave," Jessie said. "One question. How many people died here?"

"We're still finding bodies, forty-seven so far. We are missing at least ten more.

"Where were they killed?"

"There was just one bomber, and he stood at the front of the church near the altar. The blast killed almost everybody within a twenty-foot radius. Police were able to evacuate the rest of the congregation. But after firefighters entered the Cathedral, there was a second explosion that leveled the building. Thirty-two first responders died in the blast, the worst loss since 9/11. We got lucky."

"How do you call that lucky?" Roger asked.

"The Cathedral was full—over 3,000 people. Most were priests and nuns. The heart of the New York Archdioceses."

"Did you know any of the victims?" Jessie said.

"Sorry, I can't answer any more questions. You'll have to leave now. I'll escort you back to your van."

"But Officer Salinas, how did you know we were out here?"

"The cop at the door told me. I figured you wouldn't give up that easy."

Jessie and Roger followed Salinas back towards Fifth Avenue.

"Where was the bomber when he detonated?" Jessie asked.

"In the middle of the altar. The heat emitted from the bomb was tremendous."

As they walked, Jessie noticed something furry squashed

between two granite blocks.

"Excuse me," Jessie said. "Something is interesting there."

She pointed toward the object. To Jessie, it looked like a dead rat, a common sight in New York City.

Salinas knelt and took a closer look. It appeared to be a bird. But on closer inspection, Jessie saw wires sticking out. Salinas moved some rubble to get a closer look. Wires hung out of the bottom of the bird, revealing a green circuit board. The eyes were tiny camera lenses.

"That is one special seagull," Jessie said.

"This is not a seagull," Victor said. "It's a drone."

Jessie and Roger watched as agents and crime scene technicians surrounded the drone. One person took photos. Another technician pulled the body of the phony bird out of the rubble. He examined it then placed it in a clear plastic bag. He reached in and pulled out several more pieces and put them in separate bags. The bird's wings were still attached. Many of the feathers were peeled away, revealing a plastic substructure.

"Roger, are you filming this?" Jessie said. "We have to get this video to the station as soon as possible. We'll have an exclusive."

Victor picked up the drone and walked towards the command vehicle parked in front of Rockefeller Center.

Jessie noticed a tiny green light blinking from the bottom of the bird's body as Victor walked by.

Jessie reached out and grabbed Victor's left arm. "Excuse me. There's a light…."

Then the bird exploded.

Victor disappeared in a cloud of smoke and fire.

A wave of pressure slammed Jessie against the store's

boarded-up windows as bodily fluids and sharp objects pummeled her body. As the smoke cleared, she found herself trapped by something heavy. It took several moments for her mind to clear and realize it was the remains of Victor's body pinning her against the store.

Jessie wrapped her arms around Victor's torso and gently lowered him to the ground.

As Jessie tried to take a step, she felt a sharp pain in her left thigh and warm liquid oozing down her bare leg. She reached down to find a bone protruding from her muscle. Flesh, blood, and dark blue material hung off the bone. Jessie screamed.

Then she saw Roger lying on his back. There was blood flowing out of a gash on his head, and his cell phone was still clutched in his hand.

"Roger!" Jessie screamed. She tried retaking a step, but her leg buckled under her weight, and she fell to her knees. Pain ripped the breath from her lungs.

Jessie dragged herself over chunks of granite and bloody limbs. When she reached Roger, she saw he was unconscious. A large gash on the back of his head oozed thick blood. She placed two fingers on his neck and felt a faint pulse.

Thank God, she thought. *He's still alive.* She wanted to do more for Roger, but she didn't have any strength left. The pain was overwhelming her senses. Her vision was fuzzy. She felt so weak and cold. Jesse lay her head on Rogers' chest, then closed her eyes. She whispered, "I'm sorry, Jay. I love you, Momma. Our Father, who art in…."

Chapter 21

Jay and Jillian walked hand-in-hand back to Marty's house. They were still laughing about the look on Kyle's face when Jay surprised him.

As they walked up the grassy slope, Jay noticed a black Suburban in Marty's driveway. CJ and Gia were standing in front.

"Jill, I had a great time tonight, but I have to go."

"I had fun too," Jillian said.

Jay kissed Jillian goodnight and ran up the slope to the house. "Hey, guys, what's going on? Why are you here?"

"Get in," Gia said. "We'll tell you inside."

"I need to change out of my bathing suit and grab my duffle bag."

"Here it is," CJ said, throwing a small nylon bag at Jay.

Jay caught the bag, then got in the rear seat and slid over. Gia jumped in the front, shutting the door.

"Gia?" Jay said. "What's going on?"

"There's been another explosion. In New York outside St. Patrick's Cathedral."

Jay grabbed clothes out of his duffle bag and changed.

Gia said, "We're being picked up at Otis Air Base."

"I don't understand. Why are we going to New York?"

"Your sister. She was there."

"What do you mean?" Jay said as he pulled a t-shirt over his head.

"I'm sorry. Jessie might not make it."

The words struck like a sledgehammer. Jay struggled to catch his breath. After a few moments, he said, "How? What happened? Was anybody else hurt?"

"Yes. Jessie's friend Roger is in critical but stable condition. He has a fractured skull and internal injuries. A bomb squad member was killed. He was Victor Salinas."

"Oh man, how is that possible?" Jay said. "We were together in Boston. What happened?"

"Mack called me," Gia said, placing her hand on Jay's. "Reports are sketchy, but your sister tried to get into the Cathedral but was turned away by a cop. She was nearby when the bomb went off."

"How bad?"

"Bone fragments punctured her thigh and clipped her femoral artery. She lost a lot of blood. Mack said she's still in surgery."

CJ pulled through the guard gate at the joint military base in Bourne. He parked the suburban at the Coast Guard air station. Two orange and white rescue helicopters sat on helipads, ready to launch. Jay heard a faint whisper above the Suburban. He opened the door and looked up to see his ride approach. It was unlike anything he had ever seen before. It looked like a private jet, but instead of engines, this aircraft had three circular fans. It hovered above the airfield, then lowered to the tarmac. It reminded Jay of an oversized drone. But this plane was sleek and shiny. Jay and Gia stepped out of the truck to watch the aircraft land.

The door opened, and a ladder extended down. A moment later, Michelle Goddard stepped out. She waved at Jay, then ran down the ladder, "I'm so sorry about your sister. When McCoy called me and told me what happened, I dropped everything. Let's go. We can be in New York in an hour."

Gia climbed onto the aircraft. Jay turned to look for CJ and found him standing outside the Suburban.

"CJ, are you coming?"

"No, the Bishop requested twenty-four-hour protection. Madman and I are going to take twelve-hour shifts until you get back."

"Okay, stay in touch. I'll call you from New York."

Jay took a seat next to Michelle in the cockpit. Gia made herself at home in one of the leather seats in the cabin.

"Michelle, what is this thing?" Jay said. "It reminds me of one of the spaceships in the Jetsons."

"It's a Trifan 600 from XTI. I'm launching an air taxi business in Manhattan. This is the first VTOL in my fleet."

"What's a VTOL?"

"It stands for vertical take-off and lift. It's like the V-22 Ospreys used by the Marines. But it flies faster and lands like a helicopter. I'm using it for flights between New York and the other northeast cities. What do you think?"

"It's amazing," Jay said. "I think it's going to be a big hit."

"So do I. The bombings have people rattled. I've had executives request security guards to protect them on business trips. What do you think about working together?"

"Sounds like a great idea, but let's talk later. I'm too worried about Jessie to think straight."

* * *

An hour later, they landed at Bellevue Hospital in Manhattan.

Michelle opened the door and hugged Jay, "Everything will be okay."

"Why are you doing this for me," Jay said.

"Are you serious? You tried to save Michael's life in Pakistan, and you stayed with me when he died. For days you held me and never complained. For God's sake, you were a pallbearer at his funeral. I'll always love you for that. Now I'm praying that Jessie survives. I'm going to return the trifan and will be back as soon as I can."

"Thanks, Michelle," Jay said. "I don't know what to say."

Jay was escorted to a family conference room with a small couch and two chairs. GNN was on the TV. The headline read *Sister of Priest Murderer Injured in a Bomb Blast.*

After fifteen minutes, a female Asian doctor came in and shut the door.

"Mr. Mendes, my name is Doctor Chin. I'm the trauma surgeon who operated on your sister."

Jay looked at the doctor. Something was wrong. She seemed very nervous. "What's going on?"

"Your sister is alive but in grave condition. She's lost a lot of blood and has severe internal bleeding. We've been able to get the bleeding under control, but her leg is the main concern. She has severe tendon damage, and a bad infection is threatening her life."

"So, are you going to be able to fix it?" Jay said. "She's a kid."

"No, I'm sorry. We can't save the leg and keep your sister alive. I need your permission to amputate. And I need it now."

Jay stared at the doctor. *He couldn't believe what he heard.*

And now he had to give permission to remove his sister's leg? Will it ruin her dreams to be a journalist? Will she ever be able to forgive him? But how could he let her go? Then he thought of Jojo. He never had a chance to save him.

"Mr. Mendes, please," Chin said. "We don't have much time."

"Will she survive if you don't amputate?"

"No, sir. She won't."

"Then you have my permission."

Chapter 22

Kyle paced the apartment, waiting for a call from Brendan. He told him he was going to pick up Carla and Charlotte. Did something happen? Did Art show up? Kyle's mind was spinning. There was a knock on the front door. Kyle opened the door to see his three friends standing there. He could see on their faces that something was wrong.

"Where have you guys been?" Kyle asked. "I thought something happened."

"We were at the house waiting for you," Brendan said. "You said you were coming over."

"No, you said you were coming to get me."

"Stop it, you two," Carla said. "Did you see the news on GNN today?"

"No. I never watch TV."

"Oh my God," Charlotte said. "You mean you don't know what happened last night? They've been reporting non-stop."

"I don't know what you're talking about."

"Come on then," Brendan said as he grabbed Kyle by the arm and dragged him out of the door.

"What's going on?"

Nobody said a word as they walked across the driveway

and went to enter the house when Brendan stopped short. Lindsey was sitting on the sectional sofa talking on the phone.

"Shh," Brendan said to the girls and Kyle, who was still outside the door.

"You're not going to fire, Jay? Why? He's a killer." Lindsey said. "She said Jay killed that priest in cold blood. He's a murderer, and you're running around with him like he's a hero? Marty, you're crazy. You need to do something about him. He can't come to this house again." Lindsey slammed the phone down. She wiped tears from her eyes, then got off the couch and went down the basement stairs.

Kyle's eyes opened wide. The guy he thought was a rental cop. Then a hero was a killer.

Kyle followed Brendan and the girls into the family room. They sat down on the couch and waited while Brendan pulled the report up from the DVR menu.

"Here, watch the report," Brendan said. "I recorded it this afternoon."

Kyle stared at an aerial view of a smoking Saint Patrick's. "This is Kathleen Amejian reporting from Bellevue Hospital in New York City. Reliable sources confirmed the identity of the shooter at the Cathedral in Boston. He is former Navy SEAL, Jay Mendes. Mendes now works for Maravista Security in Falmouth, Massachusetts. Our source told us Mendes shot the unidentified priest from point-blank range. We also learned the person Mendes was protecting, Bishop Ramirez of Fall River, was also shot. We cannot confirm a rumor that the priest Mendes shot was wearing a suicide vest. We've asked FBI officials about Mendes, but they refuse to comment."

"I can't believe she's saying those lies," Kyle said. "Jay would never shoot anybody in cold blood."

"Wait," Carla said. "It gets better."

"We also learned Mendes' sister, Jessie Mendes, a journalism student, was injured in the blast at St. Patrick's today. Mendes was flown to New York by Goddard Aviation President Michelle Goddard. Goddard's public relations department claims Goddard and Mendes are mere friends. But my sources claim their relationship is more complex. Should one of the richest women in the world be associated with an alleged killer? This is Kathleen Amejian from GNN."

* * *

Brendan turned the television off.

"How did Kathleen find out about Jay being the shooter?" Kyle said to nobody in particular. He looked at his friends, but nobody said a word. "Come on. We were talking about Jay last night."

"Okay," Brendan said while he fiddled with the tv remote. "I mentioned to Carla that I overheard my Dad talking to Jay."

"Then I shared the news with Charlotte," Carla said. "And I posted it on Snapchat, Facebook, and Twitter."

"My mother read my Snapchat feed this morning," Charlotte said. "I'm sorry. She told her friends at the ad agency."

"Who is friends with Kathleen," Kyle said as he stood up and walked into the kitchen. "What do we do now? Jay is going to kill us. Literally!"

"How will he know we were the source of the news story?" Charlotte said. "We can try to keep it a secret."

"Yeah, we're great at keeping secrets," Kyle said.

"We can tell him the truth," Carla said. "We didn't do it on purpose."

"Okay, that's a great idea," Brendan said. "Tell the world's deadliest man we were the ones responsible for revealing his identity. That should go over with a bang. To our heads!"

"Brendan," Charlotte said. "Stop it. You're scaring me."

"Charlotte, he's teasing," Carla said. "Jay wouldn't hurt us."

"How do you know?" Kyle said." "Do you know the man? We know he was capable of shooting that priest, and he's killed other people before."

"He was a soldier," Brendan said. "That was his job!"

Charlotte put her face in her hands, "Exactly my point. He's a professional killer. What have we got ourselves into?"

Kyle put his hand on Charlotte's back. "Charlotte, it's okay. My Uncle Marty and my mother will make sure nothing happens to us. I promise. I don't believe he's guilty. We need to do something to prove Jay is innocent."

"What can we do?" Charlotte said. "We're kids."

"Oh my God," Carla said. "I know what we can do."

"What's that?"

"I saw a video on TikTok. A boater spotted four men getting off a small rubber raft on one of the Elizabeth Islands. He thought they looked like military types. There's an old, abandoned mansion on the island. People online said they were squatters."

"So, what are you saying?" Brendan said. "What does that have to do with us?"

"We could go out to the island tonight and use your drones to take pictures," Carla said. "They may have something to do with the attacks."

"What if they're like Jay?" Charlotte asked. "They could kidnap us or worse. They could kill us."

"Or the mansion is a haunted house," Brendan said. "Charlotte, you could see some ghosts. Whoooo."

"Stop it, Brendan. I'm serious. We're not soldiers. Tell your father. Let the police handle it."

"I agree with Brendan," Kyle said. "We'll send in the bots, take pictures and leave. They'll never know we were there."

"How are we gonna get there?" Charlotte asked.

"My dad has a boat," Brendan said.

"Your mother won't let us go," Charlotte said.

"Who said we are gonna ask," Brendan said. "You know the saying the adults always use. It's easier to ask for forgiveness than to ask for permission."

"We have to get home by midnight," Carla said. "How long will it take us to get to the island?"

Kyle pulled up a Google map on his iPad. They looked at the distance from their home to the island. "It's about seven miles. The boat travels at twenty knots. We should be there in twenty minutes."

"It's eight-thirty now," Carla said. "If we hurry, we can get there and back in two hours. "We'll be home by eleven."

* * *

Kyle and Brendan ran across the driveway and into the carriage house. They ran down the stairs into the basement.

The carriage house had a fieldstone foundation and dirt floor. Two bare lightbulbs hung from the ceiling. One side of the basement held boxes and furniture owned by Kyle's mother. On the other side of the basement, three tables lined the wall. The first table held a laptop computer, two monitors, and a tabletop 3D printer. The second table had a line of small tools and two rows of bins hanging from a pegboard. Three microbots, a large one, and two small ones, sat plugged into a charging station. The third table held two black carrying cases with foam inside. One case was empty, while the other case had three microbots in it.

"Grab the microbots off the charging station and put them in the empty case," Kyle said. "Then bring the case, VR headsets, and iPad upstairs. I'll put them in my backpack. I'm going to change. And Brendan, don't touch anything else."

While Brendan grabbed the bag with the bots, Kyle ran upstairs. He saw his mother sleeping on their couch in front of the television. If Kyle woke her up, she would tell him they couldn't go. If he let her sleep, she would be mad he didn't tell her. He decided to send her a text and say they're going for a walk and will be back in thirty minutes.

Kathleen Amejian was on television saying how Jay Mendes was a threat to national safety. The FBI should arrest and question him. She wondered if he was part of the terrorist plot instead of a hero. Kyle wanted to throw something at the TV, but he took a deep breath, picked up the remote, and shut the TV off.

Kyle ran down the stairs and yelled, "Let's go. It's getting late!"

Brendan ran up the stairs and handed the gear to Kyle, who stuffed it all into his backpack.

"I'm going to change," said Brendan.

Kyle joined the girls at the fire pit.

Carla wore a black t-shirt featuring eighties, hard-rock band Def Leppard and jeans. Charlotte wore a pink blouse, white shorts, and flip-flops.

"Charlotte, don't you think you might want to wear something a bit warmer? And darker?" Kyle asked. "It can get pretty chilly on the ocean."

"I didn't bring anything else," she said. "I thought we were hanging out by the fire pit."

"You can keep her warm," Carla said, punching Kyle in the arm. Kyle and Charlotte both blushed.

Brendan came out of the house and ran over to the fire pit.

"Shit, Brendan," Carla said, laughing. "You look like a Starbucks barista."

"What?" Brendan said, looking at his black shoes, pants, t-shirt, and a black knit cap to cover his blonde hair. "I'm trying to look like Tom Cruise in *Mission Impossible*."

"You guys spend too much time playing with your bots," Carla said. "Now, let's get going."

Brendan led the way to the dock and climbed onto the Boston Whaler. He helped Charlotte and Carla climb on board then asked Kyle to untie the bow and stern lines. Kyle did what he told him to do and jumped onto the boat.

While Brendan searched in the center dashboard for the keys, Kyle and Charlotte sat down on the seat in the bow. Brendan tried to start the engine, but it coughed out a bit of smoke.

"Are you a complete moron?" Carla said. "We're drifting away from the dock."

Kyle looked out and saw the dock twenty feet away.

Charlotte grabbed Kyle's hand. "I'm getting nervous."

Carla reached down inside the console, turned on the gas pump, then turned the key. The engine roared to life. "You always start the engine before you untie the lines, you idiot,"

Carla said.

"I know," Brendan said. "I forgot."

"I thought you said your family went boating all the time?"

"We used to. It's been a while since we've taken the boat out, and my dad always drives."

Brendan took the wheel back and cruised out of the harbor. When they cleared the Nob, he gunned the engine.

The small boat skimmed over the calm evening waters. The blowing wind was chilly, and Charlotte snuggled up close to Kyle. He could tell she was cold, so he pulled off his hoodie and wrapped it around her shoulders. She smiled at him and snuggled even closer. Kyle took the hint and wrapped his arms around her.

"This is fun," Charlotte said. "I'm glad I came with you. You make me feel safe."

"There's no reason to feel scared. There's nothing on the island, and I'm sure that video was fake. We'll go out and play with the bots for a few minutes and come back."

"You're so nice to me," Charlotte said, staring into Kyle's eyes. She closed her eyes and puckered her lips.

Kyle closed his eyes and leaned forward to kiss her. Then the boat jerked, sending Kyle and Charlotte sprawling to the floor.

Kyle found himself lying on his back with Charlotte's feet in his face. He heard Charlotte screaming. "You're such a jerk!" Then she jumped up and punched Brendan in the arm. Carla was laughing so hard. She couldn't breathe.

Kyle realized what happened. When Brendan saw Kyle try to kiss Charlotte, he yanked the wheel to the right, knocking them over. Now it was Kyle's turn to punch Brendan. But as Kyle got up off the deck, Brendan slowed the boat down.

They were approaching the island.

Brendan pulled up to an ancient, rickety-looking boathouse. It had a partially collapsed roof and moss growing on the outside of the rotting shingles. Carla placed one foot on the dock, then gave a thumbs up.

"The boathouse looks like it's going to fall any moment," Carla said. "But the dock is safe."

Brendan maneuvered the small boat closer to the dock, and Carla jumped off.

"Kyle, throw me the bowline," Carla said.

Kyle threw her the line and watched as she tied it off on a rusty deck cleat.

Brendan handed Kyle the backpack then jumped onto the dock.

"Okay, Charlotte, you can go next," Kyle said. "Brendan will help you get off."

Brendan held his hand out to Charlotte, but she didn't move.

"Charlotte, come on," Carla said. "It's getting late."

"I thought you said the island was empty. I'm... scared," Charlotte said. "I don't want to go."

"What's the matter?" Kyle said. "I told you I'd take care of you. Nothing's going to happen."

"No, you're playing a practical joke on me. It's a prank. I'm not going with you. I'm staying on the boat."

Kyle realized there was something wrong. The cute girl he almost kissed was changing in front of his eyes. Charlotte's eyes darted back and forth. She wrung her hands and chewed at her fingernails.

"Are you okay? Is something wrong?"

Charlotte backed away from him until she was up against

the center console. She swung her head back and forth, looking to escape.

"Kyle, I... I... I want to go home. Take me home."

Kyle reached out with his hand out to touch her shoulder.

"No!" She screamed, batting his hand away from her. "No! No! Leave me alone. I want to go home. Get me away from here. I can't stay!"

Charlotte put her hands up against her face and tried to wipe away the tears. She slid down against the center console and pulled her knees up against her chest. Kyle sat down on the deck of the boat with her.

"Can you tell me why you're so scared?"

Charlotte shook her head.

"Is it the dark?"

She shook her head again.

"Are you scared to get left alone?"

She looked at him. Then nodded.

"I'm here with you. You don't have to go inside the mansion. We'll stay outside. My bots will go inside. You'll get to see what they see. It will be fun."

"We don't have to go inside?"

"That's right. You don't have to go into the mansion. I'll stay with you."

"Okay, I guess. I'll go."

Kyle stood up and held out his hands. Charlotte reached out and grabbed them, and pulled herself to her feet.

She walked over to the side of the boat, then stopped.

"What's the matter?"

"They're not here."

"What do you mean they're not here? Who's not here?"

"Carla and Brendan."

Kyle turned towards the dock, and she was right. It was empty. He looked to his right and couldn't see anybody inside the boathouse.

"Brendan!" Kyle yelled. "Where are you guys?".

"We're outside the boathouse. You've got to see this!"

Kyle turned to Charlotte. "Are you ready to go?"

Charlotte nodded.

Kyle stood up on the side of the boat and jumped onto the dock, "See, it's easy."

Charlotte nodded and put her foot onto the side rail, and jumped off onto the dock to join him.

* * *

They walked up the dock and passed through an empty doorway onto a gravel path. Brendan and Carla were standing in front of an iron gate. A twenty-foot-high granite wall faded away into the darkness. An old chain and padlock held the gate shut, but the chain was long enough for the kids to squeeze through. Beyond the gate, Kyle saw rows of overgrown hedges and what appeared to be the remnants of a formal garden.

Carla and Brendan squeezed through and proceeded into the garden.

Charlotte stood staring at the gate.

"We can stay here," Kyle said.

Charlotte shook her head and walked towards the gate, slipped through the narrow opening, and waited. Kyle squeezed through and joined her.

The silhouette of a massive three-story mansion rose out of the mist. Rotting plywood covered the large windows.

The second-floor windows had porches in front of them.

Kyle and his friends continued down the path and stopped at the next hedgerow. Brendan knelt behind a hulking green mess of branches and put the backpack on the ground. He pulled the three microbots out of the black styrofoam packing material. He lifted the larger bot, which was shaped like a soda can with a flared-out bottom. The bot's top section had a smooth, shiny surface that appeared black in the dim moonlight. Kyle turned the bot upside down and flicked on a power switch. A small green light lit up. He then pulled out the two smaller bots and placed them next to the larger one.

Kyle reached into the backpack and pulled out a remote control handset. The same type of control is used for any hobby-style drone or RC airplane. He then pulled out the VR headset. It looked strange, but the one-hundred-eighty-degree view it provided the operator was phenomenal.

Brendan passed out the other headsets. "Put these on so you can see the video feed."

Kyle pushed a small button on the base of the large bot to check the battery power. The bots should have had a complete charge, but only two green LED lights lit up.

"Brendan," Kyle said. "Which set of bots did you bring?"

"Why?"

"Because these only have fifty percent power. These were the ones in the backup case."

"So, what does that mean?" Brendan said. "We can't use them?"

"No, but the batteries will only last about ten minutes."

Kyle pushed the left joystick forward, and the bot lifted off the ground a few feet and hovered. The two small bots started buzzing and lifted to the same level as the big one.

"Why didn't Kyle move the joystick to move the small bots," Carla asked. "They lifted on their own."

"That's because they mimic what the large bot does," Brendan said. "The small bots follow the mothership."

"Wow, that's so cool."

Kyle pushed the left joystick again, and the three bots lifted until they were above the hedgerow. He could see the video image in his headset. The picture is split into three frames. He couldn't see much, though, because the display was in the default daylight mode.

"Brendan, are you ready for the real test?"

"Do it up."

Kyle pressed the voice control switch and spoke into his microphone, "Bot one, night vision."

The screen in Brendan's headset came to life in a ghost-like green image. But now, he could see a sweeping view of the mansion and the island in the distance.

"Wow," Charlotte said.

"This is so cool," Carla chimed in.

Kyle smiled. It took him months to develop the night-vision technology, "Let's go tour the island."

The bots revealed a grown-over flower garden and crumbling concrete fountain. Green, murky water sat in the basin of the fountain.

As the bots approached the mansion, the three images merged into one wide-angle view. A set of granite stairs led up to a dark, wooden front door.

"No sign of entry here," Brendan said. "We need to look for an open window or another door.

"Who owns the house?" Charlotte asked.

"A wealthy family from Boston once owned it," Brendan explained. "They still own most of the islands. My Dad said they built a new home on another island about ten years ago and abandoned this one."

"They just left it here?" Charlotte said. "Seems like such a waste of a nice home."

Kyle surveyed the windows on the second floor until he found one with a broken board. It was wide enough for one bot at a time to pass through.

"Bots, single file," Kyle said. The small bots obeyed and lined up behind the mother. The image on the screen switched to a single view. Kyle moved the bots through the window, careful to avoid the ragged plywood.

The bots entered what appeared to be a large bedroom. Now empty, it had a ten-foot-high ceiling and a large stone fireplace on the center wall. Dark, peeling wallpaper covered parts of the wall. Kyle turned the bot in a 360-degree circle to show the entire room. It seemed that the room's door was open, so he flew the bots through the door into the hallway.

The bots hovered at the top of a broad, wooden staircase—the treads covered by a threadbare oriental runner. The stairs descended one flight to a landing. Kyle flew down to the landing. At the bottom of the stairs, he could see a wooden floor.

"Wow," Charlotte said.

A large parlor spread out in front of them. Opposite the stairs was an enormous floor-to-ceiling fieldstone fireplace filling the entire wall. The marble surround wrapped around the base of the fireplace. Large, square pillars stood ten feet apart and rose three stories high to the ceiling. Along the far wall, next to the fireplace, were four military-style folding cots. Backpacks leaned against the cots. In front of each cot sat small Sterno burners, plates, and utensils.

"It looks like somebody is living here," Carla said.

"Do you think they're squatters?" Charlotte asked.

"I don't think they're squatters," Brendan said. "Too neat."

"Who are they then?" Charlotte said. "Are they still here?"

"Let me see if they've been cooking," Kyle said. "I'll change to infrared mode. It will show any heat in red."

Kyle switched the screen mode. The Sterno stoves showed small red circles.

"It looks like somebody was here not too long ago. The cans are still hot.

"But where are they now?" Charlotte asked.

"Kyle, you have to turn back," Brendan said. "The batteries are down to one light."

Kyle switched back to night vision mode, swiveled the bots around, and flew back up the staircase and into the bedroom. He stopped so they could line up and exit the window in a single file. But when he pulled back on the joystick to increase the altitude, the main bot didn't respond.

"Something's wrong," Kyle said. "I can't control the main bot. Let me try voice command. Bot One, increase the altitude by three feet."

"Low battery power," Brendan said. "You need to get them out of the window.

But before Kyle could say another command, the screen went black.

Kyle stared at the blank screen, "Shit, my bots are dead. What are we going to do now?"

"What the hell?" Carla said. "Where did they go?"

"The battery died," Kyle said. "They're stranded in the

mansion."

"We have to go get them," Brendan said. "We can't leave them inside. You know the saying the SEALS have, no bot left behind."

"This isn't a time for joking, you jerk," Carla said. "Let's go!"

Kyle knew they needed to retrieve the bots, but he also knew it could be dangerous.

"You should go in and get your bots," Charlotte said for the first time. "I'll stay here while you three go in the house."

Brendan, Carla, and Kyle all turned to look at Charlotte. "I'm sorry, I can't go inside. I'm too scared," she said.

"C'mon, Kyle, let's get going before it's too late," Brendan said. "We have to find a way in."

"No, Brendan, you and Carla go. I'll stay here with Charlotte. We can't leave her alone. We'll watch you from out here."

Brendan looked at Carla, who was nodding her head. "Okay, you guys stay here," Brendan said. "We'll come back to this spot."

"Okay," Kyle said.

"Only one question," Carla asked. "How do we get inside?"

"That's the easy part. Follow the bots."

Carla said, "You mean to climb up to the balcony on a rotting old house that might collapse under our weight at any minute?"

"Yeah."

"Cool. Let's go."

Kyle watched Brendan and Carla turn the corner around the hedgerow and disappear.

"Shouldn't we find someplace where we can watch them?"

Charlotte said.

"Right. Why didn't I think of that? I have an idea. Let's crawl through the bottom of the hedgerows until we reach the first row. Then we can watch them but stay out of sight."

"We'll get dirty. I just bought these shorts."

"Seriously?"

"No, JK. Just joking."

"The term is just kidding."

Kyle pushed his way through the first row of hedges. He went through the far side of the shrubbery to find dead grass and another row of hedges.

"How many of these hedges are there?"

"I don't know. It seems like some sort of maze. Let's keep going. You're not claustrophobic, are you?"

"No. I actually like small spaces. They make me feel safe. My dad made me a secret hiding space in my room in each of our houses. A place where I could play with my dolls and pretend I had a different family."

"You wished for a different family?" Kyle said.

"I mean, I love my mother and father," Charlotte said, "but I hate feeling like an only child."

"Don't you have a brother or sister?"

"I have an older sister, but I never see her. She's a scientist and lives in Seattle. How about you?"

"I am an only child. I know how you feel."

"Oh, I'm sorry. I didn't mean anything bad."

"I know you didn't. I didn't take it the wrong way."

Kyle and Charlotte passed through two more hedges until they finally came to the end of the garden. In front of them, they could see the front of the mansion. They stayed inside the hedge and peered through the branches. All Kyle could see was the enormous front door.

"Can you see Brendan or Carla?" Charlotte asked.

"No, but I hear them. Let's listen."

Kyle thought he heard noises from above. He heard what sounded like wood scraping. He realized it was the plywood covering the window where the bots flew in.

He heard groaning, and someone say, *you hold it, and I'll crawl through. I'm in. He* heard Brendan say.

There was a loud crash as the piece of plywood smashed to the ground right in front of them.

Kyle jumped back as dust filled the bushes.

A minute later, Kyle looked up to see what looked like Brendan's body lean over the porch rail above.

"Kyle, can you hear me?" Brendan said. "I got them. We're coming down."

"We should move back to the spot where we said we would meet them," Kyle said.

But before they could move, two giant hands grabbed Kyle under the arms and pulled him out of the hedgerow. Kyle could see a second man pull Charlotte out and wrap massive arms around her tiny waist.

She screamed once. Then there was silence.

Kyle screamed, "Charlotte!" but a giant, gloved hand covered his mouth. He struggled to get loose, but the man was too strong. The more he struggled, the tighter the man's hold got. Kyle stopped resisting when it felt like his ribs would collapse. The giant man picked him up and carried him away.

* * *

Brendan scanned the garden from the balcony, but Kyle and Charlotte were gone.

"Where are they?" Carla asked. "I can't see them."

"I saw them go around the corner of the house."

"Let's go," Carla said as she scrambled down the side of the mansion. Brendan followed. They ran along the front of the house, then turned the corner. A large fallen tree lay against the siding of the house. Some of the branches broke through the windows, forming a large canopy covering the lawn. Brendan saw movement under the tree branches.

Brendan and Carla stopped in the thick, uncut grass before they reached the tree.

"They went underneath," Carla said. "I can't see any movement."

"We have to go inside."

"No. We don't know how many are in there. We need to wait before we rush in."

They lay down in the grass and peered through the immense tangle of branches. Brendan saw movement. It was the large man, and he was holding Charlotte in front of him. A second man dragged Kyle into the mansion.

"Let's go," Brendan said. "They're going into the house." Brendan sprung up to his feet and ran towards the tree.

"Brendan, stop," Carla said as she jumped up and ran after Brendan. She tackled him to the ground as the sound of automatic gunfire erupted from the trees. Bullets whizzed over their heads. A second later, and they both would have been dead.

"You kids, get out of here now," the man said in a strange accent. "Or you'll all die."

Brendan and Carla got up and backed away until they got

past the corner of the house. They turned and ran down the path towards the front door. The front door smashed open. The man who grabbed Kyle stood in front of them with a sawed-off shotgun.

Brendan grabbed Carla's arm, and they took a sharp turn into the garden of overgrown hedgerows. They ran through the maze of branches and thorns for what felt like hours. Men were shouting, but he didn't look back. They got to the gate and squeezed through, then ran down the path to the boathouse.

"Stop!" Brendan heard the man yell. "Come back here."

Kyle turned to see the man stuck at the locked gate.

Brendan and Carla ran to the dock at full speed, then jumped on the boat. She started the engine, but the vessel didn't move.

"Untie the lines!" Brendan said. "Hurry!"

Carla jumped back onto the deck. A loud blast made her jump, and splinters flew from the dock only a foot away. She untied the lines and jumped back onto the boat. Another shot blew the cleat away from the pier.

"Gun it, Brendan," Carla said as she ducked down below the side rail. "He's shooting at us!"

* * *

Unlike their ride over when the water was calm, the waves were now rough and choppy. The wind picked up, and whitecaps adorned the tops of the waves.

"Brendan put a life vest on," Carla said. "We may be in for some wet weather. And don't go too fast, these are dangerous conditions. Keep your eye out for larger ships."

"Carla, have you seen Kyle's backpack?" Brendan asked.

"It's on your back, you idiot," Carla said with a grin. She pulled the backpack off his shoulders and placed it on the deck.

Carla took the wheel.

Brendan rummaged through Kyle's backpack. All three bots, VR headsets, and RC control were there. He found Kyle's cell phone, which still had a little battery power.

"Kyle's cell phone doesn't have a signal. We have to call the police."

Carla pulled out her cell phone and pushed several buttons. "No signal," she said.

"I didn't bring my phone," Brendan said.

"Why wouldn't you bring your cell phone? Who doesn't bring their phone everywhere they go? Where's your boat's radio?"

"I don't know. My Dad said something about replacing it with a newer model."

"So there's no radio? What else could go wrong?"

As if on cue, Brendan heard the roar of thunder in the distance. He looked at Carla, who shook her head and held on to the wheel.

Brendan put his arm around Carla, "Don't be scared. I'll keep you safe."

Carla smiled, "I don't need you to keep me safe, but you can keep your arm me. She leaned over and pecked Brendan on the cheek."

The waves grew, battering the small boat. The fierce wind gusts blew stronger as the lightning flashes got closer. They were in open water, and there was no place to get shelter.

Wood Hole was only seven miles away, but it could have

been a thousand miles in this storm. Brendan hoped they could make it to shore before the storm hit.

All hopes faded when the engine died.

"Now, what happened?" Carla screamed into the wind.

Carla stared at the gauges on the dashboard. Then she punched Brendan on the back.

"You idiot! We ran out of gas!"

The small boat bobbed in the ocean as the waves whipped up higher and higher.

"Hold on tight!" Brendan yelled.

Chapter 23

Jessie, the bombshell television reporter, was now Jay's kid sister again. The last time Jay sat in a hospital with her, she was seven and had broken her ankle jumping off a swing set. But, it was different this time. The doctors said she would have phantom feelings and wouldn't know her leg was gone. They also said Jay was the best person to break the news to her.

Jessie began to wake up. Then, after a brief visit from a nurse to check her vital signs, she said, "What's going on? What happened to my leg? It feels weird."

"Hey, Jess," Jay said. "Do you remember what happened?"

"No, I was outside Saint Patrick's with Roger. I saw some type of seagull drone. The bomb squad guy said it was clear, and they were bringing the seagull drone to their van. It's a blur after that."

"The drone exploded. It killed Victor and injured a dozen other people."

"Where's Roger?"

"Roger's okay. Pretty messed up from the shrapnel. He's here at the hospital on another floor."

"Jay, my leg feels weird. There's a sharp pain in the sole of my foot. Can you take a look?"

Jay froze. He didn't know what to say or do.

"What's the matter? Can you look at my leg?"

"Jessie, you suffered several major injuries last night. You had internal bleeding and a bad infection. Unfortunately, they had to do major surgery to save your life."

"Do you mean it's in a cast? Can you lift my blanket so I can see it?"

"No, it's not in a cast."

"What are you trying to tell me, Jay? What's going on?"

Jay couldn't put his feelings into words, so he pulled the blanket off her leg. A bloody gauze bandage wrapped the stump of her leg above the knee.

Jessie peered at her leg without saying a word. Instead, she squeezed Jay's hand as she processed her new reality.

"Where is it, Jay? Who took my leg? Are they going to put it back on?"

"No, Jess, they couldn't save it."

"What do you mean?"

"The leg was too damaged to save. The doctors gave me no choice."

"You mean you gave them permission to cut off my leg?"

"Yes, I had to," Jay said. "You were dying."

Jessie stared at her stump for a long moment. "Can I touch it?" she said. "Why does my ankle hurt? It's not there. Oh God, why did this happen to me?"

Jay sat on the bed next to Jessie, holding her as she mourned for her leg. She cried until her tears ran dry.

* * *

Doctor Chin watched from the doorway. When Jay stood

up, she stepped into the room. A nurse followed her.

"How are you doing, Jessie? My name is Doctor Silvie Chin. I operated on you last night."

"I'm okay, I guess," Jessie said wiping the tears from her cheek with a tissue. "Shocked and scared. I don't understand why my foot hurts even though it isn't there anymore."

"Your brain plays tricks on you. We call it phantom pain. It's common with amputees. Do you feel any pain from the amputation?"

"No, it throbs a little bit, but otherwise, it seems okay."

"The bomb damaged your leg beyond repair. We focused on your internal bleeding to keep you alive. By the time we focused on your leg, it was too late. It developed a bad infection."

"What do I do now?" Jessie said. "How long do I have to stay in the hospital?"

"We're fighting the infection with antibiotics. Tomorrow you will meet with people from physical therapy and pros- thetics. Then, when you can travel, we will transfer you to Cape Cod."

"Oh dear," a woman's voice said in the doorway. "What happened to my baby?"

"Momma," Jessie said. "When did you get here?"

Jay's mother, Maria, walked into the room. Marty Hernan- des followed her in.

Jay stood up and hugged the sixty-seven-year-old family matriarch. Then, he moved out of the way so his mother could hug Jessie.

"Jay, are you doing okay?" Marty said. "The press is going wild. They're demanding your arrest for the shooting in Boston."

204

"I saw the earlier reports, but I turned it off. The FBI cleared me. It's Kathleen. She's generating the hype to drive ratings. Where's Gia?"

Marty pointed to the door. Gia slept in a chair across the hallway from the private room.

"Heck of a security guard," Jay said. "She let you walk right in."

"Yea, I'm a real threat," Marty said, laughing. "She's had a long night fending off reporters."

"What do you know about the bomb?"

"It was a weird bird drone. Jessie found it in a pile of debris. But we don't know anything else. Her friend Roger is here in the hospital. He might be able to shed some light."

Jay and Marty stepped out of the room.

Jay knelt next to Gia and shook her shoulder. She opened her eyes to see Jay staring at her.

"What the fuck," Gia said. "Did I fall asleep? I'm so sorry. How's Jessie?"

"It's okay," Jay said. "Jessie's doing fine. Marty and I are taking a walk. Would you mind keeping an eye on my mother? Tell her we'll be back in a few minutes."

* * *

Roger's room was on the tenth floor of the massive hospital. Jay waited for a doctor and a group of medical students to finish their exams. When they left, Jay walked inside.

Roger was a mess. A white gauze bandage wrapped around his head, and a patch covered one eye. Hundreds of bandages covered his chest and torso. Nevertheless, he was sitting up in the bed and seemed to be in good spirits.

"Hey Roger, do you remember me?" Jay said.

"Sure, you're on every news station in town. They're saying you murdered a priest in cold blood."

"Don't believe everything you hear in the news. I can't tell you what happened, but I didn't murder anybody. How are you feeling?"

"I'm okay," Roger said. "I have a fractured skull, and my body's filled with shrapnel from the bomb. How's Jessie?"

"She's going to pull through. It was touch and go for a while. I don't know how to say this gently. Roger, they had to amputate her left leg."

Roger stared at Jay for a long moment, tears running down his face. Then he pointed at the closet next to the bed.

"Can you get the bag with my personal items in it? I want to give you something."

Jay retrieved the bag from the closet and handed it to Roger. He dug through the bag and pulled out a large iPhone X.

"You know someone in the FBI. Can you give this to them? It's broken, but the video files should still be on the SIM card."

"If I give it to the FBI," Jay said. " They'll keep it as evidence. You won't be able to sell it to a TV station."

"I know. I care about catching the person who nearly killed Jessie. I heard a bomb squad officer died. He was from Boston. Did you know him?"

Jay nodded, "We served together overseas. Victor was one of my closest friends."

"I'm sorry to hear that. When can I see Jessie?"

"I'm not sure. I'll tell the doctor you want to visit her."

"Hey, Jay," Roger reached out and grabbed Jay's hand as he was leaving. "She's a great girl. She always says how proud she is of you. You're a real hero in her eyes."

"Thanks, Roger. But you guys are the heroes. The videos on the phone might be the big break we've been looking for."

* * *

Jay and Marty stepped out of the room. "Marty, call Mack and tell him about the phone. He'll send a local agent to pick it up."

"Okay," Marty said. Then his phone rang. "Hi, Jill, what's happening. What? I'm sure there's an explanation. I'll call the Coast Guard and start a search. Jill, stop crying. We'll find him."

"What's going on?" Jay asked after Marty hung up the phone.

"Kyle and Brendan are missing. They took my boat last night and haven't returned. Jillian's freaking out because a thunderstorm is passing through. I'm calling the Coast Guard station in Woods Hole so they can begin a search. I don't know where they went."

As they stepped onto the elevator, Jay's phone rang.

"Hi, this is Jay Mendes, Maravista Security."

"Mr. Mendes, my name is Charles Cranmore. I understand you provide private security services?"

"Yes, sir, how can I help you?"

"I received a call a few minutes ago from an anonymous person. He says he is holding my daughter Charlotte and a young man hostage. He's demanding a million dollars for each of them. I have forty-eight hours to provide the money. If I call the police, he'll kill both of them."

"Do you have the money to pay the ransom?"

"Yes, but I don't want to pay."

"You know I'm not a hostage negotiator."

"I don't want you to negotiate with the bastard," Cranmore said. "I want you to rescue my daughter. I'll pay you the two million dollars if you bring my daughter home alive. Can you help?"

"Yes, of course. Now tell me everything the caller said."

Marty waited for Jay to finish the call, then said, "What was that about?"

"Well, I know where Kyle is. But it's not good news."

* * *

Water from the powerful thunderstorm filled the bottom of the Boston Whaler. For some miraculous reason, the small boat managed to stay upright as it rode out the storm. Since the engine died, the bilge pump also died. Carla and Brendan spent the night scooping water from the bottom of the hull. Soaked and cold, Brendan was glad to be alive.

As the sun began to rise in the east, Brendan heard sounds above. Within moments, a white and orange Coast Guard helicopter appeared overhead. A searchlight filled the sky, and within moments a flare landed in the water next to them.

The rotor blades churned the water, making it difficult to see the rescue swimmer drop into the ocean. Brendan was thrilled to see the diver crawl over the side of the boat.

The diver took off their helmet and introduced herself as Ensign Jennifer Willows. She asked if they were injured. She then called the helicopter on her radio, and they lowered a rescue chair. Carla got on first, and a few minutes later, Brendan had his turn.

The helicopter landed at Upper Cape Hospital, and Carla and Brendan were brought to the emergency room. Carla's Dad and Marty met them a short time later.

Brendan told Marty about their adventure and what happened to Kyle and Charlotte as they were driving home. He then reached into Kyle's backpack and pulled out the iPad used to control the bots. Finally, Brendan found the file he was looking for, the video taken inside the mansion.

"Dad, you have to view this video and get it to Jay Mendes as soon as you can."

"Why Jay? What does this have to do with him?"

"You'll see when you look at it. Dad, everybody is saying Jay murdered that priest in cold blood. But I, I mean we, don't believe them. I want Jay to see this video before anybody else does so he can use it to prove his innocence."

"Jay's already been cleared by the FBI. But I'm sure he'll appreciate watching the video. And by the way, Brendan, you're grounded for the entire summer, and you're going to spend it fixing the Boston Whaler and scraping barnacles off the cigarette boat. Is that clear?"

"Yes, Dad."

Chapter 24

Mansion Island

J ay slipped off the rigid hull inflatable into the waist-deep water. Gia, CJ, and Madman followed him as he waded ashore. He flipped down his night vision goggles and scanned the island. The door to the kitchen was two hundred feet away. A wall surrounded the back of the abandoned mansion, leaving a small service gate as the only barrier to entry.

Jay and his team sprinted towards the gate and slid up against the granite wall. First, CJ cut the rusty chain securing the gate. Then Jay pulled the gate open wide enough for them to slip through.

In between the wall and the back door was a field of overgrown grass. They worked their way through the waist-high weeds looking for potential booby traps. When they reached the house, CJ stopped to check the backdoor. It was locked. He sprinted to the corner of the main house and looked around the corner. When Jay and the rest of the team caught up to him, CJ said, "There's a black tarp covering the opening where the tree fell into the mansion."

"CJ, lift the corner of the tarp to let us in," Jay said. "Madman, follow CJ. Be careful. They could be waiting for us."

After a few tense moments, Madman reported in, "Chief, the first room is clear. It looks like a library."

Jay and Gia followed Madman through the smashed window into a wood-paneled room with empty mahogany bookshelves lining three walls. Jay walked across the room, opened the door, and peered around the corner into a vast, empty corridor. There were three doors on the opposite side of the hallway. The main house was straight ahead.

Jay and Gia turned the corner and moved along the hall's right side while CJ and Madman sprinted across, taking up positions on the opposite side.

The team checked each door, clearing any open rooms.

When they reached the end of the hallway, they entered the large, three-story parlor. It looked exactly like the room Brendan showed him from the microbot video. To his left was a wide staircase leading down from the second floor. To his right was a massive fireplace. Interesting, Jay thought, no cots or personal gear. Was the assault team still here?

A loud crack answered his question.

The bullet blew wood splinters flew from the wall inches above Jay's head. He dropped to the floor, and used his night scope to scan the room for the shooter. Even though the rules of engagement were now satisfied, Jay didn't fire back. He didn't know where the shot came from.

"CJ, can you see the shooter through your scope?" Jay asked.

"Negative, Chief."

"I want to get into the kitchen on the right. There are two

swinging doors on each side of the fireplace. CJ, see if you can move up behind one of those large columns. When we're ready to move, Madman lay down a quick burst of cover fire towards the staircase. Gia will stay with me."

"Roger."

"Three, two, one... now."

Jay and Gia sprinted towards the fireplace as CJ took up his position behind the closest column.

The kitchen door opened, and a kidnapper stepped out. Jay froze. The man saw Jay and lifted his rifle. Then a shot rang out. The man crumpled to the floor. Jay turned to see Gia lowering her rifle. He gave her a thumbs up.

A blast of automatic fire erupted from the staircase. Jay dropped to the floor, using the body of the dead kidnapper as cover. CJ and Maman returned fire as Jay and Gia crawled through the swinging door into the kitchen. Then the gunfire stopped.

"Jay, we got the guy on the staircase," Madman said. "All clear out here."

"Good job," Jay said. "Join me in the kitchen."

Jay pushed the first swinging door open. He swung his rifle back and forth, but the kitchen was empty. The backside of the stone fireplace sat to his left. The cast-iron ovens still in place. There was an enormous food preparation island in the middle of the kitchen, while empty food pantries and china cabinets adorned the walls.

Jay was about to leave when CJ tapped him on his shoulder. He put his index finger to his ear.

At first, he didn't hear anything. Then faint sobbing. Like someone with a gag over their mouth. The sound was nearby.

CJ pointed to Jay's right. Oh right, Jay thought, the walk-in refrigerator. Every mansion kitchen had one. Kyle and Charlotte might be in there. But one of the kidnappers could be in there too. Jay had to take the chance and check it out.

Jay motioned to CJ to move up to the large stainless-steel door. Jay crouched low, and Madman slid in behind him, standing up. Gia stayed back, covering the entrance.

Jay nodded, and CJ pulled the door open. Jay swiveled around the corner. Madman followed. On the floor at the back of the refrigerator were Kyle and Charlotte. They sat back-to-back with their knees up against their bodies.

Jay laid his rifle on the floor and approached the pair. They were tied together. Kyle stared at him with a look of horror. He shook his head. Charlotte had the same terrified look on her face.

He pulled a flashlight from his utility belt and looked closer, studying the plastic ties holding their arms. A small red and white wire ran down from the plastic ties. Jay followed the wire. It ran through a small hole in the floor.

"Hi guys," Jay said. "Don't move."

"CJ, take Gia and find a door to the basement. Go down and look for a bomb."

"A what?" CJ said. "Not another bomb."

"I'm afraid so," Jay said. "Madman, clear the rest of the mansion. We're missing two of the kidnappers."

"I'm moving."

Gia led CJ down the stairs. The basement was unfinished. Piles of empty wood pallets lay spread around the floor. Empty steel shelves lined the walls. In the middle of the cellar stood three rusty steel barrels. On top of the barrels sat a bundle of dynamite. A small wire hung down from the ceiling.

Gia approached the barrels. Attached to the top piece of dynamite sat a small, yellow sticky note. Handwritten were the words, "Hi Chief... BOOM!"

"Jay, we have a problem," Gia said on the radio.

"Can you tell if the bomb is on a timer or a detonator?"

"Let me take a closer look. I don't see a timer."

"It must be a direct trigger tied to the kids. I need to take a closer look at how the wire is attached."

"Guys," Jay said to Kyle and Charlotte. "Please be careful. I need you to scoot your bums forward just an inch or two."

Kyle and Charlotte both nodded. First, Charlotte pressed her back against Kyle's and slid her butt forward a few inches. Then Kyle did the same.

Jay laid on his stomach and shined his flashlight in. He could see the wire wrapped around both plastic ties. There wasn't much slack so that any upward movement would trigger the bomb. Jay needed to clamp it off so the wire didn't move.

"CJ, do you have a C4 breaching charge in your backpack?"

"Yes, Chief."

"I need you to roll a small amount into a ball and bring it over to me. About three inches in diameter."

"What are you going to...."

"Don't ask any questions. After you hand me the C4, you need to go to the beach and get ready to evacuate. This order applies to everyone."

"No way, Chief," CJ said. "We're not leaving you behind."

"I'm not asking. I'll bring Charlotte and Kyle out with me."

CJ brought the ball of C4 to Jay, then went out the back door. Gia knelt beside Jay and placed her hand on his shoulder. She whispered into his ear, "You're the bravest man

I've ever known. Please stay alive." She left the refrigerator, and Madman followed.

Jay took a deep breath and slid the ball of soft explosives between Kyle and Charlotte's bodies. He felt the wire with the tips of his fingers. Stretching as far as he could, his arm began to go numb.

Jay pressed the ball of explosives up against the wire and pinched the wire into the malleable ball. He kept pinching until he worked the wire halfway in.

Now was the time of reckoning. If his plan worked, they would escape. If not, he wouldn't live long enough to find out.

Jay pulled his fingers off the wire.

Nothing happened.

He slid his hand out from between Kyle and Charlotte. Sweat poured down his face. He took a second to wipe his forehead with his sleeve, then removed his desert dagger from his pant leg.

Jay reached back between Kyle and Charlotte and felt for their wire ties. He had to hold the sharp knife between his fingers then slice through the ties. The knife slipped, cutting Jay's middle finger. He flinched in pain. He tried again, this time cutting through Charlotte's tie. He kept his arm in and cut Kyle loose.

The ties fell to the floor, but the wire stayed in place. Jay pulled his arm out and put the dagger away. He stood up and put on his backpack. Then he helped Charlotte and Kyle up, removing the tape from their mouths.

"Thank God you're here," Kyle said as he hugged Jay tight.

Charlotte joined in the hug and said, "How did you know where to find us?"

"Your father received a call from the kidnappers," Jay said. "He called me. Then Brendan showed me the video from the microbots.

"Brendan and Carla are okay?" Charlotte said. "How did they get home? The thunderstorm hit right after we were kidnapped. The thunder shook the mansion."

"They were lucky, considering their boat ran out of gas. A Coast Guard chopper found them drifting out to sea. We need to get out of here. Wait for me by the back door while I clean things up."

After they left, Jay reached into his backpack and pulled out a detonator and timer. He pushed the ignitor into the C4 ball and attached it to the timer. He set the timer for three minutes, then ran to the door.

"Okay, let's get out of here," Jay said.

Jay grabbed Charlotte and Kyle by the arm and pulled them out the door. As they ran towards the back gate at full speed, automatic gunfire erupted from the mansion. Bullets tore up grass all around them.

"Hurry," Charlotte screamed. Then a single bullet pounded Jay in the back, slamming him and the kids to the ground. Luckily, the bullet struck his body armor, knocking the wind out of his lungs. Jay gasped for air while steel rained down around them.

The gunfire stopped. Jay pulled his M4 off his shoulder, rolled onto his back, spun around to face the mansion, and opened fire—spraying bullets towards the second floor of the estate.

Tracers coming from the beach streamed over his head toward the second-floor balcony. The red needles of fire tearing the siding off the old mansion.

"I thought I ordered you guys to evacuate the island? Jay screamed into his headset. You disobeyed a direct order. Ceasefire!"

"Let's go," Jay said, pulling Kyle and Charlotte to their feet. They sprinted through the gate and dropped to the ground behind the wall.

"Are you guys okay?" Gia asked Charlotte and Kyle as she inspected them for injuries.

"My wrists are bleeding," Charlotte said. "From the plastic ties, I mean. They didn't hurt me."

"Let me see," Gia said. "I'll wrap it in gauze and take you to the hospital when we're back in Falmouth."

"Now run to the inflatable," Jay said. "When you get in, lay flat on the deck."

Charlotte and Kyle raced across the beach and dove into the closest inflatable. Jay and his team piled in behind them. Madman fired up the outboard motor and gunned the engine away from the island.

Within seconds, Jay felt the explosion. A deep rumbling through the ocean floor. Then the sound wave and finally a bright red flash. He turned to watch the mansion disappear into a black, roiling mushroom cloud.

* * *

Jay secured the inflatable to Marty's dock in Quissett Harbor. His team followed and piled into the Suburban for the two-minute ride back to their office in Woods Hole.

McCoy was waiting with a full cooler of cold beer and three large pizzas. The assault team devoured the food as they briefed him on the mission.

"How did they know we were coming?" Jay asked. "The note on the bomb said, "Chief... Boom."

"Kyle told me the man who kidnapped him had a funny-sounding British accent and strange gray eyes."

"The island was a perfect base for launching that attack on the Bishop," CJ said. "It's only a few miles away. Do you think he had anything to do with the Papal bombings?"

"It's hard to say," McCoy said. "There's no evidence to tie him to Boston or New York. He could be a paid assassin."

"But why kidnap the kids?" Gia asked. "They didn't do anything. And why send Charlotte's father the ransom demand? If he was an assassin, why didn't he kill them?"

"And why didn't he kill me at Olivia's apartment?" Jay said. "He had the chance to kill both of us, but he left. It seems more personal. Like he's taunting me, or he has something to prove."

There was a knock on the door. Jay looked at his watch. It was four-thirty in the morning. Not exactly business hours. He grabbed his sidearm and went downstairs to answer the door. He opened it and looked into the chest of a huge man standing on the steps. Jay looked up to see a young bald man who could have been a superstar pro wrestler.

"Are you Jay Mendes?" he said in a low, guttural voice. "Someone wants to talk to you."

The man turned and walked down the stairs to a black stretch limo sitting in the parking lot. He opened the back door, and a short, overweight man dressed in a ratty t-shirt and ripped jeans stepped out.

"Jay Mendes?" the man said. "I'm Charles Cranmore. It's a pleasure to meet you. Do you mind joining me in my car for a few minutes?"

"Sure, I guess," Jay said.

"Give me your gun first," the bodyguard said. Jay handed the man his gun and slid into the back of the limo. The guard closed the door behind him.

Cranmore handed Jay a plain white envelope then extended his hand. Jay accepted the envelope and returned the handshake.

"What you did for me tonight was incredible," Cranmore said. "I never thought I'd see Charlotte alive. She told me what that creep did to her and how you disarmed the bomb. Impressive, I must say."

"Thank you, sir," Jay said. "Your daughter was courageous. She must have been terrified."

"She was. Charlotte already suffers from anxiety. She's had it all her life. It's an awful disease and prevents her from doing many things you and I take for granted. We've taken her to specialists around the world. I don't know why she went with those kids to that island in the first place, but she'll never go back."

"What do you mean?"

"I'm moving her back home to Portland, where I can keep a closer eye on her. Put her back into a private all-girls school. I'm done with all this Catholic mumbo jumbo. Her mother insisted. It was her idea to move to Cape Cod. What a mistake this has been. Now she gets caught up with a bad crowd and almost killed."

Jay was furious. "Her friends weren't the problem, Mr. Cranmore. They risked their lives to help her. The boy Kyle, who was kidnapped with Charlotte, he's a genius. Her friend, Carla's dad, is one of my best friends. And the other boy Brendan is the son of the Falmouth deputy police chief. Not exactly a bad crowd. So don't blame Charlotte's friends for what happened. And as far as that Catholic mumbo jumbo, I was raised Catholic and proud to call the Bishop of Fall River my friend. People like the man who kidnapped Charlotte are evil, and they want to destroy the church. While I appreciate your compliments, I don't need your money." Jay handed the envelope back to a stunned Cranmore and left the limo.

* * *

Two hours later, Jay was back on Michelle Goddard's Trifan jet. She stared at him with a look of amazement as he told her about his encounter with Cranmore.

"Are you bloody crazy?" Michelle said. "You turned down two million dollars? You are insane. You could have used the money to expand your business."

"Thanks, but I don't need it. The Catholic church is hiring us to protect all of the Bishops and Cardinals in the U.S. and Europe. Marty's hiring agents like crazy. All I care about is getting back to see my sister."

"She's one tough cookie," Michelle said. "She's already up and walking."

Chapter 25

One Month Later

Brother and sister walked hand-in-hand through Woods Hole village. After Jessie moved back home to recuperate, Jay drove her to physical therapy and watched her learn to use her artificial leg. He saw his father's grit and determination in every step Jessie took.

"Where are we going?" Jessie said as they turned into the parking lot of the Woods Hole Aquarium.

"I want you to meet somebody."

Jay opened the front door of the small brick building. He waved at the volunteer at the front desk, who handed him two guest passes. Then he led Jessie through a maze of marine life exhibits. The door to the office was ajar, and Jay walked right in.

"Hey, Jay," a blonde woman said from the back of the cramped work area. "Who's your friend?"

"Stephanie, I'd like you to meet my kid sister, Jessie. "Jessie, this is Stephanie. She's a marine biologist."

Stephanie wore a dark blue slicker to keep her dry. She was leaning over a small pool with two baby sea otters splashing around.

Jay said, "How's my buddy doing? I stopped by yesterday, and you guys weren't here."

"Yeah, Jojo and I took a road trip to the New England Aquarium in Boston. He had a physical exam and played with some of the penguins."

"Are you still thinking of transferring Jojo to Boston?"

"Yeah, I'm not sure what to do. Jojo's outgrowing our facility here. Plus, we have a hard time keeping the water temperature cold enough for him. New England Aquarium has a colony of penguins from the same ecosystem as Jojo. It's a natural fit for him. I hate the idea of letting anyone else care for him."

"Who's, Jojo?" Jessie asked. "Is he named after our brother?"

"Of course," Jay said with a smile. "Come on, and I'll introduce you."

Jay took Jessie's hand and led her to the outdoor pool area. Jojo was two-hundred-fifty pounds and filled the pool. He swam back and forth, rolling over and over to the delight of the small crowd gathering outside the demonstration area. It was getting close to feeding time, and Jojo was showing off.

Stephanie handed Jay and Jessie a blue slicker. "You might want to put these on. Jojo likes to splash around."

* * *

Stephanie knelt next to the pool and slapped her hand on the top of the water. Jojo responded to the cue by reversing direction and sliding up onto a platform. The forty-five-degree water splashed Jessie, causing her to scream.

"Wow, he's so cute!" Jessie said. "Look at those big black eyes. He likes you, Jay."

"He should. I rescued him." Jay gave Jessie a quick story about his trip to the Falkland Islands and explained how he pulled Jojo from the net.

Jay patted Jojo on the head and tossed a handful of small fish into his mouth. Jojo responded by squealing and barking, then rolled onto his back so Jay could scratch his belly. The seal barked even louder.

"Stephanie, let me know when he's going to Boston so that I can throw him a bon voyage party."

"He'll love that, Jay," Stephanie said. "Nice to meet you, Jessie."

They watched the rest of the show, then strolled back towards the village.

Jessie slowed down, then stopped. "Sorry, I need to stop for a few minutes. My leg is killing me."

"Of course, Jessie, there's a bench in the park along the water."

When they sat on the bench, Jessie removed her prosthetic leg. She rubbed the stump and adjusted the gauze liner.

"Sometimes, the liner bunches up and gives me a blister. It's like having a stone in your shoe. Thanks for understanding."

"You amaze me," Jay said. "You're the strongest woman I've ever met. And I know, I've met some amazing women."

Jessie blushed at the compliment. "I didn't do anything special. I survived a bomb blast, but you're the true hero in the family. On the other hand, you save people's lives on a regular basis. Look how you rescued Charlotte and Kyle from the island. But you're still the most humble man I've ever met. You never boast, and you always give everyone else credit."

"I received a lot of training and gained plenty of experience in the military. Now it's my turn to give back. But enough about me, what are you going to do about your career? You're not giving up, are you?"

"No way. I love journalism. I'm not stopping now. My career hasn't started yet, but there's one thing I need to ask you."

Sure, anything. What do you want?"

"I want you to meet Andy. He's on his way to pick me up. He'll be here in a few minutes."

"He is?"

"Jay, don't be an over-protective big brother. Please be nice to him and give him a chance to prove himself. You'll see, I promise."

The silver Tesla convertible pulled into a parking space in front of the park. Andrew stepped out. He was tall, close to six feet four inches. He kept his sandy brown hair cut short and wore a US Army sweatshirt over a faded pair of jeans. Even though the sweatshirt was bulky, Jay could tell Andrew was in good shape.

Jessie jumped up and hopped on one leg into Andrew's arms. He picked her up and swung her around like a schoolgirl as she squealed with joy. Andrew lowered Jessie to the ground and helped her back to the bench. Jay shook his hand and invited Andrew to sit down with them.

"Andrew and I want to ask you for a special favor," Jessie said after they sat down. "Jay, will you…." Jessie stopped mid-sentence, choking up with tears.

"Let me ask, Jess," Andrew said. "Sir, my father raised me

to show respect and honor. I want to ask for your permission to marry your sister?"

Jay smiled and shook Andrew's hand, "First, I have a question to ask you."

Jessie looked at him with a scowl.

"How are you going to support Jessie? What are your career plans?"

"I have to honor my commitment to our country. I went through Army ROTC at Brown. I leave right after the Labor Day weekend."

"What unit?"

"82nd Airborne, sir. I'm a combat medic. We're deploying to Pakistan for training and treating injured kids in Afghanistan. After the service, I plan to be a surgeon."

"Despite the fact you're an Army grunt, I guess you pass the test," Jay said with a big smile. "I'm sure you'll do well. And yes, you have my permission to marry Jessie."

"I have a question," Jessie said. "Will you walk me down the aisle? Stand-in for daddy?"

Jay reached over and hugged his sister, "Of course I will. Where's the wedding?"

"At the Rosecliff Mansion in Newport. The wedding is on the third Saturday in July."

"Wow, nice place," Jay said. "How many guests?"

"Just under four hundred," Andrew said. "My father has a lot of friends. The Governor of Rhode Island and the Mayor of Providence will be there."

"And what about the church?"

"The wedding service will be at the Cathedral of Saints Peter and Paul in Providence. The Newport churches weren't big enough."

Jay walked Andrew and Jessie back to the car. He hugged her and wished her well.

* * *

It was eleven forty-five. Jay was meeting with McCoy and Marty at two o'clock. Enough time for him to get in a run. Jay jogged to his car across from the aquarium when he heard a blood-curdling scream.

"No, oh no!"

Jay recognized Stephanie's voice and ran at full speed across the street to the aquarium. He slid to a stop inside the seal enclosure.

Stephanie knelt next to Jojo's body on the pool deck. Deep red blood poured from a deep gash in the seal's neck. She held towels against his neck, trying to stem the flowing blood.

Jay choked back his emotions and pulled his cell phone out of his pocket. He dialed 911, then walked around the blood and knelt next to Stephanie.

"Why, why would anybody do this?" Stephanie said. "Who would kill Jojo?"

Jay tried to console her without success. People stood outside the fence surrounding the pool. They were taking pictures and inching closer to the pool of blood. Jay walked around the blood and asked everyone to stay back so the police could enter. A minute later, a Falmouth police cruiser pulled in with lights flashing. Marty Hernandez got out with another officer.

"I heard the call and came as fast as I could."

The police officers squeezed past the growing blood pool. Marty knelt next to Stephanie and helped her to her feet. He then pulled her back away from the lifeless seal. The second officer took pictures of the crime scene with his cell phone.

"Tell me what happened," Marty said to Stephanie when she stopped sobbing.

"I was out here taking a blood sample for the New England Aquarium veterinarian. We were going to transfer him to Boston next week. I went inside to answer a phone call. When I came back...."

"How long were you on the phone?"

"Five minutes at the most."

"Did you see anybody suspicious around here?"

"No. Nobody. How could anybody do this?"

"Did you receive any threatening phone calls?"

"Of course not. Everybody loved Jojo. He was the star of the aquarium."

As Marty spoke with Stephanie, Jay scanned the crime scene. A news truck from Hyannis pulled up to the curb, and the sound of a helicopter buzzed overhead. Jay looked up to see a red chopper with the letters GNN on the side. A flock of seagulls hovered over a boat docked next to the aquarium—the day's fish delivery.

"Excuse me," the reporter said. "Can you answer a few questions?"

As Jay pivoted to face the reporter, his foot slipped on a puddle of water and fell to the ground.

He felt the air pass above his nose then heard a sharp crack. Concrete shattered from the wall, inches from Jay's head.

"Someone's shooting at us," Jay said to the reporter. "Get down!"

Jay looked around at the buildings surrounding the aquarium. He scanned the roof of the Marine Biology Lab across the street. Then turned to look at the NOAA building next to the aquarium. The shot came from the vicinity of the fishing boat. Jay ran out of the gate and out to the parking lot next to the aquarium, squatting behind Marty's squad car.

There was another crack, and a bullet shattered the police car's windshield.

Marty ran out from the pool area with his gun drawn. "Jay, what's going on?"

"Marty, get down. There's a sniper somewhere by the fishing boat. But I can't see anybody. The shots are coming down from an angle."

Marty flopped down next to Jay, with his handgun drawn. He went to hand Jay his gun.

"Here," Marty said. "You're a better shot than I am. I'll get the long gun out of the trunk. I'll call for backup first."

Chapter 26

Woods Hole

J ay kept staring towards the fishing boat, but the sun's glare made it difficult to see any details.

Another crack. The bullet hit the police car's tire, which exploded from the impact.

Jay saw the muzzle flash. It was coming from above the fishing boat. Then he saw a glint of sun. The shots came from a seagull hovering above the fishing boat. It was too far away to hit with the handgun. Marty opened the trunk of the squad car and pulled out an AR-15 rifle. Another crack and a bullet struck the trunk of the cruiser.

"Marty, give me the rifle. Quick!"

Jay took the AR-15 from Marty's hand and stood up behind the car. He leaned his left elbow on the roof of the patrol car and aimed the rifle at the seagull drone. Jay saw a red light flash by his face. A laser designator. Jay saw the source of the red laser through the scope and fired off two quick rounds.

The first bullet smashed one of the seagull's eyes. The second penetrated the drone's body. A small puff of smoke appeared from the body of the gull. Then more smoke. The drone was on fire.

The seagull lurched away from the aquarium and flew inland. Jay followed the trail of smoke through the rifle's scope.

"I got it," Jay said. "Now we have to catch it."

Marty tossed Jay the keys to the squad car. "Let's go get it!"

The other police officer opened the rear door to get in, but Marty turned to him, "Stay here and guard the crime scene."

Jay slammed the car into gear. The sound of metal rims grinding against the asphalt pavement brought Jay back to reality. "Shit Marty, the seagull, shot the tires out. Let's take my car."

Jay and Marty piled out of the police car and ran into the street. Andrew's Tesla Roadster stopped right in front of him.

"Jay, what's the matter?" Jessie yelled out the passenger side window.

"I need your help," Jay said. "Andrew, get out of the car."

Jay yanked the door open, then stepped back to let Andrew exit the car. Jay jumped in and closed the door. Without saying a word, he put the car into gear and pushed the accelerator to the floor. The Tesla took off, snapping Jay's head back. The silent electric engine caught Jay by surprise. "Shit, this thing has pickup," Jay said as he whipped the car around the corner. He took a left onto Woods Hole Road at sixty miles per hour.

"Jay, what the hell are you doing?" Jessie said. "Where are we going?"

"We're chasing a seagull drone. It tried to shoot me. I hit it twice, and it took off."

"I saw it. It flew across the street and towards the golf

course."

Jay saw the cart path crossing for the Quissett Country Club coming up. He slammed the brakes and spun the wheel at the same time. The speedy Tesla clung to the road and sped down the cart path onto the golf course.

"Hey, it's not your tee time," yelled an elderly man in a pink polo shirt and khaki shorts. Then, realizing Jay wasn't stopping, he dove out of the way. But it was too late, as Jay smashed his golf bag, sending clubs flying in the air. Trying not to create any more casualties, Jay weaved around astonished golfers and scattered flocks of Canadian geese.

"Over there," Jessie said. "On the other side of the fairway."

Jay yanked the wheel, and the car slid onto the pristine fairway. The wide tires dug deep grooves into the manicured lawn, spewing mud and sod high into the air.

"The drone's headed for that water hazard," Jessie said, pointing to his right. Jay saw the dark trail of smoke. "Someone's there to grab it. Hurry, Jay, we don't want him to get away!"

A green golf cart stood between Jay and the water hole. A man in a white hat, pink polo, and white shorts waved a plastic flag.

Jay couldn't react fast enough. The low front bumper of the Tesla caught the golf cart's front edge, spinning the cart around in a three-hundred-sixty degree circle. The man screamed, but Jay and Jessie were too focused on the drone to notice.

A fountain of steam and water erupted where the drone crashed. The man with the green overalls scooped the seagull up with the net and threw the drone into the back of a dark-green utility cart. Noticing Jay speeding towards him from across the fairway, the man jumped into the cart and took off.

The Tesla overtook the golf cart in seconds. Jay slammed the cart's rear bumper sending it crashing into a pine tree grove bordering the fairway. He jumped out of the car. Then reached into the cart, pulled the man out, and threw him down on the ground. The man resisted, trying to squirm free, so Jay punched him in the face then pressed Marty's handgun against the man's forehead.

"Who do you work for?" Jay said. "Tell me now, or you're dead."

"The golf club."

"I don't believe you! Show me an ID card!"

The man stayed silent. His blue eyes were cold and vacant. Jay pressed the handgun harder against the groundskeeper's head. "Tell me now," Jay said. "Or I'm pulling the trigger on the count of three. One, two…"

"Jay, don't!" said Jessie. "There's a…."

"Jessie, not now. I'm busy."

"Put the gun down and put your hands above your head," a male voice said from behind Jay.

"See, Jay I told you. You never listen to me."

Jay turned around to see two Falmouth police officers. Their handguns pointed at the back of his head. Jessie stood facing the side of the Tesla with her hands in the air."

"Officer, you need to arrest this man," Jay said as he placed the gun down on the ground and raised his hands. "He's involved with the Papal bombings."

"You're talking about this groundskeeper?" the closest cop said. "What are you, some nut job?"

"No, this bird tried to kill me," Jay said. The second cop

laughed.

"No, I'm serious. It's not a bird; it's a drone. It's equipped with a rifle, and it tried to kill me at the aquarium. So I shot back at it and hit it."

Both cops laughed. "Now that's a good one," the first cop said. "You shot the bird in mid-air from, let me guess, a hundred yards away?"

The cops buckled over in laughter—their faces bright red. Jay saw tears streaming down their faces. Jay stayed quiet, waiting for them to gain some control. Then, he glanced over at Jessie, who was leaning against the Tesla. She was laughing too.

"No, it was more like two-fifty yards, you idiots," Marty said. The cops turned around to see their Deputy Chief standing with his arms on his hips. The second police officer pointed his gun towards Jay and the groundskeeper.

"I was there," Marty said. "The drone shot up my patrol car. Mr. Mendes used my long gun to shoot it. Now arrest the groundskeeper and let Mr. Mendes go. Joe, the drone needs to be preserved as evidence. Frank, make sure you put gloves on when you pick it up. Be sure to put it in an evidence bag. Someone check the golf cart for weapons and evidence."

Marty pulled out his handgun and walked past the two officers. He trained his weapon on the groundskeeper so Jay could get off. The other officer then rolled the groundskeeper onto his stomach and placed a pair of handcuffs on his wrists.

"Read him his rights and take him to the station. The FBI will be here soon."

"Jay, did he say anything before these two morons interrupted your conversation?"

"No," Jay said. "He's a pro. You won't get any information from him.

"I heard from your buddy McCauley at the FBI. His forensics team is on the way down from Boston to check out the crime scene at the aquarium and the bird drone."

Jay glanced over at Jessie, who was leaning against the Tesla. Her face was pale, and Jay could see she was in a lot of pain. "Jess, I'm sorry. Get in Marty's patrol car. He'll drive you back to the aquarium."

"It was worth it if this guy had anything to do with the bomb that nearly killed Roger and me."

"Tell Andrew I'm sorry about the car."

"He won't care," Jessie said. "His father will buy him a new one."

Jay and Marty helped Jessie limp to the patrol car. She sat down in the front passenger seat.

"Jay," Jessie said. "Did Roger give you his cell phone?"

"Yes," Jay said. "I gave it to the FBI."

"You know the bird drone. It looks like the one that blew up in New York."

"Marty, wait!" Jay said. "Don't touch the drone. In fact, stay far away from it. Call the bomb squad."

* * *

Marty dropped Jay off at the aquarium then drove Jessie home. Yellow crime scene tape fluttered in the light ocean breeze. Jay walked over to the gate of the seal's performance area. Stephanie was on her knees scrubbing blood off the blue ceramic tiles.

"Hey Stephanie, need any help?" Jay said. "I'm good at

cleaning up messes."

Stephanie turned to see Jay and smiled. "Hold on. I'll unlock the gate."

Jay noticed the smudged mascara on Stephanie's face and her swollen eyes.

"Are you okay, Jay? Did you find the guy who killed Jojo?"

"Maybe. We found an accomplice, but I don't know how much information we'll get from him. Where's Jojo? I mean his body."

"The FBI investigators took him back to Boston. They're going to do an autopsy to look for evidence. Cause of death is pretty clear."

"Was there a security camera tape?"

"No. There aren't any cameras outside the aquarium. They're all inside where the fish are. Jojo never came out to the pool area by himself. There was always someone with him.

"How did someone kill him if you were in the pool area?"

"My phone rang. It was in my office, so I ran in to grab it. The caller ID said it was Olivia, but when I answered the phone, nobody was there. So I came back out, and Jojo was, you know."

Stephanie began crying. Jay wrapped his arm around her shoulders. As they walked back towards the bloodstain on the ground, a thought came into Jay's head. Did the rapist take Olivia's phone the night he attacked her? Jay never thought to ask Olivia about that. Or did he call her with a different phone and use a phony caller ID. Either way, Jay now knew who killed Jojo.

"Stephanie, it's not your fault. Someone did this to hurt me. Actually, he knew I would respond. So he tried to kill me."

"What do you mean, Jay?"

"I know who's responsible for Jojo's death. I can't prove it, but it now makes sense. It's the same creep who raped Olivia and tried to kidnap the Bishop. He's hurting the people and animals I care about. Playing with my emotions in a very sick way."

"Aren't you sad?" Stephanie asked, "You don't seem emotional."

"Yes, I'm sad. He was my only connection to Olivia."

"I did call her," Stephanie said. "After the killing to tell her the news. She was devastated. But she was more concerned about you, Jay. Why don't you visit her in San Diego? She really misses you."

"I'll think about it. But I need to catch this maniac before he kills anyone else I care about."

"What are you going to do?" Stephanie said. "I mean when you find him."

"I'm going to make him pay."

Chapter 27

Jay and Marty drove back to the Quissett house. When Jay got out of the car, he saw Kyle run out of the carriage house door towards the harbor. Jay went upstairs to Jillian's apartment. The door was open, and he saw Jillian sitting on the couch crying.

"Is everything alright?" Jay asked.

"I'm sorry," Jillian said. " It's probably nothing."

"What's nothing?"

"Kyle," Jillian said.

"What about Kyle?"

"I shouldn't bother you with this. You're busy."

"Jillian, please tell me what's going on."

"I don't know where to start. I argued with Kyle, and I'm concerned about him."

"I'll go find him," Jay said. "What's the problem?"

"I'm worried about him. He won't talk, but I know something's wrong."

* * *

Kyle sat on the granite bench at the end of The Nob. It was a sunny day, and Buzzards Bay was filling up with boats.

He didn't care or notice. He enjoyed being alone for a few minutes. The occasional hiker or family with little kids came up the hill to enjoy the view, but Kyle didn't pay attention. He looked out at the water and wondered, *Was my mother, right? I don't want to hurt myself. I never thought about it before. Why would I? Maybe because I was an only child without a father or because I was bullied at school daily. Why would that bother me? Is it because I survived a terrorist attack, got kidnapped, and now my best friend. No, correction — my only friend — is shipped off to a loony bin? That's what every teenager goes through. Right?*

The thing is, I never thought about these things. Not until Mom told me Charlotte wasn't coming home. I miss her so much. Her quirky smile. Her shy innocence. Her gentle touches when I needed them. I can't believe she will stay away. She has to come back. I need to say I'm sorry.

"Kyle?"

Kyle turned around and froze. Jay Mendes stood at the top of the stairs.

He looked back at the water.

"What are you doing here?" Jay said. "Your mom asked me to look for you."

"What do you want?" Kyle said.

"Your mother is worried."

Kyle laughed, "Tell me something new. My mother always worries."

"She's worried about your state of mind."

"Are you a shrink? I don't do shrinks." Kyle backed up closer to the edge of the headland. He stepped onto one of the granite blocks.

Jay stepped forward and held his hand out. Kyle backed away.

"I don't want to hurt you. I saved your life on the island. Or did you forget that already?"

"I'm sure that's what you tell your victims all the time," Kyle said. "I know what you guys do to people who cross you."

"Kyle, what are you talking about?"

"Uncle Marty said who you were and that you kill people."

"He was joking. Teasing me. I was a soldier, but I never killed a person in cold blood."

"What about the priest in Boston. Kathleen Amejian says you shot him."

"Yes, I did, but there was a reason. He was going to hurt people."

"How was a priest going to hurt someone? Bless them to death? Drown them in holy water? Get God to hit them with a bolt of lightning?"

"It's an ongoing investigation. But I will tell you it was a clean shooting, and the FBI cleared me. Now come away from the edge before you slip down the rocks."

Kyle reached out and grabbed Jay's hand, then sat down on the granite bench.

"Do you mind if I sit down too?"

Kyle shook his head.

Jay sat down on the ground a few feet away from Kyle, "So what's going on? Why did you run out on your Mom?"

"I don't know."

"It's Charlotte, right?"

Kyle turned away from Jay and put his head in his hands, and cried.

Jay waited until Kyle stopped and wiped the tears off with his sleeve, "How did you know? I never told anyone how I felt about her."

Jay sat next to Kyle and said, "Her father hired me to rescue her. I met with him after the rescue, and he told me he was sending her back to Oregon."

"He's a jerk."

"I agree," Jay said.

"Did you ever lose anybody you loved?"

"Yeah, too many to count. Buddies I fought with. My mentor in the military. My girlfriend. She didn't die. She went away, like Charlotte."

"Why did she leave?"

"She said she left to take a job. But I believe it's because of the shame she felt."

"What do you mean?"

"She was drugged and sexually assaulted."

Kyle didn't say a word.

"What are you going to do now that she's gone?" Jay asked. "Do you play sports or have a hobby?"

"I don't know."

"I know you like robots and electronics. Your microbots are pretty slick."

"Thanks. I like programming and designing bots. I guess it's my thing."

"Have you thought about patenting them?"

"No. I don't get all that IP stuff."

"Patents protect your inventions from getting copied by others. It gives you an advantage if you decide to sell them."

"Why would I do that?" Kyle said. "Nobody is going to buy them."

"Don't be too sure about that. The bots saved lives and provided important intel. They can be valuable tools for the military or search and rescue teams. I've never seen anything like them, and I've tested a lot of surveillance and weapons systems."

"You have?"

"Yes. Special operations teams often test the new gear first. Then, we try it out in the field before the military decides to buy them in large quantities. I've tried a lot of similar systems that never worked. They bombed. Your system works. But I do have a few suggestions to make it better."

"See, you don't like it," Kyle said.

Jay shook his head, "That's not what I said. Listen, show me how you design and build the bots. Then, I'd like to show your system to a few of my friends."

"Okay, I guess," Kyle said. "But I have a question first."

"Shoot."

Kyle laughed.

"What's so funny?"

"You said shoot. My friends say you're the world's deadliest man. Is that true?"

"Not at all. Many people are much deadlier. But, I'm good at my job."

"Like killing? Were you an assassin?"

"Sometimes, you need to kill bad people to save good people."

"Like in the Boston Cathedral? Or on Mansion island?"

"Yes, you can say that."

"Then you saved my life. Twice."

"What do you mean?"

"I was in the Cathedral," Kyle said. "Part of the choir up in the loft.

Jay perked up. This was the type of information he was looking for. He asked, "Did you see anything that might help the investigation?"

"I don't know. I was videotaping the opening scene with my cell phone."

"Can I watch the video?"

"Sure," Kyle said. "Let me get my phone out, and I'll show you."

Kyle dug into his pocket and pulled out an old smartphone. Kyle scrolled through a set of photos and videos to find the one he was looking for.

"Here you go. This is the video where you shoot the priest."

"Let me see. I'm going to tell you something I'm not supposed to. I'm sworn to secrecy, so if the word gets out, I'll know you talked. Understand?"

Kyle nodded.

"The priest was an imposter," Jay said. "5He killed a real priest in New Bedford and stole his vestment. He was wearing a suicide bomb vest like the bombers in New York and Rome. Look, you can see he's holding the detonator. And he yells something right before I shoot him. Kyle, can you send me this video? This is evidence. It could help the investigation."

"Sure, whatever you want."

"And one last thing. I wasn't an assassin. I was part of a hostage rescue team, and we saved people's lives. So you don't have to worry."

* * *

Jay and Kyle walked back to Marty's house. Jillian and Lindsey were waiting for him.

Jillian screamed, "Oh my God, you're alive!" Kyle turned

around, burying his head in his hands. Jay laughed and wrapped his arms around the teen's shoulder.

Jillian ran over and hugged Kyle tight. "Is everything okay? I was so worried. You didn't answer your phone. We couldn't find you."

"Mom, can you stop? You're embarrassing me."

Jillian stepped back. "You were kidnapped and traumatized. I thought you were going to commit suicide. I won't apologize for loving you. But you need to start talking to me. Or someone who cares."

"Okay, mom, I get it. Now leave me alone!" Kyle ran into the carriage house, slamming the door behind him.

"I don't know what to do," Jillian said. "I'm so scared I'm going to lose him too. He's all I have."

"I talked with him. He's been through a lot lately. He's sad Charlotte was sent away. He blames himself."

Jillian stared at Jay. "He told you that?"

Jay nodded.

"He never told me he liked Charlotte. I didn't even know her name. Are you saying he loves her?

Again, Jay nodded.

"Oh my God, that's awful! He never tells me anything!"

Jay found Kyle in the carriage house basement, staring at an image on a computer screen.

"What are you doing?" Jay said. "It looks pretty cool."

"I'm running a simulation program. I'm trying to improve the design of my microbots."

"Why are you doing that? I don't know much about drones."

"They're not drones. Drones only fly. The microbots are flying robots. They also swim and do other things. I'm trying

243

to make the bodies lighter, so I can add more functions and battery life."

"How does the software help you?"

"You type in the parameters you want. The software runs millions of options until it recommends the best design. Then I print out a prototype and try it."

"What do you mean, print it out?"

"I use a 3D printer. That's how I built the microbots. I print the bodies and assemble the printed circuit boards."

"That's amazing," Jay said. "But how did you learn this? Don't you have to go to engineering school?"

"I guess I'm a fast learner. I look up stuff on the internet and ask questions. I did have a mentor when we lived in Canada."

"When did you live in Canada?

"My mom studied maritime engineering in Newfoundland for four years. She graduated last spring, and we moved back to Cape Cod in July.

"What did the mentor help you with?"

"Electronics and robotics. He taught electrical engineering at the university."

What was his name?"

"Professor Harris."

"Are you sure his name is Harris?"

"I'm positive. We lived in his guest house."

Chapter 28

Fame had its rewards. Owning luxury homes around the world was at the top of the list. Privacy and anonymity were a close second. And then, some people had it all.

The warm breeze fluttered the paper umbrella in Angelica Bonham's frozen cocktail, but she didn't notice. Instead, she lounged in the sun next to the pool of her twelve-room villa. The view of Cannes and the Mediterranean Ocean was one reason she bought this home. The remote location at the top of a hill was another reason. Thick underbrush grew on both sides of the winding driveway and dozens of security cameras assured her security team would never be surprised. The front of the house sat on a cliff's edge, dropping several hundred feet on the ocean side. The back of the house sat embedded into the base of a granite face. In the case someone was able to breach her defenses, Angelica's companions were capable of providing an aggressive defense.

Ivan, her bodyguard, and occasional lover was a legendary Soviet sniper and a pay-for-hire assassin. Her new boyfriend,

Darius Jacba, was a Polish drug lord with an extensive organization in France. He loved mixed martial arts and even convinced her to build a fighting cage in the basement.

The privacy of the villa allowed her to have special guests. The kind she kept away from the paparazzi stalking her every move. Her newest friend, Kathleen, was a famous news correspondent. They met at the Golden Globe Awards several years ago and bonded almost immediately. Kathleen had her own problems and was involved in her own steamy affairs, but it seemed her life was a bit quieter these days. Her boyfriend, a Brit named Farrity, had steely gray eyes, salt-and-pepper hair, and was quite handsome. However, he did have a bad limp. Kathleen explained she was nursing him back to health after an unfortunate accident. But it didn't seem like Kathleen was doing any nursing at all.

"Angelica darling, it's time for the daily briefing from The Master," Jacba said from the veranda above. "We can't miss the updates."

"Can you record today's message?" Angelica said without opening her eyes. "I'm quite tired. You wore me out last night.

* * *

As the women soaked in the sun, the three men chatted on the upper veranda. Jacba, a slim, fit man with pale skin and long, white hair pulled back in a ponytail, poured 18-year old scotch for the group. A valet delivered a tray of escargot and peeled shrimp which Jacba devoured with his hands and washed down with a full glass of the precious liquor.

Farrity took his time eating in the more civilized British

manner by using a fork and knife. He detested drug dealers and preferred Ivan's company, but he had to be polite to his guest. "How is the movement progressing in Europe?"

"We are having great success recruiting cell leaders into the family," Jacba said. "We start them out as drug runners, then mold them into operatives. It is a particularly challenging process. But, if they survive, they become strong and loyal leaders."

"Why drugs?" Ivan asked.

"It is profitable and, in most countries, considered a minor crime. It is also easy to bribe local officials to look the other way. In fact, in France, the government is the number one supplier of methadone. We steal their inventory and resell it in other countries."

Farrity was intrigued, "How do you train your recruits?"

"We use MMA fighting techniques, with our own twisted rules," Jacba explained. "It is an excellent conditioning routine and teaches them to be ruthless and fight without constraint. By the time we introduce weapons, they are already trained killers."

"Who's idea was it to use MMA?" Ivan asked. "It is not taught in the military."

"Angelica," Jacba replied. "She is a big fan and enjoys the competition."

"Angelica Bonham is an MMA enthusiast? But she makes her money based on her beauty. What if someone breaks her nose?"

Jacba laughed, "You don't understand. She never lost a match. Nobody even gets near her face."

You said you have your own twisted rules," Farrity asked. "What are they?"

"There are no rules. No tapping out. Winner takes all."

"You mean a fight to the death?"

"The only way. Do you want to try? In fact, my trainer, Conrad, is downstairs now working with a team of recruits."

"No thanks," Farrity said with a nervous laugh. "I'll stick to my form of mayhem."

Jacba smiled and finished off another glass of scotch, "Speaking of mayhem, did you dispose of Mendes yet? He is a royal pain in our ass. Unfortunately, stopping the Boston bombing set back our plans."

"No, not yet," Farrity said. "But I will shortly. In fact, I need to leave and head back to the States. I have explosive plans to end his illustrious career."

Chapter 29

Fourth of July, Cape Cod

J ay scanned the serene waters of Buzzards Bay through his sniper scope. Unfortunately, his view was obscured by the evening haze hovering over the water like a translucent blanket. Despite the cool night temperature, he was tense but not nervous. Jay lay prone on the bow of the twenty-five-foot Coast Guard patrol boat. Behind him, an MSST member operated the .50 caliber machine gun. The Coast Guard Marine Safety & Security Team was responsible for anti-terrorism operations. Tonight, their job was to apprehend one of the terrorists responsible for the Boston Cathedral attack before he harmed any more innocent people.

Petty Officer Kathy Brennan peered through a set of high-powered binoculars.

"Jay, I appreciate your help on this mission," Brennan said. "You are the highest qualified sniper available. But remember, as a contractor, you're not cleared for boardings. So let my team handle that."

"Roger," Jay said.

"Chief, do you see anything?" asked Mack over Jay's radio headset.

"Negative, no sign of the boat."

"What's your twenty?"

"We're three hundred yards north of the Nob. The water is calm tonight. A light haze is settling over the water."

"Our stakeout team said the boat left Barnstable Harbor an hour ago. They observed one person on the boat."

"What kind of boat is it?"

"A lobster boat. White with a blue hull. Traveling at eighteen knots."

"Where is it headed?" Jay said.

"It's heading your way. Our GPS showed it exited the south end of the Cape Cod Canal five minutes ago."

"What do you think they're planning?" Jay asked.

"We're not sure, but we heard a lot of internet chatter the last few days about an attack. But, of course, the biggest crowds are on the Fourth of July at the oceanfront fireworks displays."

"That leaves a lot of possibilities. Every town on the Cape and South Coast has fireworks on the ocean."

"We know, but Falmouth has the largest crowds right on the beach. Plus, we're expecting at least a thousand boaters anchored offshore. So it is a target-rich environment."

Brennan was listening in on the same radio frequency. "Do we have probable cause to board the fishing boat?"

"Not yet," Mack said. "Right now, we have the statement from the guy we arrested in Falmouth. He told us he picked the drone up from this fishing boat. There wasn't anybody on board when he was there."

"It sounds like probable cause to me," Jay said. "Since the

drone tried to kill me."

"Jay, cool down. We have to do this right if we want a conviction."

"Who said I wanted a conviction," Jay said. "The only way we know this bastard won't harm anybody is to put him in a watery grave."

"Cool down, Jay," Mack said. "I know you have a lot of reasons to kill this guy, but now that the FBI is involved, we have to do it by the book."

"Roger, that," Jay replied. "We're dealing with a psychopath. There are thousands of people's lives at stake. We can't let that boat anywhere near Falmouth."

"Then it has to be a security case," Brennan said. "If the boat is a threat to public safety, I have the authority from the Coast Guard Regional Command Center in Boston to board or stop the boat as I see fit."

"What about Falmouth Police?" Jay said. "They'll need time to evacuate the beachfront."

"There won't be time to evacuate ten thousand people," Mack said. "We need to keep that fishing boat away from the beach. I'm more concerned about the boaters. But I agree. Let's loop Marty into the comm circuit. We'll want to make sure emergency response teams and the local hospitals are on standby."

Jay's stomach tightened from the anticipation. The fishing trawler was five minutes away, but the time dragged by. He saw deck lights from the boats passing by. He also heard loud music and singing as people sailed towards Falmouth Heights. A distant boom startled Jay. Then he saw the distinctive flash of fireworks—one of the towns on the opposite side of Buzzards Bay starting their celebration.

251

"I got him," Jay said. "Lobster boat with a blue hull. Traveling south, southwest. Coming right at us."

"Roger," Brennan said. "GPS confirms that's our boat. We'll let him pass and fall in behind. MSST prepare to board."

Jay scanned the fishing boat through the sniper scope. The view was a bit foggy, but he could see the pilothouse. Strange, he thought. It's empty. Alarm bells rang in his head.

"Brennan, do you see anybody on the fishing boat?"

"Negative."

"The boarding team leader is Lieutenant Salerno. He's in charge. Got it?"

"Roger that," Jay said.

Jay held on as the boatswain mate increased the speed and pulled up tight to the fishing boat's stern. Jay sat at the bow of the patrol boat as it bounced over the light chop. He flipped down his night vision goggles to get a better look at the lobster boat. He saw a small derrick and chain pull located near the aft. Steel mesh lobster traps lay strewn across the deck.

The assault team pulled alongside the lobster boat

"Salerno, board the fishing boat," Brennan said.

"The deck is too small for the full team," Salerno said. "I'm taking Jones and Murray. The rest of the team will stay alert and ready to go.

The boatswain mate sped up to match the speed of the lobster boat. They pulled up against the lobster boat's port side, and the assault team members climbed over the rail.

Jay watched Salerno as he tried to enter the pilothouse, but the door was locked. Jones smashed the window with the butt of his assault rifle and opened the door from the inside. Salerno entered the pilothouse and reported, "All clear. We're going to check the cabin."

Murray kicked the door in and entered the cabin.

Jay heard the sound of a single rifle shot.

Salerno and Jones rushed into the cabin. There was more gunfire. Then Salerno emerged, pulling Murray out with him. Jones followed behind, covering their retreat.

Salerno waved for the rest of his team to board, "He took a shot in the head, but his helmet stopped the bullet."

Before any of the remaining assault team members moved, Jay leaped over the side rail onto the fishing boat. He grabbed Murray by the collar and dragged him aft until an assault team member pulled him onto the patrol boat. Then Jay picked up Murray's M4 and joined Salerno in the pilothouse.

Brennan yelled into the radio, "Mendes, what the hell are you doing?"

"You can't risk losing any more of your team members. This guy is a psychopath."

"That's what we do. It's our job. Now get off! That's an order!"

"I'm not on your team, remember."

"But I can arrest you. Salerno, place Mendes under arrest and bring him back to the patrol boat.

Suddenly, the lobster boat sped up and turned hard to port. The sudden turn knocked Jay and Salerno to the deck.

"Who's piloting the boat?" Brennan asked. "You're heading straight towards the fireworks barge!"

"Nobody," Jay replied.

"Salerno and Mendes, you need to get off," Brennan said. "We need a clear shot for the .50 cal."

Jay struggled to regain his footing as the lobster boat accelerated to almost thirty knots. "What the hell is powering this boat?" he said. "We need to get the shooter and get off the boat!"

Salerno shouted to be heard over the rushing wind, "I'll throw in a flashbang, and then we can go in."

Salerno tossed the flashbang through the hole in the door created by the previous gunshot. The cabin lit up with a bright flash and loud explosion. Salerno kicked the door then opened fire with his assault rifle.

Jay heard the return fire then went in. Two sets of bunks lined each side of the cabin. A small desk sat knocked over on the floor. Salerno was on the deck, trying to crawl out of the way.

"He got me in the shoulder. I'm okay."

Jay sprayed the cabin with gunfire, then grabbed Salerno by the collar and pulled him out.

Two members of the assault team jumped onto the fishing boat and pulled Salerno back to safety.

"Evacuate the boat, Mendes," Brennan called over the cutter's PA system.

Jay ran back into the cabin.

"C'mon, you bastard," Jay said. "I know you're the one who attacked the Bishop and kidnapped the girl! Now come out and fight like a man instead of hiding in the shadows like a little pussy."

That worked. The assailant jumped off the bunk, landing on top of Jay. He ripped Jay's rifle from his hand and threw it across the deck. Then he pulled Jay to his feet and placed his handgun to Jay's head.

Jay slammed his fist into the man's face, knocking him back against the bunk. He twisted the gun from his hand. The man grabbed Jay around the head and pulled him out of the cabin and onto the pilothouse deck. Jay wrapped his arms around the man's waist. He then lifted and smashed him onto the deck. But the attacker didn't let go. The two warriors rolled on the deck, entangled in each other's bodies. Neither man gaining an advantage.

Meanwhile, the lobster boat plowed towards the fireworks barge. Pleasure boats scattered in all directions, slamming into each other.

"Mendes, we're firing," Brennan yelled into the radio. "Get off the boat!"

Jay struggled to escape the attacker's steel grip. Grabbing at his mask, Jay pulled it off. The familiar grey eyes stared back at him.

The man smiled and said, "It looks like we're going to die together, Chief."

"Not yet, you bastard. You have to pay for your sins."

With all his strength, Jay kicked the man off his body. Jay jumped to his feet, then wrapped his left arm around his neck and yanked him to the side of the boat.

Then a roar erupted as the .50 caliber opened fire. Flaming red tracers streamed past Jay's body. Razor-sharp wood splinters and smoke filled the air as the gunner adjusted his aim down towards the deck and the engine compartment.

Jay pulled the attacker with him towards the boat's stern but had to stop to stay away from the gunfire.

"Ceasefire," Brennan ordered. "We need to help Mendes!"

Then the boat exploded, throwing Jay and his assailant overboard.

* * *

Kyle, Brendan, and Carla sat in the Boston Whaler a half-mile away. Marty was at the helm when they witnessed the fishing boat explosion. He piloted as far away from the fireworks barge as he could get. The move saved their lives.

The blast created a tsunami wave, wreaking havoc among the small boats. Dozens of boats capsized, washing boaters into the sixty-five-degree water. Those with life jackets bobbed in the water. Others were not so lucky.

Then the call came out across the emergency radio channel. The Coast Guard called for volunteers to rescue victims. As they scanned the water with a searchlight, Brendan spotted a body in the water. Marty slowed down to investigate. Kyle used a grappling hook to pull the body closer.

"Oh God," Carla said when she saw the headless body. She turned and threw up over the side of the boat.

The next three bodies were in worse condition. There was nothing they could do for these people now, so they left the bodies in the water.

Brendan slowed down as they reached the blast scene.

"Help me!" said the voice of a young child in the water. "Please help me!"

Kyle pointed the searchlight towards the calls for help. He spotted a small mound of blonde hair in front of them. "There, Brendan. She's right in front of us."

"We see you," Carla yelled. "We're throwing out a life ring. Grab onto it.

Brendan turned the wheel, so the boat turned to starboard. Kyle threw the round preserver into the water. He saw the girl grab it, and he pulled her in. Carla reached over the side, pulling her on board.

"Are you alright?" Carla asked. "Are you hurt?"

"No, I don't think so. I'm just cold."

Kyle wrapped her in a large beach towel while Carla hugged the girl to keep her warm.

Brendan turned the boat towards the shore and kept going. They picked up five more survivors. They also found a young boy with a large gash on his leg. Kyle tied his belt around the boy's thigh to slow the bleeding and wrapped the wound in gauze.

"I can't take any more people on the boat," Marty said. "We're at our limit. I need to go back to shore. Brendan, call the Coast Guard to find out where we can offload these people."

Brendan tried calling with his cell phone but couldn't get through. He tried the radio patch he was on before and reached Brennan.

"You can go into Green Harbor marina," she said. "There are several ambulances there."

"Okay, thanks."

Brendan turned the boat south.

"Brendan, wait," Kyle said. "There's another body out there. It's dressed in black. It could be one of the Coast Guard assault team members."

Brendan eased the boat up close. The person was on their back, held afloat by a black life jacket.

"Oh my God," Kyle said. "It's Jay Mendes. He's unconscious and not moving."

"That's too bad, but unfortunately, we're full," Marty said. "We'll call for someone else to retrieve his body."

"Wait," Brendan said. "He said something."

"What?" Carla said. "He's alive?"

"Help me," said a faint voice. "I can't move."

"Jay, is that you?" Kyle yelled. "What do you mean?"

"I can't feel...."

"Feel what?"

"Anything."

"Oh no, he's paralyzed," Kyle said. "We can't leave him in the water. He'll die from hypothermia."

"He can't grab the life ring either," Brendan said. "How is he going to pull himself in?"

"He's not." Kyle grabbed the life ring and jumped overboard.

Kyle swam slowly through the cold water.

"Hang in there, Chief," Kyle said when he arrived. "We're gonna get you out of the water. Can you breathe?"

"Just... barely," Jay said in gasps. "It's hard... for me... to get... a breath."

Kyle wrapped one arm under Jay's waist and held onto the life ring with his other arm.

"Carla," Kyle yelled. "Pull me in. Real slow."

Carla pulled Kyle and Jay back, and two of the adults lifted Jay into the boat.

"Marty," Kyle said. "Let's go! As fast as you can go without capsizing the boat."

Chapter 30

Boston General Hospital

The sensation was strange. Jay heard the noises of the ICU before he opened his eyes. The continuous beeping from the monitors. The voices of nurses and doctors talking about his condition and recovery like he wasn't there. He felt the oxygen feeding into this throat through the automated ventilator. A constant pattern. Air in. A pause. Air out.

When he did open his eyes, he saw ceiling tiles and fluorescent lights. A dark metal frame surrounded his head. He couldn't feel much, but he could feel the pinches of the titanium screws in his scalp. The one thing he couldn't do was move. He could twitch his nose and blink his eyes. He felt a slight sensation in his fingertips and toes, but that was it. He also felt a dull pain in the back of his neck.

He lay with his eyes open for a long time before someone noticed. Then, finally, the nurses came in and checked on him but never looked at his face. They checked his pulse, listened to his heart with their stethoscopes, and injected medicine into his IV bag. But they didn't know he was awake.

At first, Jay didn't care. The pain medication kept him sleepy and dizzy. But after some time, he got annoyed. Annoyance turned to depression. Why was he even alive? Couldn't they let him go? He didn't want to live like this. But he wasn't in control anymore. He was at the mercy of the doctors.

Then he felt a tingling sensation in his hand. Like needles poking his skin. Could he recover? He felt warmth like somebody was holding his hand. He tried to squeeze, but nothing happened.

"Jay?" a soft voice said. Then her face appeared in his field of vision.

"Jay, are you there? Can you hear me?"

It was Olivia, looking beautiful and healthy. Her cheeks were red from exposure to the sun and wind. Was he dreaming? He wanted to respond but didn't know how to communicate. He tried to talk, but his lips wouldn't move. He wanted to hug her and kiss her. Tell her how much he loved her. But he couldn't.

"Jay, blink twice if you can hear me."

Jay blinked the best he could. Tears ran down his cheeks.

"Oh my God!" she screamed. "Jay, you're there. Do you understand me?"

Jay blinked twice again.

"Oh, thank God. It's a miracle!" Olivia said. "Jay, we didn't know if you were brain dead or not. I flew in last week from California. I'm not leaving. Ever again. We've been waiting for days for you to wake up. We didn't know if you would. I love you."

Jay blinked twice. More tears rolling down his cheek.

"Let me find a nurse. They want to tell you what's going

on. Hold on."

Jay watched Olivia scramble out of the room. A few minutes later, she came back with two nurses. They adjusted his bed so he could see better. It was a small, intensive care room filled with instruments and a crash cart. The nurses wiped his face with a warm face cloth and cleaned him up.

When done, a male doctor came into the room.

"Hello, Mr. Mendes," the doctor said. " My name is Doctor Sandeesh. I'm the head of neurosurgery here at Boston General. If you can hear and understand me, blink twice."

Jay blinked twice.

"Good. That's a great sign. We removed several bullet fragments from your neck and shoulders. One fragment was pressing against your spinal cord, which caused the paralysis. There's a lot of swelling from the surgery. You will continue to have a loss of feeling until the swelling goes down. But we are quite confident you will recover most of your strength and mobility. Do you understand?"

Jay blinked twice.

"You are probably wondering about the metal frame around your head. That is a skull halo and keeps your neck from moving. We will remove it later today. We'll also remove the ventilator so you will be able to speak. Understand?"

Jay blinked twice.

"Good. You have had a lot of visitors. But unfortunately, there are also reporters and law enforcement officials anxious to speak with you. You do not have to speak with anybody unless you want to. Your recovery and health are our priorities. They should be yours too. Understand?"

Jay blinked twice.

261

"You are a lucky man. I hope you appreciate your friends and family."

Jay blinked over and over again.

"Now, get some rest."

* * *

The next few days were a blur. Jay endured numerous procedures and tests. One test known as an electromyogram (EMG) reminded him of his anti-interrogation training. Technicians attached probes to his fingers and toes, then transmitted electric shocks through his nerves. He wanted to invoke his Geneva Convention rights. Luckily, the tests didn't last long, and he was allowed to leave.

Olivia stayed with him through everything. She told him she left Falmouth at six in the morning. Then stayed at the hospital until nine in the evening to avoid the traffic back to the Cape.

Jay loved how Olivia cared for him. She spoke with the nurses and relayed information to him. But, she never asked for anything in return.

Mack visited Jay as soon as he was able to speak.

"The bullet fragments from your neck matched bullets that killed the Goddard pilots. They were from a .380 handgun."

"A .380?" Jay said. "We didn't recover any guns that small in the cave. al-Mujadin carried a Makarov and an AK47. My team used standard military-issue Beretta .9 mils. A .380 is a concealed carry gun."

"We're at a dead-end without the gun. But there was something else. The bullet had traces of Matthew's DNA on it."

Jay stared at Mack. He couldn't believe his ears. If Mack was right, there was no way Jay could have murdered Matthew. And now Jay thought he knew who killed him.

"We have to go back to the cave," Jay said. "We have to find that gun."

"Jay, you're not going anywhere for a long time."

Mack also talked about the seagull drones, "The one you recovered in Falmouth matched the design of the drone found in New York. Our forensic specialists were able to rebuild ninety percent of the drone. It appears the drones were controlled by a satellite download and relayed signals to the bomb control boards."

"You mean the bomb triggers were for show?" Jay asked.

"It appears that way," Mack replied. "We also learned the shrapnel found in the liquid bomb packets were ceramic pieces made by 3D printers. The ceramic withstood the heat of the blast because of its 4,500 degrees Fahrenheit melting point. Interpol tracked the source of the ceramic powder to a company in France. They were still looking for the printer manufacturer."

"How did the bombers beat the metal detectors?"

"We're not sure, but we did learn the wiring used plastic conductors. But the circuit boards contained metal components and circuitry. So it's still a mystery how they passed through the x-ray machines without detection."

"What about my attacker?" Jay asked after the debrief. "Did he survive the explosion in Falmouth?"

"We didn't find him," Mack said. "The Coast Guard searched for his body without any success."

"Is it possible he survived? He has a knack for that type of thing."

"He could have. We did have one report of a mysterious man stealing a small motorboat after the explosion. Unfortunately, there was a lot of mayhem that night, and we can't confirm the story."

"Have you spoken with Jillian McPhee?" Jay said. "Marty's sister. She knows someone who matches the man's description."

"Why didn't you tell me that sooner?" Mack said, then paused. "Oh right. You haven't exactly been available."

"Jillian's here at the hospital. She went downstairs to the cafeteria to get a bite to eat. She'll be back in a few minutes."

"Have you had a chance to thank Kyle yet?"

"What do you mean?" Jay said.

"Kyle and his friends saved your life. He pulled you out of Vineyard Sound and transported you to Upper Cape Hospital. Kyle, Brendan, and Carla took turns performing CPR. You wouldn't be alive without those kids."

"He didn't tell me that," Jillian said as she walked into the room.

"Hi, Jillian. I'm Special Agent John McCauley. Everyone calls me Mack. I need to ask you questions about a Canadian college professor named Dwight Harris."

"I knew him a few years ago. But not well."

"What can you tell me?"

"Well, he was a professor at the Marine University in St. John's, Newfoundland. He said he knew my husband and allowed us to live in a guest house on his family's farm."

"Did you interact with him much? Did he ever say or do anything suspicious?"

"I didn't since I was in school. But Professor Harris spent a lot of time with Kyle. He was polite and well-groomed. He

264

wore wool sport coats with a bow tie."

"How did he know your husband? "

"Daniel did some joint research projects with him at the Maritime Institute. He was working on his doctoral thesis in robotics when he disappeared."

"What was the research topic?"

"Daniel was trying to mimic animals. Birds in particular. He liked seagulls since there were many to study on Cape Cod."

"Did you ever see any of the seagulls?"

"Sure. Daniel left behind several prototypes. He could never get them to work the way he wanted them to. That's how Kyle got interested in robotics. He studied the old prototypes. Actually, it was more than studying. Kyle dissected each one. He learned how the circuits worked and analyzed every moving piece. Kyle learned like a sponge, and before I knew it, he was building his own drones and robots."

"Is it possible for me to see the prototypes?"

"Of course, you can ask Kyle to show you. I'll call him."

"Jillian," Jay asked. "Tell us about your husband. Marty told me he disappeared."

"I met Daniel when I was sixteen years old. I was attending a summer program at the Marine Institute. I loved boating and spent every summer taking students out on small boats. Daniel was a graduate assistant at MIT during the summer. He was brilliant and quite cute."

"How often did you see him?" Mack asked.

"Every day for a few weeks in July. After the program, he went back to Cambridge where he had an apartment close to the MIT campus."

"When did you start dating?"

"When I was in college. I went to Emmanuel in Boston to study nursing. I hated it. Missed the water too much. We ran into each other in a bar one Friday night, and he asked me on a date. He took me out on a small boat, and we spent the day exploring Boston Harbor."

"We understand you had Kyle when you were twenty years old."

"We were dating for six months when I learned I was pregnant. I lived in a dorm on campus but spent the weekends at Dan's. My parents didn't know we were dating. My dad was an old-world type of guy and very religious. He lost his mind when he found out I was having premarital sex."

"Did you consider an abortion?" Mack asked.

"Oh no, I would never. I was thrilled to be pregnant."

"How about Daniel?"

"Daniel was supportive. He never suggested abortion, but he never appeared happy either. His parents came to visit when they learned the news."

"What did they say?"

"That I was ruining their son's life. And that I was a floozy trying to hook a rich guy by getting pregnant. That wasn't true, of course. My father was as rich as anyone I knew. I didn't care that Daniel had money. In fact, Daniel never talked about his family. I didn't even know he was from Newfoundland."

"Where in Newfoundland?" Mack asked.

"Gander. It's a tiny place."

"So, what happened next?"

"I left school and moved back to my parent's house in

Falmouth. My brother inherited it when my father died. My father instructed Marty to allow me to live here rent-free if I wanted to."

"Didn't he leave you any inheritance?"

"Yes. It's in a trust fund for Kyle. It will pay for his college tuition when he is eighteen."

"Tell us about your marriage?"

"It was casual, to say the least. Dan visited during the summer when he was working at the institute. He would play with Kyle, and we would go out on my father's boat. We got an apartment in Woods Hole when he graduated from MIT. Kyle was four. I was planning on going to NE Maritime Academy in the fall and wanted to have fun. Dan landed a job with some defense company.

"Did Dan ever mention the name of the company?"

"No, he never talked about his work. He said he couldn't tell me who they were. It was a top-secret project. He would leave for weeks at a time and then return without telling me. Then he disappeared."

"What happened?"

"He took Kyle to Woodneck Beach. It's near the house. Kyle played in the salt marsh, and Daniel worked on one of his projects. I expected them home for supper, but I went to the beach looking for them when they didn't return. I found Kyle playing with a drone in the water. There was no sign of Daniel."

"Did you call the police?"

"I didn't have to. My brother's a Falmouth police officer. They brought in the State Police, who used helicopters and dogs to search the marsh. The Coast Guard searched all of Buzzards Bay. We never found a trace."

"Has Daniel contacted you since? Any types of messages?"

"No. Nothing. I never heard Daniel's name mentioned until you asked."

"One last question," McCauley said. "Why didn't you end your marriage?"

"How could I? He's Kyle's father, and Daniel wasn't declared dead. I never gave up hope he would come back or... I would learn his fate. Not knowing what happened has always been the hardest part."

"You never met another man? I mean, one you wanted to have a relationship with?"

"No. Not until I met Jay."

Chapter 31

Veterans Rehabilitation Hospital, Charlestown Navy Yard, Boston

I t was his reckoning day. Jay's physical therapists told him he was making significant progress. He could sit up on his own and could stand using a walker. But Jay wasn't satisfied. He wanted, no, he needed to walk independently, without help from the therapist or anyone else.

Every day he watched other patients conquer the parallel bars. Now it was his turn. Twenty feet. That's how far he needed to walk without a helping hand.

Jay stared at the bars with intense determination. He always exceeded people's expectations. His own was much harder to overcome. Some people called him a perfectionist. He needed to dot every I and cross every T. It drove his Infinity Squad teammates crazy. It also kept them alive. Many people called him the perfect warrior. But Jay knew the truth—he was far from perfect. It was that drive for perfection that motivated him to perform where others failed.

The physical therapy room got hushed. Other patients stopped their own work to watch. Jay felt his hands sweat and wiped them on his sweatpants.

"You can do this, Jay," Olivia said from behind the wheelchair. "The doctor said once you walk, you can go home." She patted him on the shoulders and gave him a quick kiss to the top of his head.

Jay lifted his feet off the wheelchair footrests and placed them on the floor without any help. A simple task he needed help with two days ago. Jay leaned forward and put his hands on the parallel bars. Next, he had to do a single dip, lift his body weight with his arms, and lock his elbows. He performed thousands of dips in the Navy. They were part of his daily exercise routine. Fifty dips, fifty pull-ups, two hundred push-ups, one hundred sit-ups, a five-mile run, and a two-mile swim. Now a twenty-foot walk was stressing him out.

Jay took a deep breath and pushed himself up with all his strength. He struggled to lock his elbows and almost collapsed back into the wheelchair. But Jay locked them in place. Finally, he stood for the first time in four weeks.

Now came step two, putting weight on his legs and trusting they would hold him up. His arms shook from the strain of holding his bodyweight. Sweat poured down his forehead as he transferred his weight to his lower body. Jay relaxed his arms until his legs were holding him up. His ankles bowed, and his knees wobbled, but he remained standing.

Now he needed to take his first step. It meant putting his weight on his right leg without collapsing.

"Come on, Jay," said a familiar voice. "You can do it."

Jay looked up to see Jessie standing next to Jillian at the

end of the parallel bars.

Another voice yelled encouragement. Jay looked to see Kyle and Brendan standing at the edge of the room. Then someone started clapping. Before he knew it, the entire room was cheering for him. He couldn't let them down.

Jay lifted his left foot and moved his right hand at the same time. He remained standing, completing his first objective. He repeated the process one painful step at a time. He heard more familiar voices. The deep baritone voice of Gunny Mack. The friendly, teasing voice of his best friend, McCoy. He even heard Gia's delightful middle-eastern accent in the crowd.

"What are you guys all doing here?" Jay said. "Doesn't anybody need to work?"

He heard laughter, and it motivated him to take his next step. He ignored his burning muscles by staying focused on his task and developed a cadence, like marching in formation. Then, someone turned on a radio to the Rocky theme song. It was corny, but it worked. Jay focused on the high-energy rhythm instead of the pain and agony within his body.

He reached the end of the bars and stopped. Now the most challenging move, the dismount. Jay had to turn around one hundred and eighty degrees so he could sit down in the wheelchair. Usually, the therapist grabbed him under the arms and lowered him into the chair. Jay's arms and legs were burning more than he ever felt in the past. He was beyond exhausted and wanted to stop. He released his left hand and reached for the right bar. But his hand missed and slid down the outside of the bar, crashing down onto his armpit. His legs collapsed, leaving him hanging from the bar.

There was a gasp from the crowd. Then, the cheering

stopped, and someone shut off the radio.

The physical therapist stepped behind him to help, but Jay shooed him away.

"No, let me do this," Jay said.

"Jay, you're exhausted, and you accomplished your goal. So let me help you."

"No!" Jay said. "I got this!"

Jay pulled his legs underneath him and placed his right hand on the bar. He pushed himself up until he was standing sideways, then moved his right hand back so he was backward. His pivot was complete. He let himself drop back into the wheelchair, and the room erupted in applause. Olivia handed him a towel then gave him a huge hug.

* * *

Olivia wheeled Jay out of the therapy room and down the hall. She turned into a darkened conference room.

"Olivia, what are you doing?"

"Wait, you'll see."

Jay heard voices behind him and sensed people coming into the room but couldn't see what was going on. Then someone turned on the lights.

"Surprise!" Then a chorus of people broke into the happy birthday song.

Jay sang along and laughed at all his friends and family squeezed into the conference room.

The conference table contained boxes of pizza and a large birthday cake. First, Olivia placed a paper Burger King crown on Jay's head. Then she put an oversized plastic bib around his neck.

Despite being exhausted, Jay enjoyed seeing his friends. McCoy filled him in on the bombing investigation, and Gia gave him an update on business operations.

Jay looked to see Marty standing there with a few people behind him.

"Hey, you didn't save me any food," Marty said with a chuckle. "You didn't even save me any cake."

"Cake is the last thing you need," Jay said, patting Marty's enormous belly. "How are you doing?"

"Great. I couldn't miss my partner's birthday party. But I had to take a detour."

"What do you mean?" Jay said.

Marty moved out of the doorway. Standing there was Charlotte Cranmore holding a bouquet of roses. Her parents were standing behind her. Charlotte walked over to Jay and handed him the flowers, then bent down and hugged him.

"I never had the chance to say thank you for saving my life, Mr. Mendes."

Jay's eyes welled up with tears. He was speechless.

"Charlotte?" Kyle said from behind Jay.

Charlotte stood up and looked at Kyle. She turned to look at her mother, who nodded her approval. Charlotte turned and embraced Kyle.

"Are you visiting?" Kyle asked after the hug.

"No, I'm moving back to Cape Cod. My therapist felt it would be good for me to face my fears and stay with my friends."

"Will you go out with me?" Kyle said in a nervous stutter. "I mean, be my girlfriend?"

"Of course, silly. I love you."

Kyle kissed Charlotte, and they left the room to find

somewhere more private to get reacquainted.

Charles Cranmore approached Jay in the wheelchair. "I want to apologize for our last conversation," he said. "Please take back my check. I don't know what I would have done if I had lost Charlotte."

"I can't take it back," Jay said. "Instead, you could donate it to this hospital. They want to build a new prosthetic lab, which will help them fill it with the latest technology. I'm sure they'll consider naming rights for a donation of that size."

"That's a great idea," Cranmore said. "My accountant says the business needs to make more charitable contributions."

"Perfect. I'll introduce you to the hospital administrator, and you can work out the details."

* * *

It was almost ten when Jay finally slipped into his hospital bed. He was exhausted from the day and excited to see all of his friends and family. A nurse came in to check his vitals and give him his nightly pain medication. She was about to turn off the lights when two people appeared in the doorway.

"I'm sorry," the nurse said. "It's past visiting hours. Mister Mendes needs to rest."

"That's okay," Jay said. "It's my sister and her husband."

Jessie looked radiant in her fire-engine red blouse and stretch lycra jeans. Her hair was pulled back from her face and braided. Standing next to her, Andrew wore his desert khakis.

Jessie limped over, kissed Jay, and then sat down in the chair next to the bed.

"How are you, big brother?"

"I'm okay, Jess. I'm sorry I missed the wedding."

"Are you crazy? I'm sorry that we couldn't postpone it so you could give me away. Andrew's father tried to, but it would have cost him two hundred and fifty thousand dollars in cancellation fees. Even though he could have afforded it, they couldn't find an alternative date before Andrew deployed. So his father walked me down the aisle instead. It was beautiful."

"What are you guys doing here?"

"Andrew deploys tomorrow morning. He has an early flight out of Logan, so we're spending the night at the Four Seasons. He wanted to see you before he left. He won't be back for nine months."

"Where will you be stationed?"

"I'm heading to Fort Bragg for training," Andrew said. "After that, we'll be stationed at Bagram Air Base."

"I know it well."

"I came here to say thank you."

"For what?" Jay said.

"For saving Jessie's life," Andrew said. "She told me how you had to decide between her leg and her life after the bombing in New York. I'll be eternally grateful for your decision."

Jay struggled to hold off the tears. He was glad he made the decision too. "You stay safe, and for God's sake, come back in one piece."

"Yes, sir."

"I have some other news," Jessie said. "I have a job."

"Congratulations. Where?"

"GNN. I'll be working out of their affiliate station, WPRV-

TV, in Providence. I'll do local coverage for training and help out with any national stories. Andrew's father put in a word for me, and they were nice enough to give me a chance. Oh, and Roger got a job as my producer and cameraman."

"They're lucky to have you. You're going to be a superstar."

* * *

Two weeks later, Jay stood next to his bed, buttoning his shirt.

"Do you need help putting your shoes on?" Olivia said.

"No, I'm good. But if you want to tie my laces, I'd appreciate it. Unfortunately, I don't have enough strength to bend down without crashing into the wall."

Olivia knelt to help him out when he heard someone clear their throat from behind.

"Your discharge papers are ready, Mr. Mendes," a nurse said, standing behind a wheelchair. You can start outpatient therapy at Upper Cape Hospital tomorrow. I'll be glad to give you a ride to the front door."

"Thanks," Jay said. "But if you don't mind, I'd rather walk."

"Well, it's against hospital policy, but as long as you don't fall, I'll let you. Don't disappoint me."

"Absolutely not," Jay said as he grabbed Olivia's arm, and they left the room.

Chapter 32

Maravista

Two hours later, Olivia pulled into the driveway of his mother's house. Exhausted and in pain, Jay didn't notice the dark green sedan sitting in front of the small Cape-style bungalow.

He walked in to find his mother and Jessie sitting with a man in a dress Army uniform.

"Mom? Jessie? What's going on?"

The man in the uniform stood up and said, "Chief Mendes? I'm Captain Victor Theopolis. U.S. Army, 82nd Airborne Division."

"What are you doing here?" Jay said as he and Olivia sat down on a loveseat.

"I'm sorry to deliver this news. Unfortunately, Second Lieutenant Andrew Bessie was killed while training in Northwest Pakistan."

The news sucked the wind out of Jay's lungs. "What happened?"

"I can't say. It's confidential pending the outcome of an investigation by the Department of Defense."

"Can you tell me something? I have a top-secret clearance."

"No, I'm sorry."

"Was it friendly fire or enemy action? Or was it an accident? Can you tell me anything?"

"All I can say is that it wasn't an accident."

"Was anybody else killed?"

"Yes, sir. Six other soldiers died. Seventeen injured."

"Have you informed his family?"

"Yes, sir. My counterpart is in Providence as we speak." The Captain stood up and faced Jessie and his mom. "On behalf of the President of the United States, I'm sorry for your loss. But unfortunately, I need to visit three other families." Then he turned and left.

* * *

The next morning, Jay stared out of the window of his office in Woods Hole. It took him almost five minutes to make it up the circular stairs to his loft, but he made it. The paperwork was piled high, and he struggled to make sense of the bills and security reports staring at him. Marty hired a part-time bookkeeper who sent out the invoices and deposit payments. But he still needed to approve expenses, review payroll, and sign the checks to pay his vendors. The whole process was maddening.

Jay found it hard to focus after the news of Andrew's death. He learned his body and those of his fallen comrades were being flown back to Fort Bragg. His father arranged for his burial at Arlington National Cemetery. Jay thought about the last time he was in Washington for General Andrew's funeral. The man dedicated his life to service. He served in the first

Gulf War, Somalia, Iraq, and Afghanistan. A brilliant leader and tactician, he was the best commanding officer Jay had ever served for. He sacrificed his life in Southwest Pakistan when he came to help in the rescue mission for Matthew Goddard. In fact, if he hadn't driven his car in front of the plane where Jay and Michelle were sitting, Jay wouldn't be sitting here. Now his brother-in-law was a member of that fraternity of heroes up in heaven.

Jay stared out the window at the sun in the sky and the blue water of Martha's Vineyard Sound and longed to go for a long swim. There was a noise below—the door. Jay reached into his desk drawer and pulled out his handgun.

"Anybody home?"

Jay recognized Mack's familiar voice and relaxed, "Up here, Mack."

"I'll come up to you."

Mack squeezed his large frame up the circular stairs and dropped into the old armchair next to Jay's desk.

"You need a real office," Mack said. "This place is way too small."

"We have one. We bought the old Cape Harbor Yacht Club. It's right next to Marty's house and has plenty of room. Unfortunately, it's being renovated after the summer tourist rush is over, so I'm stuck here until it's done. I do enjoy the view from this loft, though."

"Sorry to bother you, but I received some information I thought you would want to see. Understand it is confidential, and I'll be fired if anybody finds out I took it out of the case file."

"What is it?"

"Your attacker's dossier. His name is Reginald McFarland."

279

"Oh, shit. That name sounds familiar."

"I thought you would say that. I'll let you read it, then let's discuss our next steps."

* * *

The plain manila folder contained a picture on the left side. It was a photo of McFarland in his SAS uniform. A second photo, taken more recently, showed him leaving a conference center building on the Marine Institute campus. He was wearing a black tuxedo and was accompanied by a young, dark-haired woman in a long, sequined dress. It was Olivia.

Jay's blood began to boil, but he took a few deep breaths and kept reading.

The folder contained another picture. It showed Jay and McFarland fighting on the deck of the fishing boat on the Fourth of July. Jay didn't remember the fight or the explosion that almost killed him.

He turned to the dossier:

Reginald McFarland

Known Aliases: Dwight Harris, Ph.D., Ronald Farrity, Stuart Colburn

Date of Birth: August 11, 1980

Place of Birth: Cambridge England.

Father: Herbert McFarland, a successful Scottish engineer, inventor, and college professor. Deceased. Cause of death: terrorist bombing, October 29, 1996

Mother: Julia Parsons McFarland. Born in St. John's, Newfoundland, Canada. Emigrated to England to attend

Cambridge University. Deceased. Cause of death: Terrorist bombing, October 29, 1996

Sibling: Walter McFarland, born November 7, 1989. Deceased. Cause of death: Terrorist bombing, October 29, 1996.

Military Service: Enlisted into the British Army on October 29, 2004, and joined the Royal Regiment of Scotland after basic training. Served in Iraq for two years, then joined the Special Air Services (SAS) in 2006. Reported missing in action, Mosul, Iraq, in 2016.

* * *

Jay noticed a copy of an article from the London Evening Standard on the next page. It showed a picture and obituary of McFarland's parents and younger brother. They were killed by an Irish Republican Army (IRA) bomb in London when McFarland was sixteen and away at Morton Hall, a boarding school in Edinburg, Scotland.

British Intelligence provided the next document. McFarland's alias, Dwight Harris, appeared on the roster of the Maritime Academy in Newfoundland. He was listed as an adjunct Electronics Engineering professor. However, the US State Department couldn't find any records of Harris entering or leaving the United States. The Brits found this suspicious since there was no record of attending any university to earn his master's or doctorate. They also noted his employment at a US aerospace company under the alias Donald Farrity. The company manufactures drones for the US Navy and Army.

Jay noted the gap of one year in his background when

McFarland disappeared in Mosul and reappeared working for the drone company.

The incidents in Woods Hole and Falmouth were also noted. The last document in the file was a warrant for his arrest for the July fourth incident.

Jay placed the folder on the desk and asked, "Is he alive, Mack? Could he have survived the explosion and escaped without anybody noticing?"

"Anything is possible. You survived."

"Barely. If it weren't for Kyle and his friends, I wouldn't be here."

"We didn't recover his body, so I assume he is alive. He's too dangerous to forget about. And he has a history of surviving near-death experiences."

III

Part Three

Chapter 33

J ay stopped outside the DHS conference room when he heard his name mentioned in a heated argument.

"Marty, wait," Jay said before they went through the door.

"He shouldn't be on the team," Natalie Choi said. "He isn't even a government official."

"But he's an integral part of the investigation," a male voice said. Jay recognized it as McCoy. "McFarland has hurt him more than anyone else in this room."

"That's what I'm trying to say," Choi said. "He is too tied into this case. Come on, this McFarland guy raped his girlfriend, blew his sister's leg off, and tried to kill Jay three times. It doesn't get more personal than that."

"It doesn't mean he won't be an asset to the team," McCauley said. "Natalie, you know Jay as well as anybody. Has he ever let his emotions get in the way of his job?"

"Well, he didn't follow orders on the Coast Guard cutter in Falmouth. Commander Brennan said she ordered him not to board the lobster boat."

"But he saved the lives of the Coast Guard operatives," McCoy said. "Jay acted at the appropriate time and put his own life on the line."

"Exactly," Choi said. "And he almost died. When is he going to take a risk that's going to get others killed? Like you, Mack. I can't live with the prospect of going to your funeral or CJ's or Madman's."

"Natalie," Gia Khalil said. "You're the one getting emotional. He's not going to be doing any field operations for a long time. We don't know how much strength he'll be able to regain in his arms and legs."

Jay's face turned red as he listened to his team members talk about him. Finally, he pushed the door open and walked into the conference room. Natalie stopped talking midsentence and looked down at the table. Jay glared at her as he took his seat at the front of the table.

"If you don't want me on the investigation team, please say so," Jay said. "I don't want to be a burden to anybody."

Natalie stared at him as if he walked on water. "I didn't mean for you to hear our conversation. I just…"

"I know, Natalie. I appreciate your concern."

Jay felt the tension as the room fell silent. Finally, Mack broke the stalemate, "Come on, everyone, we have a bombing to solve."

Jay and Marty took their seats at the conference room table. Gia Khalil sat next to Marty and Mack next to Karen Whitaker from the New York FBI field office. A young, blond man Jay didn't know sat in a chair up against the wall.

"Okay, let's get started," McCoy said. "There are a few new members to our team. I'll give them a chance to introduce themselves.

A brunette woman with oversized glasses and her hair pulled back in a tight bun stood up. "My name is Amanda Brigham. I'm a Deputy National Security Advisor representing the President."

A young Asian man stood up next. "My name is Andrew Lee. I'm a Terrorism Analyst with the NSA."

The third man, a rugged-looking African American man, stood up. Jay thought he recognized him from a previous special ops mission. "My name is Roger Beasley. I'm representing the CIA."

"Thank you, everybody," McCoy said, pointing to the man sitting against the wall, "I'd like to introduce one other task force member. His name is Oleg Crishenko. He's a prosecutor with the Justice Department based here in Boston."

Jay sized up the young prosecutor. His hair was unruly, and his eyes bloodshot. His suit hung off his shoulders like it was two sizes too big. He either borrowed it from his law school roommate or lost a lot of weight in a hurry.

"Oleg," Jay said. "What cases have you worked on related to terrorism?"

"This is my first."

"Terrorism case?"

"No, my first case. Period. I graduated from Harvard Law last spring."

"Really?" Jay looked at McCoy.

"Oleg interned with me at DHS," McCoy said. "He graduated first in his class at Harvard, and he turned down offers from several law firms in Boston and New York to work for the Justice Department. We're lucky to have him as part of our task force."

Jay looked at McCoy and shrugged his shoulders.

McCoy continued, "As you know, a lot has happened since we last met."

McCoy launched a slide presentation on the front screen. A picture of Reginald McFarland appeared. "Special Agent McCauley, can you update us on the bombing case?"

Mack stood up. "Thanks to the hard work of the task force, we have a suspect in the Boston and New York bombings. His name is Reginald McFarland. In addition to the bombings and the sniper attack, we have a laundry list of accusations against this guy. He's suspected of the murders of Falmouth Police officer Bill Shannon, Father Berle in Fall River, and the attempted murder of Bishop Ramirez. We also believe he kidnapped Charlotte Cranmore and Kyle McPhee and sexually assaulted Olivia Cataldo. Witnesses last saw McFarland on the evening of July fourth."

"Do you mean he survived the explosion?" Gia asked.

"We don't know. We didn't find McFarland's body, so we assume he survived. This guy is slippery and seems to have nine lives. The FBI has moved him to the top of our most-wanted list. I won't declare him dead until I see him on the coroner's table. Consider him armed and dangerous."

"The Justice Department is convening a grand jury," Crishenko said. "I'm writing up the indictments."

"We have a new person of interest," Mack said. "His name is Daniel McPhee. He may be an accomplice of McFarland's." A junior FBI staffer handed out information sheets to the task force members.

"He may be a victim of kidnapping," Jay said. "He disappeared twelve years ago without a trace. He knew McFarland before the disappearance."

"How are they connected?" FBI agent Wilkinson asked.

"They met working at a defense contractor. McFarland was an instructor and mentor to McPhee. They're both electrical engineers with interests in robotics and drones."

"I'll need a FISA warrant to investigate McPhee's internet activity," said Lee from the NSA.

"I'll get that for you this morning," Crishenko said.

"We still have the drone catcher from Falmouth in custody," Mack said. "He's provided little information, and we don't have much to hold him on. If we don't have an indictment within 48 hours, we'll have to let him go."

"He did identify the fishing boat in Barnstable Harbor," Jay said. "Isn't that enough evidence to implicate him in the explosion?"

"It's a tough one to prove," Crishenko said. "He could have been a witness or a business associate."

"Any idea where the fishing boat originated from?" Gia asked.

"No, we haven't been able to find any registration information," Mack replied.

"I'd like permission to question him," Gia said. "I'm experienced in coercing information out of suspects."

"You're a private citizen," Brigham from the White House said. "You can't use any enhanced interrogation techniques,"

"Oh, believe me, I won't need to torture him to get him to talk."

"I didn't say torture."

"But that's what you meant," Gia said.

"I'll give you thirty minutes with him," Mack said.

"Thanks, that will be more than enough."

Chapter 34

One week later - Chance Cove, Newfoundland

C hance Cove was a sleepy village of three hundred people. Located on the Osprey Trail, the quiet town sat one hundred twenty-five kilometers west of St. John's. Small single-story white homes dotted the wooded shoreline. It was tranquil, with a few seagulls sitting on rooftops looking for scraps of fish and a lone osprey hunting for a morning meal.

CJ and Madman peered through slots in their hunting blind, hidden in a stand of thick balsams. Madman peered through his spotting scope at the cluster of buildings below.

"Chief, we have a blue-hulled lobster boat pulling up to the dock," Madman said in his headset.

"Got it," Jay said from the operations center at Maravista headquarters. "How many boats are there now?"

"That makes three."

"We need some close-up images. Is Gia in place?"

"I'm here, Chief," she said on the radio. "I'm approaching the village now."

Gia rode her trail bike up to the gated entrance of the

small fishing company. *Chance Cove Fisheries* painted in black letters on the side of a white storage building. A rusted fence surrounded the compound, but Gia didn't see a lock on the gate.

She removed her camera from its storage bag and took several photos of the compound. Two '80s era Plymouth sedans sat inside the gate. Otherwise, there was no activity.

"Looks quiet from here," Gia said. "I'll have to come back tonight to get a better look around."

"You have company," CJ said from his perch on the hillside above the village. "Looks like a police squad car heading south on Route 16."

"Roger," Gia said as she messed her hair up. She then unzipped her lycra cycling shirt to reveal an ample view of her cleavage. She leaned against the gate bent over at the waist.

The squad car stopped, and a young police officer stepped out of the driver's side.

"Can I help you, miss?" the officer said. "It looks like you're in a bit of distress, eh?"

"I'm... catching my breath," Gia said. "The ride was a bit tougher than I thought."

CJ smiled as he watched the police officer assessing Gia. He didn't hide his attempt to check out her tanned, muscular legs.

"Do you have a bottle of water?" Gia asked as she stood up and faced the officer. Sweat dripped down her neck and chest as she leaned against the gate to the fishing company. She stood at least four inches taller than the young police officer.

"Ah, sure, ma'am. Let me grab one out of the squad car."

He came back and handed her the bottle, which she drank in one swallow.

"Thanks so much," Gia said. "I appreciate your help. I'm writing a travel story about hidden gems in Maritime Canada. I thought this village was intriguing."

"I guess so," the officer said. "It's a pretty quiet place."

"Do you mind posing for a picture? It will go with my article."

"Sure, what's the name of the magazine?"

"North Atlantic Travel. You can find it at Barnes and Nobles or buy it online at Amazon."

"Barnes and Nobles, eh? There's one over in St. John's. I go there every Sunday with my folks when we go to church."

"Can you tell me about this company?"

"Sure, they were a local family-owned business up until two years ago. Operated by the Williams for three generations."

"Why did they sell?"

"I'm not sure. An overseas conglomerate bought them up. Paid them a real nice amount for the buildings and the boats."

"What kind of fish do they catch?"

"Well, that's what's interesting. The company never sells any fish. The boats come in and out, and there are a bunch of people working here. But they never talk to any of the locals."

"Where do the workers live? Here in the village?"

"No, ma'am. They stay in the buildings in the compound."

"How do you know so much about them? Do you ever go in and talk with them?"

"People in the village talk. But nobody ever goes inside the compound. We're not invited. The neighbors keep an eye on the place, and I hear them talking at the general store and in

Mabel's Coffee Shop."

"Is there anything else interesting in this town?" Gia asked.

"Well, that's the thing, ma'am. We don't get too many tourists here because this is the end of the road. In fact, you'll have to turn around and go back south if you want to continue on the scenic highway. Folks make that mistake all the time."

"Well, thank you, officer. Oh, what's your name. You know, for the article."

"Oh yeah. I'm Sheriff Pete Jones."

"You're the head of the local police force?" Gia said. "That's impressive."

"I am the police force. We haven't had a serious crime here in ten years. Some kids broke into a house last week, and once in a while, we have a car accident. Otherwise, it's pretty quiet. If anything serious happens, we call the Mounties."

Gia waved as the officer drove away.

"We go in tonight," Jay said over the radio. "Gia put Kyle's bots in a safe spot and rendezvous with the rest of the team. CJ, did you see anybody get off the fishing boat?"

"Negative," CJ said. "But I can only see half the boat. The warehouse roof obscures my view."

"See if you can find a better vantage point. Get going now, so you're in place when the tactical team goes in tonight."

"Roger," CJ said.

"What time is the team going in?" Madman asked.

"At 02:00," Jay replied. "We're waiting for the RCMP team to arrive from Gander. Can we get a drone scan every thirty minutes starting at midnight? That will tell us if anything has changed."

"Wouldn't it be easier if the RCMP provided a Reaper

drone?" Gia said. "They can stay aloft for hours."

"The RCMP team is bringing a small one. But until they get here, Kyle's bots will work great."

"As long as you keep them charged between flights," Kyle said.

* * *

At midnight, Jay watched the feed from the drone on their VR headsets. Kyle made a visual pass with night vision. The images showed the compound was quiet, and two fishing boats sat at the dock.

"Hey, CJ," Jay said. "There are only two fishing boats now. So what happened to the third?"

"I don't know. There were three when we changed positions. One must have left during our transition. We've been watching non-stop since we settled into our new hide."

"Kyle, let's do a pass with infrared."

"Okay," Kyle said, smiling. Jay could tell he enjoyed being part of the team.

The new sensors Kyle installed penetrated the wood sidings of the buildings. Jay watched the infrared images. He expected to see several heat signatures from the workers inside the houses. But the sensors showed little activity.

"I see a single light-red signature. It's not moving and on the floor of one of the buildings.

"Look for a way to get inside."

The drones flew low around the building. Bars covered the windows and secured the doors.

"No entry points visible," Kyle said. "There is a ventilation shaft I can try to squeeze the main bot through."

"We don't have a choice," Jay said." If somebody's injured, we need to know."

"I'll return this set of bots to Gia. Then send a single bot to go down the vent pipe. It's going to be tricky."

"Do you have another alternative?"

"I have one. There's a new feature, but It's not tested yet."

"What is it?"

"It's a sonic wave blaster. It emits an ultra-high frequency sound wave to break the glass. It's not subtle, but we'll be able to get in the building."

"Try it. We don't have time to mess around."

"Okay. Remove your headset, or you'll lose your hearing."

"Are you serious?"

"Yes, sir."

Kyle flew his microbots up against a pane-glass window on the front of the main building. He maneuvered them within inches of the window.

"Okay, here goes," Kyle said. "Main bot, screech."

At first, Jay didn't hear anything, then a piercing, high-pitched noise came out from the main bot. The sound was maddening even without the headsets on. The windows fractured, but they didn't break.

"Screech stop," Kyle commanded. "Sorry, Jay, it didn't work. The glass appears to be too thick."

"That's okay. The RCMP team is coming up the road. Pull the bots out."

"Roger."

* * *

Four armored tactical trucks drove through the tiny village at breakneck speeds. They didn't slow down for intersections or use sirens. Instead, the lead track blasted through the gate, stopping in front of the main building. Tactical officers streamed out of the back of each truck. They split off into teams of two and lined up outside the doors of each building.

"We're in place," Mack said. "Commander, Fry, we're ready when you are."

The RCMP special operations commander surveyed his team, "Okay, go, go, go."

Agents smashed the doors with battering rams. Then the teams streamed through the doors. Jay saw the flashlights shining through the windows. He watched for movement outside the buildings but didn't see anything.

"Chief, I have movement on one of the fishing boats, CJ said. "A single person. It looks like he has a shotgun. He's leaving the boat."

"Commander Fry, we have a lone gunman approaching your location with a shotgun."

"I will send one of my men out to investigate."

"CJ, do you have a shot?"

"Yes. It's a long one. About twelve hundred yards, but I have one."

"Prepare to fire on my command."

"Roger."

Jay watched the RCMP agent leave the house closest to the dock. Finally, he ducked out of the door. He stopped, surveyed the yard then ran to take up a position behind a parked car.

The gunman saw him running and opened fire with both barrels. The first shot blasted the windshield out of the car. The second one knocked the agent to the ground as he dove for cover.

"Officer down," Jay said. "Repeat. Gun fired, officer down." Jay saw four officers rush out the front door right into the shooter's fire zone.

"CJ Fire! I repeat. Fire!" Jay said into the microphone.

CJ focused on the gunman's head. Then, when the shooter stopped reloading, CJ squeezed the trigger.

The bullet smashed through the gunman's skull.

"Target down," Madman said. "Nice shot."

"Thanks," CJ said as he reloaded.

"Target neutralized, Commander Fry. But your man is down."

"All clear inside the houses," Mack said through the radio. "We have a situation."

"What's that," Jay said.

"We found the employees. But, unfortunately, they're all dead."

"Not from gunshots," Kyle said. "We would have heard them."

"No. The victim's throats were slit. Fresh wounds. McFarland must have killed them within the last few hours."

"Damn, he escaped. Keep searching the compound in case he's hiding. I'll call the Canadian and U.S. Coast Guards and tell them to be on the lookout for that fishing boat."

"Roger that one," Mack said. "Gia, where are you?"

"I'm in the big storage buildings with an FBI team. The building is empty. But something isn't right. It's too clean."

"Look for hidden rooms."

"We will."

* * *

Gia searched each building and house. She came up empty. She was sure the 3-D printers were going to be here. Her prisoner in Boston gave her all the information he knew. She was sure of that since nobody could resist her interrogation techniques. The location was accurate, but somebody knew they were coming. Who tipped them off? It couldn't be an RCMP officer. The only one who knew the target of the assault was Commander Fry. He was with Mack the whole time. Then it occurred to her, the police officer. Perhaps he was on the payroll of the fishery owner.

"Mack," Gia said. "Can you have one of the RCMP officers place a visit to the town's sheriff?"

"We got him," Mack said. "He was the gunman who came off the boat. The one CJ shot."

"Damn, he tipped them off after he talked with me. He must have been suspicious."

The planks on the floor of the storage building were rough two by six planks. Gia walked every inch of the building studying the floor and walls. The floors were free of debris and dust. Then she looked up. Gia saw a chain fall hanging from a beam towards the rear of the building. She pointed her flashlight at the piece of equipment and noticed recent use wore off the paint on the tip. Then Gia saw plywood between the rafters near the ceiling.

"Mack, ask the RCMP agents to bring a ladder into the storage building. A tall one capable of reaching three stories high."

Gia waited a few minutes until the agents arrived. Mack followed.

"Look up there. I almost missed it."

The agents placed the ladder against the side of the

plywood enclosure. Then one of the officers climbed the ladder. He banged against the plywood, then called down," It's loose."

He banged against the plywood again, and a sheet fell in. He pulled out his flashlight and shined it inside.

"We got it!" the officer said.

Gia climbed the ladder and pulled herself into the makeshift storage room. Inside the room stood five plastic storage barrels. The barrels had red warning stickers with the words *DANGER EXPLOSIVES*. Behind the barrels sat five desktop 3D printers and several bags of ceramic powder. Three partially made bomb vests were spread out on six-foot-long folding tables. Another table held wires and electronic components.

'Everybody out," Mack yelled from the floor. "Send the bomb squad in to inspect the whole complex and remove the explosives before anybody gets blown up."

Gia and Mack walked outside and went behind one of the assault vehicles. "Great job Gia," Mack said. "How did you know that compartment was there?"

"I don't know. Female intuition?"

Chapter 35

Zurich, Switzerland

The narrow, winding streets of Altstadt (Old Town) Zurich were unnerving at night. Residents consider the Renaissance-era district charming. Jay thought the neighborhood was creepy, with many shadowy alleyways and doorways for attackers to hide in. But Antonio promised Jay a night out on the town, and Jay had to go along.

He walked into the Aelpli, a small bar known for its lively music and alcohol-laced alpine milk. A large mural of a Swiss mountainscape adorned the back wall of the cramped room. Cigarette smoke mixed with loud accordion music created a raucous but friendly atmosphere. Jay spotted Antonio, dressed in an expensive Italian suit sitting with a slim, young, attractive woman. She had short blond hair and wore trendy, oversized Italian eyewear, a semi-sheer black blouse, and tight-fitting jeans. Antonio laughed as she attempted to down a shot of the potent Aelpli milk.

"Would you like a drink?" A waitress dressed as a traditional Swiss maiden asked in English. He wondered how she knew he was American, then realized he was still wearing his Boston Red Sox hat.

"Pellegrino, please," Jay said, pointing to the corner booth. "Could you deliver it to that table?"

Antonio Borracci was a fascinating intelligence officer. Most spies keep a low profile so they can blend in while practicing their spycraft. Antonio was known as Switzerland's best downhill skier and snowboarder. He was the first Swiss athlete to win gold in both downhill sports. Antonio had multiple sponsorship deals from Ferrari, O'Reilly Snowboards, and Luxottica Eyewear and even hosted his own sports podcast. Antonio had a habit of both coaching and dating upcoming female skiers and snowboarders. And thanks to three high-profile divorces, he managed to keep himself in the tabloids.

But Jay knew Antonio had a darker side. They met in Iraq during Operation Enduring Freedom. Antonio helped rescue a young family kidnapped by Al Qaeda fighters. Then led a mission to track down the roadside bomber who almost killed General Andrews. The police never found the bomber. Antonio was also a master of disguises who loved to mingle with the rich and famous. And he put his skills to good use by trolling the seedy financial world that funded terrorism. Most important, he knew how to have a good time.

Jay squeezed through the crowded bar and slid into the booth next to Antonio without saying a word. Antonio was so engaged in conversation. He didn't notice Jay sit down. The woman smiled as she listened.

"I was climbing Hillary's steppe on the south face of Everest when the storm blew in. I held on to my rope for three hours as Sherpas attempted to rescue me."

"You're so full of shit," Jay said. "You've never been close to

Everest."

Antonio turned to see Jay sitting next to him. "When did you arrive?"

"Long enough to hear three of your bullshit stories," Jay said with a smile. "How are you, Antonio?"

Antonio laughed. "It's great to see you. You look great, considering what you've been through."

The woman stared at Jay. "Are you going to introduce me to your handsome friend?"

"Of course," Antonio said. "I'm so rude. I'm pleased to introduce Jay Mendes. His friends and most of his enemies call him Chief. Jay, this beautiful and brilliant woman is Silvie Bruehner."

"Nice to meet you," Jay said as he extended his hand to Silvie.

"No, the pleasure is mine," Silvie said as she accepted his handshake.

Jay's eyes locked with Silvie's for the first time. Her cobalt blue eyes were stunning. She stared back for several moments, then broke her gaze.

"How was your trip to Zurich?" Antonio said. "I hope your plane didn't incur a lot of turbulence. I'm surprised you traveled so soon after your surgery?"

"Surgery?" Silvie said. "I hope it wasn't serious?"

"No," Jay said. "It was a minor procedure."

Antonio choked on a glass of Aelpli milk.

"You know," Silvie said. "Your face does look familiar. I saw you on GNN. Didn't you shoot a priest in Boston?"

Now it was Jay's turn to choke on his drink.

"A case of mistaken identity," Antonio said. "Let's take a walk. My friend and I need some fresh air."

"All right," Silvie said. "I'll meet you outside. I need to freshen up."

Jay and Antonio worked their way out of the bar and out the front door onto Ankengasse Strasse. Antonio lit up a cigarette and offered one to Jay.

"Antonio, you know I don't smoke. When did you start?"

"I only smoke when I'm out drinking with beautiful women."

"So that's every day?"

Antonio laughed. "Not anymore. I'm a happily married man. Soon, I'm going to be a father."

"Congratulations," Jay said. "That's great news."

Jay spotted Silvie step out of the Aelpli and look around. He waved at Silvie, and she joined them. She wore a stylish black leather coat and carried a small Prada purse.

"Come, let's go down by the river," Silvie said. "The view of the city at night is spectacular."

They walked down the narrow street and crossed onto a wide promenade next to the Linmat river. Across the river, the buildings of downtown Zurich reflected off the calm water.

Silvie grabbed Jay's right arm and Antonio's left arm and proceeded to walk towards Lake Zurich.

"You never answered my question, Mr. Mendes," Silvie said. "What brings you to Zurich?"

"I'm looking for information. The sensitive kind."

"I see. What type of information?"

Jay hesitated. Antonio insisted he could trust Silvie. But asking the question can get him arrested in Zurich.

"I need to know the owner of a Swiss bank account."

"You know that information is secret," Silvie said. "We have a national privacy law that protects bank account owners."

"I understand. But the account owner might be linked to the Papal bombings in New York and Boston."

"Any chance they were involved with the bombing in St. Peter's square?"

"There could be, but we haven't been able to connect them yet."

"I may be able to help you. But not tonight. I need to make a few phone calls. Where are you staying?"

"I'm at the Swissôtel on Schulstrasse."

"I'll pick you up tomorrow morning at six. Wear active gear. I'm going to show you how the Swiss workout. My car is parked on the next block."

They stopped at a dark blue Audi SUV with a government license plate. Silvie gave both Jay and Antonio a quick kiss on the cheek then got in the car.

As she drove away, Jay and Antonio continued walking towards the lake.

"What did you say Silvie does for work?"

"She's a criminal investigator for the Swiss Federal Police."

"And I asked her to break Swiss privacy laws?"

"Silvie doesn't work for the Finance Ministry. She's in the major crimes division."

"So why would she break the law to help me?"

"You'll find out. She has her reasons."

* * *

Silvie pulled up in front of the hotel at six o'clock sharp. Jay threw his duffle bag into the back seat of the SUV then climbed into the passenger side.

"Good morning," Silvie said. "I brought some hot coffee and croissants."

Jay smiled as he sipped from the strong coffee. The croissant was filled with melted Swiss chocolate.

"Man, this is delicious," Jay said. "It melts in your mouth."

"My mother bakes them fresh every morning. I stopped by my parent's house to pick them up."

"Where do they live?"

"Not far from here. My father's a surgeon at the University Hospital. I have my own flat a few blocks away."

"I'm curious," Jay said. "Why are you helping me?"

"I have my reasons."

"That's what Antonio said. Would you like to share?"

Silvie hesitated. Jay thought he noticed tears welling up in her eyes. "I will. Soon enough. Let's get to our destination before the traffic gets too heavy."

Silvie sped down the I-14 motorway at close to one hundred miles per hour. They passed by beautiful Lake Lucerne and climbed into the Alps. When they reached Interlaken, they turned up into the mountains. After going through several fear-inducing switchbacks, Silvie pulled into a gravel parking lot. They sat at the base of the famous Swiss mountain known as the Eiger.

Jay cringed as he looked up at the thirteen-thousand-foot-high mountain.

"We aren't going straight up, are we?"

"No, that's the north wall. It's known around here as the Mordwand. In English, you would say the murderous wall. It's for serious climbers. Over the years, sixty-four climbers died up there."

"Are you a serious climber?"

"No. I've attempted the climb once. I made it halfway up before the weather turned. We had to come back down. Come on. We're going to a spot where we'll get a better view."

She handed Jay a backpack and a pair of walking sticks. "The bags contain snacks and extra clothes. Okay, let's go."

They jogged up a winding path through the alpine meadows and up into the mountains. Several times they stopped to let other runners pass.

"Do they always run up this mountain?" Jay asked at one of their breaks.

"They're training for the Eiger Ultra Trail. It's a 101-kilometer cross-country race that crosses over the top of the mountain."

"Do you run that race?"

"No, I don't have time to train for that. I did compete in the Panorama and Couples trail events. It's quite fun."

Jay pressed through the pain and exhaustion to keep up with Silvie. He wasn't going to let her see him struggle.

Silvie stopped when they reached a large meadow with beautiful alpine ponds. She pulled a blanket from her backpack and placed it on the grass. The view of the surrounding mountains was breathtaking.

"This is a good place for us to talk," Silvie said as she handed Jay an energy bar.

"What do you mean?"

"There's no cell phone service in this spot, and I'm sure we weren't followed."

"Why all the cloak and dagger stuff?"

"I want to make sure we can speak without fear of my employer monitoring our conversation. The Swiss government is very serious about protecting its secrecy laws. They'll go to extreme lengths to ensure their client's identities remain secret."

"Why are you concerned?"

"It's why you are here, right? You told me you need the name of the account holder. I want to help you. Let's say we have a mutual interest."

"What do you mean?"

Silvie didn't respond right away. She gazed out at the mountains in silence for several moments.

"This is the spot where I met Hermann Koenigg," Silvie said. "We were on a social trip. I didn't want to go, but one of my co-workers insisted. He was a handsome man. Very athletic. He was a competitive triathlete and soldier."

"Where did he serve?"

"Swiss Army in special operations. He was a member of the Swiss Guard. One of the Pope's personal bodyguards."

"Impressive. I've heard the Guard's training is second to none."

"Yes. Hermann was very proud of his accomplishments. Only one hundred Swiss soldiers are selected for the honor."

"Silvie, you said he was a Swiss Guard."

"He was killed at the Vatican by one of the suicide bombers. He was standing right next to the man dressed as a monk. Over thirty Guards lost their lives that day."

"Were you there? In St. Peter's square?"

"Yes. Hermann invited me and my sister, Abbie. We were far away from the Pope at the entrance of the square. But we saw the bombs explode—five at once. The sight was horrific. We were almost trampled to death by the panic. Abbie pulled me to safety. She saved my life."

"That's terrible. I'm so sorry for your loss. Abbie must be

a special girl."

"She has Downs Syndrome. Many people are mean to her because of her disabilities. They assume she is stupid because she speaks and looks different. But she is exceptional. I'm blessed to have her in my life."

"So that's why you're willing to help me? You know, to identify the secret account?"

"Yes, that is one reason. But I'm also very frustrated with the Secrecy laws. They forbid law enforcement from accessing the names unless we can first prove a crime.

"How hard is that to prove?"

"Very hard. We have to know who the account owner is first before they will issue the search warrant. We can't search the accounts. In fact, we don't have access to the accounts."

"What do you mean? There isn't a central database?"

"No. Each bank has its own list, and they protect it like it's the Holy Grail."

"So how can you help me? We don't know the name of the account owner. That's what we're trying to find out."

"I know. But there is someone who can help who has a list of accounts. Based on the account number, it should be on the list."

"Great, how can I contact him?"

Silvie reached into her backpack and pulled out a business card. "Call the number on the card. I heard they would help. Be prepared to pay cash. Be careful. It may be a trap by Swiss counterintelligence."

"What will happen if the Swiss government finds out you helped me?"

"You'll never see me again. You need to find out who's

responsible for the bombings. You must find Hermann's killer."

Chapter 36

The Swiss Alps

Fear filled his gut as Jay held on for dear life. He told Antonio he wanted to take a commercial flight to Ascona. But of course, Antonio insisted on driving his Ferrari Monza SP2.

The sleek sports car barreled through the winding roads of the Swiss Alps at unheard-of speeds. Jay tried to converse with Antonio, but the g-forces and wind in the open cockpit made it too loud to speak. So he held on for dear life and enjoyed the view.

Antonio ran up the rear of a tractor-trailer. Without hesitation, he downshifted and passed the truck without slowing down. Jay closed his eyes as a second truck barreling down the hill in the other lane blared its air horn. Antonio cut the wheel as they slipped between the two trucks with inches to spare.

Three hair-raising hours later, they arrived at the picturesque lakeside village. Jay peeled himself out of the passenger seat, wanting to kiss the ground.

"Wasn't that fantastic?" Antonio said as he pulled a leather briefcase out of the car's tiny trunk. "This is the best handling Ferrari ever built."

"If you say so," Jay said. "Do they serve wine at lunch?"

"Of course they do."

"Oh, thank goodness."

Jay devoured a plate of spaghetti and meatballs. He washed it down with a delicious bottle of Dolcetto, a full-body Italian red wine. The tranquil water of Lake Maggiore, a popular summer destination for Milan's wealthy residents, sparkled in the afternoon sun. The mountain air was crisp and refreshing despite the warm temperature.

"When did this person say he was going to meet us?" Antonio asked. "We've been here an hour and a half."

"He didn't say."

Antonio spied Jay's empty glass, "Should I order another bottle of wine?"

"Not for me. I want to stay alert."

Another thirty minutes passed when a young boy stopped at the table and handed an envelope to Jay. Inside, a note read, *follow the boy. Come alone.*

Jay stood up and followed the boy without saying a word to Antonio. He weaved through the narrow streets of the village until the boy stopped in an alleyway. Then, without warning, someone placed a bag over Jay's head. A robust set of arms wrapped around his torso, tying his hands behind his back. A second person grabbed his legs, and they threw him into the trunk of a car.

By the sound of the engine, Jay knew they were climbing into the mountains. The endless twisting and turning threw him around the trunk. He swore Antonio was behind the wheel. Then the car slammed to a stop. The trunk opened, and the two people carried Jay onto a boat. The boat left the dock and traveled for several minutes. Then the engine stopped, and someone pulled the hood off his head.

Jay was on a wooden motorboat in the middle of a small cove surrounded by tall mountains. The shoreline was barren.

Next to Jay sat a large, dark-haired woman dressed in a black t-shirt and pants. Her long hair was pulled back from her face by a black leather barrette. Tattoos covered her arms down to her fingers, and a black stud earring pierced her nose. She pointed a Beretta handgun in his face.

"My friend has agreed to provide the information you need for one hundred thousand Euros. Did you bring the money?"

"Yes," Jay said. "It's in my backpack. You have to take it off my back."

The woman pushed him forward. Then, realizing she had to untie his arms, she pulled a fish-scaling knife off her dashboard and slit the ties. Jay let the bag slide off his back. He wasn't going to screw around with this woman.

She opened it and peered inside. "Good," she said. Then she handed Jay a piece of paper with a name on it. The account name *TyreBT06* didn't make any sense to him, but he memorized it.

"The paper disintegrates in water."

The woman grabbed Jay by his collar with one hand and pulled him out of his seat. Then, before he had a chance to react, she grabbed the waistband of his pants, lifted him over her head, and threw him overboard.

By the time Jay surfaced, the boat was gone.

* * *

"Did you see that?" Kyle said as he watched the drone feed. He sat at his computer console at Maravista headquarters. "She picked him up and threw him at least twenty feet. She must be on the WWWF tour."

"I don't think so," Gia said in the headphones. "But she is a nasty one."

"How long until we pick him up?" McCoy said. "The sun's going down, and he'll suffer hypothermia from the cold water."

"Michelle's inbound from Aviano airbase as we speak," Gia said. "Ten minutes at the most."

"Alright, keep an eye on him. Were you able to see the account name on the paper she handed him?"

"Negative," Kyle said. "The print was too small."

"Any luck tracking the GPS in the backpack?" McCoy said.

"Negative again," Kyle said. "She pulled the money out and threw the backpack in the lake right after she tossed Jay."

"That's okay. We shouldn't know who the informant is."

"It won't help the prosecution's case," Oleg, the Justice Department attorney, said. "But if we can crack the account code name, we may not need him."

"Hey guys," Kyle said. "Michelle is approaching the lake."

"Is Jay still in the water?"

"Yes, he's about one hundred yards from the shoreline."

* * *

Michelle flew Jay back to Antonio's house in Interlaken. Antonio was displeased. He had to drive back through the Alps by himself. When he returned, Antonio found Jay lounging in the hot tub on his second-floor deck.

"The FBI, with the help of the DHS and Vatican, convinced the Swiss to give them access to the bank account record," Jay told Antonio. "It's a blind trust. They're tracking down the trustees as we speak."

"Any chance they can trace the source of the informant back to Silvie?" Antonio said. "She put her life and career on the line for us."

"So far, so good. The Swiss authorities asked, but the FBI said it was a confidential informant."

"That's good. Did you know your team was monitoring your every move?" Antonio said. "They had me fooled."

"Of course I did. Gia wouldn't let me travel here otherwise. It's only been three months since my surgery. They didn't want me to go on the trip, but I insisted. I needed Gia to run the operation in the U.S. I knew you wouldn't trust anyone else with this type of request."

"Did you hear anything about the owner of that account yet?"

"No, not yet, but there is something I want to discuss with you."

"What's on your mind?"

"You're aware the Papal bombings devastated the Swiss Guard. They lost seventy percent of their Vatican security force. So Bishop Ramirez, our liaison with the Vatican, asked me for a proposal. They want us to provide security for twelve months and help them train a class of recruits. They're also concerned about the safety of the Italian Cardinals and Bishops."

"That's a good thing for you," Antonio said. "Your business is growing."

"You're right. It is good. But I need to expand my

management team. I can't run a European operation from the states. I need someone I can trust."

"What are you saying? You know I am quite busy with coaching and my sponsorship appearances."

"I'm asking you to head up my European operation for at least the next year. I'll pay you well and give you equity in the business. It will be a partnership. We'll work together to hire and staff the operation. And you can do it from this home right here. What do you think?"

"How am I going to recruit operatives? I'm not connected like I used to be?"

"I have a resource in the middle east. His name's Steve Bonner. He's compiling a list of candidates. I'm going to Bahrain tomorrow to begin the interviews. I'd like you to go with me."

"You are very convincing as a businessman. But I'm not sure I'm ready for a new job. Being a new father brings a lot of responsibility. And besides, this type of job could be dangerous."

"You won't have to do fieldwork. Instead, I need you to hire and train a security and hostage rescue team. Do you think you can do that for me?"

"I would be honored, my friend."

Antonio and Jay shook hands. "When do we start?" Antonio said.

Antonio's wife, Francesca, poked her head out of the patio door. "Antonio, you have a call from a Special Agent McCauley. He is asking for Jay. Is everything okay?"

"Yes, dear," Antonio said, laughing as he climbed out of the tub. "Nothing to worry about."

Antonio grabbed a towel, "Your timing is impeccable."

Antonio led Jay to the top floor of the chalet. He punched a code into a keypad, placed his thumb on a fingerprint scanner, and opened the door to a command center. He turned on the computer console and pulled up a chair for Jay to sit next to him. Mack was on one screen. McCoy was on the second, and Gia was on the third.

"Hey, Antonio. Hi Jay," McCoy said. "Sorry for the interruption. Did you guys have your talk?"

"Yes," Jay said. "We're all set."

"Great, I'll add Antonio to the temporary security list until we process the paperwork. We have a development. Mack is going to update you.

"Our forensics team confirmed the bullet fragments removed from your shoulder are consistent with the other .380 caliber bullets. The federal prosecutor needs the gun to build the case against al-Mujadin."

"It's not al-Mujadin," Jay said. "It must be Kathleen. She's the only one in that cave who may have been carrying a .380."

"It's a nice theory, Jay," Mack said. "But how are you going to prove it? We never recovered a handgun in the cave. Our forensic and intelligence teams scoured the whole underground complex."

"I don't know. It's a hunch. Somehow we need to find physical evidence linking Kathleen to Matthew's murder."

"Be careful. You're trying to fit the crime to a suspect. It's the other way around. You find a suspect based on the evidence. Without a gun, we don't have a connection."

"Don't you have enough evidence to question her?" Antonio said. "Perhaps she'll confess or at least slip up under questioning."

"We could," Mack said. "But there's only one problem. We

don't know where she is. She hasn't filed a news report in weeks. She's vanished."

"How about McFarland?" Jay said. "Any sign of him? I'm hoping a fisherman catches a shark, and we find his remains in its stomach."

"That's morbid," Gia said. "Think of the poor shark swallowing that evil bastard. I am sure it had terrible heartburn."

"Alright, guys," Mack said, laughing. "Jay, what's your next step with Antonio?"

"We're going to Bahrain tomorrow to meet with a recruiter and shop for equipment and supplies. We need to stock up."

"Make sure you watch your budget," McCoy said. "We know what kind of taste Antonio has. We don't need armored Ferraris. Land Rovers or Suburbans will do."

Chapter 37

Northwest Pakistan

"Michelle, what's your twenty?" Jay said.

"We're 100 kilometers out. We'll be over the cave in thirty minutes. We're using a new military-grade Trifan for this mission."

"How is it different from your other plane?"

"It's similar to the commercial model, but it's armored and has a capacity of sixteen passengers."

"What about armament?"

"It's equipped with an air-to-air defense including a missile avoidance system. For firepower, it has a mini-gun with a 300-degree fire zone for air-to-ground suppression. It also has a pod of hellfire anti-tank missiles."

"Thanks for the report, Michelle," Jay said. "Stay safe. Is Gia on the line?"

"I am here."

"Are you all set?"

"Yes, Karen Whitaker and three FBI investigators are here to help me find the gun and any other evidence."

"I thought an Army intelligence team scoured the cave

318

before?"

"They did, but the gun is still there. The team didn't find anything."

"Did we clear the mission with the State Department and the Pakistanis?"

"Yes, we are legal until a firefight breaks out. Then all bets are off."

"Are you expecting trouble?"

"You never know. That rogue Taliban tribe linked to al-Mujadin is still out there."

"They shouldn't be a problem," Jay said.

"I do not know about that," Michelle replied.

"What do you mean?"

"I heard from a friend in NATO intelligence that it was Andrew Bessie's unit that was searching the cave."

"He told me he was training to be a medic."

"That was his cover story," Michelle said. "The Taliban tortured and killed him."

Jay didn't answer as he processed that information.

* * *

Gia led the FBI investigators into the underground complex. Michelle landed two hundred yards downhill from the cave entrance. At the same time, CJ and Madman went into the mountains to set up a sniper position with a good view of the valley.

"Everyone stay close behind me," Gia said. "Don't wander. There are many branches in the cave, and it's easy to get lost."

Gia led the team through the maze. The air was cold and dry. At the bottom of a long descent, Gia stopped. She waited for the rest of the team to catch up.

"We're outside of the large chamber. Let's search the whole cave. Concentrate along the back wall where the hostages were."

One investigator waved a metal detector back and forth over the cave floor. A second investigator scanned the walls with an infrared camera.

Several minutes went by without any results. Then, while one investigator pulled out a small shovel and dug up some dirt along the back wall, Gia searched the cave wall for hidden pockets.

Gia stopped. "Over here," she said.

Gia found a small crevice in the wall near the floor of the cave. She lay flat on her stomach, reaching in.

"I feel something," Gia said. "The crack runs in about six inches then curves upward."

Gia pulled off her heavy assault jacket and stretched her hand into the small crack. She scooted herself up against the wall of the cave and spun around onto her back. She contorted and twisted her body in a myriad of directions. Then she stopped.

"I feel the grip of a gun," Gia said as she strained to reach. "I can't seem to find a way to grab it."

Gia nudged the gun with her index finger. It didn't move. She stretched a little more and nudged it again—this time, the weapon released and fell against her hand.

Karen pulled the gun out, removed the magazine, and cleared a round from the barrel. Then she dropped the gun and ammo into an evidence bag. She wrote some notes on the outside of the bag.

"Chain of custody is established," Karen said. "Thank you,

Gia."

Karen shined a flashlight on the gun. The barrel was light gray steel with a dark mahogany handle inlaid with hundreds of jewels. It was not a typical weapon. It was beautiful. Gia noticed a piece of black velcro taped to the side of the barrel.

Gia led the team back to the cave entrance, where she could get a radio signal.

"We got it, Jay. We got the smoking gun. And there's no way a man could have pushed the gun that far into the wall. His hand would never fit."

* * *

CJ watched the five technicals drive up the road. A quick shot could take out the lead driver. The disabled truck would block the road and prevent the rest of the trucks from surrounding the cave. But he didn't have the authority to make the shot. So instead, he watched the convoy approach. Madman took close-up photos of the drivers and gunmen.

"Jay, we have visitors," CJ said into his mike. "Five technicals with .50 caliber machine guns mounted on their beds. At least five fighters per truck. They're all armed with AK-47s."

"Hang tight. We don't know what the Taliban's intentions are yet. They may not be hostile."

"Are you kidding me?" Madman said. "Everybody in this hell hole is hostile."

"Michelle," Jay said. "Can you lift off and hover over the cave entrance? We have visitors approaching."

"Roger. But I can't stay exposed if they have RPGs."

"I understand."

Michelle lifted off and maneuvered her trifan over the cave entrance. She couldn't see any of the rocket-propelled grenade launchers, so she moved up closer. To be safe, she activated her air-to-ground weapons and missile defense system. The firing computer locked onto the lead truck.

Gia stopped inside the entrance, "We're ready for extraction."

"Hold tight. We have a problem. Technicals are approaching on the mountain road.

"Can we evacuate before they get here?" Karen said. "We're ready to go."

"Negative. It's not safe."

CJ chimed in, "If we engage them now, we'll have a better chance of escaping."

"Can't do it," Jay replied. "Against our rules of engagement. They have to shoot first."

"That's great," Gia said. "We have to wait until they blow us up, then we can fight back?"

"You got it. We're a civilian force here at the invitation of the Pakistan government. We have the right to defend ourselves, but not the right to attack others."

Jessie watched the technicals drive up and surround the cave entrance.

"Let's see what they want," Jay said.

Gia trained her M4 on the lead truck. She watched a man carrying an AK-47 step out of the pickup. He walked up to the cave entrance.

"We know you are in there," the man said in English. "We are not going to harm you. Please step out of the cave so I can look you in the eyes."

Gia scanned the trucks through her rifle scope. None of

the fighters had their weapons trained on the cave entrance.

"I'm going out to see what he wants," Gia said. "CJ, if anyone lifts their rifle, shoot them."

"Don't go out," Karen said. "They'll kill you."

"No, I don't think they will." Gia handed her rifle to Karen.

Jay watched the technicals. He needed a plan of action if Gia's negotiations failed.

"CJ, target the leader," Jay commanded.

"Roger," CJ responded. "I have a clear shot."

"Michelle, target the trucks closest to the cave."

"Got it," Michelle responded.

"Let's hope this doesn't turn into a firefight," Jay said. "Everybody, keep your safeties on until I say so. We don't need anyone jumping the gun."

Karen watched the lead terrorist through the scope of Gia's rifle. The man was tall, about six foot three, and wore an all-black keftu and head wrap covering his face. But she could see his eyes. They were black as coal. He pointed the rifle at Gia as he approached.

Gia walked up to the lead terrorist. She stopped five feet away from him and raised her hands over her head, "I'm not armed," she said.

"I know," the man said. "But your security team is. Tell them to drop their rifles. Especially your sniper on the mountain. I have men watching."

"Jay, can you hear what he said?" Gia said into her headset.

"Yes, we're standing down. Everybody confirm that you've dropped your weapons. CJ?"

"Affirmative," CJ said.

Jay thought about his options. First, he had to know who he was dealing with. Was it random, or did they have a plan?

"Gia, try to get him to remove his face mask. I want to identify him."

"We do not want to harm you," the man said. "We want to know what you are doing here?"

"I will tell you," Gia said. "But remove your face covering. I want to see who I am talking with."

The man hesitated. Gia knew Muslim men didn't believe in taking orders from women. She saw her demand unsettled him. He unwrapped the black scarf and dropped it on the ground.

She thought she recognized the man. Then she remembered, and it all made sense to her.

"Thank you," Gia said. "What do you want?"

"Why are you in Pakistan? Are you stealing something?"

"That's none of your business," Gia said. "We're here on official business approved by the Pakistan government."

"Then why did you come here at night? Why are you dressed in black uniforms and carrying weapons? You look like a military team. Or perhaps you are spies."

"Your men attacked the last team that came here. We are not taking any chances."

"They were soldiers. We thought they were here to attack us, so we defended ourselves."

"We are here seeking evidence. But, unfortunately, we were not successful."

"I don't believe you," the man said. "Tell your team to come out so we can search them."

"He knows about the gun," Jay said. "We can't let him take it."

"Karen, can you take a picture of the man's face and upload it to our server? Quick, we need to identify him."

In thirty seconds, Jay was looking at the man's face. "Kyle, run this man's face through the FBI database so we can identify him."

"What are you talking about?" Kyle said. "We don't have access to the FBI's database."

"I meant to say send it to Mack at the FBI. He'll do it."

"Why didn't you say so. I'm on it."

* * *

Gia turned and walked towards the cave.

"Stop," the man said. "Or I'll shoot you." He pulled a handgun out of his belt and pointed it at Gia's head. She kept walking.

"I said stop!"

Gia stopped at the cave entrance, then turned and faced the man. She held her hand behind her back and opened her palm.

Karen knew what she wanted. She placed the evidence bag in Gia's hand.

"Is this what you want?" Gia said, holding the bag up in front of her face. "You can't have it." Gia ducked back towards the cave. A gunshot rang out. Gia screamed as a bullet punctured her lower leg. Falling to the ground, she pulled herself into the cave on all fours.

The man followed her into the cave. "Give me the gun," the man said. "Now, or you all will die."

"It's right here," Gia said in short gasps. "Come and get it."

The man walked up to Gia, pointing his gun at her face. "Hand me the gun!"

Gia held the bag with the gun in it and extended her hand.

325

"No!" Karen said. "Don't give it to him!"

The man turned and swung the gun towards Karen. "Be quiet, or you'll die first."

Karen stood her ground. She stared at the terrorist with a look of defiance.

Gia slammed her injured right leg into the man's groin. Then, with her other leg, she kicked him in the side of the head. The man dropped his gun, writhing in pain.

Gia tried to stand up, but she couldn't put any weight on her wounded leg.

The man straightened up. He pulled his second handgun from his waist belt and pointed it at Gia.

Karen kicked him in the side of the head. The man dropped the gun. She jumped onto the man's back and wrestled him to the ground. He tried to shake her off, but she managed to remove her handgun and smashed him in the head with the gun's grip.

One of the investigators ran out from the cave's interior and grabbed the man's arm—the other wrapped plastic ties around his wrists.

"Somebody get me a tourniquet and a shot of morphine," Gia said. "Let's get out of here."

"We can't," CJ said in her headset. "Two of the technicals drove right up to the cave entrance. One of their fighters is approaching the entrance."

"Is he armed?" Gia said.

"Of course, he's armed."

"That guy shot me in the leg. That satisfies the ROE."

* * *

326

Karen heard Michelle's Trifan hover overhead. First, she heard a single shot echo off the canyon walls. She crawled out to the cave entrance and spotted the fighter's body lying on the ground. A large opening in the side of his head confirmed her intuition. He was dead. Then she heard a series of whooshes, and she scampered back inside. Loud explosions rocked the valley. She waited a moment, then peaked out the cave entrance. Clouds of flames and smoke engulfed the technicals. Karen froze as she saw a tall, hulking figure approach the cave entrance. The man held a large gun pointed towards the ground. Black makeup and a thick black beard covered his face.

Karen gasped when she saw him. She crawled next to Gia, then pulled out her gun, trained it on the cave entrance waiting to shoot the intruder as soon as he entered the cave. Sweat poured down her forehead as she held the gun with both hands.

"It's okay," Gia said as she placed her hand on Karen's arm, forcing her to lower her gun. "You can relax. It's CJ. He's on our side."

"Oh my God, you scared me," Karen said as CJ entered the cave. "I'm happy to see you."

"We're ready to evacuate," CJ said. "I'll carry Gia out. But we need to hurry since there may be reinforcements on the way."

CJ leaned over and picked up Gia. He cradled her body in his arms and squeezed out of the narrow cave entrance.

Chapter 38

Bahrain Commercial District

The area around NSA Bahrain has evolved since Jay's last visit. The seedy, rundown neighborhood in Manama now housed gleaming skyscrapers. He looked at the address on his text from Bonner. It said 50 Financial Harbor Tower. He compared the address to his GPS and realized the building was on the island's north side. After driving in bumper-to-bumper traffic, Jay found the building. The colossal skyscraper towered above the Bahrain skyline.

Everything about the building was shiny, from the floors to the marble front desk. Antonio and Jay rode the elevator to the 50th floor, stepping into a stark but stunning lobby. The view from the floor-to-ceiling windows took Jay's breath away. Unfortunately, it also caused a bit of angina from the dizzying heights. An attractive receptionist offered the two guests a seat. Before they could sit, Steve Bonner walked into the reception area.

Bonner, a slim, tall man with graying hair, greeted Jay with a big grin and a handshake, "Jay, it's great to see you again.

How are you feeling?"

"I'm feeling great. Recovery is coming along smoothly."

"I have a full slate of interviews for you, and your first candidate is already in the conference room. Please follow me."

They entered a large room filled with a solid mahogany conference table with ten chairs. A slim, hawk-nosed man sat in the last chair, his back to the door.

"Jay, Antonio, I'd like to introduce you to Francois Benoit, our first candidate."

The slim man turned, stood up, and snapped to attention. He looked like he wanted to salute, but caught himself, then stuck out his hand to shake. Antonio and Jay shook his hand, and all three men sat down.

"Let Anna, the receptionist, know if you need anything," Steve said, closing the door. "She'll call me when you're done."

"Mr. Benoit, you have an impressive resume," Antonio said. "Please tell me in your own words about your work experience?"

"Very well. I am Adjudant-Chief Francois Benoit. For the last 25 years, I fought with the French Foreign Legion. For the last ten of those years, I was a member of the 13th Demi-Brigade stationed in Djibouti, Africa. I was on the hostage rescue team who recovered the schoolgirls kidnapped by the Boko Haram terrorists."

"What was your role?" Jay asked.

"I was a platoon leader and cavalry specialist."

"Besides the hostage rescue team, did you see combat action?"

"Oh yes. I fought in the Gulf War in Iraq, the Gulf of Aden, and Africa. I received the French Medal of Valor for saving my platoon leader's life in Mosul, Iraq."

"Impressive," Jay said. "Why did you leave the Foreign Legion?"

"My unit returned to France, but I did not want to return to civilian life. I have no family besides what you say, my comrades in arms. I am proud to be a soldier."

"Very good," Antonio said. "Thank you for your time. We will contact you shortly with our decision."

"Excellent," Benoit said. He stood up, executed a perfect turn, and marched out of the conference room.

After several minutes, Steve Bonner entered the room. He led a blond-haired man about six feet tall. In excellent physical condition, Jay could tell he was a real operator.

"Our next candidate is Abraham Moses Pugatsky. He's a former Lithuanian special operations platoon leader."

"Hello," Pugatsky said. "I am pleasured to meet you. Please pardon my poor English. I started only to learn last year."

"Don't worry about your English," Antonio said. "We're not hiring linguists."

The man stared at Antonio with a blank look on his face.

"Okay, do your best to tell us about your military experience."

"I join Lithuanian Army in 2002. That is year they formed SOP. My job is in advanced warfare and counter-terror unit. I fought in Afghanistan with NATO and with hostage rescue in my home country."

"Did you receive any awards or distinctions?" Jay asked.

"I got medal for being injured in combat. But best, I obtained Zaliukas, the highest qualification in SOP."

"Any special skills?" Antonio said.

"I am a sniper. I attended the U.S. Marine Sniper school. Learned from Sergeant Bonner. My team won the competition the year I attended in 2015."

"That's two years after I won the competition," Jay said. "Congratulations. It's tough to do."

"Thank you. I heard a lot of good things about Maravista Security. I like to work with you. You work with honor."

"We are very interested in working with you," Antonio said. "We have a few more interviews and will contact you."

Antonio and Jay interviewed several more candidates then took a break to eat. After lunch, Steve joined them in the conference room.

"We have one last candidate. You'll be impressed." Steve opened the door, and a petite, brunette woman walked in. She wore a tailored, black suit, more fitting for a New York lawyer than a special operations soldier. Black-rimmed oversized glasses framed her dark-brown eyes. Something about her looked familiar, but Jay couldn't place her face.

"May I introduce Renee Cohen, our final candidate."

"Nice to meet you, Ms. Cohen," Jay said as he shook her hand. "Please have a seat and tell me about your work history and why you want to work for Maravista Security?"

"Mr. Bonner and Mr. Borracci," Cohen said. "Would you mind leaving the conference room for a few minutes? I need to talk with Mr. Mendes in private."

"There's no need to," Jay said. "They have the right to hear your answers to my question."

"That's okay," Bonner said. "We'll give you a few minutes with Ms. Cohen."

Jay watched Bonner, and Antonio leave the room then said, "Please begin."

"My name is Renee Cohen. I am Israeli. I completed my mandatory military service and attended university in Tel Aviv. I majored in psychology and criminal justice. When Hezbollah fired missiles into Israel, the Army activated my reserve unit. We fought in the 30-day war. The fighting was bloody, and I lost many good friends. After the war, I graduated and joined Mossad, the Israeli Intelligence Agency. I worked with the CIA and Jordanian intelligence. As part of my job, I monitored Iranian intelligence activities in the Middle East. They kept me very busy, and I infiltrated an Iranian intelligence unit, securing a vital asset. This asset told me about an operation in Bahrain. They were organizing demonstrations to protest the U.S. Navy base. The demonstrations were effective until the leader of the Iranian unit disappeared. Then, the demonstrations suddenly collapsed."

"Thank you for sharing this information, but why are you telling me this?"

"The information I'm about to tell you is for your ears only. If you tell anyone, I'll be forced to kill you. Do you understand?"

"I do, but I'm not sure why."

"Mr. Mendes, you killed the Iranian agent."

"I did what?"

Chapter 39

Eighteen months earlier - NSA Bahrain

J ay watched as two young female sailors walked out the front gate of the naval base. One was a slim, African-American woman, and the other was a petite white woman with long, dark hair. They wore blouses and khaki pants, nothing provocative. Several of the Muslim women stood in front of them, blocking their way. Jay thought he heard the words Jew and nigger mixed in with Arabic. This was not good. He stepped off the curb toward the crowd.

Bonner asked, "Mendes, where are you going?"

"To help them. Are you coming?"

Jay pushed his way through the crowd, ignoring the angry stares and taunts. He understood Arabic, listening to their hate-filled remarks. Someone pushed Jay, and Jay pushed back. He reached the two women who seemed to be standing their ground.

"Get out of our way," the African-American woman said. "We don't care about your problems. We want to get a drink."

The women blocked their way. "It is forbidden to drink alcohol. Go back to your own country," one woman said in broken English.

"I said, get out of our way."

Jay saw the second woman wasn't so bold. She was a petite brunette with straight brown hair and glasses. More of an intellectual than a sailor. She cowered behind her friend. One of the men in the white robes grabbed her and pulled her out of the crowd. Jay saw what he did and followed. He heard screams and shouts of let go of me. Then he heard slapping noises and silence.

Jay pushed after them. He saw the man with the white robe turn a corner. He followed them down a narrow street. He heard Bonner and the African-American woman behind him.

The woman caught up to Jay. She tugged on his sleeve and said, "My name is Marcia. I'm a Navy Communications Officer. My friend is Renee. She's with the Israeli Ministry of Foreign Affairs. They can't find out. They'll kill her."

They ran through a series of winding, narrow streets. Then they disappeared into a seedy apartment building. Jay lowered his shoulder and broke the door down. He ran up a flight of stairs and stopped. Two robed men stood on the landing in front of him. Each held a large knife. The man who grabbed Renee was behind them. He had her pinned face-first against the wall. One hand held her in place. His other hand was pulling his robe up.

Jay punched the closest man in the stomach, then stepped back as the second man lashed out with his knife. Jay ducked, grabbed the man's wrist, and twisted until the knife fell. Then he pulled the man towards him and let go. The man flew down the stairs face first, landing at Bonner's feet. Steve punched him several times in the face until the man didn't move.

The other robed man tried to punch Jay again. This time Jay punched him back in the face. The power of the blow shattered the man's nose, and he fell back against the wall. Jay grabbed his head, pulled it down, and brought his knee up into his face. The man dropped to the floor like a sack of flour.

Jay picked up the knife from the floor. Then walked up to the man who held Renee against the wall. His underpants were on the floor, but she wasn't letting him get his way.

"Let her go now if you want to live," Jay said in Arabic. The man turned and spat in his face.

Renee saw what her attacker did to Jay. Twisting and turning, she struggled to get out of the man's grip without any success.

Jay watched the meek woman transform into a trained killer. She spun herself around and drove her elbow into her attacker's temple. The man screamed and backed off. Renee slammed her foot onto his instep. Then elbowed him again, slamming him back against the railing. Pressing her back against the wall for support, she kicked him between the legs. When he bent forward, she kneed him in the nose. Blood spurt everywhere. Renee and her attacker both saw his knife on the floor. But the man was quicker, grabbing the knife a split second before she could. He whipped the combat knife in a wide arc, slicing Renee in the forearm. Instinctively, she grabbed her arm, and the man punched her in the face. Renee collapsed against the wall, stunned by the massive blow. He grabbed a handful of her hair and pulled it up.

Renee screamed, "No!" as the man exposed her slim neck.

"Now is the time to visit Allah," the man said as he pulled the knife back behind his head. Jay leaped forward and grabbed the knife with both hands. The man was tall and powerful. But not as strong as Jay, who twisted the man's arm until he heard the bones in his forearm break. Jay ignored the man's screams as he turned the arm, pointing the knife at the man's rib cage. Then, with one mighty push, Jay drove the knife deep into the man's chest. They tumbled to the floor in front of Renee. Jay pulled the knife out and buried it in the side of the man's neck. A gusher of blood spurted from the gaping wounds.

Sitting curled against the wall, Renee shook and sobbed. Jay used the knife to cut a strip off the dead man's robe and wrapped the cloth around Renee's wound.

Bonner bounded up the stairs, grabbing Jay by the arm. "We have to go. I can hear angry shouts outside the door. They'll kill us if they catch us. We have to find someplace to hide until we can call the MPs

"No MPs," Jay said. "Let's get out of here."

"Marcia, call for a clean-up team," Renee said as Jay helped her up. "Have a tactical team meet us behind the building. We need to get out of here as soon as we can."

"I take it you two don't work for the Navy's PR department," Bonner said.

"We can't confirm or deny anything," Renee said with a smile. "Let's get out of here, and I'll explain later."

Angry shouts came from the front door. Jay went to the dead man and searched his body.

"No gun."

"They're illegal in Bahrain," Bonner said. "Let's go up."

Jay followed Bonner up the stairs to the next floor. Bonner kicked in the first door he saw and ran in. The apartment was dark and empty. He went to the window and opened it. A narrow alleyway sat four floors below. Too far to jump.

Renee and Marcia joined them in the apartment. Pointing at a clothesline strung between the apartment across the alley, she said, "That will work."

Bonner looked at her. "It might for you, but I weigh over one hundred kilos."

"It will hold." Renee pushed Bonner out of the way and sliced the clothesline with the attacker's bloodied knife. She reeled in the line and tied one end around the leg of the kitchen table. She

wrapped the rope around her waist and then between her legs. She threw the end out the window and watched it land on the ground. "It's long enough."

Jay watched Renee crawl through the window and repel down the side of the building. In twenty seconds, she was on the ground. "You guys are next. Hurry."

Bonner looked at Marcia, "Ladies first." She pulled the rope back up and repeated the process. She was a bit bigger than Renee but still managed to get to the ground in less than a minute.

"Mendes, you go. If I'm too big, I'll break the rope, and you'll be stuck here."

"Great, and if the rope breaks, you're landing on top of me."

But Jay didn't argue. He pulled the rope back up, tied it around himself, and crawled out of the window feet first. He looked down to see a black van pull up below the window. Four soldiers in black assault uniforms piled out, taking up defensive positions around the van.

"Come on, Jay," Marcia said. "We need to go."

Jay pushed off the wall and let the rope slide between his legs. His right hand controlling his speed as he bounced off the brown stucco siding until he reached the ground.

Marcia met him and helped him remove the rope. "Get into the van," she said.

Jay followed orders and jumped inside. It had no markings and looked like a normal cargo van, except for the two rows of steel benches.

A minute later, Bonner piled in with Renee and Marcia behind him. The tactical team followed and closed the doors.

Chapter 40

The memories shocked Jay. Now it was starting to make sense.

"Why did you drug me and send me to the bottom of the world?"

"I had my agency clean up the scene, and Steve and I arranged for you to leave the country for your own safety. The Iranians were furious. They brought in hundreds of agents, but you were thousands of miles away in the Falkland Islands. Steve made the arrangements and kept an eye on you. One of his contractors worked on the ship as the executive officer."

"That was Dora Williams?"

"Yes."

"So why are you telling me this now? Do you want to work for me, or is this all an elaborate cover scheme?"

"No, I retired from Mossad. I live in Israel, and I want some action without working for the government. I know Gia Khalil, and she's confirmed what I already knew — you're a great guy, and your company is growing. I want to be part of your success."

"Does Gia know about what happened in Bahrain?"

"No, only Steve knows since he was there. He contacted

your friends when you disappeared so they wouldn't worry but never told them why."

"Does he work for Mossad too?"

"Who, Steve? Oh no, they use him to transition retiring agents back into civilian life. Many friendly intelligence agencies use him because he's professional and loyal."

* * *

"What do you think?" Steve asked Jay and Antonio after Renee left.

"I like Benoit and the Pugatsky guy," Antonio said. "They seem like solid operators. Benoit's a leader, and Pugatsky's a sniper and has personal protection experience."

"What about the girl?" Jay said. "She has a lot of great connections in the intelligence community."

"Do we really need another intelligence agent?" Antonio said. "You have Gia and me."

"I know, but Gia is my second-in-command in the U.S. I need her to manage my field operations. And you'll be doing the same in Europe. Having a dedicated intelligence operative with contacts at the CIA, Mossad, and Jordanian intelligence will be beneficial."

"Well, you are the boss," Antonio said. "I'll go along with your suggestions. Steve, what are the next steps?"

"I'll present the offers to the three candidates. If they accept, I'll help you onboard them, and the rest is up to you."

Jay and Antonio rode the elevator down and retrieved their car from valet parking.

"What's next, boss?" Antonio said. "I like the sound of that word. We will make quite a team."

"I agree with you, Antonio. Actually, I had a thought about one other candidate."

"Who's that?"

"Silvie Bruehner. She's professional and intelligent."

"She is brilliant, but she doesn't have any special operations training. I'm afraid she might not have the skill set we need. She's an investigator. Remember your fallen hero back in the States."

"Who, Bill Shannon?"

"Yes, you weren't going to work with part-time police officers because they didn't have the same training special ops soldiers had. I believe Silvie falls into that category."

"Okay, that's a good point. I'll trust you to work with Steve to find more agents."

Chapter 41

The DHS command center was bustling with activity. FBI and NSA agents hovered around computer screens listening to covert audio recordings. It seemed the clash in Pakistan increased internet chatter.

Jay approached Mack as he scrolled through new situation reports. "Did you have any luck finding out who the owner of the Swiss bank account is?"

"No, I haven't heard anything," Mack said. "They told me Tyre is a coastal city in southern Lebanon near the Israeli border. It's known as a base for Hezbollah, the Iranian-backed terror group. But they can't identify a particular person or group. We're searching our databases for Hezbollah leaders who may still be alive and active."

"Why would they attack the Catholic church?" Jay said. "Isn't their beef with the Israelis?"

"Yes, it doesn't make sense."

"How about the guy Gia brought back from Pakistan. Did we get any information from him?"

"No, Gia interviewed him twice, but he's not talking. She

341

thinks he looks familiar, but she can't remember where she saw him."

"Show me his picture again."

Mack pulled up an image on one of the computer screens. He showed Jay the picture of a dark-haired man with a long, matted beard.

"Wait, something about him does look familiar. Let me make a call."

Jay pulled out his cell phone and said: "Siri, call Natalie Choi." He waited a minute until Natalie answered.

"Choi here."

"Natalie, it's Jay. I need your help."

She hung up the phone.

Jay called her back. This time she let him speak.

"Do you remember the final mission in Dubai when Gia was undercover as the Princess?" Jay asked. "Gia sent us photos of two security guards at the hotel. If I remember, you found them in the FBI's terror database."

"Yeah, one was al-Mujadin. He was posing as Kathleen's bodyguard."

"Right," Jay said. "Who was the other guy?"

"He was al-Mujadin's second in command. "His name was al-Shalil. He was Pakistani."

"Whatever happened to him?"

"I don't know. I assumed you killed al-Shalil during the rescue operation. Wasn't he one of the guards in the cave?"

"No, he wasn't. I'm having Mack send you a picture. Can you compare it to the database picture?"

"Okay, I have it," Natalie said. "Let me pull up the database picture from my phone's memory. Jay, you're right. He's the same guy."

"Thanks, Natalie. I owe you one."

"You owe me more than one, Mendes. I'll never forgive you for leaving me in Bahrain."

Jay didn't say anything. He couldn't tell her the real story, and why bother making one up. He hung up the phone and went back to work.

"I have a thought," Mack said. "Did it ever occur to you that al-Mujadin and al-Shalil weren't trying to kidnap Kathleen? But they were working with her?"

"Mack, what are you saying?"

"What if Kathleen planned the kidnapping herself? What if she married Goddard to get access to his fortune and bolster her career?"

"That's crazy," Jay said. "Kathleen was already a successful reporter. She didn't need to marry him to get rich."

"But what if she had a different motivation?" Mack said.

"What do you mean?"

"She's Lebanese, right?"

"Yeah, but her name is Amejian. That's Armenian, and most of them are Christians."

"But her mother was Muslim," Gia said as she approached the two men on a pair of crutches. "The interview she did with Joanne Roberts the night I was in Dubai. My memories of that night are unclear because of the carbon monoxide poisoning. But I now remember her saying something about a wedding and bombing."

"I remember," Mack said. "She was visiting her mother's family in South Lebanon when Israeli bombs destroyed her cousin's home. She was the only one that survived."

"Was that town Tyre?" Jay said. "Mack, can we find out?"

"I can reach out to our Embassy in Beirut and see if there

are records of people killed in the bombing."

"That explains why al-Shalil knew we were coming back for the gun," Gia said. "He knew the gun was in the cave, and if we came back for it, we were getting closer.

"Closer to what?" Jay asked.

"What if she planned to kill Goddard all along?" Gia said. "Did Kathleen use you to cover up the murder?"

"Gia, you're a genius," Jay said. "Mack, can you find out who bought the gun? I doubt Kathleen bought it herself. If we can connect her with al-Shalil, we can charge him with conspiracy to commit murder. That may change his mind about talking. In the meantime, I'm going to dig deeper into Kathleen's relationship with al-Shalil and al-Mujadin."

Jay spent hours sifting through footage of Kathleen's background. He learned she reported on the wars in Syria and Afghanistan. Then he had a thought and called Antonio.

"Did Renee and the other two guys accept our offer?" Jay said.

"Yes, they did," Antonio said. "They're going to Switzerland to start training."

"Tell them to go to Beirut instead. Have Renee call me."

"What's this about?"

Jay filled him in on their theories and his brainstorm.

Antonio paused for a moment, then said, "It might work. I also know who we can target."

"What do you mean?"

"I spend a lot of time with the financial apparatus supporting Al Qaeda. There are two brothers, Sammi and Rajji Nasharif, in Tyre, who have close ties with Hezbollah. Some people even believe they're part of the leadership team. Sammi is a big car enthusiast. I met him at the grand opening of the Ferrari dealership in Beirut."

"What are you suggesting?"

"We conduct a little field intelligence work."

"I'm coming to join you."

"Jay, you're back in the states. You can delegate this work to your intelligence team."

"Yeah, how did that work in Dubai? I'm bringing CJ and Madman with me. I want to be close by in case your plan goes sideways."

Antonio laughed, "What could go wrong?"

Chapter 42

Lebanon

The sleek Ferrari Portofino hugged the winding coast road from Beirut to Tyre. Jay stayed a safe distance behind the six hundred horsepower beast. Antonio insisted on driving with the top down to enjoy the 'driving experience.' He could tell Renee enjoyed the wind in her long, straightened hair. They did make an attractive couple.

Halfway down the Lebanese coast, they stopped for lunch at a beachside resort. The cool ocean air provided slight relief to the blazing middle east sun. Jay joined Antonio and Renee for lunch. CJ and Madman ate in the Land Rover while Benoit and Moses patrolled the resort grounds. To an outsider, Antonio appeared to be a well-known celebrity with a team of bodyguards. Not too far from the truth.

Jay sipped sparkling water with Antonio while Renee freshened up in the ladies' room.

"Your Israeli friend seems to be enjoying her new job," Antonio said. "She seems to relish the role as my female companion."

"She's supposed to be your Marketing Director, not your

escort," Jay said with a smirk. "But yes, she does look amazing. A true transformation from the Wall Street look she exhibited in her interview."

"That's why she makes a good spy," Antonio said. "She can transform herself to play any role we need her to play. And considering she speaks seven languages, I do agree she'll be a valuable team member."

"Now you're admitting I was right to hire her?"

"No, I'm saying you got lucky. We better change the subject. Here she comes."

Renee strolled across the patio turning the heads of male guests at the other tables. Her short, skin-tight silver dress displayed her toned, attractive legs. Black high-heels and designer Versaci sunglasses completed the look.

"Look, those two young guys are pointing at you and taking photos with their phone," Antonio said as she sat down. "They think you're a celebrity."

Renee smiled. "I should provide a nice distraction for you when we meet with the Nasharif brothers. I hope I'll have enough time to break away and search the house."

"With six bedrooms and three floors, you'll have to move fast," Jay said. "If they catch you in a private area, you'll be in danger."

"I don't plan to get caught. Are my microphone and camera working?"

"Let's do a test," Jay said. "CJ, time for a sound and video check."

"Roger boss. I hear you loud and clear. But all I see is your ugly mug in the camera. Renee, can you move around so I can get a better view?"

"How's this?" she said as she turned toward the beach and

ocean. A pair of bikini-clad women walked through the screen.

"Ah, much better. Thank you."

"Great," Jay said. "Let's review the plan again before the waiter brings our lunch, then hit the road."

Two hours later, Jay pulled the Land Rover to the side of a narrow road overlooking the city of Tyre. In front of him, a sprawling stucco mansion surrounded by iron gates and security cameras. Antonio followed the Ferrari to the front entrance. Benoit and Moses pulled behind the red Ferrari in their black BMW sedan. Their job was to guard Antonio and smash the gate down to make a speedy escape if needed.

The gate opened, and the two cars rolled through.

"Here we go, everybody," Jay said. "Madman, launch the microbots. Let's try to get some eyes inside the mansion."

"Roger," Kyle said on the headset. "I'll control the bots."

Madman rolled down the backseat window and held his hand out. The mother bot flew out the window, followed by the two children bots. Kyle used voice commands to navigate the bots over the wall. He landed them behind a thick green hedgerow.

Two men stepped out of the front door. Dressed in dark designer suits, they looked like a pair of European businessmen. Then, Jay noticed several burly security guards standing inside the front door.

Antonio stepped out of the car as one of the men approached. He had a receding hairline of thick black hair. Specks of gray scattered through his well-groomed beard. "Welcome, Mr. Borracci. I'm Sammi Nasharif. It's an honor to see you again."

Antonio greeted him with a handshake and a hug. "The

pleasure is all mine. Driving this gem down here from Beirut was a true pleasure."

The second man opened the door for Renee. She swung her legs, catching Rajji's attention. The two bodyguards in the front door stepped out to grab a glimpse. Jay thought he heard Arianna Grande's name mentioned. Renee did strike a remarkable resemblance to the petite pop star.

Renee played the part, flipping her long brown hair away from her face. She held her hand out for Rajji to help her out of the car.

"Who is your lovely companion?" Sammi said to Antonio. "You must introduce her."

"This is Renee Giovanni. She's the Director of Partnerships for Ferrari. She flew here from Italy to join me and meet our next dealer in Lebanon."

"Ciao," Renee said, extending her hand to Sammi.

He held her hand with both of his. "It's a pleasure to meet you," he said in Italian. "You traveled here from Italy?"

"Sì, naturalmente," Renee replied. "Sei famoso in fabbrica."

CJ looked at Jay, "What did she say?"

"You are famous back at the factory."

"Before we let you test drive the new Portofino," Antonio said. "We would like to show you a special video Renee produced. Is it possible to go inside the house? Unfortunately, the sun is too bright to view our iPad screen."

"Yes, of course," Sammi said. "Ladies first."

Renee turned to walk up the stone steps but stubbed her toe, falling forward onto the stairs. She scraped her knee in the process and let out a loud swear in Italian. The two bodyguards rushed down to assist her.

"Go, Kyle," Jay said.

Kyle maneuvered the bots through the front door of the villa. He flew them into a stark foyer with marble floors and stucco walls. He took a sharp right into a large parlor and parked the microbots behind a plush, leather couch.

"Is the wifi hotspot activated on the bots?" Jay said.

"Yes, Chief, we have access to the internet."

"Perfect."

Renee and Antonio followed the two bodyguards into the parlor.

"I will get my first aid kit," one of the bodyguards said.

"That will not be necessary," Renee said. "Can you show me a ladies' room? Then, I'll be able to clean myself up."

"Follow me, please." The bodyguard led her through the foyer and down a staircase to a lower level. "You may use the bath in our guest suite. Take your time and come up the stairs when you're ready."

"Thank you so much," Renee said. "You were so sweet to help me." She stepped on her tippy toes and kissed the large man on the cheek. His skin turned a bright red.

Renee shut the door to the guest suite and locked the door behind her.

"Okay, I'm in," she said to Jay in her microphone. "Are the bots inside?"

"Yes," Jay said. "I'm sending them upstairs to see if there are any more guards."

"Good. I'll activate my electronic device scanner. But, first, I want to make sure there aren't any cameras or listening devices in here."

Renee pulled out her cell phone and started talking in rapid-fire Italian. As she walked around the room, her phone sent a signal to Jay's laptop.

"There's a hidden camera above the closet door," Jay told her.

She pulled a small travel-size can of hairspray from her purse. Then, she stood with her back in front of the camera and sprayed her hairspray towards the camera port.

"Perfect shot," Jay said. "Now, see if you have access to the wifi system."

Renee grabbed her pocketbook and went into the bathroom. She pulled out an iPad Mini and clicked on an icon for a gaming app.

"Okay, I can see he has several laptops, a desktop, and a dozen iPads connected to the wifi," Kyle said. "He also has a Dropbox online storage account. I can insert a file into the online cloud accounts and copy the data onto Renee's iPad. But, unfortunately, there are too many files to upload them all to our server."

"Hurry," Jay said. "We don't want the guards getting suspicious."

As if on cue, someone banged on the door to the guest suite.

"I'll be right out," Renee yelled. "Just a minute, please."

"Kyle, is the download done yet?" Jay asked. "She needs to get out of there."

"I know, Jay. It's almost done."

"Ms. Giovanni, our housekeeper, has bandages for your knee," the guard said. "Please let her in."

Before Renee could reply, she heard the door open. She stuffed the iPad into her pocketbook, then opened the door, took the towels, and said, "Grazie."

Renee pulled the iPad out of her pocketbook. The files included hundreds of documents and image files. Everything

351

related to Sammi's car dealerships. She was ready to put the iPad away when she noticed an unmarked folder. She clicked on the icon and found dozens of links to a private YouTube directory dating back to 2006. A knot grew in Renee's stomach. She clicked on one of the links and found it was password protected. Renee tried the TyreBT06 account name as a password. It worked.

The file appeared to be a security video of an apartment building in Tyre. One second the building was peaceful and quiet. Then a loud explosion, and the screen filled with smoke and debris. The loud sound startled Renee, and she almost dropped the iPad. When the smoke cleared, the building was a pile of rubble.

The second video featured an Al Jazeera news reporter. Dozens of people sifted through the rubble, looking for survivors. Renee heard the sounds of women crying in the background. Workers struggled to pull concrete and cement blocks off the pile. Then, in the background, Renee listened to another sound. Dozens of young Lebanese men chanting 'Death to America' in Arabic. The reporter explained they were Hezbollah soldiers vowing revenge.

Renee struggled to hold back tears. As a soldier, she passed by dozens of similar bombed-out buildings during the war. But to see the tragic impact on the innocent victims was heart-wrenching.

A pair of young men carried what looked to be a teenage girl out of the rubble. Her face was bloody, but she appeared to be alive. The reporter stopped the men and asked who the girl was.

A familiar but younger face appeared in the camera. It was Rajji. He was crying.

"The bomb struck our family's apartment. We were preparing for my daughter's wedding tomorrow morning. The women were together with the bride, but this girl is the only survivor we have found so far."

"Was she the bride?"

"No. She's the daughter of my cousin visiting from Beirut."

"What's your niece's name?"

"Kathleen," The man said. "Kathleen Amejian. The Americans did this. They sell the bombs to the Zionists who use them to kill our women and children. They must pay."

Renee almost fainted. Sammi and Rajji were Kathleen Amejian's uncles. They had the motive to want to kill more Americans. Renee sent the link to Jay and put her iPad away when she saw another document.

The file name said Tyre Blind Trust, and it benefited the survivors of the bombing. It listed a local attorney as executor and four trustees: Sammi, Rajji, Kathleen, and Mohammed al-Mujadin.

353

Chapter 43

Southern Lebanon

J ay watched Sammi jog down the front stairs and onto the driveway. He swept his hands across the Ferrari's shiny red paint job. Rajji followed but in a more reserved manner. He was the negotiator. He knew Rajji couldn't act excited like his brother and still demand a better deal from Ferrari. Antonio and Renee followed. Antonio appeared happy, but Renee seemed stressed. She glanced towards him from the driveway, but she wouldn't say anything on the radio. It must be serious. Jay sensed she needed to talk but now wasn't the time. It was time for the test drive.

"Okay, so here's the plan," Renee said to the brothers. "Ferrari requires a factory representative to be in the car at all times. Since you both want to drive, I'll sit in the back. Antonio will ride with our associates. Please obey the speed limits and traffic regulations. I know you will want to test the power, but we don't want you to get a ticket from your policia."

"It is not a problem," Sammi said. "The policia, as you say, know us very well. We sell them their patrol cars."

"Very good, but please drive safely. We need to return the car to Beirut. Oh, one other thing. We want to take photos with you and the car. We will use it as part of your new dealer promotions. Is there a picturesque spot in your city? Perhaps by the ocean?"

"We can go to the Hippodrome," Rajji said. "They are ancient Roman ruins. Very popular tourist location by the ocean."

"Perfect," Renee said. "It is late afternoon. The sunlight will be perfect by the time we arrive there."

Rajji opened the passenger door and helped Renee get in the cramped back seat. Antonio handed the keys to Sammi and sat down in the passenger seat of the BMW. Benoit backed out of the driveway so Sammi could exit. Then followed the red sports car.

Jay waited to retrieve the microbots, then joined the procession.

* * *

Sammi weaved the Ferrari through the narrow streets of the Christian district. The deep sounds of the powerful engine echoing off the walls of the ancient stucco homes. When he reached the ocean, he turned left onto the wide two-lane boulevard wrapped around the peninsula. They zipped by the toney resort hotels, designer clothing stores, and western-style restaurants.

"We can stop at the Tyre lighthouse if you wish?" Sammi said. "Or we can show you our other dealerships?"

"Let's keep driving," Renee said. "Your city is lovely."

"We opened our first Renault dealership ten years ago,"

355

Sammi said. Now we own five dealerships and a chain of gas stations. The economy is strong without war. We hope peace continues so prosperity can thrive."

"That depends on the Jews," Rajji said, turning towards Renee. "They need to respect our borders."

Jay heard a different tone in Rajji's voice. The Afghans spoke the same way about outsiders. A chill ran down his spine.

"Well, I'm not sure what the Israelis will do," Renee said. "I'm sure they want peace too."

Jay had a feeling something was going to happen, and it wasn't good.

"Benoit, stay close to the Ferrari," Jay said. "And keep an eye out for chase cars. I'm going ahead to scout the Hippodrome."

Sammi continued his tour of the city, pointing out local landmarks.

"Turn here, Sammi," Rajji said. "Go by the tower."

Sammi turned to Rajji and said, "Is that necessary?"

"It's part of our history," Rajji said. "She must know about our family tragedy."

Now Renee felt tingles down her spine. Did Rajji know something about Renee? Was her cover blown?"

Sammi turned into the Muslim district down streets lined by apartment buildings. Many seemed new, built within the last ten years.

"Pull over here," Rajji said. "My turn to drive."

Renee looked behind her. She saw Benoit stop in the BMW. She wanted to get the iPad to him but didn't know how to do it without Rajji witnessing the exchange.

"Renee, come here," Rajji said. "See this building. It sits on the site of my mother's home."

"What happened?" Renee said.

"Israel bombs destroyed it in 2006. Killed my mother and four sisters the night before my sister's wedding. We defended our homes, fighting the Israelis in the streets. Held them off for thirty days until they retreated. Then we rebuilt our city. The Italians, Americans, British came back. They loaned us money to rebuild, then built their stores and sold their clothes. Brought back their western ways. But did they care about how we felt? About the family, we lost?"

"I'm so sorry for your loss," Renee said. "It must have been terrible."

"Did you ever lose family?"

* * *

Renee remembered her friend, partner, and lover. Yashim was a handsome Mossad agent from Tel Aviv. They met at the university and went through military training together. He was tall and athletic. As a member of the Israeli volleyball team, he traveled around the world. Renee traveled with him to the 2004 Olympic Games in Athens. It was the best two weeks of her life. Then the war broke out two years later. Hezbollah fired rockets into Northern Israel. The IDF fired back. A sergeant in the IDF, Yashim, led a squad into the village of Bint Jbeil. Ambushed by Hezbollah, he lost three soldiers in the first ten minutes of fighting. They fought bravely for three hours. When their ammunition ran out, they were overrun. Renee didn't see Yashim's body until Hezbollah returned it in a prisoner exchange at the end of the war.

* * *

As the memories returned, tears welled up in her eyes. She was grateful to be wearing oversized sunglasses to cover her tear-soaked cheeks.

"Not the way you did," Renee said. "I was lucky to have a peaceful childhood in Italy."

Rajji stared at her for a long moment.

Renee froze. Then, Rajji turned to walk back to the car, and Renee sighed in relief.

* * *

Jay parked the Land Rover across the street from the entrance to the Hippodrome.

"Guys, let's stretch our legs and check out the ruins. Let me know if you see anybody suspicious."

CJ and Madman exited the back seat and jogged across the street while Jay stepped out of the car and looked around. The neighborhood was quiet. He reached under the front seat to remove his handgun and place it in the holster under his arm. Then pulled on his light windbreaker and closed the door.

The Hippodrome, a small coliseum, dated back to Roman times. A small section of the stone stadium sat next to an oval track. It reminded Jay of the movie Spartacus. He imagined gladiators fighting to the death in front of cheering fans. The area was flat and open, without many places to hide. With only one way in and out, it looked easy to secure.

CJ and Madman returned from surveying the grounds. "All clear, Chief," CJ said. "No signs of any trouble."

"Good. I'll be happy when we get out of here."

"There's a change in plans," Antonio said on the radio.

358

"Rajji is going to a different archeological site. The Egyptian port site. It's about a kilometer from your location."

"Shit," Jay said. "Okay, we'll meet you there."

"Let's go, guys. Change of plans."

* * *

Rajji drove the Ferrari into the archeological site. He passed through the parking area then down a stone drive surrounded by ancient Roman foundations and pillars.

Renee scanned the area for tourists and visitors but didn't see anybody. In fact, it was eerily quiet. Antonio stayed close behind in the BMW, but there was no sign of Jay.

Rajji parked the car in front of a line of ancient columns. In front of them was a spectacular view of the ocean.

"I thought this was a better location for a photo," Rajji said. "Unfortunately, the Hippodrome has no water view."

"It is beautiful," Renee said. "Let's get out and find the perfect angle. The sun is getting low in the sky. Antonio has my camera and tripod in the trunk of the BMW."

Renee walked towards the BMW. When she saw Rajji was out of hearing distance, she whispered, "You need to get my iPad to Jay as soon as possible. Where is he?"

"He was scouting the Hippodrome. He's on his way."

"Tell him to hurry."

Antonio helped Renee pull the camera equipment from the trunk.

"Benoit and Moses spread out and scan the area."

Moses removed a compact Uzi submachine gun and hid it under his sports coat. Then, he handed a second gun to Benoit.

"Okay, let's grab a few shots with you in front of the ruins," Renee said. "Then we'll take some shots with the ocean in the background."

Sammi and Rajji stood in front of the Ferrari as Renee snapped photos. She peered through the lens, trying to find the best angle. When a cloud of dust rose near the historical site entrance, she thought Jay was coming in to join her.

Then she realized it wasn't Jay. Instead, it was a flatbed tow truck leading four pickup trucks down the path. Jay's Land Rover was nowhere in sight. Her heart almost stopped when she saw men standing in the back of the pickups holding rifles.

"What's the matter?" Sammi said. "You look like you've seen a ghost?"

"Turn around," Renee said.

Sammi looked at the trucks approaching, then turned to Rajji. "What have you done?"

Rajji said nothing. He waved to the lead truck, which pulled off to the side of the stone path. A flatbed truck pulled up and stopped behind the Ferrari. The four pickups stopped on both sides of the road.

A large man with a rotund stomach and white beard stepped out of the passenger door. Renee recognized him as Yaseer Benrazah, head of the Southern Lebanon Hezbollah party.

"Rajji, Sammi, it is so nice to see you," Benrazah said. "You must introduce me to your beautiful friend."

Renee smiled and approached Benrazah with an open hand. Antonio stood out from behind the BMW and joined her. The large man planted a kiss on her left cheek, her right cheek, then her left cheek again. Renee smelled cigar smoke and liquor on his breath. She smiled and returned the embrace.

"Renee Giovanni from Ferrari Motors," she said. "This is my associate Antonio Borracci. It is a pleasure to meet you, sir."

"You know who I am?" Benrazah said. "How do you know me?"

"Of course, I would know you are the Minister of Parliament for southern Lebanon. You have a reputation as a fair and honest politician. A rare find in the Middle East."

"You are not afraid to speak your mind, Miss Giovanni. That is quite brave for a young woman. Now we must discuss your business arrangement."

"Excuse me, sir, our business is with the Nasharif brothers. How are you involved?"

"I must approve any ventures requiring public infrastructure improvements. Building a new dealership requires these improvements. Right Rajji?"

"Yes, of course, Yaseer."

"How much do you need to meet your requirements?" Renee said.

"About two hundred fifty-thousand American dollars," Benrazah said. "That is the value of this gorgeous automobile. No?"

"He wants the car," Renee whispered to Antonio, who shook his head.

"We can't give him the car," he said. "I mortgaged my house as collateral with the dealership in Beirut. My insurance company wouldn't give me a binder."

"Who could blame them," Renee said. "We don't have a choice. Twenty armed men are surrounding us. We're in

Hezbollah territory, for God's sake."

"I did bring a backup policy."

"Who Jay and his two men? How are they going to get us out of this situation? We can't shoot our way out of here, Antonio. They'll kill us. We have to give him the car."

"No, you need to tell him we can't give him the car."

Renee turned to Benrazah, "I'm sorry, Minister Benrazah, I do not have the authority to give you this car. But I can speak to my manager at the factory and see if we can make arrangements to build you a custom vehicle."

"I'm afraid that will not work. I will take the car. You and your associates will stay as my guests while we investigate your true motives for coming to my city."

* * *

Renee grabbed Antonio by the collar and pulled his head down so she could whisper in his ear, "We can't let Hezbollah know who I worked for or take me hostage. I still know too many active agents in the field."

"I'll make sure that doesn't happen," Antonio replied.

"Come on, Antonio, let's go," Renee said as she walked toward the Ferrari. "We're done here. Sammi, will you get my camera?"

Renee heard the sound of twenty men cocking their rifles.

She watched Sammi reach for the camera. Suddenly, the camera exploded. A fraction of a second later, the crack of a rifle shot rang out. Sammi fell to the ground covering his head. A return shot from Moses blew out the window of the flatbed truck.

The driver of the truck jumped to the ground. He raised his

AK47 towards Renee. Benoit released a burst of automatic weapons fire from behind the BMW. The driver crumpled to the ground. Renee grabbed Sammi off the ground and dragged him behind the BMW. Then gunfire exploded around them—Antonio dove for cover behind the Ferrari as bullets tore into the sports car's body.

Renee watched Rajji guide Benrazah to safety behind the tow truck. She ducked when bullets smashed into the raised trunk of the BMW, inches from her face.

"Give me a gun," she said. "I want Rajji."

"Do not kill him," Sammi said. "He's angry, but he's a good man."

"He double-crossed us, Sammi. He's trying to kill us."

"Not me. You and your men. Let me go, and I will convince him to release you."

"No chance. You're our insurance policy."

"I'm not worth much. Rajji won't care if I die. I'm not one of them."

"What do you mean?" Renee said as she covered her head from shattering glass. The gunfire was deafening.

"I'm not in Hezbollah. I don't believe in fighting. It's bad for business."

"What good are you?"

"I know a lot about Hezbollah. They meet at our house. I have recordings and videos. I will give them to you. You give them to your people, whoever they are."

"Where are they? At the house?"

"No, they are digital files. I store them in a secret Lockbox folder online."

Renee realized her pocketbook with her iPad and the video files were in the backseat of the Ferrari.

"Antonio, I need my pocketbook. Can you get it from the Ferrari?"

"Are you kidding? They'll rip me to shreds."

Moses handed his Uzi to Antonio. "Cover me," he said.

Antonio sprayed bullets towards the Hezbollah fighters moving towards the car. When they ducked for cover, Moses crouched low and ran for the Ferrari. A curtain of bullets smashed the windshield. As black smoke poured out of the hood, Moses slid to a stop behind the car. When the gunfire stopped, he leaped into the backseat. A moment later, Moses emerged with Renee's pocketbook. He rolled out of the backseat and sprinted back towards the BMW. When he was about twenty feet away, the Ferrari burst into flames knocking Moses to the ground right next to Renee. She grabbed his jacket and pulled it with all her strength. But the large man didn't move.

"Antonio, Benoit, help me!" she yelled. She looked to see Antonio watching the Ferrari burn. He turned to her with tears in his eyes. "What will I tell my wife when they come to take our house?"

"Don't worry about that now," Renee said. "Help us!"

Benoit dropped his rifle and grabbed Moses under his arms. He pulled with all his strength, dragging the beefy Lithuanian to cover behind the car.

Renee saw Hezbollah fighters appear in front of the blackened remains of the sports car. They were closing in.

Renee grabbed Sammi around the neck. She pressed her handgun against his temple.

"What do you know about your niece Kathleen Amejian and Muhammed al-Mujadin?"

"Everything. I presided over their wedding."

"We need to get you out of here in one piece."

"That does not look possible," Sammi said. "Rajji will call in reinforcements. They will kill you."

"I have my own reinforcements, and it looks like they're on their way now."

* * *

Jay drove the black Land Rover down the ancient causeway. CJ and Madman hung out the back seat windows tearing up the fighters in the pickup trucks with their automatic weapons. By the time they reached the flatbed, flames, and smoke rose from both sides of the road. Benrazah pulled a rocket-propelled grenade launcher out of the side of the truck. But before he could load it, bullets ripped his body in half. The rocket shot out of the launcher over the roof of the Land Rover. It smashed into a Roman column, sending two-thousand-year-old rocks flying everywhere.

Jay stopped the Land Rover behind the flatbed and jumped out. Renee saw Rajji lift his rifle and point it at Jay. Unlike the other Hezbollah fighters who carried AK47s, he held an HK433. It was one of the world's most advanced weapons. The laser finder danced on Jay's forehead. Before he pulled the trigger, Renee pushed Sammi to the ground, then fired two rounds into the back of Rajji's head.

Renee pulled Sammi up and ran up to the Land Rover. She pushed Sammi into the back seat. She turned to Jay and said, "What took you so long?"

"Somebody gave me wrong directions," Jay said. "Anyways, it looked like you had things under control."

Renee smiled as she pulled her iPad from her pocketbook

and handed it to Jay. "Upload the files on the iPad as soon as you can. We need to get out of here before Hezbollah comes looking for us."

"Renee, nice shooting back there."

"Thanks. Now we're even."

Chapter 44

After thirty minutes of high-speed driving through southern Lebanon's hills, Jay felt confident he escaped from the Hezbollah fighters. He found themselves driving through a heavily wooded region overlooking the Bekaa Valley. The road was windy, limiting his speed. The yellow low-gas light had been on for some time. The complaints of his passengers didn't help. Jay needed to find a place to pull over.

"We need to stop," Sammi said from the backseat. "Please, I need to go to the bathroom. Plus, I feel sick."

"I need to go too," CJ said. "My legs are cramping."

"Jay, pull over," Antonio said. "I won't be able to stand the smell if Sammi throws up."

"Everybody be quiet," Renee said. "You sound like a bunch of schoolchildren. We must not let the Hezbollah catch us. They will kill Sammi. We must keep going."

The wooded road Jay drove on was secluded, and Jay spotted a dirt area at the corner of a hairpin curve and pulled the Land Rover over.

"Alright, enough arguing. Everyone get out," Jay said, "Go into the woods, do your duty, and take up defensive positions. CJ, make sure Sammi is out of sight."

Jay grabbed his weapon and jogged to the edge of the treeline. He spent a few minutes finding a sightline where he could watch the road and see the SUV, then scanned the road through his rifle's scope.

Antonio and Renee kneeled next to Jay. Each trained their rifles on the road and watched for their pursuers.

"We must cross the border into Syria," Antonio said, "then back into Israel. The Golan Heights is our only option at this point. It's too dangerous to return to Beirut."

"I agree," Renee said. "But, Syria is not an option. There are thousands of Hezbollah and Hamas fighters between us and the border, and they are all looking for us."

"What do you propose we do," Jay said. "We're out of gas."

"Let them catch us," Renee said. "I have a plan."

* * *

Ten minutes passed before the first Hezbollah pick-up truck appeared on the road. It drove past their hiding spot.

Jay held his breath, waiting for the next truck, which wasn't far behind the first. The truck slowed down, then turned off the road. He released his safety and aimed at the driver's head. Then waited.

The man from the passenger seat appeared to be the team's leader. One of the fighters from the truck bed jumped out to stretch his legs.

"Ahmed, where did they go?" Jay heard the fighter ask his leader.

"Look around, Samir. They didn't have much time to go very far."

The two men looked into the empty vehicle and seemed

confused. Then, Samir walked directly towards Jay's tree. Jay trained his laser sight on the man's forehead and waited.

Samir stopped at the tree, slung his rifle over his shoulder, and pulled down his zipper to relieve himself.

Jay could smell the urine but didn't move. Then, before Samir finished urinating, Antonio jumped out from behind his tree, clasped his hand over Samir's mouth, and dragged him back into the woods. One down.

Achmed looked puzzled. "Samir, where did you go?" He waved to the driver, "Come out here and help me find Samir. He was standing by that tree."

The fighter from the passenger seat approached Renee's tree looking for the other fighter. He looked down at the ground and saw a trail of urine disappearing into the trees. He signaled the driver and the other fighters who left the truck to join him. They stepped into the treeline following the urine trail, giving Jay and his team the opportunity they were waiting for.

Benoit jumped the driver and pulled him to the ground. Then, CJ smashed the passenger in the face with the butt of his rifle.

Achmed stopped, confused by what was happening. Jay crawled out from behind the tree and put the barrel of his handgun against Achmed's temple and the blade of his dessert dagger against the man's throat. He didn't resist.

"Drop your gun and kneel on the ground," Renee said in Arabic. "Take off your uniform. Boots first."

Achmed sat and untied his boots. CJ pulled them off his feet.

"Your top."

The man unbuttoned his uniform, and Renee pulled the

sleeves off one at a time."

"Now, your pants."

The man smiled. "You pleasure me like a whore?"

"Shut up," Renee said, punching him in the face. "I'll cut your balls off if you say another word."

"Make sure you tie them up and tape their mouth's shut," Jay said after his team stripped the fighters. "We need to get going before they are missed. I hope there is enough gas in their truck to get us back to Tyre."

* * *

The smell of salt air and a healthy sea breeze helped calm Jay's nerves as Antonio drove the technical up to the UNESCO security gate. The seacoast road was once a popular tourist route. It scaled the magnificent white cliffs extending from south of Tyre to Haifa across Israel's border. In 2006, after the tragic thirty-day war, the United Nations created a buffer zone to prevent Hezbollah militants and Israeli defense force troops from attacking each other. The new border, known as the blue line, was disputed by both sides. The UN forces that controlled this region consisted of troops from various countries, mostly Africa. They were more lenient towards Hezbollah, and Jay planned to exploit this fact.

Renee promised a friend in Mossad would help them once they were in Israel. The hard part was getting across the border. She insisted she knew a route that was safer than trying to cross at the main gate.

Jay, Renee, and Antonio sat in the cab of the small Toyota pickup. In the back, canvas sacks covered Sammi and the rest of the assault team. Just in case the UNESCO guards spotted them, they all wore the dark camouflage uniforms of Hezbollah's regular forces. All except for Renee, who wore the same dress she had earlier in the day—now dirty and covered in blood. It worked for their plan.

A guard wearing the blue UNESCO helmet and khaki uniform approached the truck. In the passenger seat, Jay held his gun against Renee's stomach. Antonio rolled down his window.

"What is your business?" the guard asked in Arabic.

"Just looking for somewhere to have a little fun," Antonio replied, also in Arabic. "Our friend here is feisty, and we need somewhere remote to calm her down."

"I cannot do that. The border is closed."

Antonio gazed at the camera behind the guard watching his every move. Finally, Antonio waved slightly, and the guard approached.

"We don't want to cross the border. Just find a quiet spot near the water. Perhaps we can offer a small gift to your commanding officer for looking the other way for an hour or two? So we can have our fun."

"Do not do it!" Renee screamed. "These men are bastards, and they are going to rape me!"

"She is just kidding. We mean her no harm."

"He is lying! Do not listen to him."

Antonio turned and slapped Renee across the face. She fell into Jay's lap and stayed still.

The guard laughed. "You showed her who is boss. Your offer is tempting, and I would enjoy joining you, but my partner called in sick, and I must stay at the gate."

Antonio handed an envelope filled with cash to the guard, "We will go several miles down the road. You will not see us or hear from us, and we will return well before light."

The guard pocketed the envelope, then turned and lifted the gate. Antonio drove through.

* * *

The rusty strands of wire tore into Jay's hands as he traversed the side of the white, chalky cliff thirty feet above the churning waves. The path, initially created in the late eighties, was used by Mossad to train new agents. But, since the border closed, it was no longer maintained.

"Are you sure this is the safest route to cross the border?" Sammi said.

"We can try crossing the minefield in front of the border wall," Renee said. "I'm sure their marksmen will not be able to spot your Hezbollah uniform."

"Is that why you all changed into civilian clothes, and I'm still wearing the uniform?

Renee smiled, "You are an observant man, Sammi."

"Will you two stop," Moses said as the big man struggled to maintain his balance on the narrow path. "I am, how you say, height scared."

"The term is scared of heights," Renee said. "You will be okay. Do not look down."

"Ha, easy for you, my petite little friend."

"How long until they find the pickup?" Benoit asked from the end of the line. Will they think to search the cliffs?"

"We told them we would be there for an hour or two," Antonio said. "It will likely take another hour before they realize we aren't coming back. After that, they will probably use a helicopter to search for us."

Jay saw the path was heading around a steep headland jutting out into the ocean, "If you all don't stop talking and focus, we'll be swimming for our lives."

"This is a difficult section," Renee said. "The path goes very close to the water."

The path was little more than six inches wide as it descended below a large outcropping. Jay held on tight as the waves battered the stone cliff only a few feet below his feet. The cold spray felt refreshing. Unfortunately, it also made the path wet and the safety wire even more rusted and frayed. If it broke and they fell into the ocean, the surf would pound them against the cliff.

"We are approaching the border," Renee said, pointing ahead. "The tower up above holds wires for a cable car. It is located at the Rosh Hanikra grotto in Israel. The path will ascend from here. Finally, it ends at the entrance to a grotto where we can cross under the border."

"Why doesn't Hezbollah use this path?" Jay asked.

"Because of Israeli patrols... Help!"

"Renee!" Sammi yelled as he grabbed Renee's hand.

She screamed in terror as she hung from Sammi's arm in midair. Apparently, a rockslide washed out the path.

Jay grabbed Sammi and Antonio grabbed Jay. Then, in a split second, the entire team clung to each other like a barrel full of monkeys anchored by Moses at the back of the line.

"My grip is slipping!" Renee screamed. "You need to pull me up!"

"Reach down and grab her by the shoulder!" Jay yelled at Sammi. "I've got you."

Sammi looked back at Jay with a look of dread. "What if I drop her?"

"You won't! Now hurry!"

Jay wrapped his hand around Sammi's waistband and held on tight. Then, he lowered him down, holding his entire body weight with his right hand as his left held onto the safety cable.

Sammi grabbed the collar of Renee's dress and pulled her up until she could wrap her arms around his neck. Then Jay tried to pull them both up.

"Antonio. Everybody! You need to pull me back up! I can't hold them!"

* * *

The image from the Reaper drone was useless at this time of night. Even though the newer models were equipped with night vision equipment, the mist rising off the ocean obscured the image. Kyle was scared. Jay and his team were in trouble, and he was hopeless to do anything.

"Any sign of them?" Gia asked as she paced the Maravista command center. We have to do something."

"No, I lost them when they took the path down towards the ocean. The screen is blurry, and the drone can't go any lower."

"What do the tide charts say?"

"Low tide was two hours ago," Kyle said. In less than an hour, the path will be underwater. They need to traverse the rockslide zone if they want any chance to survive. Are you sure that wire rope will hold them?"

"No, but my friend in Mossad insists it is safe," Gia said. "So they continue to use the course for training. Just not at night. It's too dangerous."

"Great, we have six operatives and a Hezbollah defector on a path too dangerous for Mossad to use. So we have to rescue them! Plus, we have a development in the investigation, and we need Jay back here."

"I'll make a call. But you have to leave the command center, Kyle. It's highly confidential."

* * *

Like a highly tuned tug-of-war team, McCoy, Benoit, Moses, and Antonio pulled simultaneously. Jay held onto Sammi's waist, who, in turn, held onto Renee.

Jay felt a tremendous force pull him back towards the path.

"Sammi, grab the cable," Jay yelled over the roaring surf, now rising closer and closer to Sammi's feet.

"I got it, but Renee won't let go of my arm!"

"She needs to. She must pull herself up the cable towards the top of the cliff. It's our only way out."

"I can't do it," Renee said. "I'm exhausted. I need a few minutes to gather my strength."

"We don't have a few minutes. But, the tide is rising, and we will soon be underwater."

Renee looked at Jay with tears streaking down her face, "Jay, if I could do it, I would. My arms are rubber. Please, you go first. I must rest."

"I can't. There isn't enough room on the path to get past you."

"But if I go up and the cable breaks, you will be stranded. I cannot bear the thought of all of you drowning."

"We won't, but you must start climbing."

Sammi held Renee steady as she reached out to grab the

safety cable, which dangled in the air above the washout area. It rose at a forty-five-degree angle and disappeared into the mist hovering over the rising ocean. She grabbed the cable with her left hand, pulled herself up, and grabbed the line with her right. Then, with both hands on the cable, she stepped off the cliff.

Jay gasped as the cable dropped precariously close to the waves. Renee hung on for dear life as she whipped back and forth until the cable settled. Then she began to pull herself up, hanging on by sheer grit and determination.

She disappeared into the mist, and Jay held his breath. It seemed like hours, then he heard her voice, "I'm safe! Send Sammi!"

* * *

It was Jay's turn to go.

He stared at the cable and prayed his arm wouldn't fail him. Then he focused on his mission and stepped off the cliff. The drop towards the wave took his breath away. He sunk into the surf up to his waist, then the wire sprung back up, and he hung a few feet above the waves. He reached up with his right hand and let go with his left—no pain in his neck or shoulder. Jay breathed a sigh of relief, then methodically pulled himself up the cable until he reached the opening to the grotto. Renee and Sammi reached out to pull him up, and he let go of the cable.

"Antonio, you can go!" Jay yelled.

* * *

Jay and his team stood inside the grotto, looking down at the tide engulfing the narrow path they stood on just moments earlier. He was grateful his arm survived the brutal climb. His next move was to figure out how to cross the Israeli border without getting killed by mines or Israeli border guards.

Benoit and Moses returned from a quick reconnaissance run to learn what their options were.

"We are three hundred meters short of the border," Benoit said. "The land between the grotto and the wall is filled with land mines."

"Plus, border guards patrol top of wall," Moses said. "We are, how you say in English, fucked."

"I thought we would come out on the Israeli side of the blue line," Renee said. "I was obviously wrong. So now, what do we do?"

"We go through minefield," Moses said. "I lead the way."

"Don't be stupid, Moses," Antonio said. "You'll get yourself killed, and the border guards will shoot the rest of us. There must be another way."

Jay listened to the banter and tried to figure a way to cross the border. Then he heard the familiar sounds of a helicopter approaching from the north. The UNESCO security team was searching for them.

"Can we get closer to the wall?" Jay asked. "Perhaps we can call out to the guards to help us."

"We do not know where the landmines start," Benoit said. "It is too risky. We must go back into the cave to evade detection by UNESCO."

Before they had a chance to move, spotlights from the wall lit up Jay and his team.

"Do not move. You are surrounded by a minefield," called a voice over an intercom. Then without warning, a silver Blackhawk helicopter appeared from behind the wall. A second spotlight mounted on the underbelly of the chopper lit the group.

"Is Jay Mendes in your group?" a female voice asked. "Wave your hands above your head if you are Jay Mendes."

Jay waved his hands, and the helicopter flew overhead. The light and dust from the rotor wash blinded him, but he could see a rope being lowered from the open door.

"Take ten steps back from the rope. We're dropping harnesses."

Jay stepped back as seven full-body harnesses dropped to the ground. He retrieved the harnesses and passed them out to his team.

Sammi looked at his harness with a confused look, "What am I to do with this?"

"Put in on your body," Renee said, laughing. "Unless you want to stay here and be captured by Hezbollah."

"Show me how!"

Renee grabbed the carabiner and lanyard attached to the harness's back and showed Sammi how to step into the leg straps. Then she helped him put his shoulders in the harness and adjusted the chest buckles.

"Here, hold the clip in your hand," Renee said. "You will attach it to one of the rings on the rope."

"Is everyone ready?" Jay said. "Clip onto the rope."

One at a time, each of the team members clipped their lanyard to the rescue rope. When they were all connected, Jay gave the pilot the thumbs up. Then, the helicopter lifted Jay and his team over the wall and into Israel.

Chapter 45

Tel Aviv

The Israeli helicopter airlifted Jay's team safely across the border and landed inside an IDF military compound. Waiting for them was McCoy and Yossi Curran, a Mossad counterintelligence expert.

As Sammi disembarked from the helicopter, he saw the two agents and stopped in his tracks. He grabbed Renee and said, "No, I did not agree to this. They will kill me."

"No, they will not," Renee replied. "They want to question you about Hezbollah. I will stay with you at all times, and when they are done, we will go back to Bahrain, where you will be safe."

"Who is the big man? He looks terrifying."

Jay laughed as he looked at McCoy dressed in a black commando uniform. "He's harmless."

McCoy removed his assault helmet and laughed. "I was prepared to rescue you with the Mossad tactical team, but you managed to survive on your own. I'm not sure how you did it."

"Neither am I," Jay laughed. "Let's find somewhere private

379

to talk. We learned a lot in Lebanon."

Curran escorted Renee and Sammi to a private conference room.

Sammi stopped before entering the room, "Can I please have a bottle of water, and I need to use the bathroom?"

"After we speak," Curran said brusquely.

"Sammi is not to be interrogated," Renee said. "He is here willingly and has been through a death-defying experience. He saved my life, Yossi. Please show him some respect."

"Whatever you wish, Renee. I'll have one of my men show him the facilities, and we will start in five minutes."

As Renee waited for Sammi, Antonio approached her, "I am heading back to Interlaken with Benoit and Moses. Jay and his team are heading back to Boston. Will you be joining us?"

"I will soon. I need to make sure Sammi is safe."

"You did an excellent job today," Antonio said. "The intelligence and evidence you gathered will help us make our case."

"Thank you," Renee said. "I am pleased to be part of your team."

* * *

Jay joined McCoy in a secure conference room within Mossad headquarters. Gia, Mack, and Kyle appeared on the video call. Natalie Choi was on a voice line since she was aboard Air Force One.

"Okay, everybody," McCoy said. "I understand we have a developing situation. What's going on in Rio?"

'The Pope is making his first public appearance," Mack said.

"But there's more. The President will be in Rio, too. He's meeting with the Brazilian President and the Pope about a drug eradication edict."

"Why does that concern us?" Jay said.

"Because we found Kathleen and the yacht," Kyle replied.

"Actually, Kyle found it," Gia corrected. "He did all the intelligence work. As a result, we have satellite images of the *Princess of the Sea* docked at the Marina de Glória in downtown Rio. It's located in the city's center. The airport, a shopping mall, and Brazil's Naval academy are all within the blast range of a major explosion."

"Wait, I have the Pope's schedule," Natalie said. "He's going to say mass for the Bishops at the Metropolitan Cathedral at ten o'clock. Then, after the mass, he's going by motorcade to Paris Park to make a public address at noon. We're expecting over two million people to line the streets and watch the speech."

"There's something else," Gia said. "We have satellite images of the yacht. We can identify two persons of interest on the top deck. Kathleen Amejian and Reginald McFarland. Also, there's a man with unruly blond hair and a tall brunette. We are trying to identify them now."

"That's Ivan the Terrible," CJ said. "He's a paid assassin."

"The woman is Angelica Bonham," Natalie added. "I've watched every one of her movies."

"What?" Jay said. "Did you say, McFarland? Are you sure?"

"Yes, we have a facial recognition match that's over ninety-five percent certain."

"How is that possible? Why is he even alive? Are you saying McFarland is involved with Kathleen?"

Kyle chuckled, "Based on the images, he's very involved."

Jay jumped up from the chair and headed out of the room.

"Jay, where are you going?" Mack said. "We're not finished."

"Mack, I'm going to Rio to get McFarland! You guys can sit around the table and debate a plan—but we have thirty-six hours to stop the most devastating terrorist attack this world has ever seen. So I suggest we conduct our planning session on the plane."

Chapter 46

Rio de Janeiro

Michelle positioned the tri-fan over the pyramid-shaped cathedral in downtown Rio de Janeiro. GNN was the first network to use a hybrid aircraft to report on a news event.

Jessie sat next to Michelle, preparing for her first international news report. "How long can we hover?"

"All day if we want. The electric motors are powered by solar panels built into the skin of the aircraft."

"This is amazing—the view, I mean. I can see in all directions. And the camera moves with my head."

"It's the same technology pilots use in the F 35 fighter jets. We were able to license a stripped-down commercial version from the defense contractor."

"Michelle, is there anything you didn't include?"

"Yes, the FAA wouldn't let me include any offensive or defensive weapon systems. They said it wasn't necessary. I hope they're right."

"Two minutes until you're on the air," Roger said from a control panel in the back of the cabin.

"How's the video feed, Roger? Can you see what I'm seeing?"

"Yes. The image is crystal clear. But, wait, another helicopter pulled into our camera view. It's a red helicopter with a GNN logo on it."

"What are you talking about?" Michelle said. "We were the only crew authorized by the network to report today. They agreed to a pool feed for all the affiliate stations."

"Well, someone didn't get the message," Roger said. "They're coming on the air now."

"Patch the broadcast through our intercom system," Jessie said. "I want to know who's upstaging my report."

"Coming through now."

Jessie's face turned bright red when she heard Kathleen Amejian's voice in her headphones. "No way!" she said. "Cut her off!"

"Sorry, London's controlling the broadcast. We have to wait."

"No way, Roger, find a way to break in. I want to give that bitch a piece of my mind."

"You can't do that on live television, Jessie," Michelle said.

"Just watch me."

"Okay, Kathleen is going live in three," Roger said.

"This is Kathleen Amejian reporting from GNN One. It's an amazing day here in Rio de Janeiro. The Pope is making his first international appearance since his inauguration. We're above the Catedral de Metropolitana de San Sebastian. This is where the Pope will address the Brazilian Bishops Council in less than one hour. A huge crowd is lining the route to the waterfront, where he will address his followers. I learned earlier today from an unnamed source that the

Brazilian President and the United States President will join the Pope. Now, I'm joined by Joanne Roberts from our control center in London. Joanne, what is the mood back home?"

"Kathleen, what are you doing?" Joanne said. "Why are you on the air?"

Kathleen didn't respond.

Jessie laughed to herself as Roger gave her the thumbs up. He then held his hand up with a single finger. She had one minute until she went live.

"I don't know what you mean, Joanne? I'm filing my report."

"No, I mean, why are you on the air? You're not authorized to broadcast."

"I'm sure it's a misunderstanding. However, I must continue my report. The Pope is arriving now. His motorcade is pulling up to the Cathedral."

"You must stop your broadcast immediately, or we will cut you off."

"You can't do that. You don't have the authority. I'm the President of GNN News, and I make the on-air decisions."

"Not anymore. Haven't you heard? You've been replaced."

"Jessie, get ready to broadcast," Gia said in Jessie's earpiece. We've located Kathleen's uplink signal, and the assault team is ready to go. Keep Kathleen occupied as long as possible."

Jessie didn't respond. Instead, she ran her hand through her hair one more time and stared at Roger's camera.

"Three, two, one, you're on," Roger said as the camera record light turned red.

"Joanne, this is Jessie Bessie reporting live from Rio de Janeiro."

"Wait. Who is this Jessie person Joanne?" Kathleen said. "Why is she breaking into my report?"

"Because she's the reporter I've assigned to report on today's event. She's our pool reporter."

"What do you mean you assigned her?"

"I told you, Kathleen, you've been replaced. I'm now President of GNN."

"Who appointed you?"

"The CEO of Goddard International, Michelle Goddard. She has the support of the Board of Directors. Jessie, please continue with your broadcast."

"Thank you, Joanne. I'm watching the Pope's motorcade arrive at the magnificent cathedral here in downtown Rio. He's standing in his 'Popemobile' waving to crowds of supporters lining the streets. There are hundreds of police officers dressed in riot gear lining the route, but the crowd is in a celebratory mood except for a small group of protesters who are waving signs and shouting at the Pope in Portuguese."

"What are they saying, Jessie?" Joanne asked.

"They are followers of The Master. They are denouncing the American Pope and the Catholic church. They want death to the Pope and the Bishops. They say he's responsible for the millions of people in the world who are living in poverty."

"Thank you, Jessie," Joanne said. "I understand you had a chance to tour the Metropolitan Cathedral yesterday. Could you share your thoughts?"

"It's a breathtaking building," Jessie said. "I was told the conical-shaped structure was dedicated in nineteen seventy-six and stood over two hundred feet high. Inside, four huge stain-glass windows rise from the floor to the ceiling that joins in the middle to form a glass cross. The altar sits in the center of the cathedral, surrounded by wooden benches. Today, over five thousand Bishops and priests from Latin America will attend the private mass with the Pope."

"Joanne," Kathleen said. "I was at the Cathedral three years ago for the worldwide family celebration…."

"That's nice, Kathleen," Joanne said. "We have to break for a commercial now."

"Great job Jessie," Gia said. "They're ready to go."

M aking a daylight raid was very risky, especially in the middle of a crowded marina filled with multi-million-dollar yachts. But Jay Mendes and his team were willing to take the risk to stop McFarland and Kathleen Amejian's terrorist operation.

Jay fit his dive mask over his face and gave McCoy the thumbs up. The pair dropped off the side of the Brazilian Federal Police patrol boat and into Guanabara Bay's temperate waters.

Jay last visited the yacht, Matthew Goddard's wedding gift to Kathleen Amejian, in Dubai. He was there searching for Kathleen and Matthew Goddard, who disappeared right under his nose. Goddard took Antonio and Gia, who was undercover as a Saudi Prince and Princess, on a helicopter tour of Dubai. When the helicopter returned from the yacht, it crashed into the base of the Burj al Arab Hotel. After the crash, Jay dove down to the wreckage looking for bodies but didn't find any. When a security team boarded the yacht, they also found the vessel empty. He recently learned the kidnappers whisked their victims away using a mini-sub docked in the hull.

The pair swam below the hull of the yacht, looking for

bombs.

"Kyle, no sign of any booby traps. Where is the manual hatch control?" Jay said.

"It's to the starboard side of the submarine hatch. Look for a round indentation. There's a handle in the middle. You need to turn counterclockwise."

"Okay, I see it," Jay said. He grabbed the handle and twisted it. The dual doors opened with a flush of air bubbles, allowing Jay to swim under the door.

"It's clear," Jay said.

As he climbed the ladder onto the small boarding platform, Jay noticed a set of footprints on the white fiberglass deck.

"It looks like several people left the yacht via the submarine," Jay said into his radio. "Kyle, notify the Brazilian police to be on the lookout for McFarland. Is Kathleen still broadcasting?"

"Yes, she's in a helicopter over the Metropolitan Cathedral."

"You know, I have a hunch. Ask Michelle and Jessie to take a close look at the helicopter. Try to confirm that Kathleen is onboard."

"Jay, what are you saying? That Kathleen isn't on the helicopter?"

Jay and McCoy dropped their backpacks on the deck. They stripped out of their wetsuits and placed them in their packs. Jay pulled out a compact M4 assault rifle, and McCoy pulled out an Uzi submachine pistol. When they were ready to move, Jay opened the door to the submarine bay. He peered in both directions then stepped through the door.

The lower-level corridor resembled a hall in the Palace Versailles. Crystal chandeliers adorned the ceiling. Priceless works of art decorated the mahogany-covered walls. Jay stepped gently on the hard, Carrera marble floors trying to stay silent as they went door-to-door. The crew cabins, engine room, and galley were all empty. He led McCoy up a set of oriental carpet-clad stairs to the next deck. This level was just as plush. Halfway down the hall, Jay noticed a pair of steel double doors.

"Lower deck is clear. We're on deck two, and I see the command center. Halfway down on the port side. We're going to stay here until Ernesto's team clears the upper decks."

"Chief," Michelle said. "Kathleen's helicopter appears to be empty. It's being flown by remote control."

"I knew it, "Jay said. " Someone's controlling the helicopter from the yacht."

"Who's flying a full-size helicopter by remote control?" Kyle said. "I've never heard of anyone doing that before."

There was a moment of silence on the radio. Then Jay said, "Kyle, it's your father."

A more extended silence followed. Then Kyle muttered, "What are you talking about?"

"He's not dead, Kyle," Jay said. "He was kidnapped. We don't know if he's part of the terrorist group or if the kidnappers are forcing him to cooperate. But we have evidence suggesting he's responsible for building and controlling the seagull drones."

"Who kidnapped him?"

"Reginald McFarland. The same man who kidnapped you and Charlotte."

"That's crazy!"

"I know it's shocking, but I need your head to be clear. We're in a perilous situation, and millions of innocent people can die."

"Don't kill him, Jay. Please don't kill my father. I want to speak with him. I need to know if he meant to leave us. If he still wants to come home."

"No promises. We'll do our best."

"Mendes," Ernesto Cabral said in the headset. "Team two is ready to go. Is the lower deck clear?"

"Roger. It's clear."

"We're using flashbangs when we board, so don't let the explosions spook you."

"Got it."

A second later, Jay heard the explosions above him. The command center opened, and two large muscular men carrying handguns ran out.

One man ran in the opposite direction and up the stairs before Jay could get a shot off. But the other man ran right at McCoy. Before he had a chance to react, the man pointed his handgun right at McCoy's face.

Jay beat him to the punch and squeezed his trigger twice, causing the man's head to explode in a spray of red.

"Nice shot," McCoy said. "You haven't lost your touch."

"Thanks."

"The door to the command center is still open," McCoy said as he stepped over the bloody body. "C'mon, Chief."

McCoy ran up to the door and stuck his foot in the jamb before it closed.

"Cabral, we're going into the command center," Jay said on the radio.

"Mendes, wait for us. We're one deck above you. You don't know what's inside."

"I know, but we have one foot inside the door. So we have

to go in."

Jay slammed his shoulder against the steel door, and it gave way.

The room contained television lights, computer consoles, and a bright green wall.

Kathleen Amejian stood in front of the wall holding a microphone.

In front of her, a video camera stood on a tripod. A slender, redhead man sat in front of a cluster of computer screens mounted on a single arm to her left. He operated something with a black joystick.

Jay walked up behind the man in the chair. The center screen of the console showed an empty helicopter cockpit. Outside the window was a panoramic view of downtown Rio. On the left screen, he could see Kathleen standing in front of the green screen. On the right, the image merged Kathleen's image with the view of the city. Jay pushed his rifle muzzle against the back of the man's skull and said, "Don't move."

Jay stared at Kathleen. It was the first time he saw her in person since the day of his sentencing. She glared at him with a look of defiance and disbelief. Then she looked into the camera. "Well, it looks like my broadcast must come to an end. I have a situation I must deal with. This is Kathleen Amejian signing off."

Jay held his ground. He bent down and whispered in the man's ear.

"Are you Daniel McPhee?" Jay said. "Don't say anything. Just nod your head and don't turn the camera or microphone off."

The man nodded.

McCoy stood behind the camera. His rifle pointed at

Kathleen. The red laser designator danced between her eyes. Kathleen took one step towards McCoy.

"Stop, Kathleen," McCoy said. "Don't move."

"I thought you were dead, Mendes," Kathleen said.

"You thought wrong," Jay replied. "Kathleen, why did you do it?"

"Do what?"

"The list is long. Let's start with you murdering Matthew Goddard."

"I don't know what you're talking about. You were the one put on trial for pulling the trigger."

"Yes, and I was found not guilty. "My colleagues returned to the cave. We found the gun. It had your fingerprints and DNA all over it. The bullet fragment they pulled out of my neck had Matthew's DNA on it. So the bullet came from your gun."

"Perhaps it was a mistake. A reaction to seeing your assault team butchering my men."

"We also captured an associate of yours. He tried to stop us from removing the gun from the cave. But he told us how Israeli bombs killed your family in Lebanon. I met your uncles Sammi and Rajji. Rajji's dead. Sammi spoke with the FBI. He told us everything about how he presided over your wedding and how you used the trust fund he set up to help his sister's orphans. Then he explained how you and al-Mujadin hijacked the account and funneled the money into your terrorist organization. Kathleen, we have proof your money went to building the suicide bombs that leveled St. Patrick's Cathedral."

Kathleen didn't respond. She glared at Jay. She didn't notice the camera record light was still on.

"Why did you blame me, Kathleen?" Why me? Why did you ruin my career? Destroy my team. We were in that cave to save your life."

Kathleen's eyes teared up as her anger boiled up. "Because you killed the man I loved."

"I said you killed Goddard."

"I didn't love Goddard, you idiot!" I was using him! We were going to change the world by destroying the Catholic church, then blame the Jews and the moderate Muslims. We plan to kill all the infidels, especially you holier than thou Americans. You are the ones who built the bombs the Jews used to kill my family. But no, you and your band of merry misfits had to ruin our plans!"

"You're talking about al-Mujadin," Jay said. "He wasn't your kidnapper, was he? You were the kidnapper and faked the whole thing so you could get your hands on Goddard's money. But it was more than the money. It was the power and the fame, wasn't it? You don't give a shit about jihad."

Kathleen smirked but didn't say anything.

"Now I get it," Jay said. "You wanted to be number one!" Show the world Kathleen Amejian was the best reporter. Always breaking the biggest stories."

Kathleen's smirk turned into a half-smile and said, "You always thought you were so smart, Mendes. You think you've figured everything out. Now that you've exposed me, you think the world is safe again. But you're wrong. I didn't report on the news. I created it. My coverage of the Papal bombings would have been perfect—Cathedrals burning around the world. But Mendes, you ruined it! Your stupid shot ruined the attack. I have one last chance to report the perfect story. Daniel, blow the chopper!"

"Daniel, no!" Jay said as he pressed his rifle muzzle hard against McPhee's head. "Don't do it."

Sweat poured down McPhee's forehead. Jay felt him shaking with fear.

"Blow the fucking chopper, Daniel, or I'll do it myself!" Kathleen said as she stepped towards Jay and McPhee. McCoy released the safety on his rifle.

"Don't move Kathleen, or I'll shoot," McCoy said.

Jay heard footsteps behind him as the room filled with law enforcement officials. He saw Mack standing next to Ernesto Cabral.

"Kathleen Amejian," Cabral said. "You're under arrest for the murder of Matthew Goddard."

"Fuck all of you," Kathleen said as she dove toward the computer console. Mack jumped, tackling her to the ground.

Daniel flinched, pulling the joystick to the right. Jay saw the image of the helicopter veer off at a ninety-degree angle.

"Daniel, the chopper!" Jay said. "You're losing control."

"If he dies, we all die," Kathleen said as she struggled to escape from Mack's embrace. "Everyone including the Pope and the President. And everyone on this yacht."

"What do you mean, Kathleen?" Jay said. "What have you done?"

"Tell him, Daniel!"

The man sitting at the desk shivered in fear. He held the helicopter control tight in his hand. But he didn't respond.

"Tell him, dammit!" Kathleen screamed. "Tell him what happens if that helicopter crashes. What happens if you take your hand off the joystick."

Jay looked at Daniel in horror. He realized Daniel was a hostage and the victim of a horrible crime. Forced to create weapons that killed hundreds of people. Now he could be killing millions more.

"I, I... " Daniel stammered. "If I let go of the joystick...."

"What happens, Daniel?"

The helicopter... it... explodes!"

"It's filled with liquid explosives, you idiots," Kathleen said in an angry sneer. "Twenty gallons of it. He's hovering over the Pope as we speak. But there's more. McFarland installed fifty-five gallons of explosives in the engine room of the yacht. If he lets go of the joystick,"

"I trigger the bomb," Daniel said in a whisper. "She's right. If I die, we all die."

"Don't move. I have another question." Jay asked. "Daniel, where's McFarland?"

"He's plan B."

Chapter 48

J ay and McCoy sprinted down the hallway as Ernesto Cabral and his team cleared out of the yacht. They took the stairs up to the main deck three steps at a time. When they reached the main deck, they saw an incredible sight. Hundreds of yachts filled the inner harbor. People were cheering as the Pope appeared on large televisions around the shoreline. A sea of humanity filled every square inch of land on the harbor's edge. Jay saw the President of Brazil shake the Pope's hand and wave to the crowd. The crowd exploded in excitement. Standing next to the Pope was the President of the United States. To his horror, he saw his ex-girlfriend Natalie Choi standing next to the President as part of his secret service entourage.

"Maravista team," Jay said into his headset. "I need a sitrep."

"I'm on the stage with Bishop Ramirez," Gia responded.

"Madman and I are on a rooftop overlooking the crowd," CJ said.

"I'm in the control center back home," Kyle said. "I've hacked into Kathleen's computer system and can take control of the helicopter if you need me to."

"We're still hovering over the stage," Michelle said. "Jessie is on the air."

"I'm right next to you," McCoy said.

"Mack, where are you?" Jay said.

"I'm coming up from below decks. I'll be there in thirty seconds. Cabral is taking Kathleen into custody."

"We need to find McFarland and fast," Jay said. "He's somewhere in the crowd."

"Well, that narrows it down, Chief," CJ said. "There are only two million people out there."

"CJ, you and Madman scan the high-rise buildings around the park."

"They're filled with police snipers."

"Look for suspicious ones that are pointing their rifle towards the stage. The sniper may be posing as a cop."

"Michelle, scan the crowd for possible suicide bombers."

"Gia, can you get Bishop Ramirez off the stage?"

"Negative. Not until the Pope's done with his speech. We're surrounded by other priests."

"Mendes, you and your team need to leave the yacht now!" Cabral said from behind Jay. "You must evacuate."

"How do you suggest we do that?" Jay said. "We're trapped by the other yachts."

"I'll give you a ride. Put your guns away so you don't scare people. Here, I brought three windbreakers for that purpose."

Jay, McCoy, and Mack took the dark-green jackets. Large white letters on the back spelled POLICIA on the back.

"What about, McPhee?"

"We've taped his hand to the joystick," Ernesto said. "I'm staying with him until our bomb squad arrives."

"Treat him well. His son is on my team. He's a victim, not a suspect."

"I hope you are right. I have a family to go home to."

"Let's go," Jay said as he climbed over the side rail and jumped onto the patrol boat.

* * *

Jessie ended her broadcast as the Pope started his address. She sat down in the co-pilot's seat next to Michelle.

"Jessie, grab that set of binoculars on the console. Scan the crowd for possible suicide bombers."

"You're kidding, right?"

"No, I'm not kidding."

"Oh shit," Jessie said. "Roger, can you scan the crowd with the remote camera?"

"I'm already on it," Roger said.

"Michelle, are you okay?"

"What do you mean?"

"I mean. We learned Kathleen murdered your father," Jessie said. "Doesn't that make you mad?"

"I suspected it for some time. But, yes, it infuriates me to hear Kathleen say it with her own voice. The thing that really makes me mad is that she's also responsible for killing my brother."

"How's that?"

"She orchestrated the kidnapping. That means she's also responsible for attacking our team in Pakistan. One of her men shot the rocket that blew up General Andrew's jeep. The shrapnel from the explosion killed Michael."

"I'm so sorry," Jesse said. "I know what it's like to lose a brother and a husband. Plus, we almost lost Jay. I'm glad Kathleen's going to pay for her crimes."

"Keep scanning the crowd. We aren't out of the woods yet."

"Michelle, call Jay," Roger said from the back of the plane. I spotted a red laser target on the Pope's head. There's a sniper!"

"Everybody, there's a sniper! We need to warn the Pope!"

* * *

Jay stopped in his tracks. He was one hundred yards from the podium when Michelle's words came through the microphone.

Jay repeated the warning, "Natalie, Gia, there's a sniper!"

"I'm on it," Gia said as she grabbed Bishop Ramirez and pushed him to the floor of the podium.

Natalie heard the alert and spread the word to the other secret service agents who shuffled the President off the podium. She looked up at the Pope and saw the red laser dot on the back of his head.

"No," she yelled, diving toward the Pope.

Natalie hit the Pope in mid-air and wrapped her arms around his back. Then she felt a heavy punch as the bullet slammed into the back of her body armor.

Momentum carried Natalie and the Pope off the stage. They flipped over in midair, and the Pope landed on top of her. Natalie heard the crack in her neck as she landed under his body weight. A sharp pain exploded down her spine. Then she passed out.

* * *

Jay followed McCoy and Mack through the crowd. The twin giants threw people out of their way like they were rag dolls.

Jay heard the shot and saw Natalie fall off the stage with the Pope. When Jay arrived at the stage, local police had already cordoned off the platform. But when the police saw their jackets, they let them through.

Gia and Bishop Ramirez huddled over Natalie, who laid motionless in the grass. Jay knelt next to Gia, who held Natalie's hand.

Natalie's eyes flickered for a moment. Gia squeezed her hand, but Natalie didn't respond.

"She wants to say something to you, Jay," Gia said.

Jay placed his ear next to Natalie's mouth.

"I'm sorry, Jay," she said in a faint whisper. "I can't feel anything."

"It's okay, Nat," Jay said. "Help is on the way. You'll get through this."

"Jay, it's hard to breathe. I'm getting cold. You know how I feel?"

"Of course. You're the bravest person I know."

"No, about you. I always loved you. It wasn't a workplace fling."

"I know. I love you too. Natalie. I'm sorry it didn't work out."

"Me too," Natalie said as her final breath seeped out of her lips.

Jay kissed her gently and stroked her cheek. Then he said a quiet prayer for her and shut her eyelids.

* * *

The sounds of gunshots brought Jay back to reality. "What's going on?" he said into his microphone.

"We've cornered the sniper and an accomplice in a high rise next to the park," Cabral said.

"McFarland!" Jay said as he jumped to his feet. "Gia, stay with the Bishop and the Pope. McCoy, let's go. Where's Mack?"

"He already left."

* * *

Five minutes later, Jay crouched in a stairwell on the fifteenth floor of an apartment building. Ernesto Cabral knelt next to him with a map of the building.

"The sniper's on the roof. We have him surrounded, but he's fighting back. Two of my men are dead, and another is on his way to the hospital."

"I thought there were two?" Jay said.

"Yes, but we don't know where the other man is. He slipped away."

"That has to be McFarland," McCoy said. "He's a slippery bastard."

Two more gunshots rang out from a floor below them.

"Come back!" someone yelled.

Jay sprang to his feet and ran down the stairs, pulling out his rifle as he ran. McCoy and Cabral followed close behind. Then, Jay saw a flash of black leave the stairwell onto one of the floors.

Jay vaulted over the railing onto the landing below and yanked the hallway door open. A man dressed in black kicked an apartment door open and disappeared inside.

"Shit, I hope nobody's home. We don't need a hostage situation!"

Jay slid to his knees outside the door as bullets splintered the door above his head. Jay aimed his gun at the door and was about to shoot when Ernesto yelled, "No, there may be people inside."

Jay grabbed a flashbang from his pocket, reached up and grabbed the door handle, pulled the pin, and threw the grenade in. A large flash of light followed. McCoy reached over Jay and yanked the door open while Jay stayed low and crawled through the doorway. Two young children stared back at him from under the kitchen table. Jay waved to them to come forward.

"Is anybody else here?" Jay asked in Portuguese. "We're with the police."

"Yes," a dark-haired girl about ten years old said. "My mother is on the balcony."

"Okay, go out the door. I'll get your mother."

Jay looked through a glass sliding door and saw a pregnant woman lying on the floor.

"I got her," Ernesto said. "Find our suspect."

Chapter 49

The heat of the sun bore down on CJ as he focused intently on the sniper on the adjacent rooftop. The gunman was dressed in a police-style uniform, so CJ needed permission from local authorities to shoot.

Ivan was a living legend in the world of snipers and paid assassins. Nobody else would take a contract to kill the Pope. Not once, but twice.

CJ spotted the muzzle flash before he heard the shot. Madman confirmed the distance, wind speed, and angle of descent, while at the same time, CJ made his adjustments while focusing on his target.

Without warning, Ivan whipped around and fired in CJ's direction.

CJ flinched as a police sniper on the rooftop twenty feet away from him collapsed.

When he refocused, Ivan was gone.

* * *

Jay saw the door to a bedroom on his left and a small bathroom on his right. He pointed towards the toilet, and McCoy ran in.

404

"It's clear," he said.

Jay approached the bedroom. He saw a bunk bed against the far wall with clothes and toys littering the floor. He heard a door open and dropped to his knees as bullets smashed through the closet door. Jay returned fire with two quick bursts. He heard a grunt and the rifle fall to the floor.

Jay jumped up and grabbed the closet door. McFarland jumped out and slammed Jay in the chest, knocking him to the floor.

Jay punched McFarland in the face, and blood flew from his nose.

McFarland hit Jay back on the side of the head with a vicious right.

Jay landed an uppercut. McFarland returned with a quick jab to the face, splitting Jay's lip. He threw another punch, but Jay grabbed his arm and slammed it to the floor.

Jay punched McFarland several times and rolled over on top of him. McFarland kicked him off, then jumped on Jay. He pulled a large knife out of his belt and slashed Jay in his left arm.

Jay screamed and punched McFarland again. McFarland raised his knife above Jay's head and plunged down. Jay grabbed his wrist, stopping the knife inches from his neck. Jay stared into McFarland's steely gray eyes as he struggled to keep the knife's point from piercing his skin. McFarland smiled as he pushed down closer and closer.

"You know, this is not personal, Mendes," McFarland said. "Even though you abandoned me in Mosul."

"Would you have preferred I allow twenty school children to die?"

"No, but then you crushed my arm and shot me."

"You started the shooting by killing a great guy."

"It was all part of the battle plan."

"Was raping Olivia part of your battle plan?" Jay said with a snarl.

"No, the rewards of conquest. I look forward to seeing your girl soon. I heard she's back in Falmouth. She's bringing some fur seals with her. Oh, did I forget to mention how much I enjoyed slicing the neck of your stupid pet seal?"

A primal scream emitted from Jay's mouth as he wrapped his hand around McFarland's wrist with his left hand and twisted, crushing the wrist bones. With his right, he grabbed McFarland's knife, turned the blade around, and pressed it against his throat. Blood trickled as the knife dug into McFarland's neck. Still, the former SAS commando held Jay's hand back, twisting the knife around until he pressed the blade towards Jay's throat.

Jay dug deep, holding the knife with his right hand while his other hand searched his pant leg.

"If you're looking for your desert dagger, I pulled it out of your sock while we fought."

"That wasn't what I was looking for," Jay said as he pulled his backup gun out of his pant's utility pocket. Then, he pressed the barrel against McFarland's temple, "This was."

McFarland screamed and placed all of his weight on the knife, but it was too late. Jay pulled the trigger.

The handgun shot was followed by a louder explosion—a blast from a much more powerful weapon. McFarland's head disintegrated in a shower of blood and gore, covering Jay's face.

The room went quiet, except for the ringing in Jay's ears.

Jay rolled over, dumping McFarland's headless body on the

floor. He then wiped the blood off his face with the sleeve of his jacket. He looked up to see a giant man standing over him—a double-barrel shotgun in his hands. Both barrels were smoking.

"You alright?" McCoy said, extending a hand down to Jay.

"I got him," Jay said.

"Sure you did."

"I did. I shot McFarland before you did."

"With that little pea shooter?" McCoy said. "Give me a break."

Ernesto entered the bedroom with his gun drawn. He saw Jay's face covered in blood and said, "Oh my God, are you alright?"

"Don't worry," Jay said. "it's not my blood."

"Jay, are you okay? I heard a gunshot on the radio." Gia said in his earpiece. "Did you get McFarland?"

"Yes, he's dead. We're all clear here."

"Good, because we have a situation with Bishop Ramirez."

"Is he okay?"

"I guess so. But the Bishop wants you to come back to the park. Please hurry."

Jay looked at McCoy and Ernesto. Come on, guys. We gotta go."

"Wait," Ernesto said. "You need to wash the blood off your face first."

Chapter 50

Gia watched in shock as Bishop Ramirez removed his vestment, exposing the suicide vest. He held the bomb's plunger straight over his head.

"Jay said there was a plan B. Is that you?"

"No, I am plan C. The sniper was plan B. You must bring the Pope to me, or I will detonate this bomb and the five other bombs in downtown Rio."

"But why Bishop?" Gia asked. "I thought you were a loyal member of his inner circle?"

"I was loyal to God. Now I am loyal to a new leader—The Master. He believes religion is the real evil, and I agree. We cannot have a Pope from an evil country that spreads war around the world."

"But the college of Cardinals voted him in. If there were any questions about his integrity or faith, they would have known."

"They did not know him as I do," Bishop Ramirez said. "We grew up together. Went to the same Catholic high school and seminary. He was my best friend. Then he moved up in the Boston archdiocese, and he left me behind in Fall River.

Jay listened from behind the light stand. He needed to figure out a plan.

"Kyle, are you there?" Jay whispered into his radio.

"Yes, Jay. Are you alright?"

"Yeah, I'm fine. Do you have control of the helicopter?"

"Yes, I'm flying it away from the harbor."

"What happens if you cut the satellite link?"

"I lose control, and it crashes."

"Are you far enough out to sea?"

"Not really. I'm only a mile east of the airport. The helicopter can go in any direction."

"You need to cut the feed. Now. We'll have to take our chances with the helicopter."

"What are you talking about?"

"You tracked Kathleen's yacht using the satellite link, right?"

"Yes," Kyle said. "That's how we were able to link her to the Boston and New York bombings. The satellite link relayed through the seagull drones and triggered the bombs."

"Exactly. Now I have Bishop Ramirez and five suicide bombers standing in the middle of two and a half million people. There is a remote control helicopter packed full of liquid TNT providing that same relay. I need you to kill the link. Now!"

"Got it, Chief. It's done."

Jay stepped out from behind the tower and pointed his gun at Bishop Ramirez.

"Drop the trigger, Bishop. It's all over."

"You're right, Jay. It is over." Instead of dropping the trigger, the Bishop pushed the plunger down.

Gia screamed.

Nothing happened.

Nobody moved until Ernesto Cabral emerged from behind

Jay and grabbed the Bishop's wrists. "You're under arrest, Bishop Ramirez."

Gia ran over to Jay and hugged him. "How did you know they were using the satellite link to trigger the bombs? What if they were directly wired?"

"I didn't know," Jay said. "I had to trust my instincts."

There was a loud explosion in the distance.

"What was that?" Gia said.

Jay looked at the mushroom cloud, "Kathleen's helicopter going down in flames."

Chapter 51

Six Months Later

T he Federal Medical Center was a stark, modern facility located in central Massachusetts. Jay, Marty, and Mack waited in the lobby for Daniel McPhee to be reunited with his family.

"So Mack, how is this going to work?" Jay said. "Is Daniel going to be free to roam anywhere he wants? Will he need surveillance or protection?"

"No, Federal Marshals are putting him in the witness protection program. He will assume a new identity in a different community. After the trial, he will be free to live where he wants."

"Why did they release him?" Jay asked.

"The federal prosecutor agreed to drop the charges against him in exchange for his testimony against Kathleen. So he's able to tie her to the attacks in Boston, New York, and Rio. We conducted a thirty-day psychiatric evaluation, and the doctors say he's cleared to testify. Then he can go back to a normal life."

"What's normal after being held captive for fourteen years?"

Jay said. "What does he do? Where will he work?"

"Jillian seems determined to care for him and help him adjust," Marty said.

"Does she know he's going into witness protection?" Jay asked, "That she won't be able to see him until after the trial."

* * *

Jillian and Daniel waited in a family conference room. The room was stark with gray cinder block walls and a single rectangular table with four chairs. Kyle stared at his cell phone. He mumbled something under his breath, then put the phone in his pocket.

"What's the matter, Kyle?" Jillian said as she paced back and forth.

"No cell service."

"We won't be here long. You'll be able to talk with your friends when we finish."

"Mom, what are we going to do?"

"What do you mean, honey? We're going to be a family again."

"I mean, it's going to be weird with Dad in our life."

"We were a family before he was kidnapped. We'll go back to being a family."

"I don't remember that. I was too small. Is he going to boss me around and tell me what to do? I don't even know him."

Jillian wrapped her arms around Kyle's shoulders and hugged him. She ran her fingers through his unruly hair and smiled.

"He may want you to get a haircut," Jillian said. "Just saying."

Kyle laughed, "I'm not talking about that kind of stuff.

412

What I mean is…."

The door opened. Daniel McPhee stood in the doorway in a light gray t-shirt, jeans, and loafers. He didn't look like the same spirited man Jillian knew before he was kidnapped. Instead, Daniel looked sickly, with shaved hair and pale skin.

"Oh my God," Jillian exclaimed. "Daniel, I can't believe it." She rushed to Daniel and wrapped her arms around him.

He stood motionless for a moment, then hugged her back.

Jillian stepped back to see tears streaming down Daniel's cheeks.

"Honey, what's the matter? It's okay now. We're back together."

"I, I, never…," Daniel stammered as he wiped his face with his hands. "I never thought I would see you again. I was certain I would die before holding you in my arms."

"Oh, Daniel, I never gave up hope. I mean, we never gave up hope, right Kyle?"

Kyle stood behind his mother, "Hi, Dad."

Daniel reached out and grabbed Kyle's hands and pulled him toward him. Kyle hugged his father for the first time in fourteen years and let the tears flow.

"You made me really proud, son. I watched you grow up from a distance. And the way you took control of the helicopter was truly amazing. You saved so many lives."

"What do you mean, you watched me grow up?" Kyle said. "You were close by?"

"Yes, I was never more than a few miles away from you and your Mom, but I was locked up and never allowed to leave without somebody watching me. It was so terrible. I wanted to scream!"

"Why didn't you try to escape," Jillian asked.

"Because they threatened to kill you, as well as Marty and his family. I couldn't take the chance."

"Dad, what do we do now?"

"I'm not sure. I need to go into witness protection until after Kathleen's trial."

That could take years?" Jillian said. "I can't wait that long to spend time with you. Can we go with you?"

"The marshalls said we could go as a family. They will give us new names, jobs, and a house to live in."

"That's what we'll do then. Is that okay, Kyle?"

Kyle didn't answer. He was crying again.

"I don't want to go," Kyle said. "I can't leave Charlotte and my friends. Plus, I'm going to MIT in the fall. So where would I go to college?"

"You will make new friends," Daniel said. "We'll find a college for you to go to for your first year, and then you can transfer to MIT after the trial."

Kyle shook his head, "No, I don't want to go. Please, Mom. Let me stay with Marty and Aunt Lindsey."

* * *

Jay waited for Jillian to come out of the family conference room, but when the door opened, only Kyle stepped out.

"What's going on?" Jay asked. "Where's your mother and Daniel?"

"They're going into witness protection."

"Both of them?"

Kyle nodded and said, "They wanted me to go, too, but I insisted on staying. I guess I need a ride home."

Jillian stepped out of the room and came over to Jay. He

hugged her. He didn't know what to say.

"Thank you for everything, Jay. You brought Daniel home. I'll never know how to thank you. Can you help Marty watch over Kyle? He's staying on the Cape."

"Of course, I'll look after him. He's part of our team now. We'll all look after your boy."

EPILOGUE

Jay kept his promise and took good care of Kyle. In fact, the entire Maravista team kicked in. Gia was Kyle's personal trainer. She woke him up at 5:00 A.M. for a three-mile run. Then McCoy and Jay showed him how to rescue swim in the ocean. Every afternoon, Carla took Kyle and Brendan to her Dad's gym and taught him mixed martial arts. He even spent a weekend in New Hampshire, where he hiked the white mountains with CJ and Madman. The crazy pair taught him how to shoot everything from a BB gun to a sniper rifle.

Charlotte kicked in by giving him dance lessons. At first, Kyle was embarrassed by how clumsy he was. But, by the time they were ready to leave for college, he could dance the tango, swirl to a waltz, and even two-step to a country song.

He didn't neglect his microbots and even applied for a patent. Marty also agreed to help him start his own business, and Kyle named it *Maravista Technologies*.

As the summer came to a close, Kyle looked and felt like a new man. His body was tanned and fit. He eventually cut his hair to a short, military-style cut and looked like one of Jay's special operators.

Kyle and Brendan took the girls for a night out in downtown Falmouth to celebrate the end of summer.

As the two couples walked down Main Street, Art McCaskill and Tony stepped in front of them.

"Hey, Charlotte," Art said. "Aren't you going to say hi? Or are you too good for us local kids now that your boyfriend is famous?"

"Art, bug off," Carla said. "You're such a loser."

Tony walked up close to Carla and said, "Who asked you, miss dyke?"

"I'd shut up if I were you," Brendan said.

"What are you going to do about it, frat boy?" Art replied.

Carla pushed Brendan back, "Guys, cool down. You don't need to get in a fight over us. We can take care of ourselves."

Carla nodded to Charlotte. The two girls moved in unison. Charlotte turned and kneed Art in the balls. Carla followed up by punching Tony in the face. The girls stepped to the side, allowing Kyle and Brendan to finish the two bullies off. Art and Tony laid on the ground writhing in pain as the two couples stepped around them.

"Okay, let's go. I'm hungry," Charlotte said with a massive grin on her face.

* * *

Jessie jostled for the best camera angle outside the Boston federal courthouse. Hundreds of TV crews from around the world waited for the verdict of the most-watched trial since O.J. Simpson. It was a sunny day in the Seaport District of Boston. Abnormally cold for a May morning, Jessie shivered in her designer dress.

"How long is it going to take?" she asked Roger, who stood behind the camera. "The bailiff said the jury was coming out ten minutes ago."

"Joanne said the jury is sitting down now. She's going to

share her audio feed with us."

* * *

Jay sat with Olivia, Kyle, and Marty in the front row of the spectator gallery. McCoy, Mack, and the rest of his team sat scattered in the rows behind him. Jay watched Kathleen walk into the courtroom dressed in a dark gray suit. Her long dark hair was straight and limp. She wore no make-up or jewelry. Kathleen stared at the floor, unwilling to make eye contact with Jay or anyone else.

Mack was right. Her defense team didn't let her testify. So instead, she listened to Jay testify about the bombings and their investigation. Sammi described the night the bomb destroyed their family, and Kathleen vowed revenge. He also described presiding over Kathleen's secret wedding in Pakistan to al-Mujadin.

Then Daniel McPhee took the stand. Jillian sat with Jay and Kyle and listened to how McFarland kidnapped him off the beach while Kyle played in the sand. He described how they tortured him and threatened to kill Jillian daily. McFarland bragged about how he lured Jillian to Newfoundland to attend the marine academy and mentored young Kyle in electronics and robotics. Daniel was forced to watch his family on video but never allowed to see them or talk to them.

Then Kathleen met with McFarland and Bishop Ramirez in Boston. She recruited them to participate in a plan to wipe the Catholic church off the planet. They coordinated their attack in the United States with another terror cell in Italy. When Jay foiled the attack in Boston, Kathleen was hysterical. She ordered McFarland to kill him, his friends, and his family. But McFarland was insane, Daniel said. He wanted to play with Jay's mind. Torture him by attacking the people around him.

* * *

Jessie heard the verdict in her earpiece. She faced the camera and waited for the light on Roger's camera to go on.

"This is Jessie Bessie of GNN reporting live from Boston. The verdict in Kathleen Amejian's case is in. The jury found her guilty on all counts. I repeat, Kathleen Amejian is found guilty in the Papal bombing case. We'll have reactions from the Attorney General and the United States President coming up shortly. The next stage is sentencing. A second jury must decide if Kathleen will get a life sentence or face the death penalty."

"That's a wrap," Roger said. "Let's go inside and find some people to interview."

"Go ahead, Roger. I want to see Jay."

* * *

Jessie found Jay standing at the water's edge overlooking Boston harbor. Seagulls hovered overhead, looking to snare their next meal. She looked up at them to make sure they weren't targeting her. Then, she put her arm around his shoulder and hugged her big brother.

"Jessie, I can't believe it's over. For now, at least."

"It is over, Jay. Kathleen is never stepping out of jail. After that, you should be able to sleep better."

"I don't know, Jess. I have a feeling we haven't heard the last word from Kathleen. For instance, we still don't know who was responsible for the Vatican bombings. Plus, they never found the sniper who shot Natalie. And who the hell is The Master? Were they connected to Kathleen? All I know is I want to head back to the Cape and go fishing."

"Sounds like a plan, big brother."

* * *

Like what you read? Please leave a review at Amazon.com.

* * *

COMING SOON!

THE MASTER
A JAY MENDES THRILLER, BOOK THREE

About the Author

A Boston native (and rabid Red Sox and NE Patriots fan), Ken has spent most of his professional career writing marketing content and helping small businesses grow by implementing effective marketing communications programs. Earlier in his career, he traveled extensively around the U.S. and Europe discovering the natural beauty and culture abundant in each country. Ken also enjoys serving others through his membership in the Knights of Columbus, supporting prostate cancer research (as a prostate cancer survivor), and volunteering for a variety of charities.

You can connect with me on:
- ☉ https://kenwsmith.com
- 🐦 https://twitter.com/KenWSmithAutho1
- 📘 https://www.facebook.com/kenwsmithauthor

Subscribe to my newsletter:
- ✉ https://kenwsmith.com

Also by Ken W. Smith

The Final Mission, a Jay Mendes Thriller, Book 1
As the leader of a covert hostage rescue team, Jay Mendes is responsible for finding and saving people who have been kidnapped for political or other nefarious reasons. But when his own team members disappear, the mission becomes personal.

While Jay is on a rescue mission in Europe, his commanding officer learns terrorists may kidnap a billionaire business-man and his celebrity wife. Jay's boss assigns two intelligence officers to go undercover to prevent the kidnapping, but the mission goes awry, and the agents disappear along with the couple they were charged to protect. Jay flies halfway around the world to lead the search and rescue. After attempting a treacherous rescue-at-sea, Jay risks his life more than once to bring them home safe. But his nemesis has other plans. In a surprise attack, the hostages are snatched away for a second time and the team suffers an agonizing loss. A devasted Jay, refusing to give up, soon tracks down the hostages, only to learn the kidnapper is not his only enemy.